P9-BXZ-394

Sins of the Mothers

Non-Fiction works by Brenda Webster

YEATS: A PSYCHOANALYTIC STUDY

HUNGRY FOR THE LIGHT:
THE JOURNAL OF ETHEL SCHWABACHER
(Edited with Judith Emilyn Johnson)

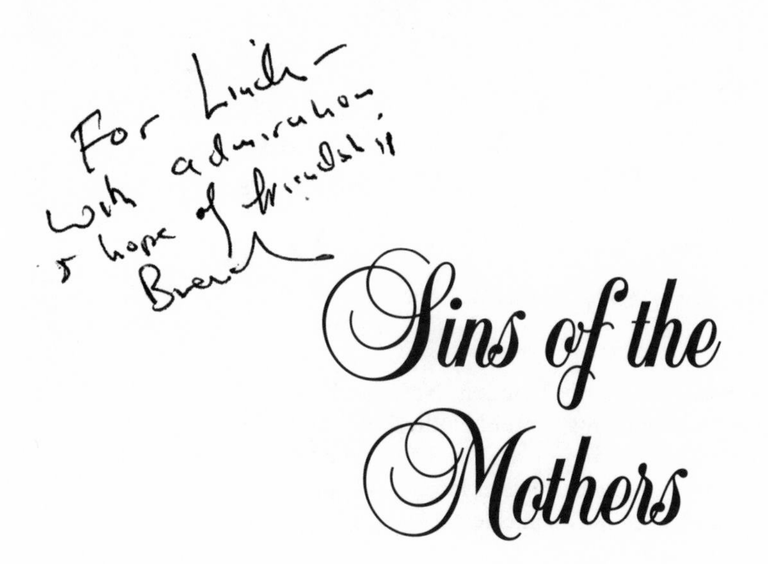

Sins of the Mothers

A Novel By

Brenda Webster

This book is a work of fiction. Names, characters, places and incidents are either the product of the author's imagination or are used fictitiously. Any resemblance to actual events or locales or persons, living or dead, is entirely coincidental.

BASKERVILLE Publishers, Inc.
7540 LBJ/Suite 125, Dallas, TX 75251-1008

Library of Congress Catalog Card Number: 93-70943
ISBN: 1-880909-05-7

Manufactured in the United States of America
First Printing

In memory of
Sara Vogan

Winter

1974

One

Why do dentists always talk to you when your mouth is full of cotton? Connie's dentist had jabbered at her for a full hour about Nixon's erased tapes while he reamed out the rotten core of her tooth. The dentist got so excited about what a shifty bastard Nixon was that Connie had been afraid the drill would slip. Now her jaw was just beginning to give out tiny sparks of renewed life. She leaned a bag of groceries against the door and rummaged in her purse for the key. As she turned it in the lock she wondered whether her daughter Sarah had taken advantage of her absence to run down to that seedy record store she loved to visit. When she heard Sarah's sweet, clear voice talking to her brother, she was flooded with absurd gratitude.

That was the Sarah she knew—her warm, helpful girl, not the moody creature who slammed out of the house in a temper when she was told she couldn't go to a rock concert. Connie couldn't begin to explain to anyone how it felt having Sarah gradually turn into a stranger. Just like the end of any passion, it left her feeling disoriented. She'd found herself dreaming of Sarah as a baby sitting in her high chair triumphantly offering her mother a spoon of apple sauce, Sarah not frightening her with the thought of going away.

"Hello up there," she called, setting her bags of groceries on the landing.

"Hi, Mom," Sarah called back from the top of the stairs.

"You're late. How was the dentist?"

"I'm rootless," Connie yelled. "Rootless in Berkeley."

"It's better than being toothless." Sarah jumped the last step and started walking towards her mother. Wiggling, rather. My God, Connie thought, doesn't she have any idea how provocative she looks in those short shorts with her long legs and that flaming brush of hair? No, she probably doesn't, poor baby. An image came to Connie's mind of boys on the street shouting after her when she was sixteen, "Hey, baby, put some salt in that shaker," and she looked at her daughter with sudden annoyance.

"Give me a hand with the groceries," Connie said, struggling with an impulse to tell Sarah to go upstairs and change her clothes.

"Why always me? Why not Mischa? Because I'm a girl?" She grabbed one of the bags by the top and looked provocatively at Connie as the brown paper began to tear. "When Dad comes back you should tell him you've got some new plans for him—like setting the table, or shopping once a week. Remember, Mom, it's the seventies. Women aren't doing all the housework anymore. You could tell him you got your consciousness raised while he was away." She shoved the juice and milk into the fridge, not bothering to move the old bottles to the front.

"Fat chance." Connie thought of the take-out food she'd been indulging in, deli chickens, shrimp salads. It had been such a pleasure doing just what she liked about food for four months. One night she'd even brought home a ham baked with cloves the way she'd had it as a child. It would have outraged Howard. Not eating pork was the only dietary restriction she'd agreed to when she married him. But she didn't care. He liked being thought of as a pious Jew but Connie had long ago decided that he only observed the rules that pleased him. If he'd wanted to eat pork, he'd have renamed it chicken.

She set her bag down next to Sarah's and, taking out two

red peppers, unloaded the rest of the vegetables into the plastic bin.

"You could negotiate. You'll stop cooking him leg of lamb until he agrees." Sarah lobbed the empty egg carton into the trash.

"I'll think about it," Connie said evasively. She had always thought parents should present a united front. But she wasn't looking forward to a return of the old regime any more than Sarah was. She wondered what Sarah would think if she knew about the assertiveness class Connie had been taking. Would she think it was ridiculous? Or would she be pleased her mother was learning how to stand up for herself? At the last session, she'd pretended one of the men was Howard and told him off while the class cheered her on. The question was whether she could do it in real life. She straightened up and unbuttoned her sweater. "Sarah, it's boiling in here. Turn the thermostat down, will you?" Sarah couldn't seem to get it through her head that they were in the midst of an energy crisis.

"I was freezing to death." Sarah rubbed her bare leg with her hand. "You had it set at sixty."

"Our gas bills were astronomical last month. If you'd cover up a little, you wouldn't be cold. January isn't exactly the time for shorts." Sarah nudged the dial down a notch and slouched against the counter looking offended.

Connie rinsed a red pepper, sliced it and handed some to her. "Peace offering," she said biting down on a slice. Then she grimaced.

"Hurt your tooth?" Sarah hoisted herself onto the kitchen counter and sat dangling her legs, thumping her heels to some inaudible tune.

"Yes. The dentist slipped and got my gum. It's sore as hell."

"Maybe you should have had them all pulled and gotten false ones. That's what they do in Australia."

"Thanks. But I think I'll hold on to them for awhile." She

smiled wryly. "I'm not ready for retirement yet." What had Sarah said the other day? That she didn't see the point in people making life changes after forty because they were almost dead. Well, she was forty-two, but with new gold centers, her teeth might even outlast Sarah's.

"Don't take it personally. It was just an interesting fact." Sarah kicked off a clog and casually raised her leg over her shoulder, showing off her dancer's extension. Her shorts cut into the curve of her thighs. The skin was milky white with a single freckle right in the middle. Like an exclamation point, Connie thought. Look here!

"Oh hey, I forgot to tell you." Sarah crunched the pepper. "You had a message. Some guy has been calling since I got home." She looked at Connie curiously. "He said if you got home after five, you could call him tomorrow. Anyone I know?" Connie felt herself flushing, embarrassed at her own feeling of pleasure. So Marc had called after all. Well, why shouldn't he?

"It was just someone I met at Jane's party," she told Sarah. "I'd promised to find out about schools for his daughter. I guess that's why he called."

"No," Sarah said matter-of-factly as she went upstairs clacking her clogs together like castanets. "He wanted to have lunch."

While Connie was getting the chopped meat out of the fridge, she couldn't shake her sense of minor triumph that he wanted to be her friend. Though it was irritating that he thought being a specialist in adolescence made him particularly good with his daughter—when he clearly wasn't—she was glad he had called. He'd been thinking of sending his daughter to a convent school in France. Just because she was a little wild. It made no sense. At least he didn't resent her telling him what she thought. She wondered if he was attracted to her. Her friend Jane told her he had a reputation for womanizing at the Medical School in San Francisco where he taught psychiatry. The thought made her laugh: in seventeen years of marriage she'd never come close to having an affair. She'd given all that up when she decided to marry Howard.

Marc did have a charming way of smiling though, with his whole face and eyes. When she'd caught his smile over the heads of the other guests, she'd posed herself in the kitchen doorway like Isabel Archer, tilting her head and putting one leg forward to show the slimness of her ankle. Marc didn't lower his eyes after a minute the way most people would have. He just stood there looking surprised and pleased. There was something open and unembarrassed about his pleasure, like a little boy at a birthday party. Though he was anything but little. He must have been at least 6'2". Whatever it was this tall, beautiful man wanted, Connie simply felt like seeing that smile again. She touched her cheek pensively then unwrapped the meat. Marc's face was suprisingly small for his long, lean frame. It was triangular, a little like a fox's, she thought, with coal black eyes under a shock of black hair. She kneaded the beef gently between her hands, sculpting it into round generous shapes.

Even though she disliked cooking, it made her feel virtuous. Nurturing. Like a good woman. By which she meant as unlike her artist mother as possible. While her mother had shut the door of her studio and left Connie outside crying, Connie let her children interrupt her even in the middle of a sentence. She knew her more liberated friends thought she went too far, but she couldn't help it. She never wanted her children to feel that they were interfering with more important work. Besides, being a good mother was intensely gratifying. But somehow Sarah's growing up was beginning to change things.

The hamburger started to spit grease. She jumped back, but not before she'd gotten a spot on her skirt. Damn. She'd never understood women who could cook without getting their clothes dirty. She dabbed at the grease with a sponge and called Sarah and Mischa for dinner.

Mischa threw himself into his chair and reached for the bread. Connie could see he hadn't washed his hands. Two bright, black, beady eyes peeked from between the middle buttons of his shirt.

"Mischa, dammit. You're not supposed to bring that rodent of yours to the table." Connie pressed the sore spot in her mouth gingerly with her tongue. "It's unhygienic."

Mischa pushed the hamster's head down. "Evel's not here. You must have imagined it." He'd named his hamster after his hero Evel Knievel.

"The last one died because you kept him in your shirt like that." Sarah hugged herself, mocking him. "He's not a teddy bear, you know. You shouldn't have a pet if you can't take care of him properly."

The hamster struggled up and flopped with a bound onto the table. Mischa grabbed him with seven-year-old fervor, knocking his peas onto the mat in the process.

"Oh for heaven's sake," Connie exploded, "How many times do I have to tell you something before you hear me? Get him out of here before I wring his neck." She shut her mouth hard and a sharp pain shot through her tooth. This wasn't the night for shenanigans. But then her children always seemed to pick the worst times. They had an infallible instinct for it.

Mischa scrambled after the hamster, who was scurrying across the table. When he stopped, peering, whiskers twitching over the edge, Mischa picked him up and shook his finger under the hamster's nose. "See what you've done," he said menacingly, in Howard's voice. Then under his breath, "you filthy little beast." Connie looked at him, shocked; he sounded so like his father.

"Quit it, Mischa, that's not funny," Sarah snapped as he headed upstairs with the hamster held tightly in his fist. She turned to Connie, her brown eyes narrowing. "It's bad enough that Dad says that stuff to Mischa without his imitating it."

"He doesn't mean those things, you know." Connie swept the scattered peas into a heap with her napkin. "It's just his way of letting off tension." She believed that was true. Once when they were having a fight she had asked Howard straight out, "Do you want Mischa to hate you the way you hated your father?" He'd gone white. "Do you think he hates me?" he'd asked miserably and she'd felt a wave of pity for him. But he couldn't seem to stop saying cruel things. They escaped from him like steam from a pressure cooker.

"He should get a punching bag." Sarah jabbed the air. "Beat up on that."

Connie envied the vigor in Sarah's voice. In the four months since Howard had been in Israel working on plant physiology, Sarah seemed to be getting more self-assured. She'd never said things like this before. Connie had the fleeting, disloyal thought that they were all better off without him. Mischa had been calmer—until now, when Howard was about to come home and Mischa started doing these little imitations.

After dinner, Connie sprayed her skirt with Spot Off to see if she could loosen the grease. While she was changing into her night clothes, Sarah was looking through her mother's closet for something to wear with her slacks. She was going out with Jeff. Watching her, Connie felt her skin prickle with irritation. She didn't see why Sarah had to pick the fastest boy around when there were so many sensible boys her own age. She felt like snatching her silk blouse from Sarah's fingers, but she knew that wouldn't help.

"You know what I'd really like? That black leather jacket you were trying on last night. The one you said you wore at college. Where'd you put it? Leather's really in now."

"Is it? I hadn't noticed. I thought it was those flowered granny dresses. Anyway, I put the jacket back in the trunk and I'm not about to go looking for it now." Her college outfits seemed like costumes now. She could hardly remember how it felt to be on a motorcycle weaving between cars, her face tight against her boyfriend's back.

"Okay, okay. Don't get uptight." Sarah started rummaging through Connie's jewelry box. "You should get your ears pierced. I'm going next week, you should come with me. Then you could get some great earrings."

"So you can borrow them?" Connie asked a little too sharply. She knew Sarah was softening her up so she wouldn't insist on her being home early. Still, Sarah knew how to charm when she wanted to.

Sarah laughed. Then she picked up Connie's hairbrush and began to brush her mother's dark bangs to the side, cocking her head to see if she liked the way it looked.

"I wish Dad wasn't coming home," she said suddenly. "He's just no fun." She kept brushing, fluffing out the back of Connie's new, short cut. The stroking of the brush was so soothing. Connie made a noncommittal sound in her throat. "All my friends think it's pretty weird the way he acts," Sarah persisted. "Why don't you go with him some night when he goes out? Keep him company. Or you could hide under a blanket in the back of the Pinto and pop out and surprise him."

Funny, a friend had suggested that too. But what was she going to find? All her instincts told her he wasn't having an affair. In any case, she wasn't about to discuss it with Sarah. "Speaking of cars," Connie said, "I'd like you home by a reasonable time tonight. Say 12:00."

"Mom, that's ridiculous. We're going to a concert. It won't even be over 'til midnight."

"Concert! What concert? I thought you were going to a movie."

"A friend gave Jeff tickets. It's just the Beach Boys. Nobody even does drugs at a Beach Boys' concert." She hummed a bar from *California Girls*. It did sound fairly innocuous compared to some of the things she listened to.

"That's not the point, Sarah. If you're at a concert for three hours, you can't tell me he's not going to drink. I know he drinks when he drives."

"Who told you that? Chrissy's mother? Well, she's full of it. Maybe he has a beer once in a while. So what? Besides, he's a great driver. Better than you are." She scowled at her mother. "Since Dad's gone you've been clamping down on me. I didn't even have a curfew last summer."

"You weren't going out with Jeff then." She didn't want to be waiting up all night worrying they'd had an accident. "Look, Sarah, I'm not in the mood to thrash the whole thing out now. And I don't want to be unreasonable. Make it 12:30. But that's it. If you have to leave early, leave."

"Leave? You must be crazy. Do you want him to think I'm a baby?" Sarah threw down the hairbrush and ran out of the room, slamming the door. Connie sighed and went into the bathroom to look for the aspirin. She took two and began examining her mouth in the mirror. The temporary filling seemed to spill sloppily over the side of her tooth. Maybe it would have been easier to have it pulled instead of hanging on to it. But that wasn't her way. She stuck to things.

Just then the doorbell rang. "I'll open it. Let me," Mischa said, running downstairs. While she watched, he struggled with the difficult lock.

Jeff's shockingly big shape loomed in the doorway. His body seemed to go up endlessly, topped by wildly curling hair. She felt an irrational impulse to shut the door in his face. "Oh it's you, Jeff. Come in." How could her child be old enough to be going out with this creature? He wanted to wait there, he told her, shuffling his feet awkwardly. In back of him she could see his red sports car. Connie felt like grabbing Sarah and locking her in her room for five years until she turned twenty-one. Keeping her safe. There are no second chances if your brains are splattered all over a freeway. For one long minute she wished Howard were there. Jeff might be more intimidated by a man.

"Is it supposed to be a good concert?" she asked conversationally.

"Yeah, we're going to meet some friends there. It should

be cool." He stood there stolidly waiting for Sarah.

Connie fingered her cheek nervously. These kids don't realize how little alcohol it takes to mess up your reflexes. Remember your curfew, she started to say but didn't.

"Mom," Sarah said coldly, "don't sweat it. We'll be fine."

"Have a good time darling," Connie reached out to hug her to make up but Sarah slipped under her arm, grabbed Jeff's hand and practically pulled him out the door.

She stood there watching as he gunned the car and took off around the corner. It looked like rain. Connie couldn't see any stars and the moon was half hidden behind a cloud.

She shut the door and went back into the house. Before she went into the kitchen, she turned on the outside light so Sarah could see her way to come up the path. Then she set the dishes in the rack to dry and put some salt in a glass with hot water. She swished the salty water around in her mouth, feeling her lips pucker.

"Time for bed, Mischa," she called when she'd finished. He had parked himself in front of the T.V. and was flipping the channels. "Everything was Watergate," he said, disgusted. "I just found a Western. Can't I watch? Please."

"Nope." She walked over and put a hand on his shoulder. "Let's go." One look at her face told him she meant business. He gave a windy sigh, clicked off the set and got up.

She had just gotten him tucked in and was downstairs with her feet up watching T.V. when the doorbell rang. All she needed now was one of those petition peddlers with their sincere faces. Sign here for clean air, free clinics, the salvation of endangered species. She grabbed her robe and looked for a dollar to give. It would be easier than talking.

She lifted the shade and peered out. Marc's face smiled up at her. "Good heavens, Marc," she stuttered opening the door. She pulled her robe tight and tied the belt.

"Hi. I hope I'm not disturbing you." He looked at the money in her hand. "Were you expecting pizza?" He was wearing gray slacks and a suede jacket in a soft, pleasing earth tone.

"Gosh, I was just going to call you," she said. It seemed so odd. The way he'd materialized on her doorstep. She wondered if he did this sort of thing often. She slipped the dollar into her robe pocket. She wished she'd put on her Japanese robe instead of this bunchy terry-cloth that accentuated her hips. She shifted from foot to foot. Maybe she could slip into the bathroom and put on some makeup.

"I know it's crazy, but I brought you some lemons." He proffered a huge bag. "My tree is full of them. They're bouncing around my yard like tennis balls."

"Thanks." She opened the bag and put her face close to the lemons. They gave off a tangy, fresh smell. Should she ask him to sit down? Let him look at her more closely in this state? She put the bag down on the landing, deliberating. "Do you give lemons to all your dinner partners?" Marc had sat next to her that night at the party.

He laughed. "Actually, I gave some to my wife—my ex, I should say. We're separated. And some to a woman who's been tutoring my daughter—she likes to make lemon meringue pies. And some to you." He leaned nonchalantly against the banister. "It was great talking to you the other night. I hadn't even been sure I wanted to go to Jane's party. But talking to you made my evening."

"I'm glad." She wondered what he wanted from her. More advice about girls' schools? Band-aids for some quiet desperation? But he didn't look unhappy. He kept beaming at her.

"Come on in." She started into the living room, her polka dot slippers flopping like clown feet every time she took a step. He followed her and sat down on the sofa. "What are you watching?"

"I don't know the name." She moistened her lips. Her mouth felt as though it was stuffed with cotton. "Just something I turned to when I got tired of hearing about doctored tapes." The press had been full of the tapes for days. Every blip and beep. The national detective story.

"They should just impeach Nixon and be done with it," Marc said with conviction. Connie remembered Marc saying he'd been involved in the Resistence ever since he and the other protestors had been hosed down the stairs of the Federal building. She'd been frantically studying for her qualifying exams at the time, taking care of Sarah. No left-over energy for causes.

"You think so?" It all seemed so overblown and sordid.

"Well, aren't you embarrassed to have a petty criminal as President?"

Connie thought the President's misdemeanors were only an exaggerated version of what went on all the time. What had Howard said before he voted? Better a thief than a fool in the White House. "I don't take it that personally," she said. Certainly Marc hadn't come just to talk politics and unburden his lemon tree. She got up and turned off the set.

"You know, I found the name of that hotel in Switzerland for you." She offered him a tidbit of useful information. "The one with great views and good food."

He smiled at her. "That was sweet of you to do it so quickly."

She tried to smile and got a stabbing pain in her jaw. "I envy you going. It's so beautiful. I think I even have a picture of it in my photo album." She moved over to the book shelf and started hunting. "I know I saw it here just yesterday."

"You'll show me another day. I have worlds of time." He came after her and put a hand on her arm. "I'm not going until spring vacation. As long as the price is reasonable and there's access to the ski slopes, I'll be happy."

"I've always meant to learn, but Howard doesn't like the cold."

"Skiing's less a sport with me than a necessity. I actually prefer cross-country. Snow camping. Being completely surrounded by white. I went up to the Sierras over Christmas vacation. I was feeling really pissed off at this damn neighborhood group down in the flats. I'm on the board of a half-way house for disturbed adolescents. We finally found a place that's safe and not too expensive and what happens? One of the neighbors finds out, tells the others and before you know it they're trying to keep us out." He made an exasperated tisking sound. "Thank God for snow."

He was looking at her swollen cheek and it made her nervous. She put up her hand to cover it. Maybe he thought Howard had come back from Israel and belted her in the jaw. "My dentist believes in doing everything at once," she said, touching her cheek.

"Jesus, why didn't you tell me? I feel terrible barging in on you like this when you have a toothache. I'm going to make a quick exit. Will you let me take you out to lunch next week to atone for being such a boor?"

"Oh, sure," she said, walking him back to the door, "I'd like that." Maybe then she'd find out what he wanted in exchange for the brown paper bag full of overripe fruit.

Two

Connie curled the long phone cord between her fingers impatiently as she listened to her mother's clear, rich voice, the voice of a young woman.

"What are you doing, darling? You sound a little harassed." Connie had an image of her mother sitting on her bed, leaning forward trying to see across three thousand miles.

"I was sweeping the kitchen." What difference did it make what she was doing? Was her mother planning to swoop down from the sky to see if she'd left dirt in the corners?

"Doesn't the housekeeper do that?"

"She doesn't come in today and I'm having a friend to tea." Connie eyed the Italian teapot she'd set out on the counter.

"Oh. Is it...ah...What was the name of that lovely English friend of yours? The one we had such a nice tea with last time I was there. Sue? Jane?"

"Jane. Is it so hard to remember?" Oh God, here we go again, Connie thought. "Did you see the papers this morning, Mother? Patty Hearst's been kidnapped. They dragged her out in her bathrobe. Stuck her in the trunk of the car. She lived about ten minutes from me." There, that should distract her. Give her something juicy to think about besides her daughter's social life.

"That's dreadful! I didn't imagine she was so near you.

They said on the radio that the men were part of some radical gang. Is it likely to be dangerous?"

"You mean for you? When you visit? Of course not. We're hardly in that class. What a thought." She imagined her mother trussed up like a sausage in the back of a car. Wouldn't it have been terrible if Patty's mother had been visiting and they had taken her too? Tied them together. Back to back. Never a minute apart even to pee. She shuddered. The idea was worse than the kidnapping.

"You know, it's been so long since I've made a trip. I've been wondering if I should come after all. Maybe it would be more sensible to stay home."

"I thought it was all settled. You'd gotten the tickets." Connie chewed at her lip. She hated the way her mother seesawed to and fro.

"The storms are so bad this year. Flying in turbulence makes me ill."

"For heaven's sake, don't come then." Connie gave the phone cord a vicious yank. Who did she think she was, Maria Callas?

"That's not very friendly. After you begged me to visit."

"I asked you two months ago. Not now when Howard's just coming back. You're not that fond of him anyway." She paced back to the phone table and set the phone down with a bang.

"You don't need to be nasty. You know how much I want to see you and the children."

"Your cat was sick. Wasn't that why you wouldn't come before?" Why did they have to go through this farce? Elsie hated to travel. She always got the runs before a trip. Or cancelled at the last minute. Like last summer after the Japanese jet was hijacked by the Palestinians. But she wouldn't this time, Connie was sure of that. Because it was so inconvenient, she'd be sure to show up.

"Let me bring you something pretty. I saw a beautiful yellow sweater at Valentino's."

Connie thought wryly of the last unflattering dress her mother had bought her. "You know yellow's not a good color for me." Elsie chose colors she liked in her painting, but none of them went with Connie's skin. "Don't bother."

When she hung up, she quickly cleared the counter. She wanted tea with Marc to be perfect. She'd even made a cake with lemon glaze from his lemons. Since he'd brought them over, she'd gone to lunch with him twice, and they'd taken a long walk on the fire trail in Strawberry Canyon.

She pushed the squeezed-out lemons into the disposal, but when she turned it on, it gave off a faint whir and died. She tried again. Now not even the water was going down. It backed up and filled the sink. She stuck her hand in and tried to feel if there was anything stuck between the blades. Egg shells and coffee grounds floated to the surface. When the doorbell rang she didn't hear it until Marc leaned on it. "My disposal just went on the blink," she said apologetically, wiping her hand on her apron. She noticed he'd brought back the paper on George Eliot that she'd given him. "Excuse the mess."

"No problem. Let's have a look." He walked over to the sink. Took off his jacket and rolled up his sleeves.

"Nothing's stuck. I checked. It has no excuse to break. It's a brand new '73 model."

"Have you tried pushing the button?" He knelt on the floor and peered underneath.

"What button?" She crouched next to him trying to see too. Her arm brushed against his and she felt the warmth of his skin.

"Usually there's a reset button under these things. He reached under and pushed a small red button on the bottom of the disposal. "Try it again." She turned on the switch but this time there was no sound at all. "It doesn't sound as if there's any current coming through. Do you have a screw-driver?"

"Yes. But I didn't ask you over to fix my plumbing. We

were going to have tea."

"Where's your screwdriver?"

She got it out of a drawer and watched fascinated while he took off the switch plate and started to examine the tangle of wires behind it. Howard wouldn't have had the slightest idea how to do that, even if he wanted to. He had trouble changing a light bulb.

"You look like a pro," she said.

"In my family, if you couldn't do a job like this you were dead. My girlfriends thought I was a gold mine. They loved me to fix things for them. But my wife was too competitive. Alix had to do everything herself. A real ball-breaker, that one." He grimaced, tightening something. "See, it's just a loose wire. There." He screwed the plate back on. This time it worked. He pushed the lemon peels down the drain with a wooden spoon. She looked at him gratefully. "Thanks."

"I had chores a mile long when I was a kid," he said. "I wasn't grateful then, but I sure learned a lot of useful things. Now, of course, I have a housekeeper."

"I do too. Two mornings."

"I don't like letting someone else do my shit work, but I just don't have time anymore." The disposal whirred loudly as it chewed up the rinds. It gave off the smell of lemon blossoms. Standing next to him, her head barely reaching his shoulder, she noticed how trim he was. Trim and taut, no fat anywhere. His shirt was open at the neck letting her glimpse the curling hair of his chest. He didn't seem conscious of his beauty. If he had, she would have been put off.

While he was rolling his sleeves back down, he noticed a piece of trim that had come off the counter and picked it up gleefully. "Oh good, something else to fix."

But this time she was firm. "I'm not going to let you do a thing more. You've done enough. We can have some cake while we wait for the pot to boil." She motioned him towards the dining room table and followed him bringing the cake on a tray.

He picked up her article from the counter and sat down. The kettle gave a burbling shriek. Connie filled the teapot, brought it back to the table and poured them tea. She handed him a slice of cake and he bit into it and smiled. "Hey, this is good. My lemons?"

She nodded and sat down beside him with her elbows resting on the table, looking up at his face. "So, do you like my article?" She'd found it was so much easier to work with Howard away. Usually a piece took her months but she'd polished this off in a few weeks.

"Very much. Your style is great. So many critics ram their points down your throat. Your prose has a transparency that makes you feel the material is speaking for itself. You really convinced me." He gave her a warm smile. "Sorry I didn't read it sooner but I was working on an article myself. I'm still trying to figure how to combat Freud's idea that women have weaker superegos than men. I've been looking at it developmentally and I'm convinced they just have different priorities."

Connie flushed, pleased. It warmed her inside to have someone care about what she thought, to listen and be listened to. She hadn't had that with Howard for ages. The sense of intellectual companionship. Howard was always telling her what crap her work was, whenever she got the energy to talk to him about it. Besides, even when she didn't agree with Marc, she loved the intensity in his voice when he talked about ideas. It was sexier than talking about sex. "In George Eliot's case, she was as hard on herself as any male Puritan. I'd love to write a biography of her showing what a fascinating woman she was. How tormented by self-doubt. Her work is a mass of scruples. She won't let her heroines have any sensual pleasure. Even being pretty seemed faintly criminal." Connie thought Eliot would probably have made her an anti-heroine. She could imagine the description. Doe eyes, pale ivory skin, slightly bewildered expression.

Marc wiped a crumb of cake from the corner of his mouth. His teeth were refreshingly uneven. It gave him character. "I always thought of her as a free-thinking, independent type. It seemed pretty gutsy back then to go off and live with a married man. I like unconventional women."

Connie noticed the way his eyes lit up at the thought. A strong woman. An unconventional life. She wondered what that meant in practical terms. Someone who'd go off to Alaska at the drop of a hat? What could he see in her, then? Sitting there pouring tea in her slacks and serviceable shoes. Mother of the family. She determined to get herself some new clothes.

He was leaning back in his chair now, studying the small oil painting of cows and giant flowers on the wall opposite him. "It's amazing how my aesthetic sense perks up when I have some sugar in my blood. Who's the artist?"

"My mother." Maybe I should redecorate, she thought perversely, not have Mother's paintings hanging all over the house. Maybe then people would notice some other things, like my Japanese prints.

"It must have been wonderful having someone like that for a mother. With that extraordinary energy."

"It was nice..." Looking at Marc's envious expression, Connie saw Elsie for an instant through his eyes without the aspects that tormented her.

"Nice," he echoed. "It's terrific. You're a lucky woman. How many women do you know who have something in common with their mothers?"

"Not too many," Connie said with an ironic intonation that he didn't catch. "Mother can be a pain sometimes though. Right now she's worrying about being kidnapped when she comes to visit, like Patty Hearst. But that poor girl. Can you imagine how terrified she must be?"

"No more than a lot of other people who die on the streets every day without anyone noticing. Actually, I think it's great; they should kidnap every super-rich kid in America."

"You do?" She opened her eyes wide. She knew he was a radical, but she didn't know anyone who was in favor of kidnapping.

"Yeah. Talk doesn't impress big business. Take their kids and they'll sit up and take notice. That might generate some enthusiasm for social programs. Take Trisha Nixon and Eisenhower's son and stick them in a closet together. Then we'd see some action." He gave her a wicked grin.

Connie stared at him. It was a dangerously appealing fantasy. If when you cry no one listens, take a club. Force them to hear you. Give you what you need. Despite her horror, she was fascinated.

"I hate violence." She pulled her sweater around her shoulders, suddenly cold.

"They won't hurt her. They'll use her as a bargaining chip—if they have any sense." His eyes shone. He seemed energized by the idea.

Connie shook her head. "It won't work. And besides there are some things you just don't do. At least not in my book."

"Don't get scared. I talk big but most of the time I go through the regular channels like everyone else. I don't want you to picture me making bombs in my basement."

She laughed, but for a moment she had. She could picture him in a kidnapper's hood, or a mask with only his black eyes gleaming.

"Look. Did you know I've been helping the police defuse violent situations for years. They call me when some kid goes off the deep end. Threatens to kill himself or someone else. I'm good at dealing with these people because I understand where the violence is coming from."

"You must have been a tough kid yourself." Before this, she'd imagined him as a boy Galahad, helping old ladies across the street.

"Oh, I was before Yale polished me up. Spoiling for a fight." He rapped his knuckles on the table for emphasis.

Her father had been like that as a boy in Newark, fighting

the Irish boys that attacked him after school, calling him "dirty kike."

"Does it work? Do you really get people calmed down?" Connie stretched out her arm on the table until it almost touched his hand. He moved his a fraction of an inch closer. She imagined a blue spark crackling from his little finger to hers.

He laughed. "It depends. A couple of years ago there was a Berkeley student who locked himself in the Chem lab with a bunch of explosive chemicals and I had to talk him into opening the door. It took two hours and I was afraid I'd get a face full of acid when he finally came out."

"How awful." She suddenly realized she had heard about this case from Howard.

"Not to worry. He came out like a lamb. I took him in my arms and he burst into tears." Marc draped his arm over the back of her chair. "I'm a good peace maker, but it's more fun to make love."

The room suddenly seemed too warm and she wondered if Sarah had turned the thermostat up again. "Do you stick your neck out like that often?" she asked, trying to ignore his arm. The little hairs on her skin prickled where he touched her.

"All the time. I'm a risk-taker. Not a good bet for death of old age," he laughed.

That sort of daring was what she admired about her father. She wondered what he'd be doing if he were alive now. He'd always defended unpopular types. Communists, blacks. Probably now he'd be taking gay rights cases. Like those New Hampshire students. She could imagine him parodying the trustees' worry that two boys dancing together could turn America into a nation of sodomites. She'd gone to court to watch him argue. For a while she'd wanted to be a civil rights lawyer but her mother had discouraged her. Convinced her she didn't have that kind of mind. The facts would slip out like water through a sieve. "Most shrinks are pretty reactionary," she said. "Most professors are too. I still remember the sexist comments I got when I was working on my doctorate. After my exams they told me my feminine charm made my flaws appear virtues. That's my favorite. Then they failed me on my prospectus just because they didn't understand what I was trying to do with psychoanalytic theory. And like a good girl I was too polite to tell them off."

"Didn't you fight?"

"The next time I defended my thesis wearing a black leather jacket with my hair combed across one eye. It had a definitely intimidating effect. I passed. Though as I was leaving the chairman said, 'We release you to the custody of your advisor,' and smirked at me as though I were a mental case."

"Hey, you have revolutionary potential. Unfanned flames." He smiled.

He looked intrigued, she thought. She was glad she'd told him this bit of her past instead of how much she admired George Eliot's ideas of self-sacrifice. How she'd been trying to figure out why Eliot made Dorothea, her most brilliant heroine, devote all her talents to her wizened scholar husband.

"You know," he said suddenly, "I'm developing quite a crush on you." It threw her off balance. All she could think of to say was that he hardly knew her.

"When you've been burnt as many times as I have, you develop an instinct for people."

"I always thought disasters made you cautious," she said.

"It depends how much you learn from your mistakes. I picked the wrong women too many times. I know what I want now." He squeezed her shoulder.

Mischa came in the door just then and stood looking over the stranger. The sight of him jarred her. "Mischa. You're home early." She looked at him distractedly. He was wearing his Skylab T-shirt. The bullet-nosed space station hung over a slanted earth like an uprooted windmill. Marc took his arm off the back of the chair.

"No, I'm not." Didn't he remember she'd told him not to stare? Still, he looked so manly, standing there with his hand on his hip, trying to seem disengaged. She felt an absurd rush of maternal pride.

"I'm talking to my friend. Could you get yourself a snack? I left out cookies and fruit for you." She shrugged her shoulders apologetically.

"But Mom, you've got to drive me to the sport store. I need new shoes for soccer. I'm going to make the first team this year for sure. I got the ball past Tony yesterday. Right over his head. What a jerk he is. He looked so stupid standing with his mouth open." He danced over kicking an imaginary ball and stood in front of her, avoiding looking at Marc.

God, he was full of himself. Connie hadn't been that way when she was his age. "This is my son Mischa." Connie sighed. There was no way she was going to get rid of him now. "When are the tryouts?"

"Tomorrow." He jigged from one foot to the other. "Come on. Let's go. It's almost five- thirty. They'll be closed."

"Don't be so impatient. It's rude. We'll go in a minute." She cleared the table and put the dishes in the sink.

Marc went out the door with them, chatting to Mischa about sports. She wanted Marc to like Mischa. Not just because he didn't have much of a father but because her children were the best of her put into fresh bodies, given a chance to flourish. But Mischa was talking too rapidly, trying to impress, and Marc seemed tense.

"Sorry to break things up like this." She buttoned her coat up under her chin, feeling suddenly awkward and exposed.

"It was just getting interesting, wasn't it?" He took Connie's hand, holding it longer than necessary. "That's okay. We'll take up where we left off."

While she was driving to the store she thought about his

elegant, long body and the dark line Marc had around his pupils, setting them off. She felt slightly disoriented but refreshed, as though she'd been out walking in the mountains. If Mischa hadn't been there visibly reminding her she was a mother, she might have forgotten her age.

Marc had unsettled her. Mercurial and provocative. But that was part of his attraction, his slightly adolescent charm.

Now they were driving past a funeral parlor with a hearse parked outside. It was enormous. "Look at the black Rolls," Mischa said. "And the men with a coffin. Is there a body in there?" He craned his neck to see. "I bet it would smell bad if you opened it up."

"Mischa, shush."

Howard had only gone out with Connie once when he invited her to come with him to visit the cemetery in Long Island where his grandmother was buried. It was the anniversary of her death. Connie thought it was an odd choice for a second date, but she'd ended up being touched by the way Howard had put flowers in the marble urn at the tomb and talked about his feeling for his grandmother. He'd read the proofs of his first book to her in the hospital before she died. She insisted, he'd said quietly, even though she knew she was dying. He seemed reassuringly solid, standing there in his suit and vest with the white shirt.

"Hey, there it is," Mischa yelled. "There it is, Harberts."

They were in front of the sporting goods store. Mischa jumped out before she had fully stopped the car and raced inside. By the time she joined him he was standing on the steel ruler having his foot measured by a salesman in bright tweed pants.

"Hey, Mom," he pointed at a jumble of things on a table. "I want some red flippers. They're neat."

"You're getting soccer shoes, Mischa, and besides, you can hardly swim." The salesman went into the back room and came back with the appropriate size. They looked tiny, almost like ballet slippers. But Mischa jammed his feet into the shoes and stood admiring himself in the mirror, pretending to kick, to bounce a ball on his toe, off his head. His feet were just like Howard's, she thought, with those long aristocratic toes. Maybe Howard had bought burial plots while he was in Israel. His and hers. Or a double. Like reserving a hotel room. She could imagine him doing it after Ben Gurion died, wanting to be in the same cemetery.

Mischa ran back to her. "Please can I have the flippers? I'm going to take swimming at rec camp this summer. They're having a sale. See, special." She eyed the assorted leftovers from last summer. A nicked surfboard. Flippers in garish colors.

"All right. If you'll stop nudging. Now put your shoes back on. Don't bother to wrap them," she said. "I'll just pay. And the red flippers too." Mischa gave a whoop of joy and ran to get them. The man rang it up. Gave her her change. She piled the things in Mischa's arms.

"Tony's whole family went to Hawaii over Christmas. Why don't we ever go anyplace fun together?"

It was a question she didn't want to think about. She stuck the end of the flipper in his mouth. "There, that should keep you quiet for awhile," she said. Then she put her arm around his shoulder and propelled him out the door.

Three

The day before Howard was due home, Connie drove with Marc to a fort on a spit of land jutting out into the Bay below the Golden Gate Bridge. She couldn't believe how strongly his physical presence affected her. When they stood watching the waves crash against the rocks, she was so dizzy she almost fainted. The breeze, unnaturally warm for mid-February, the natural sounds and motions—even the way the traffic pounded the bridge suggested some cosmic sex act. When they got back, Marc wouldn't come into the house.

"I can't. I've got to make a plane to San Diego. I'm going to visit a friend. I'm afraid we'll have to let our infatuation simmer on a back burner for a few days." Before he left, Marc traced the outline of her mouth with his finger.

His calling it an infatuation shocked her. True, in the last week, she had been seeing him almost every day but she managed not to think what this might mean. She liked him, she wanted to be with him, but she told herself she wasn't going to do anything foolish. He had told her enough about his women for her to see he had the hunting instinct, that he liked the chase.

"When I want something badly enough there's no way I'm not going to get it," he'd said when they were hunting for an antique store he wanted to show her on some out-of-the-way street in San Francisco. "I pursued my wife half way around the globe to get her to marry me."

"Why didn't she want to? Or is that an indiscreet question?"

"It is. But never mind. I suppose she was afraid it would interfere with her hotshot career." He pressed his lips together in a bitter line. "She probably knew she couldn't sustain a relationship with a man. She told me it wouldn't work. I should have listened to her. But no, I had to have her. I was sure once she saw how good it could be, she'd soften."

"And she didn't?" Even scornful, his face twisted, Marc was vastly attractive. Still, Connie wondered how Alix would have told it.

"Oh, at first, she'd wake up in the morning and throw her arms around my neck. Tell me how glad she was. But she was a driven woman. She didn't know how to relax. We'd be having a little warm-up volley on the court, and all of a sudden she'd start slamming balls at me. Whoosh." He mimicked the ball hurtling past him.

"But you stayed married to her for a long time." It was half a question. He'd been married almost as long as she had.

"I should have left after the first year. But I'd had so many affairs that I'd given up on, I was determined to make marriage work. And then it was too late, there was Selina. God, I'd still do anything for that kid." He looked at her, his lips trembling, and she patted his arm.

There was something self-indulgent in the way Marc told it, Connie decided, when she thought about it later that night, lying in bed, as though he'd had no part in the outcome. It seemed to her that it would be very foolish to get seriously involved with him. So the next day when she saw Howard fighting his way through the airport crowd, she was reassured. If her life had been a movie, he would have been Erich Von Stroheim. But as he got nearer and she saw him tripping over his untied shoelace, she reflected that he never would have protected her the way Stroheim did Swanson at the end of *Sunset Boulevard*, directing Norma Desmond's last pathetic walk in front of the cameras. Making it seem a triumph. No, Howard would never have saved her from painful knowledge. It would have been the other way around. Because Connie had always protected his illusions.

He walked stiffly up to her and kissed her on the cheek. Just a peck. Like distant cousins. "What's that smell?" he asked her, wrinkling up his nose.

"Perfume, *Je Reviens*, to be exact." He grunted disapprovingly. She couldn't believe that this was the way a couple reunited. His head had a thicker, more rock-like quality than she remembered. His massive neck, rigid as ever. His bald skull. Only the jowls were getting softer. He'd added another fold just under the chin. He looked as if he'd put on weight. He'd never be fat, his metabolism would never allow it, but his stomach bulged slightly above his belt. In someone else, the effect might have been a general softening, but in him it just accented his features—the huge ears like jug handles, the thin mouth, big nose, haunted deep set eyes. She took his briefcase and started towards the car.

"You look different," he said, as she was searching for the Pinto in the parking garage.

"I cut my hair. I wanted something more lively." She knew better than to ask if he liked it.

"No, I don't think it's that."

"I got a new jacket." He was still looking at her curiously. "My shoes?"

"You're wearing all those gewgaws," he pointed to her gold bangle bracelets. "You didn't used to wear jewelry."

As they drove back he told her a little about his last weeks in Israel. While Kissinger was working on disengagement, Howard had been invited to give a final presentation at the Weizman Institute on water transport across plant cell membranes. An important Israeli botanist had liked his work. He didn't say this boastfully but almost apologetically as though he feared she were bored. She found this endearing. But now he was telling her about the exodus of young people from the kibbutzim.

"It worries me terribly. The kibbutzim are the heart of the country. Its heart blood. What the founders meant it to be. Israelis weren't meant to turn into Europeans, lusting after clothes and fast cars. The Arabs are doing less damage to Israel than the credit card." He slowed down. There had been an accident at one of the ramps. They passed a crumpled sports car and a man lying on the ground, his hands over his eyes. Howard shook his head. Connie knew he was thinking this had proved his point. She looked away.

"What's wrong with wanting to shop? Go on a nice vacation? I'd go crazy always cooped up with the same people. No privacy. Not even having your children with you at night." She picked at her cuticle.

"That could be a benefit sometimes." He gave her a knowing smile. "Besides if you had a yen for children you could work in the children's house in the daytime."

She didn't feel even a twinge of desire. Dry and cold as a lump of lead. "Wheeling ten babies around in a wheelbarrow just doesn't appeal to me. Think how many runny noses you'd have to wipe."

"The kibbutz I visited was perfectly lovely." Howard's voice took on the exalted tone Connie associated with religious subjects. "On Lake Tiberias. They'd lost several men in the Yom Kippur War but they kept their spirit. After work they swam with the children or sang songs just the way they always had. I kept thinking of the ones who'd died keeping the Syrians out of the Galil." He glanced at her out of the corner of his eye. She was watching a sea gull soaring on an air current but when she felt him looking she made a low encouraging sound. He kept on talking. "They raise various crops. There's a dairy. Then at night they sit around and talk about Jewish history. I found it very moving. History," he repeated, "at night. After working in the fields all day with the threat of being blown up by terrorists. One man was writing a book about the early settlers. A half hour at a time. In the language of the Bible." His voice got thick.

Connie wasn't really listening anymore. She noticed some hairs sprouting out of his ears. Funny, she hadn't remembered them. Gray tufts like small clumps of grass in the cleft of a stone. He looked older, tired, in spite of his tan. "Did you remember your vitamins?" Connie asked.

"What?" He looked startled. "Some of the time. When Arni's wife reminded me. She has a sweet nature, that woman. She watches over him and the boys like a brood hen. One of them was home recuperating from a shoulder wound. But she wouldn't hear of me staying in a hotel; she took care of me too. I don't know why you never liked her."

"She was so sanctimonious about her kitchen, her dishes. Always boasting about cleaning the house with a feather on Passover." She'd reminded Connie of the girl in Rumpelstiltskin who was supposed to separate the wheat from the chaff before morning. Frantic. But with a permanent lunatic smile. Of course it wouldn't have occurred to Howard that she was only being polite, that she had her hands full without him.

"You're not fair," he said, hurt. "It's tradition. Just because you wouldn't do it. Besides, her strudel is fantastic."

"Sometimes I think men invented this religion just to keep the women occupied from morning to night."

"What's gotten into you? You never talked like this before. Arni's a lucky man. Deborah's a real mother of Israel." He swerved to let an ambulance pass, siren wailing. "Damn. Do they have to break your eardrums?"

There would have been a time when his praise of Deborah's virtues would have driven Connie crazy. Maybe she would have even offered to look for bread crumbs, sweep them up with a feather and burn them next Passover. Certainly she would have told him she baked hallah this morning, "for Shabbat."

"Did you?" he would have smiled at her. It was true she

had baked the twisted loaf, but she didn't even want to score a point. Let Deborah win the competition for holiest bread on the block. Kneading the dough, the fragrant smell of the bread in the oven was still deeply satisfying, but Connie had stopped thinking that her efforts could make Howard happy.

It was starting to rain. Fat raindrops falling like a curtain down into the water. Howard searched for the knob to turn on the wipers and Connie noticed his shirt cuff was flapping against the steering wheel. "You lost a button."

"It caught on something," he muttered. "Could you fix it?"

"Sure," she smiled wryly. He was like some crotchety uncle that one takes in and cares for in his old age. Sews for and tidies up after. She'd gotten used to his crankiness. She'd even gotten used to his inability to communicate his feelings.

She had strategies for making this more bearable. One was to tell herself that it was good discipline. Life with Howard was a sort of perpetual initiation into a religious order. You got detached. You tried to see the best in what you had. You kept working at what seemed impossible. That's why even though she didn't believe in God, she had been glad Howard was a practicing Jew. It had been her mission to be a good woman. "A good woman is a pearl without price," Howard had read her from the Bible after they married. At first, squeezing herself into that mold had the obscure fascination of writing poetry in a difficult form. But slowly her attention had shifted from Howard to the children, and now he was just another child to care for.

Howard was driving abstractly, humming to himself, while the rain pummeled the windshield. "Turn up the wipers," she told him, "You can't possibly see like that." How did he manage to give speeches and write his books? He seemed so helpless sometimes.

Howard didn't snap at the children at dinner but afterwards he called them into the living room for a talk. Mischa stood digging his hand into his pocket and jouncing the way he did when he had to pee. Sarah looked calm until Connie noticed she was quietly biting her lip.

"What's this about failing your Hebrew class, Sarah?" He shook a letter at her. "You have to be practically a genius to do that. The way they teach it in this town. Per-miss-ive." He drew the syllables out. Sarcastic. Connie saw Sarah wilt.

"That was before. I'm doing better now."

"How much better?"

"C." She paused studying his face. "Maybe B-." His expression didn't change. Why couldn't he give her a chance, Connie thought. She was improving.

"My daughter getting a C in Hebrew! That's awful. You'll have to have a tutor. Or I can do it myself. Yes, we'll start tomorrow. We can have a half hour every night after dinner."

"Oh, Dad. Do I have to? I've got so much schoolwork."

"Don't 'Oh, Dad!' me. Of course you have to. Now Mischa."

Mischa looked pale. "How do you say, 'I want to go to the bathroom?'"

"*Rotzeh lalechet le bet shimush.*" Mischa said promptly.

"Good." Connie saw the tension go down. "But that was way too easy for you, wasn't it? Baby stuff. Boys your age in Yeshivah already know most of the Torah by heart. Let's try something a little harder. What's the root of *lalechet*, to go?"

"*Lamed, kaph, tav.*" Mischa quavered, jigging again.

"Shame on you. It's an irregular verb—*hey, lamed, chet.* You should know that." Howard reached out and gave him a tap on the behind.

"We're not doing irregular verbs yet." Mischa said in a low voice.

"This isn't just any irregular verb. It occurs in almost every sentence you use. Learn it."

Mischa gulped. "Okay Dad."

"But I'll give you another chance. What's the gender of

even, stone?"

Connie could see Mischa scuffing his toe against the rug. He didn't know. "Stones are hard." Mischa said with a slight interrogative note. "It looks..."

"Do you know it or not?" Howard snapped.

"Masculine."

"Wrong." Howard gave him a harder slap on the rear. Mischa jumped but he didn't cry. "No soccer for a week. I'll test you again next weekend."

"I suppose you've been seeing that friend of yours while I was gone," Howard said after the children had gone to bed. "Did you sleep with him?"

"What are you talking about?" For a second Connie wondered if he was reading her mind, then she realized he meant Alfred. A dear friend she saw once a week for lunch. Had seen, that is, before she met Marc. "God, I didn't expect to hear that. I never was sexually attracted to Alfred. You know that. What makes you think of it now?"

"You never know with people. I won't be secure until you're fifty. Women don't usually run away after fifty. That's eight more years." He rubbed his jaw meditatively.

"Where am I going? Off with the circus? What makes you think I'd leave you anyway?"

"This is an age of serial monogamy. Besides you're a terrible flirt. At the Gross's costume party, when you wore that harem dress with only your eyes showing, all those old farts were after you." His face was flushed. Either with emotion or because of the carafe of wine he'd downed at dinner. Too much, she thought. I should take the bottle away.

"It was the veil," she told him. "They just wanted to see who I was. It was only play." She patted his shoulder.

"I like to think you don't mean it, but who knows."

She sat next to him on the sofa. He didn't usually come so close to admitting he needed her. Usually he pretended he didn't. Thinking about it, she felt a flash of anger. What meaning did it have if he only told her he loved her when he was drunk?

"Jane invited me to a party while you were gone," she said, looking at his knees. "Marc Price was there."

"He kept that crazy student from blowing up Stein's lab. No doubt he's a smart man." Howard frowned as though making an inner comparison.

"I think he has a crush on me." She lifted her eyes and looked him straight in the face. Throwing him a challenge.

"Doesn't he know you're married?" The naiveté of his response surprised her. She'd thought he'd do better than that. At least make it clear he was on guard.

"Of course he does." Wake up, she wanted to yell and shake him. Wake up, I'm in danger. Your roof is burning over your head. Do something.

"Well, tell him your husband doesn't want you to see him any more." His face was composed. She could see he thought that was enough. Certainly it was more than usual. You're missing the point, she thought. It's me. I want to see him. I like him.

He got up brusquely and went into his study. She went into the kitchen and cut herself a piece of chocolate cake. A small one. Just enough to alleviate her feeling of frustration. Howard couldn't admit he cared, she knew that already. In the early days after Sarah's birth when Connie had been in her mid-twenties, she'd tried hard to get more attention by making him jealous. But it had just made him withdraw more. Seem more unconcerned. Once, determined to break through his aloofness, she'd walked along an Italian beach wiggling her hips and collecting a trail of gesticulating men. "I don't like that," he'd said, finally.

"Well then, pay me some attention, dammit." She'd felt it as a triumph but it hadn't changed anything.

Trying to get his attention by being good was much harder and just as frustrating. But her mother had taught her well. She was conditioned to keep trying. She'd probably picked Howard instinctively because she'd known he'd frustrate her too.

Howard came down a few minutes later brandishing her diary. Her chest tightened.

"I'm very upset," he said now. "What is all this stuff about?" He waved it in front of her, then started reading snatches of it. "'The waves were a powerful, violent green...I shut my eyes and listened to them beat...He kept talking in a low, quiet voice right next to my ear. I could feel it pull at me like the undertow tugging at the little white shells.' This is just adolescent purple prose. Silly. But *this*, Connie! I'm not going to dignify it by reading it." He pointed to the ending passage. She didn't have to read it. She knew that she'd asked herself why she was so excited—so moved—by such an obviously neurotic man.

"Do you understand why I'm shocked?" Howard asked.

"You shouldn't go nosing in my things," she said, her heart pounding. "I don't go in your study and rummage around. Do I? It's not right." He looked as if he might hurl the book at her head.

"I don't think you understand. I'm not upset that you want a roll in the hay with someone. That really doesn't bother me at all. What bothers me is that you seem to take this man seriously. That's what astounds me. You know how I feel about shrinks." He glared at her accusingly. Then made a dismissive gesture with his hand. "They're asses, all of them."

"Always a rationalist, aren't you? Why do you have to be so cerebral? Pretending you don't care what I'm doing. Can't you admit it? You're bothered as hell." She had always felt he was like a rock. If you chiseled away at it, you would get to the secret spring. She couldn't believe he'd dried up inside.

"I thought I could trust you after seventeen years of marriage. I'm grateful. You've taught me better. You're a sneak like every other woman, starting from Eve." He gave her a withering look. "Go ahead. Tell me more. What were you really doing on those trips to New York to see your mother and that ape-necked brother of yours? Finger painting? Palpating clay balls?" He reached out and pinched her arm. She yelped and moved away.

"Dammit, Howard, you're the one who went away for four months. You didn't call or write. I don't know what you were up to. You could have been doing anything. How about your all night walks? How about that?" It made her dizzy to hear herself asking. Whatever he was doing, she hadn't thought she wanted to know.

"Why do you care what I'm doing? I'm a good provider. Most women would be glad to be in your shoes." He took his gold watch out of his waistcoat pocket, slipping it around in his hand, avoiding her eyes.

"Is that what you think marriage is about? Simply paying? I might as well be back in college. I was getting my expenses paid there too." It hit her. He really thinks this. There aren't any other thoughts hiding behind that inscrutable face of his. I've been making up dialogue for a person that doesn't exist.

"You didn't use to be a shrew. You must have taken lessons from your mother while I was gone." He forced a laugh.

"Don't you call my mother a shrew. She's an artist."

"Artist! A poor excuse for permanent hysterics. Her colors make me puke. All those horrible reds. Like the inside of a slaughtered animal." He put his hands over his stomach and bent over slightly, pretending to spit.

"You're colorblind," she said outraged. "You can't even see red." Those paintings were the only part of her mother she really liked.

"Red, green. What difference does it make? I hate those paintings. And you inflict them on me. You and that bloodsucking mother of yours."

"If you're too blind to see they're beautiful, just shut up about it. At least she gave us something. What did your mother ever do?"

He inhaled, packing his chest with air. "She raised me to be a decent man."

"You call it decent to go caterwauling around San Francisco three nights out of every five? How do I know you don't have a mistress?"

"I've told you what I do. Walk." He enunciated it as though he were giving a diction lesson. "Is that too hard for you? Do you want me to spell it?"

"Why should I believe it? Maybe you're leading a double life." She held her breath for a second, watching him.

"That's ridiculous." He went over to the liquor cabinet and took out a bottle of Grand Marnier.

She followed him. "Is it?" she asked his back. "Then why are you so stingy with me? Why do I have to ask you for five dollars every time I go to the market? I can't even buy a roll of toilet paper without asking permission."

"If I gave you more money, you'd come home with knick-knacks instead of food. A stuffed owl or a musical chamber pot."

"We're not talking about impulse buying, Howard. For years I've been telling you we need a new roof. The damn thing spritzes all over the kitchen floor when it rains. You just won't get to it. Why?"

"No one's stopping you from getting the roof re-shingled," he said dryly. "You can do anything you please."

"Who's going to pay? The Messiah?"

"You know I don't tolerate blasphemy. Are you going to stop?" He raised his hand.

She took a step back, but she kept on. "And that's just one thing. The plumbing downstairs is all rusted out. The window frames are rotten. But every time I bring something up you say 'later' in that maddening voice. Who are you saving it for? Certainly not your children. You didn't bring them anything from Israel. Not a fountain pen. Not even a candy bar. Tell me the truth," she hissed, leaning forward. "You can't afford to fix up your own house because you're paying the rent on another apartment. That's it, isn't it?" As soon as she said that, she wished she hadn't. It sounded childish. Petty.

He turned around and poured himself a glass deliberately. "Maybe I'm a bigamist. Why don't you accuse me of bigamy?" he snorted scornfully. "The truth is, the house bores me. And you're beginning to get tedious too."

She grabbed the glass away from him. "Drinking isn't going to help you. Stupefying yourself until you fall asleep on the couch. What are you hiding from?" As hard as she could, she hurled it against the cabinet. It had been an exquisite glass, one of his mother's. It shattered into slivers of rose and green. Howard drew in his breath.

"You never could control yourself, could you? How can you expect me to talk to you? You're worse than a child." The pale liquid trickled across the hardwood floor.

She felt her face grow hot. She could feel herself shrinking. Becoming an idiot, a huge hydrocephalic head on a spindly little body. It's not me, she told herself, fiercely pushing the image away. "What is it that makes you like this? Like a knife. Mocking everything. I'm trying to figure out what's wrong with us." Her mind was grinding to a stop.

"Well, you're not doing a very good job of it. You're getting yourself hysterical over nothing. That's enough. Stop. It's finished. I have no other woman and I hope you have no other man." He put his arm around her neck, dragging her towards him. She broke away and grabbed her diary out of his hand.

"Next time I won't be stupid enough to think I have any privacy." She tore out the pages he'd read, crumpled them into a ball and threw them at him. "Here. Reread them to your heart's content."

He picked them up and threw them into the trash.

"I'm sorry," he said in an angry voice. "Is that what you want me to say? Come." He steered her towards the bedroom.

"If all you care about is being a good provider, what do you want to fuck me for? Hmmm? Can you tell me that?"

"Calm yourself." He stopped propelling her and stood uncertainly.

"I can't stop being angry just like that," she snapped her fingers. "Just because you have an itch." She slipped away from his arm and went into the living room and started to pick up the pieces of Lego Mischa had left scattered under the table. She dreaded finally having to go to bed because she could see that Howard was determined to wait for her. It didn't bother him that she was still furious. It probably only piqued his appetite. Hers too, though not for him.

If Marc had suddenly appeared, she might have thrown herself into his arms. She stopped herself. Still, she had to admit that seeing him made her aware of feelings she thought were dead. It had been a long time since she really enjoyed sex with Howard. Over the years, she'd grown to believe that sex wasn't really part of his makeup. It seemed somehow incongruous, pasted on, an almost indecent addition to pure mind.

But tonight, he grabbed her as soon as she slipped under the sheets.

"Do you really want to make love to a corpse? Because that's what I feel like." She kicked him in the ankle and pushed at his chest.

"Go ahead, scratch if you want to. I like it. I like it when you're angry." His skin was so smooth, no hair anywhere. She scratched, tugging with her nails. He moaned and pulled her tighter, forcing himself into her. "That's good, do more."

She lay underneath him. Not moving. Waiting for him to finish, her teeth against his shoulder. Wanting to bite. But afraid he'd enjoy that too. Not wanting to give him any pleasure. He'd thrown off the blankets and she watched the way his hips rose and fell. Like a piston. The impersonality of it, no intimate touch or word, was almost a relief. If he wanted it that way, she'd take advantage of it. She imagined Marc coming into the room and pulling Howard off her. Forcing him to sit in a corner while Marc made love to her, slowly. She imagined him kissing her breasts, fondling them. Kissing her body all over until it revived and opened to him. Howard felt her soften. He shuddered and came.

The next day, the rain stopped and Howard invited her on a walk around the block, taking her hand in a childlike way. If she hadn't been still burning with annoyance, she would have been touched. He hadn't done that for a long while; he only offered her his arm with formal courtesy as though she were his eighty-year-old mother.

But now he was feeling rather cheerfully unconstrained. There was a family of nearly tame squirrels in the sugar pine at the corner and he'd taken some stale bread and was trying to lure them down. Love of animals had been one of the things they shared. They were without a cat for the first time in years. Their tortoise-shell tabby had been run over by a truck before he left. For a moment she felt close to him, squatting innocently on her haunches throwing out bread. Nice, she thought, he can be sweet sometimes. But why couldn't he give anything to the kids, then? Or to her? She balled up a piece of bread between her fingers and flicked it at a squirrel's nose. So he's an animal lover. Good at hand-outs to rodents. So what? They're a dime a dozen at the A.S.P.C.A. Hitler liked animals too, after all. Everyone knows they're easier to get along with than people. If being an animal lover was the only thing Howard had going for him, that wasn't saying much.

"I think I've got Stanley," he said abruptly. Connie's heart sank. Stanley was his chairman. Was he going to start this childish business again? In the months he'd been away, she'd almost forgotten how hard he made things for them. The way he insulted people, it was almost impossible to keep a social life going.

"What's it this time?" Stanley was one of the few people

in Plant Biology he still liked and who liked him. She foresaw that he was going to ruin it. Jesus, what a waste of life. Not just his, she thought angrily, hers too. Because she was the one who picked up the pieces.

"I've invented the perfect job applicant." He was delighted because his imaginary candidate was not only highly qualified in Stanley's specialty, she was also female and black. He told Connie he'd gotten so enchanted with the woman that he had already sent out several letters. "There's no way they'll be able to turn this one down. Stanley will be squirming." He rubbed his hands together, sprinkling a shower of fine crumbs on his trousers.

"My God, Howard. I feel like a seeing eye dog. I can't count on you to stay out of trouble for more than a minute. You'll be miserable if he takes it seriously." She thought of herself as Howard's guide in personal relations, but for the last few years he'd been running ahead of her, as if frantically eager to trip and hurt himself.

"Will I?" He grinned at her in a slightly crazed way.

Her shrink had once pointed out to her that sometimes she acted as if Howard was psychotic. And maybe he was, but then her mother had been pretty crazy too, so in a way it seemed normal. It was just Howard.

"Would you like Daddy to read you a bedtime story?" Howard asked Mischa that night. Mischa looked at him suspiciously.

"What?" he asked. "I'm tired of *Wind in the Willows*." Howard had read the parts about the foolhardy toad to him over and over again.

"Something special." Howard gave an odd grin.

A little later, when Connie passed Mischa's door, she saw Howard twisting his arms around each other and moaning, "Glub, glub." Mischa had his eyes closed and was holding his hands over his ears.

"Let me in," Howard whined in a high voice, imitating

some misshapen monster. "It's cold out here and you have such a lovely warm house. Let me sleep with you in your bed."

"No," Mischa shouted, pushing Howard away. "Get away from me."

"Feel my foot." Howard took out a piece of something wrapped in foil, unwrapped it and dangled it next to Mischa's face. Mischa screamed and tried to get out of bed. Howard held his arm. "Come on, it won't hurt you."

"Don't touch me with that." Mischa lunged away, shrinking from the thing in Howard's hand. Connie ran up and grabbed Howard's arm.

"Stop it. Can't you see he's frightened?" She sat down and put her arm around Mischa. "It's all right, sweetheart. Mommy's here." Mischa pressed his head against her. She turned to Howard. "What in God's name are you doing?"

"Telling him a story," he answered blandly.

"But what were you pushing at him? Give it to me," she reached over and took it out of his hand. "Liver! For heaven's sake."

"It's perfectly clean. I got it from the fridge."

"But that's ghastly, Howard. You're scaring him to death."

"Nonsense. Am I scaring you, Mischa?" Connie could tell from the way he asked, he thought Mischa's struggle had been part of the game.

"Not so much," Mischa said opening one eye and looking at the greenish liver.

"He's not an idiot. He knew it was a joke. You're not afraid of a little piece of chicken liver, are you, son?"

"Noooh," Mischa quavered, opening the other eye. Howard poked the liver with his finger.

"See? This is what he looked like when he turned into green gook."

"Leave it, Howard." She snatched her hand away. Picked up the foil from the bed and wrapped the thing up in it. "What is this story you're telling him?" Howard leaned towards her and she could smell the wine on his breath. Sour. His teeth had a purple film.

"*The Thing on the Doorstep*. Glub, glub."

"Well, I hope you're prepared to get up with Mischa when he has nightmares tonight." She stroked Mischa's head.

"It's not that bad, Mom," Mischa looked up, emboldened by her presence, "once you get used to it. It's about this three-thousand-year-old man who dissolves into a puddle of slime."

"Just a minute ago you had your eyes squinched shut," Connie said. So it was Lovecraft. That nut Howard had given her to read when they were dating, who wrote about Eldridge horrors.

"It's real scary. But sometimes I like scary things." He looked up at Howard for approval. Howard grinned at him. "It's better than Conan the Barbarian. Really." The comic book was one of Mischa's favorites. He wrapped the blanket around himself and attempted to look confident. "This is my super protective armor. Nothing can get me now."

"Have you brushed your teeth?" Mischa shook his head no. "Well then, off and do it."

"Glub, glub." Mischa imitated Howard, twisting his arms and running into the bathroom. Connie sighed. It was pitiful, it was irritating. She told herself that Howard didn't know he was frightening Mischa. He was just a big child himself, fascinated by body snatchers. People being taken over by primeval creatures. If he had a family crest, it would have been an octopus, with spread tentacles.

Howard padded off to the living room to read and she heard Mischa calling her. She went and sat down on his bed stroking his hair gently. Sitting there in the semi-dark, she wondered how she'd ever imagined Howard would be a good father. He hadn't wanted to have children. He told her so right after they got married but she'd kept nagging him. She wouldn't trade Mischa and Sarah for the world, but what a fool she'd been. He'd been petrified of Sarah from the moment he laid eyes on her.

Mischa's breathing quieted and she could see he'd fallen asleep. She straightened his covers, pulling them smooth. When she'd gotten pregnant with Mischa she'd even thought of getting an abortion. Oddly enough it was Howard who wouldn't think of it. The Arabs had killed enough Jews. They couldn't murder their own. Now she was so glad she hadn't. She took Mischa's Evel Knievel doll off his pillow. Evel's motorcycle had so many points and angles she was afraid Mischa would roll over on it and hurt himself.

Mischa murmured in his sleep and popped his thumb in his mouth, swallowing hard and sucking. He didn't let himself do it during the day. Connie withdrew his thumb gently and put it under the covers. The dentist had said it would buck his front teeth. What if she hadn't had children? She tried to imagine what it would have been like if she and Howard had just stayed with their cats. She probably would have left him years ago.

"Connie," Howard called from the living room, "Connie." She got up quickly, tiptoed to the door and shut it softly after her.

"Shhh, you'll wake Mischa. What is it now?"

"I can't find my glasses anywhere." He stood there, his arms dangling helplessly.

Connie went over to the mantle. "You're staring right at them, Howard. Here." She picked them up and handed them to him. "If you'd put them in the same place each time, you'd have less trouble." While he was away, she hadn't had to look for anything he'd lost. Hadn't had to listen to him berating her for not screwing the tops on the jam. Above all, she hadn't had him there in the background like a smoldering volcano, always about to explode.

Four

Waiting for her mother to arrive made Connie's stomach clench. Even though she knew it was stupid, she felt childishly eager. She walked over to the coffee table to check her arrangement of Dutch tulips, their heads bent like swans. Flowers had been her first language of love. Even as a child she knew she couldn't tell her mother what she felt, so she brought her flowers. The worse she felt, the more colorful the bouquet. To pass time, she picked up the *Newsweek* article she'd been reading on a series of shootings in San Francisco. People were wondering if it was tied to the Hearst kidnapping. Yesterday a young black man had walked up to a pregnant woman and shot her. The bullet had lodged in her spine, paralyzing her for life. Reading about it made Connie jumpier than she'd been before. She put the magazine down and phoned her brother Steve.

"Am I getting you too early?"

"The time is later here, remember? New York." Her brother's voice was teasing. "You must be writing something. Off in some other world."

"No such luck. I'm waiting for M." That was their nickname for her. Short for Majesty. Sometimes DM, Divine Majesty. "She's not even here yet, and I'm already climbing the walls. I don't know why she insisted on coming now when Howard's just back. We're not settled down yet. It's going to be as tense as a meeting between the SLA and Randolph Hearst." She stopped herself from telling him about her fight with Howard. It would just worry him. He liked to think things were getting better.

Her brother laughed. "Take a deep breath. M gets along pretty well with Howard. I bet the first thing she does when she gets home is boast to me about how tactful she was with you." Connie heard a buzz. "Damn, there's a call on my other line. I better take it. I have a case to take to court tomorrow, a soft-drink king who wants to disinherit his eldest son. Just remember how lucky you are not to have M with you the rest of the year. Okay? Chin up."

"Thanks, Steve, you've cheered me up. Good luck with your case." She put the receiver down gently. She never would have imagined when she'd tried to drown her baby brother in the swimming pool, how much she was going to like him later.

She waited anxiously at the gate straining for a sight of her mother's curly gray hair. The first few minutes—the first hug, the frail body, the soft, soft face—were always the best. Everything wordlessly said. Mother. Child. The illusion of hearing and being understood. Holding her mother against her shoulder, Connie felt it might be possible to get over the past, even feel some compassion. She picked up her mother's bags. They were surprisingly heavy. You would have thought she was staying a month instead of four days.

"I'm so glad you could come and get me, darling. I hope it didn't inconvenience you too much."

"Not at all, Mother." She shifted hands, putting the lighter bag on her left. Her mother knew damn well that she'd had to cancel the job interview she'd had at Saint Mary's. Elsie had refused to take the shuttle or even a cab, insisting that Connie pick her up.

"You can reschedule it, I'm sure." Elsie had said, impervious to Connie's distress. "Besides, it's not as though you seriously needed a job, darling. You told me yourself it was just a spur of the moment thing. If your teacher friend hadn't gotten sick and had to leave, you probably would never have thought of it."

Connie helped her mother into the Pinto, settled herself in the driver's seat and circled her way out of the parking garage. Elsie seemed content for the moment. She'd succeeded in getting what she wanted. Her own armored tank with Connie as personal body guard. Though she was hiding it pretty well, Connie knew how trips terrified her. She made Berkeley sound like the wilds of Africa, asking whether there was a drugstore nearby, whether she could get medicines if....

Elsie breathed deeply and smiled. "Darling, darling Connie, how wonderful to have a tan in February. It looks so beautiful against that rose blouse. Like the Ingres painting of a young woman looking into her mirror." The woman didn't look like her at all, but Connie didn't contradict her mother. It wasn't worth it. As a matter of fact, the portrait looked like her mother as a young woman. Her mother was always seeing her as someone else.

"You know I've been looking at that painting for years," her mother went on, "but last week I discovered that one arm is too long. It's all out of proportion. Isn't it odd that I never noticed before?"

"I think it's wonderful the way you keep seeing new things. I wish I could." Connie felt tension radiate down her back. She shoved the inflatable pillow lower against her sacrum.

"You do all the time in your criticism." Her mother stressed the word, setting it off. Connie knew she despised critics. Artists were the only people that mattered. "Is something wrong with your back, dear?" Connie gripped the wheel hard and straightened up vehemently. "Maybe you should do some of those old posture exercises Miss Magnus worked out for you."

"I never could figure out why you made me do those things. Even Dad thought it was ridiculous. Walking around with books on my head. He was right." Miss Magnus had made her do chin-ups until her arms ached, pressed the hollow of her spine against the door. "He wanted me to enjoy life. Do things with my friends. Ride, swim. He wasn't always worrying about health the way you do." She remembered him at the beach practicing throwing his Indian clubs. She saw him in his bathing trunks laced up the front, twirling the clubs in the air while she watched entranced. A small dark-haired man with a broad face, gypsy nose, infectious smile. Proud of himself, of his body, of his daughter.

"Let's not get off on the wrong track, Connie. I've been dreaming about seeing you for weeks, darling. I got myself a new jacket just so I'd have something special to wear to San Francisco." She adjusted her neck and shoulders, posing, straightening her jade necklace.

It was maddening that after all these years, she persisted in calling Berkeley San Francisco. Connie had a sudden crazy urge to rip the jade necklace off her throat. It lasted only a moment but it frightened her. "Your jacket is beautiful," she told her mother. She couldn't think what had possessed her. If she'd asked, her mother would probably have given her the necklace. She'd always said she didn't want her children wishing for her death. She'd rather give them things while she was alive.

"You must be tired, Mother. When we get home I'll tuck you up on the sofa for awhile and get you something to drink." Connie glanced sideways at her mother. A moment ago Elsie had been holding herself straight and taut, but even when she sat and let her shoulders round, her sharp eyes moved and penetrated everywhere. Connie sensed them now moving over her profile. Elsie's be-ringed hands, clasping each other in her lap, seemed to Connie to show her relentless will. She spoke softly, moved gracefully, but underneath was steel. It was the same with her clothes, bought at fashionable boutiques then combined with utter disregard for fashion. They both masked and revealed her artistic force.

Today, though it was quite warm, she was wearing a green jacket from Rive Gauche with full cut, blousy sleeves like an artist's smock. Underneath she had on a simple lavender dress with a flowing skirt lined in darker silk, one of a series she'd had made in different colors, like a series of abstract paintings on a single theme. She wore expensive sandals with white silk stockings that drew attention to her small feet and made them resemble the tiny bound feet of Chinese women. She apologized to Connie for them, explaining that she wore only sandals now because her feet hurt her. "But why shouldn't I do what I like?" she asked. "After all, I'm over eighty." In spite of the sandals, she still cared terribly how she looked. And what amazed Connie was that she did look striking. Or rather, she struck her as a presence. This was the genuine article. No one else could have put on those clothes and looked like that. Or so it seemed to Connie. Anyone else would have looked ridiculous. Still, Connie could see that she was feeling exposed and anxious even inside the closed car.

The children greeted them at the door with branches of flowering quince for grandma.

"It's so lovely to see you, my darlings," Elsie gave them perfunctory hugs, then installed herself on the sofa with the flowers beside her and pulled the afghan over her feet. "I've brought you presents." She took two beautifully wrapped packages out of her bag.

"Those sketches you sent me were very special, Mischa," Elsie said, while Mischa ripped the paper off his package of colored pens. "What a wonderful idea you had." Connie remembered the drawings. A squiggle that he said was the eye of God watching the world. Other squiggles that showed the sight coming out of his eyes like rays. Connie saw a bewildered look spread over Sarah's face. She'd sent Elsie drawings too. Carefully drawn and shaded. Now she put the box of oil paints Elsie had given her down on the coffee table without opening them.

"I'll draw something for you right now. Something even better than last time." Mischa ran into the kitchen and came back with a pad.

"Why don't you do it in the other room and surprise me with it later. I think that would be much better, don't you? I'm very tired," she added when Mischa looked as if he were going to protest. Sarah grabbed his arm and marched him out of the room.

"Thanks, Sarah," Connie called after her, wanting somehow to cheer her, to get that unhappy look off her face. A few minutes later, she heard the sound of Elton John's song *Goodbye Yellow Brick Road* blaring from Sarah's room. She thought she could make out Sarah singing along with it. "*You can't plant me in your penthouse, I'm going back to my plow.*" Not high art maybe, but these songs had a way of expressing feelings. Connie had read that in psychiatric hospitals the nurses paid great attention to what the kids were listening to. It was the only way to reach some of them.

"I think I'm in for a rough time with Sarah," Connie said, sitting down on the couch in the space left by her mother's feet. The music seemed to be howling now. Lonely. "She's been hanging around a record store after school. The men there all look as though they've been sleeping on the streets. And she has a boyfriend who looks like an escapee from *The Wild Ones.*" What a coward she was, Connie thought. Why couldn't she come right out and tell her mother how tactless she'd been, how she'd hurt Sarah's feelings? Why turn it around and put Sarah down?

"She's not a child anymore. You can't control what she does. You might as well just take it with good grace." Elsie took the pillow out from behind her, plumped it and put it back with a sigh.

"That's easy for you to say," Connie responded angrily. "But I'm responsible for her." How could Elsie sit there and imply that she would have done it better—had done it better? Wasn't Connie living proof of the mess she'd made?

Elsie straightened her aquamarine ring. "I always tried to leave you free to make your own mistakes."

"Like letting me ride a horse that was too hard for me, that threw me and broke my ribs? You wouldn't even believe they were broken. You were playing with Steve, remember? You thought I was just trying to get attention." Connie had always thought of herself as the expendable one. Her mother let her run wild because she just didn't care. Her brother Steve, her father, they were the ones who mattered.

"Well, you were always faking. How was I to know this time it was real?" Her mother shrugged helplessly.

"You could have checked at least. And gotten rid of the horse afterwards. Weren't you afraid it was going to happen again?" She picked up the wrapping paper Mischa had thrown on the coffee table and folded it into a tiny square.

"Now that I think of it, it was your father, it was Simon, who wanted to keep the horse. He was sure you were going to win a first in a local show that summer. And I didn't want to be overprotective. We had friends whose son had drowned ice-skating and they never let the other child do anything. It was awful. I didn't want to make you fearful." She reached down and patted Connie's hand.

"Sounds like a good idea, but I'm not sure it worked."

"I didn't mean to criticize your way of doing things, dear. I think you do a wonderful job with the children." Connie could feel the plea in her mother's voice. Don't tell me more bad things or I'll feel it's somehow my fault. That I wasn't a good mother to you.

"Actually, my results aren't so hot," Connie said plaintively. "Sarah's room's a pigpen. She throws tantrums over nothing. Mischa always thinks he's dying. When his belly aches, he says it's appendicitis. He thinks that one of his legs is shorter than the other." She looked up to see how her mother was taking this.

"Steve was a bit anxious around seven. Afraid of burglars and that sort of thing. I wouldn't worry, Mischa's such a self-confident child."

"It's mostly bluff. He's like jelly inside." Connie bit her lip. She was the one that was jelly. Her mother turned her into a God-damned jelly.

"He feels things deeply. You should be pleased. He has an artist's temperament." Elsie leaned towards Connie, intent on having her admit the importance of an artistic sensitivity.

"No doubt Mischa's a genius. I don't know about you, but I'd rather have a normal, happy child."

"Being gifted doesn't mean you're disturbed. I always thought you were a gifted child. I kept telling Simon how precocious you were. Though I admit he never believed me. But why don't you speak to someone about Mischa, if you're so concerned?"

"I am speaking to someone. I'm speaking to you." Connie expelled her breath in a sort of hiccuping sob that was part laugh. The idea that her mother might actually listen was oddly funny.

"I mean..." Elsie drew back, startled.

"I know what you mean, a psychiatrist. But I don't want to. I've had enough of that." She shook her head vigorously. "Uh, uh. No more surrogate parents." Thank God Marc wasn't one of those.

"You're not going back to Dr. Schlossburg?" Her mother looked at her reproachfully.

"No. I'm not. It wasn't getting me anywhere." That wasn't exactly true, but Connie knew it was the most hurtful thing she could say. It paid back the hurt of having a mother who'd been in analysis for thirty years. Jesus! Wasn't analysis supposed to bring you freedom? It just seemed to make Elsie better at hiding her feelings, getting what she wanted by subtler means.

Elsie sighed and lay back against the pillows, a signal that the conversation was over. Connie resisted an impulse to soften what she'd said. Take it back.

"I'm tiring you, Mother," she said, gathering up the branches of quince and offering her mother her arm. "Why don't you go in and take a nap in the bedroom. I'll tell Sarah to turn her music down."

After she'd helped her mother into the bedroom, spoken to Sarah and put the branches in a vase, Connie retreated to the bathroom and drew herself a hot bath. She poured in a capful of pine essence and sunk into the foam closing her eyes. Her therapist had told her repeatedly that the kind of conversation she had just had with her mother was a futile form of acting out, but she hadn't been able to stop herself. And where had it gotten her? Nowhere. She'd made her mother worry, that's all. Broken down her poise. Well, at least that was familiar. She knew where she stood. All that about leaving her free. Sure, her mother had done it when she was busy with other things. Because she didn't give a damn. But when Connie's father died, she'd changed completely. It was hard to believe she was the same woman. Her mother seemed to have forgotten all that. How she'd begged Connie not to leave her in the house alone, clinging to her neck like a drowning person.

Connie had felt so sorry for her mother. Left with no one to care for her. She hadn't been aware of how her mother was manipulating her. With her first boyfriend, her mother had seemed so generous, giving Connie the key to her room. And everything was fine—as long as she and Freddy were content to stay home and make love, then sit in the suffocatingly hot living room eating cookies with Elsie. But when Connie wanted to go out to the movies with him, her mother had a fit. Sobbing and throwing herself around in her chair.

"Listen, Mrs. Silver," Freddy had said, propelling Connie toward the door, "Connie has her own life. It's time she got on with it instead of sitting around here pampering you."

But though she'd gone, the chocolate cake she'd tried to eat stuck in her throat, and she didn't even get to see the movie. She'd made Freddy take her home. Her mother was lying on the sofa when Connie came back, her hands deep in her skirt pockets watching the television with the sound turned off. A perfect emblem of despair.

Connie still thought about it years later. How she should have steeled herself and kept going out. Taken that trip to Europe. Gone to a college in California. But she hadn't had the strength and now it was too late to change. She would never have married Howard if she hadn't lost confidence in herself. *He'll get me out*, was what she thought when she looked at him. But she'd just hemmed herself in again.

The bubbles were dying down. Connie scooped up a handful of foam and spread it over her chest. Her father would never have caved in the way she had. He never let himself be bullied. Not even when the street gang had broken his nose. Sitting warm in his lap, he let her feel the crooked place where the bones had set badly. She'd always assumed she'd grow up to be like him. "Chip off the old block," he'd called her. But somehow she hadn't. He made everything he did seem so easy. Paying the bills, deciding where to go on vacation. Even taking her shopping for clothes as though he knew just what little girls wore.

How could he have died of a heart attack? Abandoning her at fifteen just when she needed him most, without giving her a warning. "How could you do it?" she'd whispered into her pillow after the funeral service, "without saying goodbye." It took away her energy. She'd felt it draining out like sap from a cut tree. She'd thought it was her fault. Her father had chosen to die, to leave her because she made some fatal error.

Connie swirled the green water with her toe. It was getting cold. She turned on the tap and felt the hot water jetting down through the cooler layers towards her legs. That was where it started. Back when she was a skinny fifteen year old with metal braces on her teeth. That was where the scene of desertion had taken over her mental landscape.

"Darling," she heard her mother trying the knob. "I

couldn't sleep after all."

"Don't," she said before she had a chance to think. "I'm just finishing up. I'll get dressed and be right out." The last thing she wanted now was to have her mother watching while she dried herself. Telling her she had left wet spots on her back. She dried quickly, threw her clothes on and walked Elsie back to the living room. She had just gotten her moved back to the sofa and poured her a glass of sherry when Howard came in. She could see his look of displeasure when he saw Elsie in his favorite corner of the sofa with his afghan on her feet.

"Hello, Elsie." Howard entered briskly and gave her a perfunctory kiss. His tone was perfectly polite. "How was your flight?"

"Fine, dear. Thank you." Elsie smiled up at him.

"No weather problems? Everything else all right?" He inclined towards her like a solicitous innkeeper, clasping his hands.

"Perfect." She smiled again more broadly, willing him to see how easy she was being.

"Good, good."

"And is your work going well?"

"I'm satisfied. I think I've made progress."

Connie wondered how long they could keep up this empty exchange.

Just then, Mischa came running in. When he saw Howard, he stopped. He was holding Howard's pipe. "Look what I did," he waved it exuberantly. "I cleaned your pipe. To surprise you. It was all dirty inside." Connie held her breath. Oh God, now we're in for it.

"Give me that." Howard snatched it away from him. "What did you clean it with?"

"I soaked it in the sink. To get all the black stuff out."

Howard examined the pipe, holding it, Connie thought, as though it were a packet of explosives. "You little beast, you've ruined it. How can you be so stupid? You never put water on a pipe."

"I didn't know." She saw Mischa's shoulders sag.

"Haven't you seen me clean my pipe? Well, haven't you?"

"Howard, maybe that's enough," Connie said, trying to keep the storm from breaking. "I think he understands."

Howard ignored her. "Mischa, when I ask you a question, answer me." She noticed his jaw twitching. In a minute she was afraid he was going to grab Mischa and shake him.

Mischa looked down at his feet "With those wires?"

"Of course with those wires. They're pipe cleaners. What are you, an imbecile?" Before Connie could interfere he reached out and pulled Mischa's ear hard. Mischa yelped.

"He's your son, for God's sake, let go of him!" Connie took Mischa's arm and moved him around behind her. "Besides, he was only trying to do you a favor."

"What difference does that make? It's spoiled, isn't it? Why didn't you watch him? Keep him away from my things?" The veins on his neck stood out.

"You're his father. They're your things, why don't you teach him how to treat them? You live here too, you know."

"If I'd had my way I would have taken a belt to him, taught him some respect. But you wouldn't let me touch him, you kept blatting on about his delicate psyche. Yammer, yammer, yammer." He pinched his fingers together like a duck's bill, quacking. "You want me to do it now? Do you?" He took a step towards her.

"Don't you dare touch him. You're absurd. You don't have the slightest idea of how to treat anyone. Least of all your own children."

"What?" he stared at her surprised. "I didn't come home to be insulted. In my own house."

"You can always go back to Israel. Go ahead if you want to. I'll even call the airline for you."

"Children, children," Elsie called, clapping her hands together to get their attention. "For heaven's sake. Don't get so upset about a trifle. Let me buy you a new pipe, Howard."

She advanced regally. "Come, Connie. Let's go right now."

"After the way he's behaved? I don't feel like doing anything. You get the pipe if you're so anxious to woo him. I've had it. Actually, I don't see why you can't stick up for me for once. This isn't really helping me."

"You can't replace that pipe anyway, Elsie," Howard said gruffly. "I got it in Jerusalem. The wood was aged a hundred years." He turned towards Mischa, who was peeking out from behind Connie's back. "Do you hear that, Mischa? Do you see what you've done? In five minutes you've destroyed what it took a hundred years to make."

Mischa hung back terrified. "I thought you'd like it," he stammered. Howard raised his hand.

"I'm sorry, Daddy." He was crying now. "I was going to wash the car but then I thought...."

"Never mind what you thought. You would have botched that too. Just keep your hands off my things from now on. I don't want to see you touching anything. Is that clear? Not for any reason. You have your mother's lack of aptitude for things, apparently."

Mischa looked increasingly hurt. Connie squeezed Howard's arm. "That's enough, Howard. More than enough. There's no need to be gratuitously nasty."

"You should really give up smoking anyway, dear," Elsie put in. "You know Freud died of tongue cancer."

"That was from cigars, not pipes. That's why I switched in the first place. Because my lip was getting irritated. But I don't know why I'm telling you this. None of you give a damn."

Elsie suddenly clutched her head. "I think I'm getting one of my migraines."

"Surely not, Mother. You haven't had one in ages. I'll get you a glass of water. We'll stop this now and you'll settle down and feel fine." Connie went into the kitchen for the water. Mischa tagged after her, still sniffing. She turned the water on. While it was getting cold, she hugged him against her. "You must feel rotten," she told him, "but try to forget it."

"I can't forget it. I hate him," he said into her stomach. She filled the glass. Looking over his head she saw Howard pick up his paper and retreat towards his study.

"I don't remember you fighting like this," her mother said later. "Do you think it's good for the children?"

"They feel the tension anyway. It's probably better than standing like a zombie while he abuses them."

"I suppose," her mother said doubtfully. "Your father never lost his temper except once, when I didn't want him to go away on a business trip."

Connie had a faint image of her mother in her embroidered robe, crying and pulling on her father's sleeve. He had gone into the bedroom and slammed the door. That time it had been too much even for him.

Spring
1974

Five

"I can't come for lunch," Connie told Marc, her heart racing, "Mother's here such a short time. I wouldn't feel right running out on her." She kept her voice flat and polite because she could sense Elsie straining to hear from the other room, ready to pick up any hint of excitement.

Marc didn't seem to notice Connie's restraint. He was full of persuasive energy.

"I'll give you two good reasons why you should come today. Reason one: I'm here and I want to see you. Reason two: I think you want to see me. Besides, it's a glorious day. We can sit in the garden and sample the Domaine Chandon I picked up. Surely your mother can amuse herself for an hour or so. You can fix her something first. Tell her a friend is having problems of the heart and you have to talk to her."

"I see your problem, Milly. It's rough but I'll see what I can do." There, that should throw her mother off the track. Just listening to Marc's rusty voice excited her. She could picture the way he was moving his lips, forming the words. But why was he making things more difficult for her? She wished he had stayed in San Diego. What was he doing back early, anyway? She hadn't thought to ask.

Connie had planned what she hoped would be a nice diversion for her mother this morning, a chance to show off her expertise. She was taking her over to the neighbors to look at a painting they had on approval. Mr. Johnson taught in the art department at Sacramento State and was delighted to be meeting one of the New York abstract expressionists. He was sure she'd approve his choice of a de Kooning.

The Johnsons ushered Elsie in as if she were royalty. And she did look regal, holding her head high and nodding as though she were in a glass coach. When she was the center of attention, at least Connie didn't have to worry about her getting exasperated and rolling her eyes the way she did when she was bored and wanted to leave.

"He's not afraid to use images." Mr. Johnson pointed to the abstraction over his fireplace. "That's what I admire most about him." Connie could see that the figure, though distorted, was clearly a woman.

"Images are one thing, hatred of your subject is another," Elsie said dryly. "Look at the agitated whirls of that woman's hair," she made a whirlpooling motion with her hand, "and those sharp teeth that seem about to bite. He hates women."

Mr. Johnson bristled. "That's not hatred, that's energy. See the force of the man's brush stroke!" He stabbed his finger at the canvas, "there and there." Connie could see the nervous imprint of a brush that still seemed to move on the surface. "And his palate is as vibrant as Hoffman's."

"We both love his *Door to the River*," Mrs. Johnson added timidly, "with those wonderful yellows and blues."

"His colors are luscious, I agree." Elsie stood back, foot pointed like a dancer, ringed hand on her hip. "But I'm afraid this painting is dominated by negatives, ugliness and anger. It's disturbingly sadistic." Connie cringed. Thank God the Johnsons hadn't actually bought the painting. She tried to think of some appeasing remark. But somehow the Johnsons seemed stimulated rather than crushed. They leaned towards her mother, listening attentively.

Elsie gave them only a moment to digest what she'd said, then moved into a broader attack on violence in modern art in general.

"For me, de Kooning and Pollock, too, have a demonic quality that blows things apart. But they don't break through to create a new star." Once again Connie noticed that the artists her mother criticized were always men. Her mother had never forgiven fate for putting her, with her genius, into the body of a woman. But now she was looking at Connie for agreement, as if they were finding a new way of being women together.

"Heat and brilliance, but somehow sterile," Connie said, disappointed to hear how dull she sounded after her mother's stars and demons.

But Elsie seemed pleased that Connie agreed with her. "Yes," she said, inclining her head graciously.

"I disagree," Mr. Johnson said. "Granted, de Kooning has an explosive quality but it's under firm control. He's a master of composition." He gestured towards the painting. "Look at the way he balances the demands of the figure and the purely abstract forms. You can really see the parts of the woman's body. Every line and tone is clear. But look at that cylinder that seems to shoot rays of light into the woman's face and that freewheeling triangular shape. They act abstractly but at the same time they add emotional meaning to the figure. If that isn't creating something new, I don't know what is."

"That doesn't address the hatred," Elsie started.

Mrs. Johnson flashed her a broad social smile. "Didn't Pollock's wife have a show at the Whitney recently?" she asked, positioning herself between Elsie and her husband. "What is her name? It's on the tip of my tongue."

"Lee Krasner," Elsie said coolly. She was clearly annoyed at being interrupted and scornful of Mrs. Johnson's ignorance. It flashed through Connie's mind that Mrs. Johnson knew all about Lee Krasner, she just didn't want any more arguments. "It is gratifying to see her coming into her own. I was getting fed up with seeing her photographed in an apron. As though all she could do was cook. A good show. Better than most nowadays. But still, something missing." She looked slyly at Connie and veered back towards her earlier subject. "People should study the Greeks and the Egyptians. There is real power. Not the kind that tears apart but the kind that heals, a power that makes things grow, like sunshine pouring down."

Mr. Johnson frowned and murmured something about time will tell, but Connie felt sucked into her mother's words the way she had so many times before. The beauty of the images, the generosity of the concept. Damn it. If her mother could imagine this healing power in art, why couldn't Connie get any? Where did her mother hide it? Hoarding it up to spill it out on her canvases.

The idea of being healed made Connie think about Marc's hands with their fringe of black hair. She was tempted to tell her mother about him. Even boast a little, compare him to her lawyer father. He's interested in social justice too, she might say. She could imagine how that would irritate her mother. Elsie liked to keep up the illusion that no man resembled Simon in the slightest. After all, if there had been anyone, wouldn't her mother have found him in all those years of widowhood?

As she walked Elsie back home, Connie thought about Marc cooking for her at his house, his sleeves rolled back exposing his forearms, chopping or cutting things with deft, precise movements of those delicate hands. When her mother lay down to take a nap, Connie called Marc and told him she'd have lunch with him.

Marc's house had the steeply pitched overhanging roof of chalets in Switzerland or Northern Italy. It was perched on the top of a hill in a grove of redwoods, perfectly private. As she went up the steep steps, Connie wondered whether her mother would nap until she got back. She'd said she was tired. But it would be like her to wake up and get into a panic about something. Even if she didn't, Connie really didn't feel very good about leaving her. Still, if she'd come she might as well relax and enjoy it.

"How was San Diego?" she asked Marc.

"Lousy. I couldn't wait to get back." He took her arm walking close beside her on the narrow path. He'd been waiting for her outside in the garden.

"Excited about getting back to work on your tax returns?" She teased, leaning her hip against him slightly.

"It's certainly more exciting than seeing a bore." Inside she felt a momentary shock. The drop off was so steep it was like being in a cabin at the top of a mountain. Everything looked hand hewn. There was a big beamed ceiling and a stone fireplace. Light poured in from a window filled with the blue of the bay. Giant philodendrons threw leafy patterns across the bed.

Marc went into the small kitchen that opened onto the living room. She could see nicely browned pieces of chicken in a casserole on the stove. And the room was filled with the pungent smell of garlic and herbs.

"Sorry your weekend was a bust," Connie said after a minute. She wondered about the woman. Was she young or middle-aged? Blond or brunette? Lawyer, teacher, labor organizer? Had Marc slept with her?

He shrugged. "She wanted me to stay but it wasn't working. I shouldn't have gone down there in the first place. I hate to hurt people's feelings. Especially women's." He came over to her and gently rubbed her shoulders. "But at least I got a trip to the zoo out of it."

Her face brightened. "That is a fantastic zoo, isn't it? I love the set up." She suddenly had the ridiculous idea of going there with him. Going to the zoo, she mocked herself. That's not what you want, you idiot, and you know it. "All that space," she added, blushing slightly. "The animals can breed and mate almost the way they would in the wild. They even got the gorillas to mate. They just had a baby." She smiled at him. The birth of a healthy male gorilla in October was the first live birth in over twenty years.

"I saw him, diapers and all. There was a very pretty girl feeding him a bottle. Have you noticed people have animal affinities? Endomorphs love the heavies, rhinos, elephants. I'm a big cat man myself." He toyed with a strand of her hair. "Let me guess...you like birds. Pink flamingoes, cranes." He moved around to where he could see her face. "No. Something smaller, more delicate. Ah, I have it, you're mad for jeweled hummingbirds."

"Wrong." She shook her head, laughing. "I like monkeys. Not so exotic but more fun. I actually studied Langurs for a year."

"Don't tell me you went to Madagascar." He loaded a brass tray and set the table outside in a patch of sunshine.

"No, just up to Tilden Park. The University has a monkey station and I had a friend in Anthropology who wanted to know if langurs have an incest taboo."

"Do they?" Marc asked, amused.

Connie sat down and stretched languorously. "I never found out for sure. I got frustrated because they couldn't talk. I always wanted to interview them. 'Hey, kid, do you know that guy you're with is your Daddy?' That sort of thing."

Marc laughed, bending over her, filling her plate with food. The steam rose from the rice in a delicate spiral. He's such a perfect looking man, she thought, tall but with delicate features, nothing out of proportion. The sort of man she could never have imagined paying attention to her. She picked a chicken leg up in her fingers and bit through the skin. "What did you put in this, besides garlic? It has a great flavor." Juice trickled down her chin and she wiped it off quickly, hoping he hadn't noticed. Only women like Mrs. Waters in *Tom Jones* could drip grease and make it look sexy.

Still, Marc was looking at her mouth attentively. "Lemon juice. But it's the garlic that does it, twenty-four cloves! I'm preparing for Europe. Got my passport in the mail this morning. It's beginning to feel like I'm really going. I bought myself a tri-lingual phrase book."

"You're a lucky guy. I envy you." She picked up her knife and fork and cut a piece of chicken small enough to slip between her lips. Thank God he hadn't made a pasta that would have slithered off her fork and into her lap.

"Come with me." He flashed a mischievous smile.

She laughed. "Sure. Just give me a ticket and I'll be there like a shot." She relaxed and took a gulp of wine. Marc was unbuttoning the collar of his shirt. He had touched her shoulders. What if she reached over and put her finger on the little pulse on his throat?

"I like your shirt. You look good," she said finally, breaking off a crust of french bread. Between the sun and the wine she was feeling giddy.

"Be careful. I'll think you only want me for my body."

"I thought only women worried about that." She mopped up a bit of gravy with her bread and put it in her mouth.

"I used to hate it when women looked at me as a sex object. But I don't mind you liking my looks. I want to please you."

The phone rang suddenly and he disappeared through a door that opened on the small stone patio where they were sitting.

"They trashed the house? Well, why'd you let her have a party if you weren't going to be there to supervise?" Marc sounded furious. This must be Alix, talking to him about Selina. "I couldn't, you know that. I had business to take care of in San Diego." Some business, Connie thought, watching flamingoes with some broad. She felt a flash of sympathy for Alix. It was no picnic taking care of a teenage girl by yourself.

"She feels neglected. Believe me, Alix, she doesn't think you take her seriously as a person. If you stayed home with her more...I do see her, I see her plenty. We just went to the movies last week. Don't nitpick, Alix. Maybe it was three weeks ago." His voice was downright nasty now. "So what? I have a terrific rapport with her. And basically she's a great kid. It's no use trying to make me think she's a delinquent. I know you're just trying to shaft me, Alix...Hello. Hello?" Alix must have hung up. Connie was disappointed. Somehow, she'd imagined Marc having a mature divorce. One where the parents worked on the children's problems together.

Connie reached for the magazine that was lying open on a deck chair near the table. She didn't want Marc to think she'd been listening. While she picked at her chicken, she looked at pictures of Patty Hearst as a child in her communion dress. Pictures the family hoped would evoke pity in her captors.

Marc came out with a wooden salad bowl filled with leafy greens, set it on the table then stood behind her, bending over to hug her. His body felt incredibly warm against hers. She could feel her heart beating faster.

"Ready for the next course?" he whispered against her ear. "It's spinach salad, then my special desert."

"I'm not sure I have time for both," she said, wondering if her mother was all right. This lunch was taking longer than she'd planned.

"Sure you will." He served her a generous portion of spinach flecked with bacon.

"It's a relief to have some other tapes besides Nixon's, isn't it?" She nodded at the magazine. "I'm so glad she hasn't been hurt, though the SLA sounds like a group of crazies." The tail-end of the sixties comet, some journalist had called them. Sputtering out in the skies of Oakland.

"Patty Hearst is just one bewildered child ruined by being privileged. Nixon has duped an entire country. No president has ever been caught like this before. Jimmying open someone's door. Did you hear that fatuous State of the Union message he gave?" Connie shook her head. "Vowing to protect Americans from electronic snooping! It would be laughable, if it weren't tragic. Our country's had too many false promises for too long. It makes people crazy. The SLA is only part of a much more serious problem. They want something concrete. Food money for California's poor. When they work out a plan, I'm going to help distribute it." He looked at her face. "What's the matter, am I being too radical for you?"

"No, it's not that." Damn. Why did she have to leave just when they were getting to Patty Hearst. The girl was becoming an obsession. Connie pushed the plate away and elaborately studied her watch. "It's just, I really should go. I've left mother too long already."

"How old is your mother?" he asked, pulling his chair out roughly and sitting down again, his legs apart, hands on his thighs.

"Eighty-four. Why?" Connie was fascinated by the way the fabric of his trousers was creased under his fingers. She made herself look up, into his face.

"It's surprising that an eighty-four year old woman can't find something to do with herself for an hour."

"I should fix her lunch." Connie pulled at a loose thread on her sweater and popped a button. It lay blinking at her from the gravel path. She felt sure her mother was waking up, calling her.

"Is she disabled? Even a ten year old child can get herself something out of the fridge. On the other hand, I can't eat the rest of this by myself. Or do you want me to give you a doggie bag?" He scooped up a serving of mousse and for a minute she thought he was going to throw it in her lap. But he only put it on a fresh plate. Did he think he'd convinced her, then? Before he could serve her, she got up.

"You don't understand. Some people are always children. I've always felt responsible for her. Since I was fifteen. By now it's habit. I can't help it." She held out her hand.

"You mean you're really going? Sometimes I can't figure

you out. You seemed so eager. I thought you couldn't wait."

"My brain's all fogged up, that's all." She started walking slowly toward her car.

"Turn on your de-fogger then." He held her arm and turned an imaginary knob on the side of her head. "Or you're going to miss out on a lot more than my chocolate mousse."

When she got home, Elsie was sitting on the couch kneading her stomach with an unhappy expression. "That spice cake you made last night was delicious but it was awfully rich. My tummy's on the blink."

"It had almost no butter. I don't see how it could have hurt you." Even though Connie had figured her mother would find some complaint to hit her with when she came back, she could hear her voice going up, frustrated. Stop it, she told herself. There's no point. We'll never have a real conversation. "Never mind, we'll try to get something you like for supper. Maybe broiled fish." She'd had her hour of freedom. She could afford to be a little generous.

As they drove to the Safeway, Elsie chatted about some cousins in Long Island. Connie wasn't listening. She hadn't seen any of them in years.

They wheeled the cart through the aisles. Connie noticed her mother's balance seemed a little off. Though she still walked quickly, she was leaning against the cart handle. Now she lurched uncertainly towards a bottle of Vermouth on a shelf at the end of the aisle. At the meat counter, Connie saw Jane, the woman who had introduced her to Marc. Connie hoped Jane wasn't going to ask whether she had seen Marc again. That would be all she needed. Her mother bent down stiffly and massaged the arch of her foot through her sandal straps. Connie wished she wouldn't do that. An unbecoming roll of flesh was visible above her silk stocking. In the old days her mother would never have upended herself like that in public. Upside down that way, it was clear she was expanding, getting more bottom heavy.

Jane rushed up, gave Connie a brief hug and clasped Elsie's hand. "Mrs. Silver," she gushed, "how nice to see you. Why don't we all go out for tea?"

"I'd love to," Elsie said, "but I have to go home and lie down for awhile. My daughter's orders. I've been on my feet too long."

Jane looked disappointed. "I wanted to hear how you've been doing." She gave Connie a knowing look. "And I have some really juicy gossip to tell you. Stanley and Mary are finally going to get a divorce. I've been at her for months to do it."

Elsie gave a loud groan. "I have that pain again, darling, right in the ball of my foot. Do you think it's serious?"

"I doubt it, but we better go." Connie took her mother's arm. She was almost glad Elsie was being difficult. She didn't really want to talk to anyone about Marc. Especially not Jane.

As soon as Elsie had detached Connie from her friend she revived. "What's the matter with her?" Elsie asked. "She looks terrible."

"She's upset. Her husband's running around with a younger woman."

"So she consoles herself by intervening in other people's marriages." Elsie sighed. "I hate people who meddle."

In spite of the fact that they had ice-cream and frozen vegetables in the car, Elsie insisted on stopping at the Green Nursery. She wanted to buy Connie some flowers to brighten up her terrace.

"We need someone to help us," she said, aggressively moving ahead of a woman who was obviously waiting. The girl behind the counter stared at her.

"Mom!" Connie plucked at her arm but Elsie shrugged her off.

"We've been waiting a half hour already and I'm not feeling very well."

"Would Harvey come to the front please," the girl called into the speaker. When a young man in green overalls and a beard appeared, Elsie immediately started talking at him.

"My daughter likes bright colors. Full sun, isn't it, darling?" She didn't wait for Connie's answer but followed him into the bedding plant section. Each time she passed a new set of flats, she exclaimed over the colors. Then she looked at the herbs.

"Do you have any tomatoes?" she asked. "That way we'd get vitamins and color at the same time."

"It's way too early for that," the man said.

She tousled Connie's hair. "Remember how I used to paint you eating tomatoes, darling? The juice running over your little brown tummy?"

"How could I forget. I felt ridiculous." Connie thought she saw the young man stifle a laugh behind his hand. They went back to the beginning of the bedding plants and started all over again.

Finally, Elsie stopped in front of some flowers with paper thin petals and peered at the name. "What are these wonderful things?" She unfolded a narrow pair of glasses from her purse. Connie had never seen her mother use them before. She must be getting farsighted.

"Iceland poppies," the young man said before Elsie had adjusted the glasses on her nose.

"Lovely. We'll take a flat." She snapped the glasses shut and stuck them quickly in her purse.

"Isn't that too much, Mom? I don't have all that room."

"You have to bunch them for a strong effect." She molded the air dramatically with her hands.

"They'll get spindly." Connie insisted stubbornly. "Besides the deer will eat them." She imagined them gracefully leaping the railing and tearing the flowers to shreds.

"On the terrace? I doubt that," Elsie said, then added impatiently, "Well, half a flat then and a half of this Lenten rose. The deep rose splashed with purple is sensational, don't you think, Connie dear?"

"Fine. They're all fine." She was tired and bored. Elsie had taken forty minutes to make her choice.

They had parked next to a newspaper stand. As Connie put the bags of fertilizer and planting soil into the trunk, she caught sight of a picture of Patty Hearst in the *Chronicle*. The fragment of last night's dream came into her mind. In the dream huge tables of food were set out, plates of pancakes and sausages, and Connie was stuffing herself even though she knew it was going to make her sick. It must have been triggered by the fact that Patty's father had been offering to give food to the poor. She had the persistent after-image of a narrow closet in which Patty was chained like an animal or one of those feral children found in the jungle that people tried to teach to talk. Connie pictured her crouching naked, her blond hair matted, eating scraps off a dirty newspaper.

"Mom, get a *Chronicle* for me, would you? I want to see if there's anything new today about Patty." Elsie put in a quarter and glanced at the photo sourly before handing it to Connie.

"I don't know what they're making such a fuss about her for. She sounds like such an empty person. The SLA's probably brainwashing her the way the Communists did in Vietnam."

Connie tucked the paper in the door pocket and started the car.

"I'm not so sure. She could have inner resources we don't know anything about. Maybe she'll manage to escape. Become a heroine. Surprise everyone. I don't know why, but it fascinates me." She imagined Patty breaking her chain and climbing out a window in the moonlight. Half Frankenstein, half Joan of Arc.

"You always were interested in violence. Romantic violence but violence none the less," Elsie said dryly.

Connie felt as though she'd been slapped. "That's not true. I never was." Excitement maybe. She always craved excitement. But that was because she was left alone so much. With nurses who didn't care a damn for her. Maybe Patty Hearst wasn't going to get away after all. She was probably in a closet or cellar somewhere like a pale bulb, her eyes fastened on the crack of light under the door.

When they got back, Elsie was suddenly tired again. Too tired to help Connie put things away. Connie was still feeling stung by what her mother had said. It was amazing how she felt free to say anything she wanted and then ignore the way Connie felt about it. Connie wondered if Elsie even realized she'd hurt her. Even that would be something. She carried the flats out onto the terrace. The day had started out almost like summer but now the sun had gone behind thick gray clouds and a nasty wind had sprung up.

Connie got the afghan from the sofa and settled Elsie on a deck chair, then she knelt and started mixing the potting soil with the dirt in the pots.

"Isn't it better to throw out the old dirt and start fresh?" her mother asked, craning her neck to see.

"Maybe. But this is easier." Connie dug out a bit of clotted root and tossed it over the edge of the terrace. The stirred dirt gave off a slightly acrid smell. Like mold.

Elsie got up, clutching the blanket around her and started to tip the dirt out of one of the pots. "This isn't hard at all."

"Mom, wait. I'll help you. It needs to go over the edge." Too late. Dirt clumps rolled like tumbleweeds over the terrace. Her mother let out a moan.

"Oh damn. That was too heavy for me. I think I hurt my shoulder." She stood leaning against the railing. "Oh damn, damn." Connie dropped her trowel and put her arm protectively around her mother.

Elsie drew back with a little cry.

"What's the matter?" Connie asked, a knot of fear clenching her stomach. "Did you wrench your shoulder? Did I hurt you?"

"Your hands are dirty, darling," Elsie said softly, "I want to spare my new jacket. Wash your hands, that's a good girl."

For a second, Connie looked bewildered. She actually felt she was a child again. Her mother seemed as big as the giants in *Gulliver's Travels*. Then she shook her head. "Mother, for heaven's sake, I haven't been a girl for thirty years. Listen. Let's go inside and I'll make you some tea...."

"No, we started this, I want to finish. It's just a muscle spasm. If you'd get me a heating pad, I think that would soothe me."

Christ, Connie thought, a heating pad out here! I'll need thirty feet of cord. "Just let me finish mixing the soil first, okay?"

"Of course, dear. Is there some place I could look?"

"Second closet in the hall. Oh hell, I'll get it." What difference did it make? She washed her hands under the faucet on the deck, opened the door to the inside and went down the hall to the closet, swearing quietly to herself as she rummaged around in blankets that smelled of mothballs. When she found the heating pad, she went into her study and detached the extension cord from her electric typewriter.

"There's no need to be cranky, dear," Elsie said when she got back. "I was perfectly willing to wait." Connie attached the extension cord to the pad and plugged it into a socket in the kitchen. It was still too short so she took another one off the toaster, then trailed the whole mess back to the deck chair.

"By the way," Elsie said looking up at her brightly, "I read the draft of the paper you left me. It flows very well."

"Thank you." So she actually liked it. Connie's heart softened. She handed the pad to her mother with a smile.

"Though there is always a danger of over-interpretation, don't you think? I find critics doing that all the time when it comes to art."

"I like to lay out alternatives. It's my way," Connie said,

bending back over the plants and beginning to divide them. She felt like a balloon with a slow leak. When was she going to grow up? Stop caring so much what her mother thought of her? She plunged her trowel angrily into the dirt, severing roots.

"I'm sure you're right, dear. I don't know your field, of course. But in the art world, the critics are so busy being clever they often miss the point entirely." Swathed in the blanket that way, Elsie looked like someone on a luxury cruise waiting for high tea.

Connie massed the Lenten roses in a big terra cotta pot and added some fertilizer, breathing in the muted odor of processed steer manure. "If you think I missed something, why don't you come out and say it? I wouldn't have given it to you if I didn't want to hear your opinion." She straightened up and glared at her mother.

"Why don't you try a border of primroses?" Elsie said. Some things weren't worth arguing about. Connie silently lifted out some of the plants she'd just put in. "I wish you'd go back to writing poetry. You had such a flair for it," she sighed.

"I'm not a bad critic either," Connie flashed back before she caught herself. How childish can I be? Next I'll want to bring her the review of my book in the *New Republic*. The one that said I cast light on the dark places in Lawrence's psyche. "Maybe you just don't like my type of criticism," she said more quietly, settling primroses in the vacant spaces. "Well, never mind. I suppose I shouldn't have bothered you with it."

"Of course you should, darling. You know I'm always interested in what you do. It's just that you don't have enough confidence in yourself. In your gifts." She withdrew one of her hands from the blanket and gestured vaguely towards the pot Connie was working on.

"What if I turn out to be horribly ordinary? I'm middle aged, you know." Why can't she tell me it doesn't matter what I am? I tell my kids that all the time. Connie squeezed two more plants in along the edge of the pot and started to sweep up. The pots were horribly crowded even though most of the Iceland poppies were still in the flats. Right now she didn't care if they all died.

"Nonsense!" Elsie flared her nostrils slightly. "Van Gogh wasn't famous until he was dead."

Connie had to laugh. It was as though she'd told her mother that an article of her clothing was common. A garden variety critic for a daughter. Grubbing around in writers' complexes. Not even a poet. "Give me a break, Mother. I'm never going to be Van Gogh. See. Two ears." She lifted her hair with her dirty hands. "And I have no plans to cut one off." If she did, she thought, she'd send it to her mother.

They got into a routine after a day or so. Up by seven, day filled with visits or shopping, to bed right after supper. But on the last night, Connie wanted to do something different.

"I wish you'd let Mother take us to a nice French restaurant just this once," Connie said, adjusting Howard's tie. "Mother doesn't visit that often. And she's leaving tomorrow." She wondered why her mother had bothered to come. To get away from the snow, she supposed. The four days had seemed like a month, she thought, pulling on her softly bloused knit. It was one of the few things her mother had given her that she liked. The mid-calf length had been popular since fall. Probably Elsie succeeded this time because the styles were reminiscent of her youth. The Great Gatsby reborn in the seventies. Funny how history kept coming round again. She could imagine her mother thinking that it looked like a dress for a Jazz Age poet. The poet she wanted Connie to be. Violet with touches of rose.

"Spending more than twenty dollars a person on food is disgraceful," Howard pronounced. "Just because your mother spends money like water doesn't mean that we have to encourage her."

"She doesn't, really." They'd had this conversation many times before, but Connie could never resist it. "She doesn't buy fur coats or take trips around the world the way some people do." Connie wondered why she never let herself agree with him. Even when he was right.

"Pours out your inheritance on a psychoanalyst, that's what she does. The pity of it is, she's going to put us all underground. First your father. Next it will be me. She's got the evil eye, that woman. A real bloodsucker." He thrust his first and little finger forward like the horns of a bull. The ancient sign of the evil eye.

"Do you have to exaggerate so? It makes it unreal. Zip me, will you?" She turned her back to him calmly, hoping to distract him. His chest was beginning to puff out with the familiar epithets that gave him such pleasure. Witch. Vampire. It had become almost a ritual. Though she usually protested, she was aware of a faint forbidden thrill at this wholesale damning of her mother. She shook her head at him in mock reproach and went smiling into the living room.

"Mother, we finally decided where we're going to go. A wonderful Japanese place in the city. I think you'll like it." Seeing her mother's eyes on her, Connie was conscious of the way the dress accented her waist.

"I'm sure I will, darling, as long as it's not too hot. I tend to feel faint in overheated places." Elsie's eyes flicked over Connie's body. She reached over and made a minute adjustment of a shoulder seam.

"Hello, Elsie." Howard gave her a dry kiss, and said he hoped she'd had a nice day. He wanted to show her some of his favorite sights on the way to the restaurant. Would she like that? Their reservation wasn't until seven-thirty.

"Oh, yes. What a lovely idea. How thoughtful of you." Elsie smiled up at him.

Her mother hated driving but Connie could see she was determined to be pleasant. When Howard turned off near the Navy base for a view of the city and the bridge, her mother told him it was magnificent and reached out her hand slightly towards his arm. He drew back just then to point something out to Connie, but she saw him grinding his teeth. His jaw muscle was twitching under his skin while he smiled. His official smile always made her embarrassed for him. It didn't work at all. Besides it frightened her that he couldn't make such a human, ordinary gesture. Now, though, she felt pleased at Howard's imperviousness to her mother's charm—as artificial in its way as his smile—secure in her knowledge that no matter what Elsie did, she couldn't reach him. And she felt an added pleasure in her certainty that her mother didn't understand this.

Once they got to the city, Howard carried on a running monologue about the things they were passing. It probably was as good a way as any to avoid conversation. Connie's mother had been there several times before, so he was concentrating on some of the old houses he liked. Connie had no idea where they were. She had no sense of direction and was totally unable to read a map. Her mother was the same way. She used to tell Connie that if you took her out of a subway station and turned her around she would be lost. She was rather proud of it, as though it confirmed her artistic gift. Helen Frankenthaler was that way too, she said.

Their final stop was a Bahai temple on California street that Howard always liked to show visitors. It was wood with seven turrets, all in different styles. Some were round and swelling like the domes on Russian churches. Others seemed more like medieval steeples. A bizarre jumble, though, God knows, maybe it had some interest as an architectural curiosity. Even Elsie had trouble finding adjectives for this one. Connie imagined her running through a list. Magnificent? No. Harmonious? No. Subtle? No. "Interesting," she finally offered weakly, "very interesting."

Howard made them get out of the car and go across the street to look at the turrets from different angles. "It reminds me of a mosque I saw in Jerusalem," he said. "The one thing the Arabs are good at is building domes." Connie had always known he was passionate about Israel but this was ridiculous. The Bahai temple was a marvel of inventiveness but it had nothing to do with Eretz Israel. Since Howard had gotten back every other word was Judaism this or Jerusalem that. He was like a violin that could only play one note. She should never have let him go.

The restaurant, the Fujiya, was hot after all. The waitress wearing a kimono and obi knelt beside the table and deftly stir-fried huge plates of greens and translucent strips of beef. Howard kept shifting his legs, trying to find a comfortable place for them.

"That's quite a decent scroll painting they have in the entry." Elsie picked at a morsel with her chopsticks. "I wonder whether it's genuine." A warrior sat astride a warhorse with delicately drawn legs. Behind him, a scene of carnage.

Howard glanced at it briefly. "That's not what real warfare is like. Tanks and bombs. Men blown to bits. At the kibbutz I visited, a man had his leg blown off in the Yom Kippur War."

God, this is going to drive Mother crazy, Connie thought. She hates talking about war.

"Remember Doran?" Howard asked Connie. She nodded. "His son was killed. They couldn't even find enough of him to bury."

"That nice boy who played with Sarah? How awful. When is this senseless slaughter going to stop?" Connie shifted in her chair uneasily.

Elsie was studying the scroll with a dreamy expression. "What brush strokes! The bodies are exquisite."

Howard didn't look at her. "There was almost no one who didn't lose someone this time. Thousands dead. That's too much for a tiny country." He poured himself another cup of sake.

Elsie gave a loud sigh. "If they weren't living on someone

else's land, none of this would have happened. They should have given back the Sinai to Egypt. It's not theirs or the West Bank either. Why don't they give those poor Palestinians back their land? And the Israelis aren't the only ones who've taken what didn't belong to them. Look at what we're doing to the Indians."

Connie racked her brain for some way of getting them onto neutral ground.

"Did you see the Chagall windows this trip, Howard? Chagall's always been a favorite of Mother's, hasn't he, Mom? It's so mystical...."

"They were given that land by the British," Howard sputtered, ignoring Connie's attempt to distract him, "or else they paid good money for it. And look what they've made. It was dust and stones. They've irrigated farms, built cities."

"The Arabs were part of the desert." Elsie sipped her tea. "They lived in harmony with it. They didn't feel any need to change. They learned to get by without much water, to shelter themselves from the heat. They survived without damaging their environment. The Bedouins, Lawrence of Arabia...what marvelous romantic figures. The Israelis have ruined the aesthetics of the whole area."

"Mother, most of the Arabs aren't Bedouins. They're clerks and shopkeepers and lawyers. The Palestinians need a homeland for national reasons, not because they're Transcendentalists."

"I suppose it's romantic to want to drive the Jews into the sea, Elsie," Howard said thickly. "Or for the Syrians to fire down onto men farming their land."

Connie felt an ache at the base of her skull. What ever made her think these two could have a relaxed dinner together, let alone find something in common. "You're being just as illogical as Mother, Howard. This isn't a replay of the Holocaust. Israel isn't in danger of being annihilated anymore. It doesn't make sense to evoke those images. It's that kind of paranoia that keeps the Israelis from making peace."

"What do you mean?" Howard asked so loudly that the diners at the next table looked around. "Israel won the right to make terms. Since when does a victorious army go down on its knees to the other side? Believe me, if the Arabs had won in '67 they wouldn't have been making comforting noises to Israel. They would have been cutting people up into little pieces and hanging them in the squares. Power is the name of the game, Connie." He slowly clenched his fist.

Connie stared at him. She hadn't realized how much the Yom Kippur War had changed him. He'd never been so militant. The war seemed to reinforce a sort of Holocaust psychology. The need to stay fully armed at all times, mentally and physically. "I can't accept that, Howard. If Israel is so strong, that's all the more reason to make peace. They could compromise a little, look at their options, make concessions with dignity. War doesn't settle anything. It just leads to endless cycles of bitterness. Look at Vietnam. Tell me what we gained there except heartache."

Elsie suddenly leaned forward. "I don't feel very well." Connie stood up immediately. Her mother's skin was covered by a faint veil of perspiration. When she took her arm, Connie could feel her body trembling. "Get me to the bathroom! Get me to the bathroom!" Elsie clutched her, her eyes frantic.

"I'm going as fast as I can. Don't worry." She spoke to her as you would a child. "You'll probably feel better if you put some cold water on your face." That's what Connie had done for her mother when she got hysterics in the plane over New Mexico and started to cry and vomit. Connie winced, remembering. They'd had to give her oxygen. But maybe this time it was real.

"Hurry! Hurry! I'm going to faint." Elsie's voice took on the hysterical tone Connie knew so well.

"No, you're not." She's probably just eaten too much, Connie thought, steering her toward the faintly painted ladies' room at the other side of the restaurant. Even I feel stuffed. Maybe she'd feel better if she threw up.

"I can't go any further." Elsie stood leaning against her.

"Yes, you can. Come on. Just take one little step at a time." Why couldn't she just walk to the bathroom like a normal person? Connie took a tighter grip on her mother's upper arm and tried to propel her forward. She felt sure Elsie could move if she'd only exert herself. But Elsie slowly slid down against a soji screen and sat fanning herself with her hand.

The manager came over looking concerned. "What is it? Is there anything I can do?" he asked.

"Probably just indigestion." And nerves, she thought. Mostly nerves. Her mother hadn't even been able to visit her at camp in Colorado because every time she got near the train she started to tremble. Connie was sick of it.

All of a sudden Elsie keeled over and lay there gasping faintly. Connie knelt next to her. Her heart pounding. Elsie had made it out West this time. Was it possible her mother had come all this way just to die on the floor of a restaurant? She was over eighty, after all. Connie pushed the thought out of her mind. It was probably only a fit of hysterics. A crowd of people gathered. "Call an ambulance," a man said.

"No, no," her mother said, panicked. "Tell him no. I'm fine. I just felt faint." Howard rushed over, pushing the man out of his way, and crouched on Elsie's other side.

"She's all right," Connie said. "There's no need." But she was beginning to wonder. She knew the story of the boy who cried wolf once too often. She looked attentively at her mother. Elsie had closed her eyes. The vigor of her expression gone, her face seemed to collapse on itself as though something were drawing it in from inside. She looked small and frail all of a sudden, like a bird fallen out of its nest. Connie lifted her head in her arms. "Mama, maybe it would be better if we called."

"No!" She began thrashing her head.

"I'll get some water," Howard said, getting up.

When he came back, Connie held the glass to her lips.

"Take a sip, Mama, please. Your mouth looks so dry." Elsie opened her mouth and sucked at the edge of the glass. Her eyes were still closed. Connie's hand shook so badly that water spilled out on her mother's chin. "Do you think you can get up now?" she whispered. "I'll help you. You can lean on me." Elsie shook her head.

Howard was holding a bottle in front of Elsie's nose. "What's that?" Connie asked, confused. There was a strange droning sound in her ears.

"Ammonia," he said. "This should bring her around."

"It isn't working." Connie felt suddenly as if she were choking. Something was rising in her throat. "I don't dare wait any longer. If it's serious, we've waited too long already." She turned to the manager. "Would you call an ambulance. Tell them to hurry."

"Oh, no. Please," Elsie cried, but one of the waiters had already gone off. "I don't want to go in an ambulance. Don't let them take me away." She reached out and held Connie's shoulder in an iron grip. Her eyes were open now.

"Try to get up then." Connie put her arm under her mother's shoulders and tugged. Help me, Howard." He took the other side and between them they got her to a sitting position. But she couldn't go any further. While they were still trying, the stretcher men came and Howard helped them lift her onto the stretcher. His face was almost as pale as hers.

As the men were putting Elsie into the ambulance she stretched out her hand, calling Connie's name. At the last minute she tried to get off the stretcher. But the men held her down and she vomited over the side. "Don't worry. You'll be all right," Connie called, trying to keep control. "We'll be there when you get to the hospital."

They weren't allowed to see Elsie right away. She was in a curtained cubicle having a conference with a doctor. Connie sat with Howard on a bench in the hall.

Connie stared at the white curtain and found herself holding her breath and listening. She heard the doctor telling her mother to cough. She remembered the horrible sick feeling that had come over her when she was sixteen, a year after her father died, when she stood next to her mother's bed and listened to see if she was breathing. Then, she hadn't been relieved. She'd heard a rough rasping snore that sent shudders though her. A death rattle was what she thought. That's what it is. She'd screamed for Louise, the cook, and then she'd dialed the operator.

"Will they hurry?" she kept asking Louise. "Should we call them again to tell them to hurry?" Her mother was lying on her side on the bed with one arm dangling down. Her eyelids were bruised looking as though someone had been beating her, purple with delicate veins.

Because she didn't know what else to do, she kept shaking her mother's arm and begging her to open her eyes. Then she saw the empty bottle of Seconal lying on the floor with the cap off and her stomach lurched. She felt sick. Like throwing up. She stood by her mother's bed in her plaid tartan skirt and knee socks and looked at her watch. Surely an hour must have passed but it was only five minutes. Why did her mother do this? Connie's father had died in June. If she'd done it then, Connie might have understood. But almost a whole year later? Just when she'd seemed to be getting less depressed?

"He's certainly taking his time in there," Howard said, taking his gold watch out of his waistcoat pocket and studying it. "Do you think I should go take a look?"

Connie looked up, startled. "No, don't. It'll only fluster him. Let him do what he has to." A siren wailed, coming into the emergency entrance.

On that cloudy morning, twenty-seven years ago, there hadn't been any siren. Two fireman had run into the room, not even noticing that Connie was there. She wondered why they needed axes and slickers. Didn't they know what they were coming for? Steve pressed close to her, his hand against his mouth, not saying a word. How out of place the firemen's red helmets seemed bent next to her mother's face as they rushed her out on a stretcher.

The family doctor called and told Louise they'd put Elsie in an iron lung at Mount Sinai. It was fifty-fifty, he said. Maybe they ought to think of some contingency plans for the children.

She'd sat in the kitchen with Louise, drinking hot chocolate to stop her shivering. Steve, practical like his father even at nine, wanted to know if they were going to be orphans.

"No, of course not." Connie had said. "People are only orphans in comic books and movies. You don't know any orphans, do you?"

And though it looked for awhile as though Elsie would have to stay in the iron lung, that didn't happen. After only two weeks they said she could continue her recuperation at home. Sometimes Connie doubted that she'd ever really recovered.

Connie looked across the corridor of the Mount Zion Emergency. The curtain was pulled open a little and she caught a glimpse of the doctor's white coat. Maybe they were finished then. They'd been in there over forty minutes. Could she have had a stroke? Like Grandma? Connie got up and went towards the curtain, near enough to hear voices.

"It was the strain of seeing my daughter's family," Elsie was telling the doctor. "They didn't give me any privacy. I had to be with them all the time." Connie felt her blood boil for a minute but then it subsided. It wasn't news to her that her mother invented things. Steve was always commenting on how she told different stories to different people. But that one, of all things, when Elsie couldn't stand to be alone for a minute.

The doctor came out and mumbled something about the heat in the restaurant and the unfamiliar food. Nothing to be alarmed about. A not uncommon shut down of the system when it gets overloaded. He didn't think there was a need to keep her overnight since she seemed so dead set against it. Her vital signs all seemed normal now. But she should certainly check with her own doctor when she got back to New York.

In the car going home, Connie sat in the back seat with her mother. Elsie wasn't sweating anymore but she was rolling her eyes slightly.

"Why did you tell the doctor that you didn't have any privacy? That that's what did it." Her mother had always thought she was a goddamned saint. Put upon by everyone. Now she looked so miserable Connie wanted to put her arms around her but she wouldn't let herself. She wanted something first. Some admission. A little bit of truth.

"I don't think I said that, did I?" Her mother looked bewildered, as if she really wasn't conscious of what she'd said. Was that an excuse?

"You did." Connie felt like crying. There she goes, lying again. It would be nice if sometimes she could say I'm sorry. Sorry for everything from year zero.

"Maybe you should let your mother rest," Howard said in a gentle voice. His solicitude surprised her. But it shouldn't have. He always visited people when they were in the hospital. And he'd been so kind when she had a miscarriage. She walked her mother to the door, holding her arm, and when they were inside she took off her jacket for her and hung it in the closet. "Good night, then," she said. "Hope you feel better in the morning."

"Aren't you going to help your mother get ready for bed?" Howard whispered to her when Elsie went into the bathroom. "She's still feeling badly."

"She's all right." Connie felt faintly ashamed that for once Howard was being nicer than she was, but she couldn't help it. Let her have her privacy, if that's what she wants. She sighed, feeling even meaner. A bitchy, nasty daughter. Accused by her mother's pallor, the slight line of spittle on her lips. Elsie came out and saw them still standing there in the entry way.

"I'm sorry, darling, to be such a bother," she muttered contritely. "I'm sure it will be better in the morning."

What Connie found unbearable was that just when she decided to step back a little from her mother, Elsie made some small gesture that touched her to the quick, like poking a finger inside and stirring it around. Now it was the look of being sorry. She couldn't face that look without feeling repentant. She remembered that when Elsie had a gall bladder attack, she'd hardly made a sound. "I didn't want to frighten you," she'd said.

"You can sleep late if you want," Connie said grudgingly. "We don't have to leave for the airport until ten." Being righteously angry had been easier. These conflicting feelings of love and anger confused her. She went in with her mother and helped her take off her clothes and pack for the morning.

Six

It had finally stopped raining. Connie was reading a novel about a couple that didn't go to bed together for months. When they finally did, it was a disaster. The relationship went caput in a week. She reminded herself of that when she was tempted by Marc. She felt she needed cautionary tales because in her own case, it was getting more difficult all the time, and she had known him only nine weeks.

Marc asked her to go with him to Point Richmond—a quiet backwater port much used by lovers. They had lunch in little place hung with fishermen's nets next door to a ramshackle gray hotel.

Eating shrimp among corals and pink centered shells made Connie feel dreamy and irresponsible, like some mermaid on a rock. "To freedom soon," she said, clicking her glass against Marc's. The wine swirled richly and gave off a spicy odor.

Marc's eyes softened. "Does that mean divorce?"

She laughed. "No, no. I was thinking of Patty Hearst. She just turned twenty and they say she's fallen in love with one of the gang." Cinque. Power to the fifth. Connie imagined Patty had fallen in love with him when he'd caught her climbing through her window, trying to escape.

"I don't know why you're so obsessed with her. She's just a spoiled brat. There's so much more at stake in what's going on with Nixon. Do you know what those indictments are doing to our image abroad?"

"It's certainly not a pretty picture." Connie thought of the photos she'd seen. The Attorney General reminded her of Alfred Hitchcock, Ehrlichman looked like the Godfather, and Liddy could have been a second-rate boxer. Connie slipped back into her reverie. Cinque had thrown his arms around Patty's legs and kept her from going. Patty interpreted his violence as a form of love. Nobody had ever cared that much about what she did. Whether she went or stayed.

"It makes me ashamed of being an American," Marc was saying. He looked particularly handsome today, she thought, in a blue silk shirt he'd gotten on a trip to Bali. "It's so seamy. 'A conspiracy of silence, lubricated by lies.' They'd have indicted Nixon too if he wasn't the President. I can see the headlines in *The London Times*: 'President of the world's foremost democracy puts a premium on honesty, says offering cover up money would be wrong.' But they'll get him eventually. It's clear by now he's up to here." He tapped his throat where his collar opened. Connie noticed how well the strong color of the shirt set off his black hair.

"Here's to honesty," Connie said, leaning forward and accidently spilling a little of her wine on the table. "And to us."

"Are you getting tipsy?" Marc asked.

She shook her head. "My hand just slipped. You know, the first time I got really drunk was on my twentieth birthday. On Dago Red. I went out on the roof of the dorm and started dancing. The next day I couldn't keep down a boiled egg." Connie pictured Patty celebrating her birthday by taking a bath. Scrubbing off all that dirt. Letting her body shine again. Then maybe she'd dance for her lover. Here Connie's imagination faltered. Would the girl urge him to drink and then make a break for it, back through her window, into that cold moonlight? Or did she need him for whatever she was going to do?

"I bet you're a hell of a drunk. There's a lushness about your mouth." He took her chin and kissed her lightly.

"I always thought I looked like Joan of Arc, a militant virgin." Connie laughed, excited and embarrassed at the same time. "You know I have fantasies about Patty being a little like that. Persuading her lover to join her. Confronting her mother and father in their oppressor's castle. I picture him as a genie with gold earrings. A sort of black, giant killer. 'You've taken enough,' Patty will say to them, 'now you're going to have to give. Feeding the hungry is just the beginning.' Then she'll kiss him and her parents will have to watch."

He laughed. "Well, at least your fantasies show revolutionary potential. Other kinds too. Though you're not specific enough about your fantasy man. Is he built like Muhammad Ali or does a lightweight have a chance?"

They held hands crossing the rickety tracks between the restaurant and the water and went down to the beach. Almost every time Marc had taken her out they'd been near the water. It seemed right to her. Howard loved volcanoes and arid places. He'd dragged her up Mount Aetna and gloried in the poison gases that billowed from the crater. But Marc was a Pisces. Brilliantly scaled, quick.

Connie was excited by the sun and the sparkle of the wavelets licking the beach. She stretched high on her toes and twirled until she was dizzy. Her skirt was a blue flowered material that swelled out when she turned. Then she kicked her clogs off and waded into the cold water, her skirt tucked in her waist, the deep frills falling against her thighs. Like a woman in a petticoat, she thought. Marc stood waiting and watching until she came out, flushed and pleased with herself. Letting her body take over for once. And then he took her in his arms and she felt his tongue slide into her mouth. It was as though she'd been jolted by an electric current. The unbearable vividness of the sensation. She clung to him, her hands roaming over his back, pressing her thighs against him. Suddenly she realized what she was doing and pulled away, shocked.

"We shouldn't have done that." She stood there shaking, frightened at the way her heart was pounding.

"Why not? You enjoyed it, didn't you?"

"That's not the point. I don't feel comfortable. For one thing, I'm a married woman." Agitated, she picked up a handful of stones and threw them into the water.

"Very happily. I can see that."

"What do you know about it?"

"I saw you at Cafe Del Sol last week. He didn't pay any attention to you." He stroked her bare arm. Drawing her back. "What harm is there in a kiss?"

"One thing leads to another," she stammered. Now that he'd stopped, she wanted him to keep touching her.

"Well, what do you think? We're not going to take off all our clothes and lie here on the beach just because I kissed you." The idea seemed to amuse him. "Besides, it's too cold."

The trouble was, she could see it happening, perfectly. She was so hungry for him, she could imagine dragging him off right there behind the bushes. Opening his shirt and rubbing her face against him hard. "I don't trust you," she burst out.

"Why? You trust a man who voted for Nixon because he thought a thief was better than a fool. Or do you only consider cynics as suitors?"

"Howard wasn't a cynic when I married him, he was a Democrat."

They both laughed. There was a minute's truce.

"What else was he? I want to know what appealed to you. His brains, his money? Was he your mentor?"

"Let's not talk about him," Connie said evasively. "Let's talk about you." She thought getting more information would make her feel less threatened. Like someone going on a jungle expedition who makes lists of the dangerous animals. Cobra, alligator, puma. "Tell me why you got bored with Alix as soon as she said she'd marry you." It was more than trust, Connie thought. She wasn't sure she liked him. Marc was a robber baron, a dealer in hearts.

"Jesus. You got that ass-backwards." He frowned at her. "She was the one who was bored with me. She didn't want me to touch her. If I took her in my arms, she acted like I was going to rape her. I left her alone. That's what she wanted."

"Maybe she was frigid because you lost interest. Or because she was mad at you for something." His left eye flickered with the hint of a tic. The long black lashes brushed his cheek.

"Nonsense. She was always that way. Right from the beginning." He rubbed the back of his neck, turning it from side to side.

"Why did you chase her then, if it was so obvious?" She scuffed at the sand with her toe, feeling the muscles of her calf contract.

"That was the honeymoon stage."

"And then it started going bad? Just like that?" She moved around to where she could see his face.

A group of sandpipers scurried past them, bills cocked, watching intently for tiny crabs. "Oh, there was a woman at work who was interested in me. But I never would have taken up with her if Alix hadn't been the way she was."

Connie shivered slightly, wishing she'd thought to bring a towel. Her legs were beginning to feel cold. "You hadn't mentioned that."

"Look. That woman put herself in my path like a lady lying down in front of an express train. I would have had to be an acrobat to keep from hitting her. It was a grade B movie from the start—intern with Jane Russell silhouette leaning over the doctor's desk." He sighed ruefully. "I'm not proud of that one."

"And what's my rating?" she asked him, wrinkling up her nose.

"Don't be such a prude. This isn't the Middle Ages."

She flushed. "But why didn't you talk to Alix first?"

"Talk to her!" His voice rose. "My God, she hardly had time to say good morning. Locked up in her room until three a.m. working on her hospital systems. The efficient placing of bedpans." He snorted in disgust, "Sleeping with her was like fucking an IBM typewriter. Sex wasn't in her program, it was messy and wasted time. Work's important to me too, but not like that. I wanted someone to love." He looked out over the water.

"You sound like Hemingway," Connie said. "Bullfights and bleeding hearts. But what about all the interns you hang around with?" They'd have to build a barn to house all the girls he'd taken to bed, she thought. "Is that searching for someone to love too?"

"They like me," he said simply. "I'm a good teacher."

She brushed the sand from her toes, rubbing hard, and slipped her clogs back on. "I bet."

"Why are you fixated on my past? Try to stop, will you? Or think of something positive. Like the countless hours I volunteered at free clinics or the time I spent doing draft counselling. Helping kids with strategies." His eye flicked again, giving him a shifty look.

She touched his arm. "That's one of the reasons I like you so much. You're for all the right things—things I didn't have a chance to be involved in because I was so bogged down with my kids. But I can't just ignore the rest of it. I'm not a cause, I'm a woman."

He took her hand. "Our government made a terrible mistake in Vietnam and the killing is still going on. People make mistakes too. And I've certainly made my share of them." He smiled at her with his old charm. "But if you don't believe in change, what's the point in staying alive? Vietnam has taught us a lesson. We won't intervene like that again, the cost was too high. I know I learned a lot from my mistakes, too. I'm freer now than I've ever been. I know what I want. Do you?" He turned her hand over and explored the tangle of lines on her palm with his finger. "Look," he went on seriously, "kissing you was wonderful. And I certainly want to make love to you. But I won't unless you feel completely clear that it's the right thing to do. So there's nothing to worry about, is there? It's in your hands."

Driving home Connie felt shaken. This was a crazy way to act. What was she doing? For a second, she felt her habitual fear of Howard. What if he found out? Her next thought was, let him. If he had cared anything about her, he would have seen how unhappy she was long ago. She hadn't realized until he went to Israel just how much he neglected her. If she had a lover, he probably wouldn't even notice.

When she got home, she was too agitated to sit still so she changed into her bathing suit and went to the outdoor pool at the Hearst Gym. She needed to get hold of herself. By the end of the first lap, she felt better. The buoyant liquid, the long stretch of turquoise beneath her, even the familiar smell of chlorine, calmed her. But what she liked most was the feeling of control. She picked out a girl in a red Speedo cap swimming ahead of her in the adjoining lane and made herself catch up. She gasped with the effort, but it was worth it. She passed the girl, swimming a steady crawl, and looked back, pleased that the girl was younger. She swam another lap and did it with someone else. This time she pretended she was in a race. She imagined herself coming from behind, splashing ahead, winning against all odds. It was unexpectedly satisfying and reassuring. After the second time, she relaxed a little, enjoying her fish-like motion through the water, the way it parted on either side of her body, stroking her sides. She swam on slowly, feeling a slight chill when she entered the deep part of the pool. Maybe she'd make something special for Howard tonight. He was so easy about some things, she thought. So easy to please with food. As long as it was hot. She stopped off at Lenny's and got lamb chops—his passion.

As soon as she got back in the house she went to the phone and called Howard. Just to say hello, come home early, I miss you. Let's have a drink together before dinner. While she took a shower and washed her hair, she tried to remember what Howard had told her about the committee meeting he'd been worried about. They were hiring a new man in Biochemistry and he wanted to make it a shared appointment with Plant Biology. She'd ask him about it, she thought. Show some interest in what was going on in his life. After she dressed, she got out the Greek olives. While she listened to the news about the 400 North Vietnamese killed in the Central Highlands, she arranged an antipasto plate. It was the worst fighting since the cease fire in January. Death was our legacy, she thought, a sort of ghastly present we left behind us. Like the sons' bodies baked in a pie and served up to their rebel father by a Greek tyrant. The door opened and slammed shut.

"Hi," Sarah called.

Connie turned off the radio. "I thought you were going to Melissa's tonight. What's up?" She took an onion out of the fridge, quartered it and chopped it quickly and put it in the pot.

"She got sick. Anyway, I needed to talk to you. Something really great happened. My friend Ari's quit his job at Rather Ripped Records. I think I'm going to get it. He's talking to the manager for me." Her words tumbled out in a rush.

The note of challenge disturbed Connie and she looked up into Sarah's face. When she didn't meet her eye, she felt her heart sinking. "Would more allowance help?"

Sarah looked as though the Watergate gang had offered her hush money. "I need to earn it myself." She dropped her book bag in the corner. A copy of *Rolling Stone* slid across the floor. The lead article announced on the cover was 'How to grow marijuana at home.'

"How often will you go?" Connie asked, eyeing Sarah dubiously. She hoped for something tolerable like Friday and Saturday nights.

"Only two school nights. Saturday's the only late night. The one they have performances. If you're worried about me coming home alone, I'm sure Dad wouldn't mind getting me. He likes to stay up late." She shed her jacket, draping it over a chair. Hang it up, just once, Connie wanted to say but decided to save her ammunition for the essential issue. Sarah's idea made her want to scream. She hated the record store. And on the weekends they had live rock performances. Dressed up in leather and fringes, blaring music so loud it split your eardrums.

"Look, Sarah. There's no use pussyfooting around about it. That place is a hot-bed of drugs." She dumped a glass of wine into her onion-rice mixture and a cloud of fragrant steam rose toward the ceiling. She could imagine Sarah threading her way through the crowd, inhaling dope with every breath. Connie scraped the bottom of the pot angrily.

"Oh come on, Mom. They are drugs everywhere. If I wanted them I could get them at school."

"There's a big difference, Sarah. Rather Ripped is full of older men who know what they're doing."

"I'm not a baby. I know the score." Sarah slouched defensively, "Even Mr. Ramon thinks it would be good for me."

"Mr. Ramon? Who's that?"

Sarah riveted her with a scornful look. "God, you're spacey. He's my Spanish teacher. I've been talking about him for weeks. You never pay any attention to what I say, do you? Something's always on your mind." She picked up a fork and beat an impatient rhythm against the cutting board. Tattattatat, like a drum.

"You know that's not true, Sarah." Damn, why did she have to forget the teacher's name. It put her off her stride. But it was hard to think about the children properly when her mind was shifting around like a kaleidoscope.

"Mr. Ramon says you overprotect me. Martha's mother let her go to Europe alone last summer and she's no older than I am. Mr. Ramon says I need a chance to be independent."

That sounded like something Connie might have said herself when she was sixteen. She'd been so bitter when her mother held her back. But now she began to understand how her mother had felt. She felt herself getting angry. Whatever she did, she was a rotten mother. If she left Sarah alone for awhile, she was negligent. If she paid attention, she was smothering.

"Look Sarah. I'm all for your being independent. But there are a million decent jobs you could get. Why'd you have to pick just this one?"

"I told you, because Ari quit."

"Well, then it's easy. I know the owner of Moe's Bookstore. I'm sure he'd be glad to give you something part time."

"Shelving books alphabetically. No way. There's no way I'm going to do that. It's boring." She hit the side of a steel pot with the fork and it gave off a metallic clang. Connie winced.

"A restaurant then. You could waitress. Bonnie at Augusta's would..."

"I don't need to get a job from your friends. I found my own job perfectly well." She dinged the pot again.

"You're being unreasonable, Sarah." Connie reached over, took the fork and tossed it into the sink.

"You're so uptight," Sarah shouted. "I can't believe it."

"Hey, what's going on here?" Howard asked, walking into the kitchen and looking at them. "Sounds like a tenure committee meeting."

"You look cheerful," Connie said. "The appointment you wanted must have gone through."

"It did. To my great relief." He smiled at Sarah. "Now, what's the trouble?"

"Mom doesn't want me to take a perfectly good job at Rather Ripped Records. What do you think, Dad?" She flashed him an appealing look, wanting to make the best of his good humor.

Connie wished Howard hadn't walked in on them just then. That she'd had a chance to talk to him about it first. She set the risotto in the oven to keep warm and poured Howard a drink.

"I don't see what's wrong with a job. Working at something real will be a good experience for you. It'll help prepare you for living on a kibbutz." He winked at Sarah. "School isn't everything. You need a mixture of learning and work. The early settlers knew that." Sarah smiled back. They looked like conspirators, about to rob a bank together.

"Kibbutz?" Connie exclaimed. "I didn't know you were thinking about that. Is that what you were doing in Israel? Staking out a place for us in some Godforsaken spot in the desert? At least you could have mentioned it. Sent me a picture postcard."

"Where I go, you follow. Women are like dogs, they follow their masters." He tilted Connie's head back with one hand. "Don't you think your mother has Alice's eyes, Sarah?" Alice had been their poodle. "Anyway, it's hardly a godforsaken spot." Howard went back to his idea. "I have a perfectly God-fearing kibbutz in mind."

"That was a nasty thing to say about Mom, Dad. You better watch it. You can't go around saying things like that on a kibbutz. Women drive tractors and shoot guns. They were with the men in the Yom Kippur War. You told me so yourself. They're not like dogs. That's fifties stuff. Seventies' women aren't like that." She tossed back her red mane.

"I can see you'll like Israel, Sarah. They raise beets and chickens. You can drive a tractor to your heart's content."

"Hey, I hate to spoil your plans," Connie said, untying her apron and shoving it in a drawer, "but I have no intention of moving to Israel. We've lived abroad enough. I've had enough trekking around with suitcases, setting up house, trying to raise kids. I'd like to think about myself for awhile." She carefully poured herself a glass of white wine.

"This is different. You don't have to worry about anything. They even give you clothes. I'd like to get away from this money-mad society of ours. I'm tired of possessions. I feel like my parents. This house is full of things I can do without." He made a sweeping gesture with his arm. "I'd like to get rid of it."

"Sell our house?" Connie shouted, "You must be mad. And they're not just things. They're full of memories."

"Yeah, like my baby rocker." Sarah pointed to a small maple chair in a corner. "The one that Mom had at her farm. Or Grandpa's desk."

"You should have thought of that thirty years ago, Howard," Connie said. "That would have been the time to start a new life. Not now. Besides, I don't notice you being so sanguine when something happens to one of your possessions. What about your pipe? You were awfully mad about that." Connie drank a sip of her wine. It felt sour in her stomach.

"Did you have to remind me of that? In Israel, kids have discipline. They don't run wild like Mischa." His jaw started to work.

"Your memory's off, Howard. Mischa was trying to do something helpful."

"I don't want anyone buying my stuff for me," Sarah interrupted. "That's why I want this job. So I can get records, build up my Elton John collection."

Connie turned on her. "Sarah, I've already told you what I thought about that." She paused and looked at Howard. "The place is full of drugs and older men."

"But Mom, I'm on your side. I don't want to go to Israel either."

"Don't be fresh, Sarah," Howard said, stung. "You could really look for a decent job, you know. Or do you have to be contrary about everything?"

"I just think it's stupid to pretend you don't like things. You don't have to be money-mad. And don't worry about my job. You already said you thought it was a good idea."

"I can change my mind. I didn't know this business about drugs."

Connie thought this would be a good point to stop. Now, while they were at a stand-off, while Howard seemed to be veering over to her side. She suddenly remembered her risotto in the oven drying out. "Look, let's call a halt to this and eat before the food gets spoiled." She called Mischa to dinner and he came running in with a suspicious bulge under his shirt. Connie decided to ignore the possibility of it being his hamster. Maybe they'd get through dinner in peace. She poked at the crust that had formed on the top of her risotto and carried it to the table.

"Howard, I have an idea." Connie ventured when they'd been eating for awhile in relative silence, "Let's all go up to Calistoga for the weekend. Let's go tomorrow morning." While the kids swam or rode, she'd have a chance to talk to him. She wondered if he was really thinking of making aliyah—emigrating to Israel. She had a feeling he was. Anyway, they needed to talk.

"Did you forget I'm going to Bolinas with Matti?" Mischa asked, hurt. "We're going to sleep in his tent."

"I can't go either." Howard wiped his mouth. "I've got to write up my committee report. Why don't you take Sarah?"

"Do they have horses?" Sarah asked indifferently, toying with the rice on her plate.

Connie nodded. "Yes. Good ones." This wasn't working out the way she planned. No talk with Howard and Sarah sulking up a storm. Not a pleasant prospect. They'd probably just argue about the job. But at least she'd be away from Marc for a few days. Be able to collect herself.

"You know, Sarah, you like animals so much, you should take some veterinary science courses at Cal. They'd be really useful at the kibbutz. They need veterinarians." With a little food and wine, Howard had recovered his impetus.

"Every time there's a war in Israel, you want to replenish

the country." Connie reached for the salad. "Don't we need veterinarians too?"

"I don't want to be a veterinarian, anyway," Sarah said. "I want to study dance."

"As I've told your mother, I don't see much point in that but it's all right as long as you keep up with your Hebrew." Howard leaned back in his chair looking like Moses coming down the mountain with the definitive word.

Mischa took his hamster out of his shirt. "I could be a veterinarian," he piped up. "I'm real good with animals. I trained Evel to run an obstacle course. Want to see?" He started to put him on the table but stopped and looked questioningly at Connie.

"Sure. Your mother won't mind." Howard grinned at her the way he had when the kitten shredded her new curtains. "We're through eating." He handed his plate to Sarah to take to the kitchen.

"I do mind," Connie said.

Howard leaned back in his chair and pounded on the table. "Why make such a fuss? You're not afraid of a little dirt, are you? Your mother had a very proper upbringing," he said to Mischa. "But we men are different. We know dirt's natural. Right?" He pinched Mischa's cheek. "*Inter urinam et faeces nascimur.*"

"Yeah," Mischa said doubtfully, putting a saltcellar on its side and following it with two napkin-ring hoops. He tried to lure Evel through with a bit of salad. "Come on, boy, you can do it. Come on, Evel." The salt cellar lurched forward in a drunken roll as the animal clambered over it and Mischa let out a whoop of pleasure. But then Evel got stuck in a napkin ring and struggled wildly.

"Jesus," Connie yelled. "He's dropping shit balls all over the table. Get him, Sarah, he's right in front of you."

"Mischa, you should be a circus clown," Sarah said, grabbing the hamster, ring and all, and squeezing him through. "The kind that always flubs up and makes everyone laugh.

The only trouble is, you're not even funny."

"Howard, this was your idea. Clean it up! Dammit, you're worse than a seven-year-old."

Howard swept the little pellets into a pile with a napkin. "Life's a dirty business," he said grinning. "You shouldn't keep the children from experiencing it."

"You just like to provoke me, Howard. Don't moralize. Whatever life is, I don't need to see hamster turds on my dining room table. It's disgusting."

Sarah got up from the table holding the hamster outstretched in one hand, took Mischa by the arm and went upstairs.

They started off to Calistoga about ten the next day. Connie stopped at the pump to get gas. This was one of the few times she agreed with Howard about the Arabs. Their damned embargo! It had stopped a week or so ago, but gas was still $1.10 a gallon.

"You know, Mom," Sarah said, getting out with her, "the only reason I'm going up with you is it's the last weekend I'll have free before I start working." Connie took off the cap, stuck the hose into the tank and turned on the pump.

"Sarah, let's not start. I've told you what I think." Connie watched the numbers bounding upwards. She wished she had a hearing aid that she could simply turn off.

"And I'm not buying it."

"Well, you may have to. It's no, Sarah, no. This is not a good job for you and I don't want you to take it." Sarah stood sullenly biting her lip. Connie topped up the tank, ignoring Sarah's glare and went into the station to pay.

When she got back Sarah was waiting for her in the car. "What can you know about what's good or not? You've never worked. You know something? If you made your own money you'd probably defend yourself a lot better."

"What are you talking about?"

"Putting up with his insults, that's what I'm talking about.

For a religious man, he's sure got a mean mouth."

Connie was trying to get through a difficult intersection and didn't understand at first. "How?" She squinted at Sarah out of the corner of her eye.

"How!" Sarah's face was red, as if she was going to choke. "Don't you remember? He compared you to Alice—a dog! He said you had the same eyes." She toyed with the frayed edge of her jacket, pulling at the threads.

"He used to joke about Alice being a woman in her last incarnation. I thought he was only teasing."

"That's the trouble with you. You don't react like a normal person. You just sit there smiling that little smile while he tells me you and Alice have the same personality traits—as though everything was just fine and dandy. I had to speak up for you, tell him it was nasty. I can't stand it!"

Connie felt her stomach turn over. She wished Sarah would lower her voice. In the enclosed car, it seemed twice as loud.

After her outburst Sarah calmed down and told Connie she was sorry. "I didn't mean to yell," she said, "but it's hard having a mother you can't look up to. The only thing I can learn from you is how not to do things." She covered her eyes with her hands and leaned against the door.

"Well," Connie told her, not daring to touch her for fear she'd explode again, "you can think that now because you're sixteen. The hardest thing to learn is that as you grow up, you change. Really. Even after thirty-five. I should know, I'm doing it." Sarah gave a little laugh and Connie felt the tension drop.

"Look. When it really matters, I'll say something. Remember when Mischa broke Dad's pipe? I stuck up for him. The dog joke just wasn't worth a fight."

"You told him to clean up Evel's shitballs, too," Sarah said. "I guess that's a start."

"Well, you know," Connie said shyly, not sure how Sarah would take this, "I've applied for a job at Saint Mary's. I won't know for awhile if I've gotten it, but I think it would be fun."

"Wow." Sarah made a "V" with her fingers. "Right on. That should make Dad sit up and take notice. Do you think you'll get it?"

"I don't know. I've never taught before but I think I could do a good job." She had a momentary vision of standing in front of thirty pairs of eyes, losing her voice. Would she really have the authority to bring this off? She'd never even given a lecture. "I've already thought out what I'll teach if I get it. I may have to work twice as hard as everyone else at first, but that's okay." She had another flash of panic. "It'll be a challenge." That was the way to look at it, she thought. When Howard was away she'd found she had much more capacity for work than she'd realized, when she wasn't ground down by looking after him. For the comparative course, she was going to try love versus reason in the *Aeneid* and *King Lear*. She wanted to show the kids these authors weren't just old bores. Or worse, requirements. They had sexual itches and parental obligations too. Give it to them in a way they could get excited about.

Sarah looked at her mother as though she were an unusual animal in a zoo. "I know you've written a book and stuff. But you never talk about yourself as if you've done anything. It's confusing. You didn't even show me your good reviews until I asked for them last year."

"Girls didn't play baseball with the boys when I was growing up," Connie said. "We played ourselves down." Sarah half-smiled at the reference. The Little League had just voted to allow girls on its teams. "It was even okay to look a little stupid. It was just the thing to do. And after awhile it got to be a habit." Even now, simply mentioning her job possibility to Sarah, she had to fight off a feeling that she was being pretentious, immodest.

"But Grandma doesn't."

"You didn't know her before, when my father was alive."

Connie thought of her mother with her hair loose on her shoulders, telling Connie how she'd fallen in love with Simon. She always finished by reciting her favorite lines from *Othello*. "She loved me for the dangers I had passed, and I loved her that she did pity them." Desdemona and her princely Moor.

When they arrived, they changed into their bathing suits. The straight cut across the legs slimmed her thighs, she thought with satisfaction. She looked good. They ran into the stream in back of the ranch house. Hot water from a hidden spring flowed into it and made the water deliciously warm. After a few minutes they were playing around like kids, pushing each other into the cold spots.

That night when they were washing up before bed, Connie asked Sarah how her friend Chrissy was. She'd had a bad case of bronchitis and had to miss two weeks of school. Connie had always liked Chrissy. She seemed so pulled together.

"Oh, Chrissy, she's fine. She's been having sex with two boys at the same time." Sarah put down her washcloth and looked at her, cheerfully taking in her shock. "I think it's a good idea for sex to be casual," she said. "It always has been for boys. Why shouldn't it be for us too?"

Connie understood that she'd only make Sarah defensive if she got excited. "It's much harder for women to stay detached emotionally," she said as calmly as she could, dabbing toner on her neck. Jesus, she thought, maybe legalizing abortion last year wasn't such a great thing. Made it too easy for these kids. No consequences. She wondered if other mothers felt so inadequate when their daughters started asking them questions. She knew what she thought but she didn't have clear reasons to back it up. Just her feelings.

"Then they should practice." Sarah pulled up her nightgown and sat on the toilet, peeing noisily.

"But why, Sarah? What will they get if they do? Turn out callous like most men? It seems like a step backward."

Connie looked at her, fascinated by a line of freckles on her thigh.

"Fun, pleasure, no strings, no guilt...." Sarah pulled the flush and walked into the bedroom, bouncing onto her bed and turning to face Connie. She began to talk more rapidly. "Don't you see, it terrified me to see the way you were so much under Dad's thumb." Connie started to protest. "Yeah, I know you're trying to change but all my life I've seen you apologizing for everything—your clothes, the way you looked, everything. I don't want to give anyone that much power over me. Do you know what I mean?"

Connie did, but it hurt anyway, to have her needling into her sorest spots. She'd certainly never realized how afraid Sarah was to be like her. She couldn't think of a single time she'd criticized her mother to her face. "But you can choose a completely different type of man, Sarah."

"You don't understand. It's me I'm worried about. I want to feel good about myself. At the record store, they said they'd let me cashier. That means they think I'm responsible. They trust me. Life isn't just going to school and getting married." She paused. "I don't think I'll ever marry anyone. I can't seem to like boys unless they've got something cold about them, like Jeff. He's so much like Dad. If they're really nice I think something's wrong with them. Except for Mr. Ramon. He's awfully nice. He's helped me get rid of a lot of mental crap, like always wanting Dad's approval." She pulled the heavy comforter up from the foot of the bed.

"Oh, God, Sarah, I see what you mean. But having casual sex isn't the answer. What if you fall in love afterwards? You know you can't always control those things. Don't you think you'll be open to being hurt? If it's still just casual to him, you'll be miserable. You can't convince me you won't." She went over and stood beside Sarah. She looked so vulnerable with her scrubbed face and her shiny hair.

"Mom, we just don't play power games any more." Her voice was so movingly young, and so self-righteous. "It's all up front. I try to be honest with people. If I want to do something, I will. If I don't, I say so. But I don't try to use saying no to get an advantage." She sat up holding the covers around her.

"If a boy wants to sleep with you, he should really get to know you first and like you, like everything about you, not just your body." Connie didn't want Sarah to wake up after seventeen years of marriage feeling she'd been cheated. She wanted her to have some sense of romance, shared values, companionship. Once Connie had believed in Howard's understanding, even generosity. With a sense of shock, she recalled a poem she'd written when they were courting, about how loving him canceled out the horror of her father's death. She'd talked about angels singing. It was painful to remember.

"I guess you do have things with Dad I don't really know about. It's hard to see from outside, but maybe you talk things over when you're alone?"

Connie grimaced. What had gone wrong with them?

"That's one thing I love about Mr. Ramon," Sarah went on dreamily. "Boys are such immature jerks. He really talks to me. About politics, history, his life. He says there's nothing he can't talk to me about. He's a wonderful man. I'd love you to meet him. I think you'd like him. He's got a marvelous body too. He's a soccer player." She reached over from her bed and Connie stretched out her hand and touched Sarah's fingers.

Connie thought of Marc's blunt fingers on her arm, pressing the skin, his fingernails with their half moons. She didn't understand why Sarah was talking so insistently about her teacher. She seemed to be waiting for Connie to say something.

"I'm sure I'd like him if you do, Sarah." Connie told her. "It's wonderful to have a teacher you can talk to like that." Sarah seemed disappointed. She lowered her lashes. Then opened her eyes wide and looked at her mother.

"Mom there's something I don't get. You're letting me make up my mind about sex, why can't I decide when to come home at night? Why stick me with a curfew?"

"There have to be some rules, Sarah." Connie felt her stomach tense. How had they gotten back to this?

"And why can't I take that job?"

"That's not up for debate. No."

"I thought you were beginning to understand me," Sarah said bitterly. "I guess it was just talk. I bet you got the idea from Dr. Spock." Sarah imitated a fatherly male voice, "Talk to your teenager. Make her feel like you take her seriously. Shit."

"Sarah, cut it out. Saying no doesn't mean I don't understand you."

"Don't expect me to be rational. I'm just a teenager—incapable of making any decisions about my life." She looked angrily at Connie and switched off her light. Connie sighed and got up to go to the bathroom.

She sat there a few minutes thinking about what Sarah had said about boys and sex. And the job. She seemed to want it so much. But that record store was such a disaster area.

She sighed and picked up the paper, scanning it for news of Patty Hearst. There it was on page 4. Hearst says there will be no more money for free food after he distributes the two million. Jesus, what would she do if Sarah was kidnapped? They were almost the same age. Though why anyone should kidnap Sarah, she couldn't imagine. Unless it was a pervert or child molester. She shuddered thinking of the man who'd stolen a girl off her back steps and kept her chained to his bed post for six years. When they got her back, the flesh on her ankles was worn through almost to the bone. God, it was horrible. If anyone kidnapped Sarah, Connie would give every penny she had. That was for certain. Not like that ineffectual Hearst Daddy. A gentile version of Howard. Howard couldn't rescue a cat from a tree, let alone a woman. She thought again of the Rather

Ripped store. That was just the sort of place the Symbionese Liberation Army might come to make contacts, hang out. No, better hold firm about the job. It's too dangerous.

By the time she got back, Sarah was fast asleep. Something about the way she was lying with her head tucked into her pillow, fist against her face, reminded Connie of the way Sarah had looked as a baby. How Connie had loved wheeling her along the Viale in Italy. It was really then, Connie thought, watching Sarah's thumb brush her lips, that she entered the company of women. Other women with carriages would pause and greet her as if they were sea captains dipping their sails to each other in respect and awe of each other's prowess. The nurses were less comrades-in-arms than rivals. There were two women who always paused to examine each other's babies in more detail. A lusty male was the object of the most praise. "Look at the flesh on him," one would say, "just look." And she would uncover an enormous infant clad in rolls of fat like a Buddha. "I've been tanning mine," the other would reply. "Ten minutes a side every morning. Look." And she would lift an almost equally fat thigh to show the evenly golden skin. Connie had picked out a boy's name when she was pregnant, Cyrus Alexander—she'd imagined him twice a king, and, for a second, looking at the golden boy, she'd felt a twinge of regret. Then she'd leaned over to touch Sarah's silky cheek.

Sarah's beauty, she thought looking at her now, wasn't in her bulk—she was neat and trim—but in her features and coloring. Her mouth was a perfect rosebud, her skin pale ivory with a touch of peach and her hair red-gold. "*Oh quel angelo*," the women would say leaning over her, "a true angel come down from heaven."

The next day on the morning ride a man next to them in the line struck up a conversation. "I'm an astronomer," he told them with a slightly foreign accent, "studying Venus's veils." It turned out what he meant was the light haze shell they found surrounded Venus. The U.S satellite, Mariner II, had taken remarkable pictures of both Venus and Mercury. He looked like a man interested in Venus, Connie thought. Dark and handsome in an Eastern European way, his head covered with touseled black curls.

"This is boring, don't you think?" he asked Connie and Sarah after a half hour of ambling along. It was a big group and the leader wasn't letting them go faster than a trot. "Why don't you give your horse his head. Pretend he's run off with you. Sarah and I can give chase."

"Great idea," Connie said. She'd always thought they should let serious riders go out by themselves. She gave her horse a sudden kick and he and Sarah started up after her with a shout, cantering at right angles to the line off through a clearing. When he drew up alongside her, Connie saw that the astronomer had a good seat, his faded bell bottoms barely lifting from the saddle. The turf was soft and the horses skimmed along it without jarring. It was lovely feeling the wind in her hair, Connie thought. For a minute she wished Marc was riding beside her instead of a perfect stranger.

"I'm going to grab your horse's reins," the astronomer shouted, when they'd had a good run, "to make it look authentic." He leaned down, and pulled her horse up short. "You can faint if you like."

She laughed and patted her horse's neck. He was fat and puffing. "Sorry. I'm not the type." She wasn't about to tell this man that it had been one of her favorite adolescent fantasies. Mad gallop across a field. Swoon into a man's arms. Kiss before you were fully conscious.

"Why'd you do that?" Sarah said, pulling up next to them. "Mom's perfectly capable of stopping her horse by herself."

"I guess I'm just a dimestore cowboy," the astronomer said. "Always did want to be in the movies." Sarah looked annoyed.

"He's a pain in the butt," Sarah whispered to Connie when he went with them to the tennis court afterwards. "Why don't you get rid of him?"

"I can't stop him if he wants to tag along. The facilities are open to anyone. Besides, he says he wants to practice his backhand."

"And a lot else." She gave Connie a dirty look. "I bet he's real good with his hands."

After they had a couple of casual volleys, he challenged both of them to a game.

Sarah was outraged. "You don't have a partner!"

"I can take you both on. Two beautiful women. You'll inspire me."

The astronomer moved effortlessly on the court. He had a lightning serve. It was all Connie could do to return the ball. She lobbed it weakly over the net and he slammed it across to Sarah's outside corner. Sarah ran for it gamely but she didn't have a chance. "You're out of line," she yelled, then stopped flustered. "Over the line, I meant."

"No. He's inside," Connie shouted. "Hey, nice shot. You scored!"

"I certainly was trying to." He looked at Connie in a way that made her blush. "Fifteen, love."

"You have a mean backhand," she told him.

"Not mean," the astronomer said, "just firm and hard."

"Asshole," Sarah muttered.

When the score was thirty, love, Sarah complained of a headache and insisted that Connie take her back to the cabin.

That night, he asked Connie to go swimming with him, without Sarah. Sarah was dead set against her going.

"Who knows what he'll do. You hardly know him."

"I'll be back before you're asleep," Connie told her, putting on her clothes over her suit, "Don't worry, it's just for a dip. I'll be fine."

"How can you tell me what to do," Sarah said, jumping up and pulling on her own suit, "if you pick up guys in the stables? It's ridiculous."

"What about all those liberal attitudes you were spouting? They're all right for everyone else but not for me?"

"I was talking about people my age." Sarah pulled herself up to her full height. "Not my mother. You're forgetting your role. What kind of example is this?"

"Come then. Be my chaperon. It's fine with me."

When the man took off his jeans, it turned out he was wearing a tiny bikini. Sarah gave Connie a black look. He was clearly annoyed that she'd brought Sarah.

"See, I told you, he wants to get rid of me," Sarah whispered. "He thought it was a sex date." Sarah paddled off following the current and Connie found a deep, warm pocket and stood there with the water up to her shoulders. The astronomer slipped into it with her. "Afraid to come down here alone?" he asked, pressing himself against her leg.

"What's there to be afraid of?" His erection prodding her thigh was strangely reassuring. For the last few days, she'd been trying to imagine letting Marc see her naked and the fantasy never worked. Like some schoolgirl, she was afraid her breasts were too small and her legs too fat. This man was young and strong and he liked her body. Suddenly she realized her doubts were absurd. Marc must have noticed her shape by now. She took the astronomer's hand and rubbed it over her breast then she swam off a little and turned on her back kicking her legs.

"Where are you going, pretty one?" he asked hoarsely. "Don't you like water sports?"

"Wait," she told him. It dawned on her that she was really going to sleep with this man. It would be a sort of trial run. On the way back to the cabins they went single file up the path. Sarah in front, then Connie. The astronomer walked behind her touching her hip. She liked the feel of her flesh swaying softly from side to side. Like a rocking boat. The idea of sleeping with Marc had terrified her. She had no idea what an affair with him would mean. How much she might come to love him. Maybe it would addle her brains, the way masturbation was supposed to do in the nineteenth century. She could picture them frying like eggs over a hot fire. Dissolving. But she never had to see this stranger again. Even if it was a disaster, if he was impotent or hated her cellulite or she got her period in the middle of it, it wouldn't really make a difference.

"I'll be along," she told Sarah as they reached the top of the path. "You go to bed." She gave the astronomer her hand. She could feel a callus on the palm. This is what her friends were doing in the 60s, Connie thought as they walked towards his cabin. She could smell his hair oil mixed with the sulfur smell of the spring. It made her think of Greek beaches and retsina wine. She didn't mind missing the 60s, but she wished she'd done this five years earlier just to see if she still could. She'd never cheated on Howard before and she felt like a rusty gate, not even sure she knew how to move or come.

As they went into his cabin, she stole a glance at his chest. It was broad and manly, covered with fine dark hair. She had imagined that whatever they did would be short and fast but the astronomer seemed in no hurry. He drew off her suit and dried her with a towel, rubbing until her skin was rosy, then he kissed her gently. "Aphrodite," he murmured. She moistened. Relaxed. This wasn't going to be so difficult. He led her smoothly towards the bed. All she needed was someone who knew what he was doing. Who liked it. He began to kiss her face, her eyes, her cheeks, smothering her with kisses that set off small bursts of excitement. Howard hadn't kissed her on the lips. How had she stood it, she wondered? This man was even kissing her toes! He moved up the inside of her thighs and she could smell herself, yeasty and strong, like baking bread.

Their ardor was increased by the absolute irresponsibility of it, by the moonlight that flooded through the window and the liquid sound of a night bird. Connie stroked his back, feeling the muscles under the skin. She wondered if he did other sports beside tennis. She licked his ear gratefully. This had been lovely and easy. It had given her confidence. She'd leave tomorrow and no one would ever know.

Sarah was sitting up in bed when she came back to their cabin. "What did you do?" She wrinkled up her nose, sniffing like a bloodhound. "You smell like fish. You made it with him, didn't you. How could you? Ugh."

"You were the one who was talking about free love, Sarah. Giving me a big spiel about no strings, no guilt. I'm an adult."

"If sleeping with a guy just because he has big pecs is being an adult, then leave me out, I'm staying sixteen. The guy has nothing to offer. He is an asshole." Her voice was full of contempt.

Connie had been feeling like Rita Hayworth. Now she caught a glimpse of herself in the mirror, a flushed middle-aged woman. "Don't make assumptions about things you don't understand, Sarah. And don't be so damned judgmental." Part of her wanted to beg Sarah's pardon, the other half wanted to clobber her on the head.

Sarah followed her look. "Can't you see you're too old for this sort of thing? You're a mother. You should stick to your books." She switched out the light.

"Age has nothing to do with desire, Sarah. Or motherhood either. Being a mother isn't like being an untouchable. Maybe you'll find that out when you grow up a little." Sarah didn't answer. Connie had a sudden picture of herself in a black veil ringing a little bell to warn people off. A moral leper. I've certainly blown it with her, she thought. We're back to base one. The pits. If anyone had told her a few months before that she'd do something crazy like this—and with her teenage daughter along, no less—she'd have laughed.

Howard was in the kitchen warming a hot dog for Mischa

when Connie and Sarah came home. "Hello, all. Sorry we're late but the traffic was fierce." Connie gave Mischa a big hug. "How's my Boy Scout?"

"Mr. Grossman took us sailing. We practiced our knots."

"Good for you."

Howard looked up coldly. "Your friend Marc called when you were gone."

"Oh." Her stomach churned. What to say? "I promised him some names in Switzerland." It wasn't good but it was the best she could manage on short notice.

"What names? You haven't been there in years."

"Someone just happened to mention a chalet to me. I said I'd find out who to contact. It didn't seem like a big deal." The corner of Howard's mouth twitched once and then again. She watched it, fascinated, avoiding his eyes.

"Is Marc that guy with the gangster hat?" Mischa asked. Connie shook her head at him distractedly. Marc's soft gray fedora did look like something a thirties mafioso would wear. "I don't like him."

Oh God, that's all Howard needs to hear. That Marc's been visiting with Mischa. Connie pulled Mischa's A's cap down over his eyes. Since the A's had won the series it had become standard daily wear for seven-year-old boys.

"You're the gangster. Stick 'em up." She started to tickle him. He gave up trying to talk and began giggling.

"Well, is he?" Howard asked. Sarah was staring at them both.

"What difference does it make? For heaven's sake, Howard. This isn't even funny any more," she straightened up. "Let's stop it."

Seven

The day after they got back, Howard was working at home. When Connie took her coat, getting ready to slip out the door to visit Marc at his house, Howard looked at her suspiciously.

"Going out? Will you be long?"

"A couple of hours. I have a lot of little errands to do."

"What errands?"

"Drop off your suit at the cleaners. Check something at the library. Get some stuff xeroxed. Look for a new bookshelf for the study." She checked the urge to multiply the list. That would just make him more suspicious.

"We could get the bookshelf together on Saturday."

"I'm restless. I'd just as soon do it now."

"Is anything the matter? You seem nervous."

"Howard, do you want to come out with me? Shop with me if that will make you feel better. Come on." She took his hand.

"I've got work to do."

She kissed him on the cheek. "Don't worry."

As she pulled her Pinto out of the garage she saw him still watching her from the door. She flicked on the car radio. A man on a talk show was complaining about 1974 being named the year of women. "I mean, it's not the 60s anymore. People are tired of this stuff. Bella Abzug, Gloria Steinem, if you ask me, they should be put out to pasture."

His tone implied shooting would be better. “Not that I don’t like women. Don’t get me wrong. But they don’t fight fair.”

“It was a long two days,” Marc said, twining his fingers in hers. “I really missed you.”

He sounded as though he meant it, while she.... Connie’s face flushed. “I thought you’d be so busy getting ready for your trip you wouldn’t notice.” She nodded towards the garment bag he’d hung over his closet door.

“Trial packing isn’t a substitute for seeing you.” He pressed her hand. “It’s not even fun. I’ve been agonizing over whether to take more light-weight things. Do you think it’ll still be cold there?”

“It’ll be cold in the mountains, but Rome could be glorious—aren’t you stopping for a few days on the way?” She imagined herself doing charming, innocent things: “Innocent things like looking at the Easter displays at Piazza Navona.”

“If we get off the ground. The stewardesses are talking about striking. I don’t blame them.” He grimaced. “‘We really move our tails for you.’ An ad like that makes every businessman think he’s entitled to make a pass. And the girls have to pretend to like it.”

Connie thought his tone was faintly patronizing. The tone men use when they take up women’s causes. “Oh, they can probably take care of themselves.” Connie knew she should be quiet but she felt irritated, jumpy. “A man made a pass at me at the ranch,” she blurted out, “and I handled it fine.”

Marc seemed stunned. “You mean while I was mooning around like a lovesick kid you were up at Hot Springs Ranch making out with someone?”

“Of course not!” Connie’s heart started to thump so loud she thought Marc must hear it. “I was with Sarah, remember? Do you really think I’d do that with my daughter along? Besides, the man wasn’t interesting.”

“You don’t have to prove anything to me, you know. But maybe you were trying to find something out. Or maybe he just had a nice body. What do I really know about you anyway?" He narrowed his eyes at her, scanning her face.

She felt as though her facial muscles had suddenly gone haywire and were all pulling in separate directions. Her eyes sliding away like fish, her mouth screwing up. She wondered how much Marc could see. "Look. You don't have to believe me but I've never felt like this before. When you touch me it's like dynamite on a short fuse. It confuses me. I'm scared." That was honest at least.

"Why?" He put his hand on her neck and she shivered. "You're a big girl. You field passes from strange men like a pro. Why are you giving me such a hard time?"

"I'm afraid," Connie said. She could smell his shaving lotion, like apples and wood smoke. "I'm afraid that you'll leave me with my house collapsed around my ears, watching you walk away."

"Sounds like you've been watching too much twister news." She nodded. Maybe she had. The images filled her mind. Men and women sucked up into a roaring funnel of wind, dropped down like rag dolls. Children abandoned. The worst tornado disaster in half a century. Three hundred dead.

"Tell me." He brought up his other hand, caressing her throat. "Have I done anything since you've known me? Said anything that would give you reason? Do you want testimonials from my friends? People who've been in the trenches with me? You've made me into some sort of monster. It's not me, really. Ask them. They'll tell you. I've been fighting for Free Speech, not free love." Suddenly he stopped caressing her and began punching one hand into the other palm. "Sometimes I wonder if you wouldn't like it better if I were only some Lothario like that guy at the ranch."

"That's ridiculous." She toyed with a plate of orange rinds on his desk. They gave off a bittersweet odor.

"Is it? You know what? I don't think you're scared I'll leave you. I think you're scared I'm serious. Listen," he said, as though an inspiration had just struck him. "Why don't you make a clean break with Howard? You could get an apartment in San Francisco. Give this a chance to develop naturally." She didn't say anything. "Or is this just something you do to relieve the monotony of being a Berkeley housewife? Do you love me or not?"

"As much as I can right now," she said weakly, feeling as if their roles had been switched when she wasn't looking. For a minute she indulged a fantasy of throwing herself into his arms and telling him she'd do it. "How can I move out?" she asked instead. "With two kids to take care of? In the middle of a recession? When even our President can't pay his taxes." Marc gave a wry smile. Nixon had just been caught owing the government half a million dollars. "I'm not teasing you, I'm just trying to keep my wits. I wish you wouldn't act as if it's so easy to walk out of a marriage."

"Who knows," he said with one of his melting smiles. "It might be worth it."

"You sound like Hemingway again. A pot of gold at the end of the rainbow—read marriage for rainbow. How many times did Hemingway marry? Wasn't it four?" Connie couldn't imagine a future with Marc in the sense of furniture and children, but she could imagine a perpetual present, rich in sensuous shocks. She didn't understand why he felt he had to hint at marriage in order to get her into bed.

"What's Howard given you?" he asked in return, squeezing her hand so it hurt. "Shelter, a roof over your head, that's all. A bushman on the African plains could do as well as that. Don't you deserve better? Why don't you think about it while I'm gone?"

She wished he hadn't reminded her that he was going. In those ski resort towns, he could console himself with sexy women from all over the globe.

"I want you for myself, don't you understand?" Marc drew her towards the couch. She felt the silky texture of his shirt against her bare arm. "I don't want just a little piece of you. And whatever I am, I'm better than that jerk you're married to."

She stood still and looked at him. "It's not right to be jealous when my whole life's at stake. You're not even divorced yet yourself, are you?"

"Shhh, never mind. I'm sorry." He kissed her neck, pulling her down.

"Not now. Please, I can't." She wished she wasn't so weighed down by fear and distrust. She would have liked to turn off her brain.

"What is it with you? You act like lady pure with me and then you flirt like crazy with some guy you don't even like. Or did you like him? I'll bet you did. You attract men like flies. And then you don't want me to be jealous. You're a tease, that's all you are. You get high on saying no." He took hold of her wrist. "Come on. Be honest. Admit you want me as much as I want you." He undid the top button of her blouse.

"Stop it. I don't want to." She tugged her arm back and when he wouldn't let go, hit his wrist.

"All right then," he said, suddenly angry, "if you don't want to take responsibility for what you feel, I'll help you." Before she knew what was happening, he wrapped his leg around hers and pushed. In a minute they were wrestling on the rug.

"What are you doing? You're mad." She hit him in the shoulder and then tried to get away from him, pulling herself up against the couch. He grabbed her around the waist and got her down again, pinning her arms to the floor. She kicked at him and he climbed over her, straddling her, holding her legs quiet with his knees.

"Had enough?" he asked her. He was panting lightly. She just looked at him, stunned. Not thinking. She could feel the blood making a sound in her ears like a conch shell.

"I'm not breathing this way because I'm tired," he said. "It's because it's the first time I've been so close to you. You don't really want to fight me anymore, do you?"

"No." Her muscles relaxed. She felt heat rising to the surface of her skin.

"I can feel it in your body. You're close to me too." He leaned over and kissed her cheek. She groped for his mouth.

Marc's body had an incredible heat that warmed Connie through to the heart. She ran her hands over his thighs, his stomach, the hollow of his groin, watching his penis strain towards her. She fondled him, kissed him until he drew her into his arms. He held her under the shoulders, half lifting her from the couch, swooped her from side to side, up and down. She gasped with surprise, it was like a roller coaster. When he gathered her up, she was weightless, disoriented, helpless. When he let her drop she felt a stab of pleasure in her belly. He kept on until she felt they had fused into some sort of giant bird. Then he lowered her back against the pillows and lay on top of her, his head to her neck, moving steadily inside her. Now she concentrated on the glowing circles of warmth expanding from her center like ripples in a pool after you've thrown a stone. She could even see the green, gray water lapping softly against the gravel. Marc slowed even more until, when he hovered above her teasing, she ached inside and had to pull him down, her hands on his buttocks. Her body had only one thought, wanted only to complete the rhythm. Slowly, still holding him, she straightened her legs against the curved hard shapes of his thighs. He gripped her tighter, whispering unintelligible words into her hair. At the last minute, she arched her back and screamed. Outside her head, the sound spiraled up, shrill, birdlike, triumphant.

Afterwards, she was dizzy. The painting over the couch pulsated under her eyelids, radiating yellow light. She wanted the warmth to last. She tried not to think, not even to breathe, but it was impossible. They lay sprawled out, their clothing lying all around them on the floor. She was reassured by his peacefulness. No danger there, she thought. His energy is inside me. I am strong with it. For now nothing can hurt me.

After making love the second time, they went upstairs to the bedroom under the eaves, climbed onto his bed and covered themselves with the sheet. She didn't know where her body began or ended. Her skin felt translucent. Her senses were like antennae tuned to his slightest breath. She couldn't let him turn away from her even for a moment, even to sleep. She needed the pressure of his arms on her ribs. Without it she would fly apart into a thousand pieces. She turned to him. She wanted to burrow right through his chest, dig herself a cave in his body, curl up there and live under his heart, be with him everywhere. She lay breathing in his scent like hay with the sun on it.

The phone shrilled insistently. She was bewildered at first, not remembering. Then for a fraction of a second she was sure it was Howard. She sat up, holding the sheet in front of her. Marc answered it, sitting close to her, stroking her hair. She could hear a woman's voice and she collapsed back against the pillows.

"Hi, Alix, what is it this time?" Marc's body tensed. "Why? Uh huh." Connie could see he was worried how the call would affect her. She moved closer. "Oh come on, Alix. You have Selina with you all year. I told you a friend of mine was going to drive me to the airport. It's all arranged." His voice was getting strident. "Look, Alix, I know, thirty-one people were machine gunned in the Rome airport. Yes, we're living in a terrible time. But can you imagine the security precautions the Italians are taking now? I bet you can't open your fly without a guard asking you what you've got there. Relax. Selina's not going to be hijacked. And it will do her good to get away for awhile." Oh, Connie thought, so she's afraid of flying too. But what did she want from him? What was the understanding between them? "No, not from you in particular. From the whole social scene here. Try not to personalize everything, will you? It would make it a lot easier." He sighed, impatient, and Connie kissed his shoulder. Enough with this woman, she wanted him back. She kissed him more loudly, half wanting Alix to hear, even if it hurt. That might even make it better. Someone else hurting meant it wasn't her. "All right, all right, Alix." Marc caressed Connie's hair, distracted. "Drive us if it's so important."

"The woman doesn't make sense," he said to Connie. "She waltzes around for months as though she doesn't have a daughter and then just when I want to do something with Selina, she gets all panicked. Now she wants to drive us to the airport." He hugged her. "I hope this didn't upset you."

"It didn't," she said. "Don't worry." It was true. All she could think about was clinging to Marc's body. It seemed perfectly natural, her God-given right. Her energy was thrumming in her veins. She didn't care who called him. Not even Alix, his wife. He was with her now. She knew how to please him, hold him. She was strong, urgent. Her wishes found answering flesh. She was the lucky one.

All the way home in the car she felt dazed, sure Howard would notice something. She checked herself in the mirror before she went into the house. Her mouth seemed swollen, her face flushed. While she was walking into the living room, she felt a warm gush of liquid down her leg. She sat down in a chair, hoping he wouldn't come near her. It would be too obvious if she went in and took a bath right away. It seemed to her Marc's smell was everywhere on her body. Even her hair. When she swallowed she tasted him in her mouth.

The rest of the week they had a run of rainy weather more typical of spring in New York than in Northern California, and Connie and Marc spent most of their time together in bed. But the day before he was leaving for his trip was clear. Connie could tell it was going to be warm even at eight o'clock. She washed her hair and put on the flowered skirt he liked. Even though she'd managed to see Marc every day, the week had gone so fast she felt cheated. She felt like someone preparing for a famine. Raiding the supermarket, unloading all the shelves into her cart.

She was determined to be cheerful even though she felt lousy. If she made Marc feel guilty about his trip, he'd only resent her. Like Alix, she thought, remembering how cold Marc's voice had gotten when he spoke to his wife on the phone. Driving over she wondered what would happen if Alix had a minor accident on the way to the airport and Marc couldn't get to the plane. Better still, what if he broke a leg. Nothing serious. Just enough to keep him from going. Then Alix would have to take Selina and Connie would be left alone with Marc.

There was a cement truck blocking the street two blocks from Marc's house. Restless, she switched on the radio. A newscaster announced there'd been a new message from Patty Hearst. Connie turned it up. The newscaster's voice blared into the car. "In the most recent and cruelest communique from the SLA, Miss Hearst, who now calls herself Tania, called her father 'a corporate liar' and denounced his food give-away program as a sham. She had similar messages for her mother and her fiancé, Stephen Weed. 'I can never go back to the life we led,' Miss Hearst said, 'Love doesn't mean the same thing to me anymore. I will stay and fight.' Randolph Hearst, in a statement to the press, said that he is convinced his daughter has been hypnotised or drugged."

So it was true then, Connie thought, watching the barrel of the truck churning out liquid cement. Patty had fallen in love with Cinque. That's what had done it. Love the destroyer. She saw a machine gun getting bigger and bigger, swelling, steel hard, steel gray, until it turned into a canon. She imagined Patty riding a white horse, leading the masses. Turning the cannon against her father. His castle-keep exploding in slow motion. The fragments going up and up. That night she and Cinque would make love in the ruins. They'd find a casque of her mother's jewels and she'd put them on. Dance in them naked, the fires still burning behind her. No, better if her parents had to watch her. Watch her dancing. Watch her making love. Their faces blackened, cringing in the shadows. Reduced. Shrunk to a proper size. Seeing her appropriate their things. Seeing her change direction. In the morning they'd help saddle her horse, bowing beside her stirrup.

As Connie started the Pinto up again, she wondered what it would take to make a girl turn against her father. She thought of Selina going off to Switzerland with Marc. One mistake. One big mistake or a lot of little ones. Girls were funny with their fathers. Nothing would have made her betray her father. Even if he had made the mistake of loving her brother.

Marc came to the door in his shirt sleeves, still knotting his tie. A blue and red paisley. Connie wondered if Alix had gotten it for him.

"Come in, I have something to show you." He took her hand and pulled her along. The couch was covered with great lengths of colored silk. Purple and rose, black with gold designs, scarlet. Connie drew in her breath.

"How beautiful!" she touched the scarlet one gingerly. "Where did you get them?" They had the barely perceptible odor of incense.

"They were having a closeout sale at an exotic Indonesian store in the city. They're Balinese festival silks. I had to see this on you." He picked up the scarlet silk and threw it over his arm, excited. "Come stand in front of the hall mirror. The blouse is fine. Take off your skirt."

Connie raised her eyebrows. While she stood there hesitating, he pushed her skirt down over her hips. It slipped to the floor.

"Put it on," he coaxed, holding out the silk.

"Marc, I'm a big girl now." She laughed, embarrassed, seeing her skirt in a heap around her feet. "I don't think I want to have you dress me." Before she could move, he draped the gleaming silk over her shoulder, then down under her arms, round and round her body, falling in gauzy folds to the floor. "You look like the goddess Uma." He kissed her neck.

He was right. Even though she would never have chosen it for herself, it suited her. The colors vibrated. She adjusted a fold over her hip, wishing she didn't like it so much. "But why?" she asked again.

"Don't worry about it. They're Alix's."

"Alix's?" She started to rip the silk off. The gold border fluttered. "You said you bought them for me. If you think I'm going to wear her castoff things, you're crazy."

"Leave it." He caught her hand. "I thought they meant something to her. But she never wore them. Any of them."

"I don't care. Why do you want to dress me up in her things anyway? What's going on?" She pushed away his hand and went on unwinding the silk. Like unwrapping a mummy.

"I don't know. I just had such a strong impulse to undo something, do it over again, better. I thought you'd like them."

"That's no reason to lie," she said, resisting the look of pain on his face.

"Sorry." He hung his head. "Sometimes we do things we don't understand."

"You've been separated for years. Why do you still care whether she wore your gifts or not? What difference does it make? You seem awfully tied up with her." More like a man sinking in quicksand, she thought, unable to get onto solid ground. "You act as if she were still your wife." She folded the silk angrily.

"She infuriates me, that's all. She didn't learn anything from what happened. How to treat anybody right. Not Selina, not even another man. It's still me, me, me. She runs around racking up bills trying to make herself look good when she's just an old bag of bones." He scooped up the lengths of silks from the couch. "If you won't have them, I'll give them to Goodwill."

Connie put her hands over her ears. "Don't shout!"

"Was I?" He dropped the silks and put his arm around her. "Sorry. I don't know why I was haranguing you. It's not you I'm mad at. It's Alix."

"I know." He'd given her a lot to think about, but nothing was going to be settled right now, certainly not by nagging him. "Look, let's forget about Alix. We can talk about it some other time. We've only got two hours." She took off her blouse and dropped it on a chair, then she stepped out of her slip. He didn't let her get any farther. He carried her over to the couch.

About fifteen minutes later, they were in the midst of a passionate embrace when there was the crunch of footsteps on the gravel path.

Marc partially detached himself from her arms and looked out the window. "My God, it's Alix and Selina."

"Oh no," Connie moaned, catching a glimpse of a tall woman with a geometric haircut, deeply cleft chin and oversized eyeglasses who was talking to a girl in jeans with embroidered pockets. "I thought you said she was coming at noon and it's only 9:30." She sat up wondering if she should make a dash for her skirt. Her blouse was even farther away, on a chair on the other side of the room. Before she could do anything but grab a silk from the heap next to the couch and cover herself, Selina and Alix were in the room, eyeing her curiously. Alix had a small overnight case in her hand. She looked as though she was about to take off on a business trip. Connie licked her bitten lips. They felt abnormally swollen, as obvious as the rear of a monkey in heat.

"Alix, what the hell?" Marc spluttered.

"I know we're early," Alix said, her gaze flicking rapidly over Connie, who pulled the silk up closer to her chin. A wave of hot, zoo smell wafted from underneath her. "But I wanted to pick up my casserole dish. And I brought along the suitcase because you said the lock on yours was broken." Alix was slim and stylish in a trim suit and silk blouse with a bow. The kind of blouse Marc was always trying to get Connie to wear. Connie flushed. This was horrible. Worse than being caught masturbating by her mother.

"I told Mom I bet you'd be here," Selina said, popping a bubble of pink goop. "Looks like we interrupted something." She snapped her fingers and jigged a little in place, grunting a phrase from some obscure rock song. Something about getting down.

"Selina," Alix said sharply. She looked at Connie as though she'd like to kill her but didn't want to risk dirtying her gloves. Connie moved her buttocks slightly out of the damp spot she was sitting in. If she made a run for it, would she leave a wet trail behind her? Little globs of white on the floor?

Selina jigged a little closer to the couch. Pretty but not too bright looking. "Hey, what are you doing with Mom's silks? Using them as covers. Playing dress up? Did you see this, Mom? They're all over the place." Alix shrugged and walked into the kitchen alcove.

Marc got off the couch. "Come on, Princess, your mother couldn't care less about them." He picked his underwear off the floor and stepped into it with one foot. Connie cringed. Wasn't he embarrassed letting them see him buck naked? Apparently not. Maybe he walked around that way all the time. She looked at the hair tufting between his legs and felt as though Selina and Alix could see her naked too.

"It's still her stuff, man." Selina tapped Marc's chest warningly, tugged at a whorl of hair. "I don't think she'd like you messing with it."

"Don't worry, babe," Marc said appeasingly. Selina turned on her pocket radio and it started grinding out Eric Clapton's *I Shot the Sheriff.*

"I'm not taking anything, Selina." Connie said, combing her hair back with one hand, "and if you two would go out and wait in the car, I could get dressed and get out of here." Damn them, why did they have to come and ruin her last hour with Marc? And why was he letting them?

Alix didn't seem to hear. She was looking in the fridge. "I see the apple crisp I made you, but where's the casserole?"

"The dish is in the sink," Connie said. They'd eaten it last night. If she'd known it was Alix's, she would have thrown it out. She leaned over, trying to see if her panties were on the floor next to the couch.

Alix turned on the water and it splashed into the sink. "Are you going to Switzerland too?" she asked.

Connie felt like Alice at the Mad Hatter's tea party. All it needed now was for Alix to offer to make scones. "I hadn't planned to," she said, fishing around under her cover. If she could only find her underwear.

"I'd thought of going myself." Alix took the dish out of the sink and dried it. She looked like those women on T.V. advertising dishwashing liquids. "I have friends there," she said, walking over to Marc's desk. Connie's toes came into contact with a piece of damp silky material. She hooked it and brought it up to her hand. Thank God, her panties. While she wriggled into them, she could see Alix riffling through the mail on the desk, as though this was her own place.

"You don't have any friends in Switzerland, Alix," Marc said. "You're just giving me a hard time. Why don't you wait in the car for a few minutes and...."

Alix picked up a letter. "Oh, for heaven's sake, Harvey Lester. I don't know why people still write to me care of Marc," she said with obvious satisfaction. She opened the letter and glanced over the contents, ignoring Marc. "Men are extraordinary creatures," she went on, "always looking for new additions to their harems. Not caring who their partner is." She glanced at Connie. "It must be something retrograde in their genes, don't you think?"

Connie scrunched down and ran her foot along the crack

behind the cushions, trying to find her bra. "I haven't thought much about it."

"Every woman should. It's very instructive. Frankly, I don't think men have advanced much from the Stone Age. They've just gotten more articulate. Better at rationalizing their obsession with sex."

Marc was zipping his trousers. "So that's the kind of stuff you're telling my kid. No wonder we have problems. If you listen to your mother, Selina, you're going to end up a bitter lady."

Selina picked up two of the Balinese silks from the floor. "What about the silks?" She pulled at a gold thread that had unravelled. "They're getting trashed."

"Stop worrying about the silks, Sel. I'm giving them to Goodwill."

"I certainly don't care what you do with them." Alix gave a little sniff. "You can dress up the neighbor's dog in them. It wouldn't bother me."

Connie had found her bra. Now she lay back so she could hook it without losing the protection of her cover. "You know," she said struggling with the hook. "I didn't wear your...."

"Please, no confidences," Alix said with icy politeness. "Don't try to explain anything to me. I don't want to hear it. I have my life, Marc has his. I don't meddle. That's why we're still good friends." Good friends! My god, what an act, Connie thought. The woman was still obsessed with him. "I think we should go soon, Marc. The lines are so long now with the hijackings and the security checks." Alix spotted the suitcase near the door and knelt to open it. "I don't see why you packed this shirt. It doesn't go with your blazer."

"But two hours early, Alix!" Marc took the shirt and ties out of her hand and slammed the suitcase shut. "And leave my stuff alone, will you please."

"I needed to talk over something important." Alix bent her

head towards Selina. "But if you don't care about your daughter...." Connie saw Marc swallow his protest. Jesus, she thought, Alix just has to suggest it's something about Selina and he goes into shock.

"Of course I care," Marc said, putting his arm around Selina. "You know you're my favorite girl, don't you, baby?"

Alix gave Selina a little shove. "I'll open the trunk. Selina, help Daddy with his bags." She walked briskly off to her car, her heels clicking against the stone steps.

Connie threw back her cover and made a dash for her skirt. She slipped it over her head. Then she went over to the chair and got her blouse, buttoning it rapidly. She couldn't believe this was happening. But she kept a phony smile on her face. She didn't want to give them the satisfaction of seeing her discomfort. She moved calmly toward the street with Mark and Selina, acting as though everything were perfectly normal. On the way, Selina blew a horrible pink bubble and it burst all over Marc's suitcase.

"This has been awful for you. I'm really sorry," Marc whispered to her as they went down the steps. "But with Sel here I couldn't make a scene. Please baby, try to understand. Sel hates it when Alix gets upset. I love you. I'll call you from the airport." Then they piled into the car and Alix gunned the engine and pulled away, leaving Connie standing on the sidewalk in a cloud of exhaust fumes.

Marc called an hour later.

"I'm not even sure I want to talk to you after that," Connie said.

"Yell at me, it'll make you feel better."

"What's going on with you and that wife of yours? You still let her cook for you. You want to dress me in her clothes! And then she comes in and acts as if I'm not there."

"She's deranged. She can't help it. She's just gone off her rocker. She won't admit to herself that we're not married anymore. That's what her little domestic act was all about. She tries to pretend nothing ever happened. That she didn't end up clawing my face like a wild animal. You know she even told some woman interviewing her for a business magazine how grateful she was to her 'husband' for supporting her career. It's pathetic, really."

"She thinks I'm coming between you. That's what her snide comments were about. Barging in between a man and wife. Well, am I?"

"Of course not. We're totally finished."

"Then how come she doesn't know it? She brings you suitcases. Even checks to see if you've put in enough sweaters. My God, I couldn't believe it."

"You don't think I ask her for that, do you? It's just one of her little pretenses of intimacy."

"Why do you let her cook for you then? Go through your closet? It takes two to create a situation like this."

"I try to go along with some of it, for Selina's sake. Who knows what Alix would do otherwise. She's bad enough already. Besides, she's always been a much better cook than I am." He laughed awkwardly. "Hey, what difference does it make? Why are you making such a thing of it?"

"Because it keeps up her delusions. It keeps her from cutting free of you."

"She'd have them anyway. This just makes things a little more civilized."

"Civilized! Well, she was too polite to stick a kitchen knife between my ribs."

"I don't think people can just cancel out fifteen years of their life. Not with children."

"Maybe," Connie said skeptically. "But trying on her silks? Is it a regular routine of yours? Do you try them on all your girlfriends? Strew them around to make her cringe? Are you still that angry at her?"

"That's really going too far, Connie. I've never even shown them to anyone else—and I never will."

Connie was almost sure he was lying but, still, she wanted him so badly her legs were weak. "The past is one thing but you better be faithful to me in San Moritz. Or...." She said it lightly but she could see those gorgeous long-legged women in their après-ski outfits. She could see Marc standing next to one in front of a roaring fire, sipping a campari, making casual conversation. Starting something up.

"Or what? I don't even see other women, you know that. You can inject me with novocaine—freeze me until I get back to you. I wouldn't mind it a bit. I'm getting an erection just thinking about you. But this is it for the duration." Despite herself, Connie felt a throbbing between her legs. "This is Custer's last stand."

Eight

Sarah was late for dinner on Wednesday night. At first Connie didn't think anything of it. She turned on her T.V. and watched a report on what seemed to be a "second phase" of the cultural revolution in China. It was amazing how much energy the Chinese expended on denouncing abstractions: feudalism, capitalism, imperialism. There was something adolescent about it, like high school students solving the problems of the universe when they still can't talk to the girl next door. The newscaster shifted to Nixon. Connie wondered what would happen if the Chinese got their hands on Nixon and his tapes. They wouldn't bother with a subpoena, that's for sure. They'd handcuff him in a cell and take a good look. The minute he opened his mouth to say, "I'm not a crook," they'd hit him in the teeth. She opened the oven and was hit by the Italian restaurant smells of bubbling cheese and tomatoes. She spooned some of the sauce over her lasagna.

Mischa wandered in with a stack of baseball cards. "I'm starving."

"Why don't you organize your cards? You wanted a shoe box to keep them in, didn't you. There's one at the back of the closet."

"I don't feel like organizing, I'm hungry."

Connie looked at the top card. "Isn't that the guy who

broke Babe Ruth's record? What's his name, Aaron?" Ordinarily Mischa would have rattled off the man's whole career and Connie would have gained half an hour. But this time it didn't work.

"Hank Aaron," Mischa said listlessly. "He hit 715."

By the time Connie's lasagna began to crisp at the edges, Mischa was grouching so much that she couldn't hold up dinner any longer. They had to eat without Sarah.

"Never mind," Howard said when they finished, "you've got us. In fact, if you like we could go to a movie tonight. Let's see *The Sting*. Gangsters and jazz. Forget about Sarah. She's probably at a friend's."

Good heavens, Connie thought, what's gotten into him? He hasn't asked me to a movie in years.

"Thanks," she said, looking at him curiously, "but I think I should stick around and see what's up with Sarah. I'm worried. It's not like her to be so late. Besides, Mischa's got school tomorrow."

"I don't need much sleep," Mischa began.

"Don't start. You know you don't go to movies on school nights." She tapped him on the bottom. "It's late enough already. Go brush your teeth."

Howard started to help her clean up. He stacked the dirty plates and carried them into the kitchen. This really was amazing! First an invitation to the movies, then help in the kitchen. What *was* going on? She left him washing the dishes while she went to put Mischa to bed.

He had brushed his teeth and was drawing at his table. She looked over his shoulder. It was a cartoon which had several panels. In the first a little boy was being given a machine gun by a man. In the last he had turned the machine gun against the man, who was cowering with his hands up. The little boy had a propeller on his hat and a big grin.

"Do you get it?" Mischa looked up at her eagerly.

"Someone gave the little boy the idea that the way to get what you want is to shoot people?" She rested her hand on his shoulder. The gun was as big as the boy and colored with slashing strokes in black crayon. Too much violence, she thought. The kids are bombarded with it, and then we expect them to grow up and make peace.

"Wrong," Mischa said. "It's what I'd do if anyone asked me to rob a bank. I'd turn him in to the police. Patty Hearst did what those weirdos told her because she's a girl. Girls are easy to boss around."

Connie sighed. Patty Hearst had just robbed the Hibernia Bank. "Not all girls," she said. "Think about your sister. She's pretty strong-willed."

"Yeah, well, maybe. But if you gave her a gun I think she might shoot a few people." He gave an uneasy laugh.

"Your sister isn't Patty Hearst. She's not going to shoot you. I bet she's not even going to rob a bank." She bent over him. "Your A's cap is starting to grow mold. I'm going to wash it." She took it off and ruffled his hair. "You're the only kid I know who sleeps in his hat."

"Don't get the brim wet," he murmured sleepily. "Okay?"

She'd just finished tucking him in and hanging up his cap to dry when she heard the key turn in the latch downstairs.

"Sarah, where were you?" Connie called impatiently before she was all the way down. Sarah was nonchalantly looking through the mail. Connie touched her arm to get her attention. "What happened? I kept dinner waiting for you for an hour."

"So you were waiting. Big deal." Sarah opened an envelope and examined a large green flier.

"Sarah, what kind of answer is that?" Connie asked, irritated.

"I'm sorry. All right, something came up and I had to take care of it." Her indifference infuriated Connie. There was something deliberate in it, as though Sarah wanted to let her know how boring this was, that the crucial things in her life were someplace else. She glanced at the flier and saw the name of Peron. Somehow that added to her aggravation.

"At least you owe me an explanation. What were you doing that was so important? You know you're supposed to be home for dinner. We've never had any trouble with it before."

"Mom, I told you at the ranch, I'm not a baby anymore. None of my friends have to be home for dinner at six o'clock. I wasn't home two days last week, or the week before, for that matter. Why are you making such a thing of it now? I hoped you were loosening up a little. And it was about time." Sarah folded the flier and put it in her pants pocket.

"But you gave me good reasons. You told me you had to study for a test and you asked...."

Sarah looked at Connie scornfully and she suddenly realized that she had no idea if Sarah had really been studying with Annie. Sarah's look told her she was doing something quite different, something she wouldn't like. She had a panicked feeling that while she hadn't been paying attention the past weeks, Sarah had become a different person. She didn't feel accountable any more.

"Look, Sarah, it's really inexcusable to come in two hours late, without a word of explanation or even an apology. I don't understand why you're acting this way. But whatever your reasons, I want you home on time from now on."

Howard strolled in holding his Hebrew paper—Connie noted the picture of Golda Meir on the cover, grandmotherly even when being forced to resign—and a slim book bound in vellum. "Don't you say good evening to your father, Sarah?"

"Dad, can't you see Mom and I are talking about something?"

"What are you doing, planning a bank robbery?" he asked not unkindly. "Don't try the Hibernia. It's been done." He held out the book. "Sarah, pay attention for a moment. I brought Bialik's poems for you. I want you to read them with your Hebrew teacher. Thursday's your lesson, isn't it?"

"As a matter of fact I was thinking of dropping it. I'm starting Spanish."

Howard turned red. "This is absurd. You're a Jewish child. Do you hear me? Taking Hebrew isn't open to discussion."

"Dad, there are things that are more important to me." She touched her back pocket as if to make sure her flier was safe.

"What could be more important than your Jewish education?"

"You said after my Bat Mitzvah, when I was thirteen, I could stop if I wanted to. Well, I'm stopping."

"Are you ashamed of being Jewish? Don't you realize what a privilege it is?" Howard's voice rose. "What is this nonsense?"

Connie edged between them and put her hand on his arm. She agreed with Howard but his righteousness wasn't going to help.

"We're not forcing religion on you if you don't want it Sarah. But Hebrew's your heritage. Part of your identity. You can't just cut it off like that."

"How do you know? You didn't go to religious school. You didn't study Hebrew 'til you got married."

"I wish I had. That's the point. We're giving you a foundation you can rely on. Later, you can decide what to do with it." Connie'd hated being raised by agnostics. Nothing to believe in. No roots anywhere.

"Take this book," Howard spluttered. "Take it right now," he shook it at her. "Honor your father and mother, *Kabed et Avika ve'et Imecha.* That's what the Bible tells us."

"All right I'll take your stupid book," she snatched it from his hand. "But I don't see what's so great about being Jewish. They just threw out the one good woman they had in Israel. Now we'll go back to the old patriarchal stuff. Women as bedmakers, no more women premiers. And you want me to be grateful." She slung her bag over her shoulder and ran upstairs.

Sarah went to her Hebrew lesson on Thursday. She even came home on time but she sat through dinner in silence and then went up to her room. At first Connie was relieved. Sarah needed limits, that's all. Connie didn't have them when she was a child and it had made her feel as if she were walking a tight rope, always about to come smashing down.

If only she could explain to Sarah how important boundaries were. In college in Connecticut, finally released from Elsie's spell, Connie had been wild and out of control. Back in the 50s, she'd taken a motorcycle ride with Freddy—racing downhill the day the cycle came, before he knew how to drive it. She'd felt she was making up for lost time but the accident had practically cost her her life. She'd ended up skidding under a truck. Between the wheels. She still had the scars on her legs from scraping along the concrete.

For a month she'd had to sit with weights on her foot because the muscles in one leg had atrophied and it was weaker than the other. Her black leather jacket somehow escaped getting scratched. It scared her. She had to clamp down on herself. She went back home to New York to recover from her leg injury and enrolled in graduate school at Columbia. A year later she married Howard to make the rest of her life an atonement.

She wished she could explain to Sarah that she didn't set rules because she was mean but because she cared about her.

The next day she was getting ready to fix the loose doorknob on the front door when Sarah opened it and almost fell in on her. Connie gave a little scream. Sarah's hair straggled over half of her face and her blouse was badly crumpled. Two buttons were open and Connie could see her breasts.

"My God, Sarah, what happened? Did someone try to hurt you?" Connie reached out her arms, ready to hold her.

"No Mom, nothing happened. You freaked me out hiding behind the door like that. Mellow out. Give me a break." Sarah's face was flushed with anger. She'd obviously expected to run to her room and straighten herself up. Before

Connie could say anything, she walked past her and turned the stereo on loud. Elton John blared Sarah's theme song of defiance, *"I'm not a present for your friends to open."* Without a word she deliberately finished unbuttoning her blouse and dropped it on the floor with an insolent look, then she kicked off her shoes, peeled off her jeans. Standing there in her bra and bikini underpants, she pretended not to notice Connie but every gesture was saturated with defiance. She began moving hypnotically in time to the music, her eyes closed. The bra was much too small for her and her full breasts bulged provocatively, threatening to slip out entirely. The sight enraged Connie. She looked like such a slut.

She turned off the stereo and caught her by the arm. "Sarah." The sweet sickly smell of pot was overwhelming. "You've been smoking dope. Where have you been? What have you been doing?"

Sarah interrupted her furiously. "What right do you have to ask me where I've been? Do you tell me where you go? Out for hours on the weekends with that guy. Do you think I'm so stupid I don't know what's going on? I passed you the other day on the street and you didn't even notice me you were so wrapped up in each other. Not that I mind. It's your business if you want to have affairs. Pick up as many men as you like." Connie flushed at her allusion to the ranch. How stupid that had been. Stupid and costly. "You don't have to talk to me about it. But get off my back, will you. I have my own life to lead." She looked at her for a moment with pure hostility.

"Don't talk to me that way, God dammit." Connie lifted her hand to slap her but an image of her mother intervened, open mouthed, snarling, about to hit. She'd sworn never to do that. "Sarah," she said, "Our situations are very different. We're not roommates. I'm your mother and like it or not, you're still my responsibility. You can be as angry as you like but I expect respect from you as long as you're in this house. Understand?"

Sarah was still glaring at her coldly. "You never let me say what I think."

"That's not true, Sarah and you know it. I just want a little civility. If you have more to say, go ahead and say it."

Sarah made a face as though she were tasting a lemon. "You think you can come back any time you feel like it and have me talk to you about stuff while you feed me cookies. As though I'm still a kid. Well, you're wrong. You probably wouldn't talk to me at all if he was around. What's the matter? Did you have a fight with him or something? Not that I care if you want to sneak around like G. Gordon Liddy. I've got a lot of more important things on my mind."

"Sarah, you're being gratuitously nasty. That's enough. This is a non-conversation."

"You don't have to tell me to go to my room. I'm going," Sarah shouted. "I don't want to be here. This doesn't even feel like home anymore." She scooped up her clothes, ran upstairs and slammed the door.

Connie felt as though her life was falling apart, as though she was going completely crazy. There seemed to be no way of stopping Sarah's anger. She guessed it had been building up for years, like tension in an earthquake fault. The job, the curfew, the man at the ranch, even Marc were only the last stressors. One minute the plates were touching, contact along all their surfaces. The next, rending, turmoil, an abyss. And it had happened so fast. One minute Connie was confident, in control, and the next she was guilty and confused, sniffling in the hallway outside her daughter's closed door.

She wondered if it would make her feel better to call Marc in Switzerland. But though she needed someone to talk to, she couldn't get herself to do it. What would she tell him? That Sarah was furious because of him—that's what she had an urge to say—or that she was defying her, saying she wanted to lead her own life, running around doing....

She decided to talk to Howard. After all, he was Sarah's father. She went to his study and knocked on the door. He was sitting with his feet up on his desk, reading the Hebrew paper. Not Golda this time, her successor, Rabin. Howard had drawn a mustache on the face that made it look a little like the White Knight.

"We've got to do something with Sarah," Connie said, pulling up a chair facing him. "She's getting out of control. I think she's smoking dope."

Howard looked up annoyed by the interruption. "Send her to Israel. Get her out of here. Away from all this Berkeley filth."

"I don't think that's the answer." She rubbed her fingers over a frayed place on the armrest. If it wasn't sewn soon, it was going to come apart.

"Why not? Picking apples instead of smoking weed." He put his paper down on his lap.

"You can't just rip her out of school mid-semester. You can smoke dope there too, by the way."

"She has a chance to do something different with her life."

"Like what? Be a girl soldier? Get killed when someone throws a grenade over the wall of her kibbutz? You wanted to have Mischa after the Six Day War. To replace the Jewish boys who were killed." It was such an insane idea, raising a child for cannon fodder in a place thousands of miles away. Not even her own country. It would be different if she believed in Israel the way Howard did, totally, no matter what happened. But she couldn't. "I was a fool to let you persuade me that things would be different with another baby. That you wanted to try to be a father. You didn't mean it. Not one word. It was all for Israel." She should have followed her first impulse and had an abortion when she found out she was pregnant a second time.

"Children are only the dreams of their parents. The Jews are God's chosen people."

"Chosen for what? For centuries of slaughter? Now just because there has been another war, you want to send Sarah to a kibbutz. Is all our life going to be dictated by what happens in Israel?"

"There's not going to be another massacre. That's the whole point. Masada won't fall again." His voice got thick. She remembered the rocky fortress town high on a hill. They'd had to scale a ladder to get there, climbing in the boiling sun.

"What about the war we just had? Didn't the Arabs cross Suez and storm the Golan Heights? Didn't they surprise Jewish soldiers and kill them?"

"That's not going to happen again either. They're having a judicial inquiry. Israel will be better prepared next time. And the time after that. As long as it takes. We're raising a new generation of Jews. Jews who aren't afraid to fight." She saw his jaw clench. "Jews who won't step aside when someone tells them to step into the gutter or be driven into the sea."

"They're becoming gangsters. They can't help it. It's what happens when you get used to using force."

"Nonsense. They've got some pride now. They feel like men for the first time since the Fall of the Temple. Mischa is too soft. You spoil him. It would do him good to be a soldier for a couple of years."

"A couple of years! I saw the cemetery in Jerusalem. Those rows and rows of graves. Some of them empty. The mothers bringing flowers to empty graves. It was terrifying. There's enough to be frightened about in raising a child without that—a Holy War."

"You have war here too but it's capitalist war."

"I hate it here too." Connie hit the desk with her fist. "I hate war, period." She could hear her voice spiraling up like a crazed hummingbird. "The Johnson's son had to go to Canada. I'd want Mischa to do the same. God, Howard. We're finally getting out of Vietnam. Do you have to run and find something else? Aren't 50,000 body bags enough for you? Do you have to add Mischa or Sarah?"

"Being a Jew is what makes life worth something. When

Mischa was circumcised, I looked at him and thought, now he's a human being."

Connie hated the ceremony. She thought it was barbaric. Tied to a cutting board like some barbaric sacrifice. Her milk had knotted in her breasts when she heard Mischa screaming. "What was he before that? An animal? A changeling?"

"Less than an animal. An unformed lump of protoplasm." Howard swung his feet around and sat up.

"Protoplasm! Is that what you think of your children? And how about Sarah? Since she wasn't circumcised I suppose she doesn't count at all. You can send her off to be shot with an easy conscience. Do you really want your daughter to be a statistic?"

"She had her naming ceremony. And you're exaggerating. She doesn't have to be a soldier. She can be a mother of Israel. Have healthy sons instead of wasting her time selling records to drug addicts."

"Howard, don't pretend you care about her. Say whatever crazy thing you want but don't pretend it's for her. You're feeding your obsession. That's all." She thought she was going to start screaming and not be able to stop. Like a girl she'd seen once who'd been kicked in the head by a horse.

"Judaism has served generations of Jews. Given them a sense of direction. It gave me one. Got me away from my parents' hypocrisy."

"I don't see you packing your bags, Howard. If you care so much, why don't you go yourself instead of sending your children? How can you ask them to do what you can't do? It's not fair." The minute she said that she knew she'd made a mistake.

Howard reached for her hand. "You know I want to go. I'd go in a minute if you were willing. Come with me, Connie. Let's take the children and start again. Come back to Abraham, your father... Abraham's wife, your mother." She had the awful feeling he was going to embrace her knees, urge her to pray with him.

"Stop, Howard," she said, tugging her hand away. "Don't go on." How could he be so out of touch as to offer this after what she'd told him? Not once but over and over. "It's your dream. Not mine."

Nine

Before dinner, Connie waxed the dining room table, applying the slippery wax with a soft cloth. Near her, Howard was mixing the almonds and apples for the Seder. The purposeful movement of her hand was calming but she couldn't tell herself anymore that she was being virtuous, a "pearl without price." What solace was this religion to her, really? Would she ever turn to it if she were in trouble? Would she miss anything about it except the sense of family it gave her?

Howard opened the nearest window and a fragrant whiff of air entered the room. Even over the wax, Connie could smell wisteria. Howard threw the apple peels out into the garden. They landed on her daffodils, splotching them with red.

"Do you have to do that, Howard?" Connie asked, putting another dab of wax on the table. Once again she thought of how peaceful it was while he was away in Israel and she was spared all his irritating habits. Since he returned, it seemed to her that she was always ordering things and he was messing them up. He did everything impulsively like a child.

"Why shouldn't I?" he asked, "I've always done it."

"That doesn't mean it's right." Connie rubbed the white film off the dark wood. "For one thing, it brings ants."

"Nonsense, it's a natural fertilizer. Earth to earth," Howard said defensively, pulling his neck down between his shoulders. He had taken off his jacket and was working in his vest with his sleeves rolled up, his father's gold watch in his vest pocket.

Sarah gave her a pained look. "Oh let him do it, Mom. What difference does it make?"

Connie shrugged and rubbed away another portion of wax, making a whirled pattern. Sarah seemed to be feeling unusually sorry for Howard. Connie wondered how much Sarah really knew about her and Marc. If she knew it was serious, would Sarah side with Howard? That would be ironic after all her complaints about him, but you could never tell with kids. Their loyalties shifted in funny ways. Besides, adolescents hated moral impurity in their elders. Sarah might go on a campaign against her like the Little Generals of the Red Guard, informing on their parents. Connie heard Howard humming contentedly to himself and felt a guilty tightening in her chest. He was so engrossed in his preparations for the holiday, seemingly unaware that the structure of their lives was in danger. That Connie was building up the courage to leave.

Or was he so unaware? Connie wasn't sure. He was being more attentive than he'd been for years. She was suddenly angry that she'd had to wait so long, that all those years of breaking her neck to please him hadn't meant a thing. It was only now, when she was thinking about someone else, that Howard began to notice her. She looked over and saw that he had begun grating the horseradish. It was making him cry.

She was glad when the service finally started. She wanted to give in to the ritual, make the gestures, enact the familiar story of oppression and liberation. After Howard had blessed the family, he said a blessing for the state of Israel and her new premier, Yitzak Rabin.

"I'm going to add Kissinger tonight," he said. "May God bless him and keep him safe." Connie saw Mischa fidgeting restlessly in his seat. Oblivious to his tension, Howard proudly showed him the symbolic foods on the Passover plate, the gnarled horseradish root and the lamb shank burnt on one side.

"Do I have to ask the four questions by myself? Can't Sarah help me?" Mischa looked anxiously at his father for a moment and then began to squirm again.

"Mischa, you know it has to be you. You're the youngest son. Be a good boy. When it's time, I'll help you start." Howard straightened Mischa's cap and gave him a little pat on the shoulder.

Mischa frowned. If he felt desperate enough, Connie knew he'd make a scene. Hoping to distract him, she asked him to show them the matzot shmurot, the flat bread especially baked for Passover. Mischa lifted the white satin cover carefully and gave her a wan smile.

"Do you remember why the bread isn't risen like ordinary bread?" Howard asked. "It's one of your four questions." Connie could see he was trying to draw Mischa in, but from the look on Mischa's face, it wasn't working.

"Because the Jews were running away from the Pharaoh and they didn't have time to make it right." Mischa glanced toward the door as if the Pharaoh were hard on his heels.

"Pay attention, Mischa," Howard said with barely controlled impatience, "the matzo's right in front of you." He leaned towards Mischa and Connie was afraid for a minute that he was going to grab Mischa's ear, but he only turned Mischa's head with his hand. "Watch now," he said and held the matzo out in front of him with straight arms, crying out in a voice breaking with emotion, "Behold the bread of affliction. Let all who are hungry come and eat." It was dramatic, Connie had to admit, that strange cracked voice. Like an Old Testament prophet. Even Mischa was staring. Howard turned to him with a proprietary look.

"All right, son. It's time for the questions. Tell us why this night is special."

Mischa sat on his hands and then pulled them out and looked at them, wiggling his fingers. Come on, Connie mentally urged Mischa. She knew he remembered it, but he hated being forced. Howard leaned forward and Connie could see his jaw twitching.

"Mischa, now!" Howard said loudly, "Do you hear me?" He took his arm. Mischa turned pale and looked pleadingly at Sarah. Connie felt the tension in the back of her neck.

"You're a crybaby," Sarah said but she hummed the first note in Mischa's ear. He struggled for a minute more with his dislike of the whole business and then, sighing, began to sing in a high, sweet voice. "*Ma nishtanah halailah hazeh....*"

Connie felt a surge of relief. Her eyes caught Sarah's across the table. She could see that Sarah felt relieved too. Thank God. Maybe they'd get through the rest of the Seder without a crisis.

During the supper part of the service, Howard gave them a little talk about Israel and its mission to gather in all the Jews who had been dispersed through the diaspora. "Kissinger must see that we need secure boundaries," he was saying, his face flushed with feeling, "so the exiles can be gathered in safely. Giving back the land we won would be a disaster." He turned to Mischa. "Do you remember where Passover used to be celebrated?"

Mischa chewed his finger. "In Jerusalem," he said questioningly, "on the temple mount."

"Good boy. Just imagine, Mischa, instead of the Arab mosques there was the great temple of Solomon. Hundreds of families arriving with lambs for the burnt offerings. Wine, feasting." He sighed, his eyes looking inward. "The high priest in his white garments giving his blessing."

"Be glad God didn't want a boy," Sarah said, pinching Mischa's arm lightly, after Howard described the way the high priest sacrificed a lamb in the temple. "Remember Isaac? Abraham was going to sacrifice Isaac because that's what God wanted. Then He changed His mind. But if He hadn't...."

"Don't torment your brother, Sarah." Howard said, "That's not the Paschal spirit. And we don't have to speculate in possibilities. We know what happened. God spared Isaac."

Mischa looked as though he was going to cry. Connie wondered why Sarah was being so mean. "Abraham would never have killed his son," Connie whispered to him. "Don't worry, sweetheart."

"He would too have killed him," Sarah muttered under her breath. "Well, I think it's despicable." She raised her voice. "How can you love a God who asks you to kill your child?"

"It was a test of his obedience, Sarah," Howard said, "Abraham passed with flying colors. And because of him God made his contract with the Jewish people. To be our God forever. Because of what Abraham was willing to do. Can't you see?" Connie could tell from the way his jaw was jumping that he was getting angry, but he was holding himself back.

"What about Isaac?" Sarah's face was closed. "How do you think he felt about it? Knowing his father would have slit his throat. Just because God told him to do it."

"Later, he understood that God's will can't be questioned," Howard said, closing his fingers around the lamb shank on the Passover plate as though it were a club. What was Sarah doing, Connie wondered. Did she want him to brain her?

"It does seem strange to worship a God who asks you to put aside your most basic feelings. What makes you human. Doesn't it, Howard?" It crossed her mind that it would take more than Kissinger to make peace between Jews and Arabs. It would take a whole new concept of God.

"Not in the least. Being human is being an animal. It's what we're trying to get beyond." He looked at Connie as if she had just revealed a carefully hidden secret to his worst enemy.

"Jesus, don't you see where this argument ends? In the superhuman benefits of war. I thought we'd finished talking about that, Howard. I'm tired of lofty principles that end up killing women and children."

"You still don't get it, do you?" he said caustically. "Animals fight for turf. Men fight for their ideas. For what they believe in. If you don't care about something enough to die for it, what meaning does it have?" His kipah, his ritual cap, slipped forward and he jammed it back on his bald head, beaded with sweat from wine and aggravation.

"Nothing has any meaning if you're dead. I don't want my children joining the army. Any army. German, American or Israeli."

"How can you even think of comparing Germans and Israelis? Don't you understand that Israel is fighting to defend herself? To keep from being destroyed? Just a few days ago women and children were brutally killed at Qiryat Shemona. Do you think the Israelis should just sit back and watch that? What if you and the children were in danger? I have a picture in my mind of that kibbutz I visited, the young men and women relaxing in the sun. I'd fight to defend that. But no, my wife compares the Jews to Nazis! Think before you open your mouth, Connie." He gave her head a sharp rap with his knuckles. "Use your brain." Connie could feel the children looking at her, tensely. Waiting to see what she'd do.

"I think it's great that the Israelis let women carry guns," Sarah burst out after a minute. "I wouldn't mind learning how to use a rifle. It might come in handy." She spit out the words, throwing back her head like a soldier.

"I don't think you really mean that, Sarah," Connie said, touching her arm. "You're no Patty Hearst."

Sarah gave her a scathing look. "I do mean it, believe me. Women are still losers around here. You get your choice of being a housewife or a prostitute. I want to be something strong."

"That's the place for you, then." Howard banged his fist on the table. "You're my daughter after all. At least somebody in this family understands me. There isn't another culture in the world that gives such equality to women. You'll be making history."

"There are other ways of doing that, Dad. Working for social change, for instance. That's what my new job is all about."

Howard turned on her, his face going red. "At that degenerate record store? And what the hell do you think you're selling? Union songs from the thirties?" His anger had been building up all night, first with Mischa, then with her. Now Connie was afraid he was going to unload it on Sarah.

"I didn't take that job." Sarah drew back, hurt. "I've been working at La Peña."

"What's that?" Connie asked her, surprised.

"You mean you haven't even heard of it? It's famous all over the country as a center for Latin American culture."

Connie suddenly remembered the green flier.

"You don't mean that Spic bar down on Ashby and Shattuck with the big mural?" Howard asked.

"Don't talk that way, Howard. You sound like a redneck." Connie moved the wine bottle out of his reach. "Sounds interesting," she said to Sarah as though Howard weren't glaring at her. "How'd you get into it?" She hoped he wouldn't launch into a tirade just when Sarah was confiding in them. When she might actually have gotten a decent job.

"Through Mr. Ramon. He's Colombian. That's what makes him so sensitive. The struggle of the oppressed is part of his everyday life." Sarah straightened her shoulders.

"Wait just a minute." Howard leaned forward, the knot in his jaw jumping. "What is this Marxist rhetoric he's feeding you? You know that's passé Sarah. It went out of style a long time ago."

"I can think for myself, Dad. I don't need someone to feed me ideas. I want to work with some other people for a while, that's all. There's a group of very dedicated people at La Peña. Humanity includes more than just the Jews," Sarah's voice rose defensively.

Howard glowered at her. "And what do you do in this job, Sarah?" he asked sarcastically. "Make cushions out of Jewish skin?" Connie knew he was just venting his anger but it was an ugly attempt at a joke. None of his angry jokes ever worked.

"You're so suspicious. Does everything have to be a plot against us? I'm helping in the kitchen, for God's sake, waiting on tables, taking tickets...." Sarah opened the bag she had hung on the back of her chair and whipped out a calendar. "There are talks, concerts, all sorts of wonderful things." Howard leaned over and read the top entries. As his eye ran down the list, suddenly his expression darkened and he started to stab at the paper with his finger. "Sarah, look at this, a lecture on the PLO. Are you blind? Can't you read? These are anti-Semites. Why do you want to be mixed up with people like that?"

"Dad, it's just one lecture. It's not what the place is about, really. Can't you try to understand?"

Mischa poked Sarah with his elbow. "Dad's getting really mad," he said in a stage whisper.

"I don't care," she hissed back. "Stay out of this." She stared defiantly at Howard. Howard frowned. Then with a sigh he pulled out his checkbook and wrote a check for a hundred dollars.

"This is for you, Sarah. If you study your Hebrew and forget about La Peña."

"You don't understand anything," she said, ripping it up and scattering the pieces on the rug. "All you care about is being Jewish. You wouldn't care if I were dead." She pushed her chair back and started to leave the room.

"Don't you dare, Sarah." He jumped up and grabbed her wrist. "Don't you go stomping off like a spoiled brat. That may be the way you behave all the rest of the time. But not tonight. On the holiest night of the year. You have to finish the service." He dragged her over and pushed her down into her chair. "And I don't want to hear anymore about your working for anti-Semites."

Sarah jumped up again. "I thought Jews were supposed to be for the underdogs, to care for people. Why do you have to turn everything into an ideological battle? Can't you just be a human being for once?"

"You do what I tell you," Howard shouted, banging his fist on the table, "or you'll do nothing. No private school. No dancing lessons. Do you understand me?"

"You're impossible," Sarah screamed. "Hitler couldn't have been worse than you."

"Stop it," Connie shouted, taking hold of Sarah's arm. "I'm not going to listen to you yelling and screaming at each other anymore. I'm going out and I'm taking the kids. Mischa, Sarah, come on." Mischa stood up hesitantly and looked at Howard.

"Going out tonight? You must be crazy." Howard's eyes were deep pits of outrage.

"I told you, I've had enough." She reached for her purse. She thought of taking them for ice cream. Soothing their nerves with hot fudge. "This is no way to live. It's a Middle East battle zone here. And we're no nearer to solving our problems than they are." She gestured to Sarah to bring Mischa.

Before anyone could move, Howard grabbed the purse out of Connie's hand.

"So you're going out on the Seder, you bitch, subverting my discipline." He opened her bag and started rummaging through it frantically, throwing ball point pens and wadded kleenex onto the table. "You slovenly bitch, where are your keys?" An old tampax fell on her plate and lay there soaking up gravy.

"Give me that." Connie pulled at her purse. "You have no right." Just then Howard found the keys and let the purse go. She stumbled back against the door. With a shout of triumph, he ran over to the sink and threw the keys into the disposal.

"Howard, don't," she said, struggling to get her balance. "Please." For a second he held his hand over the switch. Then he turned it on. Connie let out a wail. There was the sickening sound of metal against metal as the blades struggled to grind what they'd been given. She ran over to the switch.

"Get away from that, Connie," Howard yelled, pulling at her arm, "I'm warning you." She reached out with her other arm and pressed. It clicked off. The grinding stopped. Enraged, Howard whirled her around and slapped her in the face.

"You hit me. My God, I don't believe it." She put her hand to her cheek, gasping. "You really hit me." Mischa started to cry and Sarah took his arm and dragged him out of the room.

"Did I hurt you?" Howard asked, pulling her hand from her face.

"Get away from me." She moved away from him, crying.

"I'm sorry, but you pushed me too far. You just pushed and pushed." He walked after her. "What can I do?"

"Nothing. Just go away. I don't want to look at you." She leaned over the disposal, fished out her scarred, useless keys and threw them in the trash.

At around midnight Connie went to check on the children and found Sarah awake listening to Janis Joplin on her little radio. *"Nobody you can count on."* The slow, sad, blues sound rose and fell over Sarah's pillow, *"get it while you can...don't you turn your back on love."*

"Sarah, you okay?"

Sarah turned a smudged face towards her. "Mom, are you going to get a divorce? Is that what's going to happen next? I know you're having an affair."

Sarah's eyes, sad, frightened, angry, set up an ache behind Connie's breast bone. What had she done? It still shocked her that she'd had the nerve to betray Howard. She was committing adultery. Something she thought only other people did, that only happened in novels. She was sleeping with two men. This had never happened to her before. She reached out awkwardly and patted Sarah's shoulder. "Don't worry. I'm not about to break up the family."

Sarah sat up clasping her knees. "Maybe you should. Your marriage is lousy. Worse than lousy. Scary, weird, awful."

Connie was stung by the contempt on her face. "What do you know? Wait till you've been married twenty years. Then tell me about it. Maybe instead of being so judgmental, you should thank me for fighting to keep our family together." Connie realized the lie as soon as it was out of her mouth. For years she'd seen herself as a sort of minor biblical heroine, a sort of long suffering Ruth, but she didn't anymore. Not after tonight.

"You want me to be grateful? For this? Pushing and yelling and fighting? I had to rub Mischa's back for an hour to get him to sleep. He was tense as a board. He couldn't even breathe right."

"Sorry you had to go through that, Sarah," she said, her throat contracting painfully. "It must have been hard for you. I know it was for me. But real life isn't like *All in the Family*. Sometimes it's pretty rotten." Her cheek still smarted from where Howard had slapped her. Adulteresses used to be stoned to death, she remembered. She had a sudden image of the stones thudding against soft flesh. Her flesh. A slap was a cheap punishment if you thought of it that way. Looking at Sarah's strained face, Connie felt as if she deserved worse.

"Have you ever seen *All in the Family*?" Sarah asked, her voice bitter. "Archie Bunker's a fascist pig. But even he doesn't beat up on his kids."

"Oh Sarah, you know what I meant. That we're conditioned by soap operas with a hug at the end of every episode. Believe me, I wish it were that way. Don't you think I'd rather be eating ice cream with you than fighting with your father?" What if she'd gotten to the door with the kids before Howard grabbed her keys? Maybe she wouldn't have come back.

"You're the one who's conditioned. To putting up with anything Dad dishes out." Sarah rocked herself back and forth, "You stood up to him for a minute tonight. Don't back down for us, Mom. That's all I'm saying." Her red hair fell forward over her shoulders.

"I don't think you realize how hard a divorce would be, Sarah, on all of us." Connie's hands were cold as ice. "Besides, I made a commitment when I married." She'd been almost twenty years younger then, wanting as much as Sarah did. She couldn't have imagined, when Howard pinned the orchid on the bodice of her dress, what a sink hole she had gotten herself into.

"I hate that word, 'Commitment.' It sounds like a prison sentence." Sarah rubbed her chin against her knees.

"Sometimes it feels that way. But what do you think, Sarah? If everyone cut and ran whenever they felt the urge, would that really be better?" I wish I could, she thought. God, I'd really like to. But she was afraid of spinning out of control, driving off a cliff instead of to a new life. She suddenly imagined Marc breaking the window, taking her by the wrist, pulling her outside, shoving her into his car....

"But there must be some reasons. I mean, Dad hits Mischa, he slapped you...." Sarah paused and looked down at her feet.

"I've always thought family meant a kind of trust that doesn't depend on behavior. It's just there." Couldn't Sarah understand how much she'd wanted to make her feel safe? "You think commitment's awful, but how would you feel if I left you? I knew a woman who did that once. Left her husband and child and went to Los Angeles to open an art gallery. What would you think of a mother who did that?" Connie didn't tell her that the woman had run off with her lover. How could she have stood the guilt? Adultery was bad enough but there should be a law that prevented you from leaving your children. If there was a shipwreck she hoped she'd stay with Sarah and Mischa, not swim off and save herself.

A look of fear came over Sarah's face. She suddenly got up and put her arms around Connie's neck. "I don't know what I think anymore. Why do people have to have families anyway?"

"I guess because they haven't found anything better. Look, sweetheart, I'm sorry if I sounded angry at you. I'm doing some mental housekeeping and it's complicated. I get frustrated." It wasn't Sarah's fault that all the beliefs Connie had structured her life around were going down the drain. She felt like the experimental rat she'd read about who got shocked when it pressed the food bar. It became paralyzed, unable to decide what to do. Connie stroked Sarah's face, smoothing her forehead with her hand. "The truth is, Sarah, there are reasons to leave a marriage, and I have them. I'm still too much of a coward to do it, that's all." She could hear Sarah sniffing. "Go ahead and cry if you want to." Connie felt a wave of protective tenderness for her. What lousy luck to have a bully for a father and a mother scared to be on her own. "These are hard things to think about." Sarah stayed there quietly, nestling her face under Connie's hair the way she had when she was a child.

For the next few days, Howard worked in his office. He didn't come home for dinner and went to bed long after Connie had curled between the sheets. She wasn't really upset by his absence in the evenings. It gave her another chance to try to talk to Sarah.

Connie was in the living room reading a magazine article about Patty Hearst and the Hibernia Bank robbery. It had big glossy illustrations of Patty with her paramilitary beret cradling a huge rifle. She reminded Connie of the Chinese girl soldiers, grim-faced, righteous, an American revolutionary. Connie wondered what it must feel like to shoot someone for ideological reasons. Did you feel full of hate? Or was it more like ritual sacrifice?

When Sarah came downstairs in her nightshirt to get a book, Connie studied her surreptitiously, trying to gauge her mood. Perhaps Sarah had been trying to make peace by telling about the work she was doing. She'd done it in good faith, not knowing all hell was going to break out.

"Sarah, why don't you sit down. Come chat with me, here," Connie patted the sofa cushion, "while I finish my after-dinner coffee."

"It's no use, Mom." Sarah put her hands on her hips, "I'm not giving up La Peña. If that's what you want to talk about, forget it." Connie didn't say anything but her expression seemed to infuriate Sarah.

"You didn't like the record store. I thought you'd be pleased that I've found something else. You know Dad's crazy, don't you?" A vein pulsed bluely at Sarah's temple. "With his mania about being Jewish."

Sarah's tightly strung voice grated on Connie's nerves like chalk on a blackboard. She took a deep breath, willing calm. "If you'd stop being paranoid and let me talk for a minute, maybe we could straighten things out. As a matter of fact, I think it sounds like a fine job. Working for something you believe in. Why shouldn't you do it?"

Sarah didn't seem to know what to do with her body now that there wasn't going to be a fight. "Gosh, I'm surprised." She flopped down on the sofa beside Connie. "Last year you wouldn't have said that."

"This isn't last year. You're growing up."

That hadn't been so hard, she thought, taking her cup and saucer into the kitchen. In fact it had been easy. Things were so much easier without Howard there to raise the temperature to boiling point. As Kissinger said on tonight's news, the important thing was to keep talking. She switched off the lights and was just turning to go when she caught a glimpse of the owl that lived in their backyard swooping on some small prey. She had always been pleased that the owl had chosen to live with them because it was Athena's bird. Goddess of wisdom. The goddess born without a mother. Straight from her father's thigh with none of the traumas of childhood. The owl was sitting immobile on a branch outside the window, its eyes catching the light. It had caught a bird in its beak and held it while tweets and squeaks vibrated deep inside its throat. Connie stared fascinated while the owl blinked its shuttered eyes and swallowed the bird alive. That's the old self, she thought with a thrill of pleasure. Down the hatch. Like Jonah into the whale's mouth. He couldn't have felt comfortable down there in the wet, dark. He couldn't have known that he was going to come out changed. There's going to be a new soul coming out, she thought, looking at the owl ruffling its feathers. She didn't know what it was going to be like yet but it was coming. That was the message writ large.

The next day, Sarah came home early for the first time in weeks. Instead of dashing up to her room with a bag of cookies, she sat down and started to eat them at the kitchen table.

"Do you mind if I put on one of my new records?" she asked, brushing some white blossoms off her backpack and extracting a record.

"Sure," Connie said cautiously, bracing herself for the rock Sarah had been listening to lately. Sarah put on a record and rhythmic male voices began to sing in Spanish. The music had a mournful sound, as though tears were condensing into speech. "Do you like it?"

Connie nodded and they sat there quietly listening. Sarah offered her a cookie and she ate it slowly, letting the chocolate chips melt on her tongue.

"Hey, that song's in Italian. I thought I recognized an awful lot of the words. Wait, I know it. It's *Bella Ciao.* That's one of my favorite songs." Connie started singing along, stressing the heavily accented syllables with relish. "*Partigiano portar me via, che me sento da morir.*" It was really too fine. The words of the dying partisan carried off by his comrades brought her close to Sarah as she almost shouted the refrain, "*bella ciao, bella ciao ciao ciao*," banging on the coffee table with her fist.

Sarah looked at her, surprised. "You're really getting into it," she said. "You're not pretending. Did you know these are revolutionary songs? *Cantos Revolucionarios*!"

"So?" Connie had sung revolutionary songs herself at college in the 50s.

Sarah looked mildly disappointed. "Just checking to see if you knew."

"I didn't but it's okay. Where'd you get the record?"

"From Joan. I met her at work. She lent me some books of Latin American poetry."

It was ridiculous how pleased Connie felt because Sarah was listening to a record with a folk song she could understand and talking about reading poetry instead of about rock n' roll. Sarah had also brought home some fat new paperback books. She left a couple of them in the living room and after she'd gone upstairs Connie eyed them furtively, wondering if she'd left them there on purpose for her to see. Usually she kept her things squirreled away in her room. Cautiously she picked up the uppermost one, *Latin American Revolutionary Poetry*. That sounded too didactic for her taste. The second was Robert Bly's translation of Neruda and Vallejo. Connie remembered that Neruda had died in September. That would explain the spate of new translations. She thumbed through the book and read one of Neruda's early love poems. "Lonely as a tunnel. Birds flew from me." If this was Joan's taste, she was going to do Sarah a lot of good. Connie imagined the two girls having deep conversations about literature, Sarah's grade point average soaring.

The next afternoon, Sarah called and asked if she could sleep over at Joan's. This gave Connie pause. She knew Joan had her own place, a studio apartment, and she never allowed Sarah to sleep anywhere without a parent there. But she knew if she mentioned that, Sarah would be furious.

"I'm not sure sleeping over's such a good idea, Sarah," she said cautiously. "Didn't you tell me your cold was getting worse? You know it always goes into your chest when you don't get enough sleep."

Sarah hawked and Connie could hear her spitting into something. Sarah said spitting got the impurities out of her system; Connie thought it was disgusting. "C'mon, Mom, I know you're just scared to let me stay with Joan because she has her own apartment. It's all right," she told her. "She's older. She's cool. We're not going to party all night, we just want to read some poetry together."

Connie was torn. It sounded innocent. Having an older friend was clearly flattering. It seemed to make Sarah feel much better about herself. On the other hand, what did Connie know about Joan, really? She didn't know her family. She didn't even know her last name. Joan might be using drugs. There might be men there. "But where's her apartment?"

"Somewhere on Alcatraz. I don't have the address yet but her number's on the phone pad. She'll drop me off at school in the morning."

"Why don't you bring her over here? I'd like to meet her."

"I'm not sure it'll work for tonight. But don't worry, you'll see her." Sarah gave a funny little laugh. "She's kind of curious about you too."

They burst in the next day with a parakeet in a cage. Sarah was talking excitedly about Neruda, but when she saw Connie in the kitchen she stopped and looked at her cautiously, as though she wasn't sure if her friend would be welcome. As cordially as she could, Connie invited them in for cookies and milk.

"A friend of mine had to go to Latin America suddenly and I'm not allowed pets in my apartment. Sarah said she could keep him. I hope you don't mind," Joan said to Connie, opening the cage and taking the bird onto her shoulder.

"Not at all." Connie offered the bird a piece of cookie. "I hope your friend had no serious trouble." The bird lunged at her finger and she drew it back.

"Shame on you, Rodriguez," Joan tapped his head. "Don't bite." She turned to Connie with an apologetic smile. "My friend left Chile after the '73 coup. A few days ago, she heard that a friend of hers whom she thought had been murdered after Allende's death was seen in a certain prison and she needed to check it out. It's a brave thing to do but I'm worried about her. She might not be so lucky this time." Connie had a strange feeling of *deja vu*—herself at twenty sitting up all night discussing McCarthy's witch hunts.

Joan had a long intense face with short, curly black hair ringing her head. She looked a little like an El Greco angel. Angular, androgynous. Sarah was looking at her adoringly and Connie could see why. She liked her too. She had enormous poise. There was something fascinating about her mobile features, her serious eyes and the gestures she made with her long hands, her long fingers stroking the bird. She was dressed in black cotton pants and a white embroidered blouse, small silver earrings, black sandals with thick cork soles. Simple but with an instinctive sense of style. She was carrying Neruda's *Canto General*.

"You're reading Neruda," Connie said, wanting this girl to like her. "I don't know much Spanish, but even in translation he's startlingly strong."

"Yes. I was just talking to Sarah about the poems he wrote before his death. The man was amazing, he kept his power right to the end. It's ironic that he died just when the military dictatorship took over. I'm afraid it's the end of socially conscious literature." Joan looked at Connie intently. "Which poems were you reading?"

"I don't remember the names. Some of the love poems...one about a woman's body...."

"He went beyond that," Sarah interrupted stiffly. "We're reading his political poems together."

"Oh, well, it must be doing wonders for your Spanish."

"Why do you have to make everything a question of utility?" Sarah asked. At the sound of a raised voice the parakeet took off, swooping like a dive bomber over Connie's head. He came to rest on a wreath of dried flowers over the kitchen door. Joan laughed.

"Easy, Sarah," she said, taking a chair and standing on it to coax the bird down. "I'm sure your mother didn't mean to irritate you...and it is certainly improving your Spanish."

Connie looked at Joan gratefully. Sarah did seem touchy. But why? She'd chosen a friend who had a good mind. What was so bad about admitting it? "Do you go to Cal?" she asked, not willing to let Sarah censor the topic of education.

"Joan isn't in school now," Sarah said triumphantly, taking the parakeet from her friend's shoulder. "You shouldn't assume that anyone who reads anything is doing it for school." The parakeet seemed fascinated by Sarah's hair. He started to groom it, running the strands through his beak.

"I've stopped out for a while. I'm making a video on women in revolution. I've been teaching Sarah how to use the camera. She's a natural."

Connie felt her heart lurch. Stopping out was dropping out, whatever they called it. "How did you get started on this?"

"Through Mr. Ramon. He was my teacher too, hasn't Sarah told you? He's acting as consultant for my video. We've been friends for years." Connie realized in a flash that they must be lovers.

"Can I go to Cuba with Joan next summer?" Sarah asked, while Connie was still digesting this fact.

"Sarah, you can't just spring these things on me." How had they gone so quickly from books of poetry to her daughter's probable martyrdom in a foreign country? She felt as though she were in a movie on fast forward. "Isn't it terribly dangerous?"

"Why would it be dangerous?"

"Because of the revolution."

"C'mon, Mom, it's been over for almost twenty years. Anyway, Joan went to Nicaragua last year, just after they had the big earthquake, and took videos. That was much more dangerous. God, sometimes I can't believe you're for real."

Joan gave her a warning look and Sarah went on reassuringly, "Don't worry so much. Joan can take care of me. Her Spanish is fluent enough, and Mr. Ramon is probably going to come too. Can I go?"

"We'll see, Sarah. Let's talk about it later."

Sarah frowned and, taking Joan by the arm, literally pulled her out of the room. The bird squawking and bouncing on her shoulder like a cartoon image of her state of mind. She turned and gave Connie a defiant look just before she went upstairs.

Sarah's clenched, closed face made her think of Patty Hearst. What influence was this woman having over her? What anger was she whipping up towards Connie? She wondered what people had inside that kept them steady, made them know themselves. This is me and no one else. I can do this but not this. What made some people so soft inside that if you broke their connections, they'd forget who they were? She imagined Mizmoon, dressed in feathers like Papagena in *The Magic Flute*, offering Patty a feather mantle. Laying it at her feet. Kissing the arch of her foot. Connie could see it white as Sarah's with a little toe that was slightly bowed. Flattering her. Telling her she was a young Amazon who ought to be Queen. Getting her to go through the fire with her. Robbing the strongholds of the rich. Bringing them down with a rat-tat-tat of flesh piercing shot. Patty in her feather mantle waving a machine gun.

Connie really liked Joan but she was jealous. She was afraid Joan had bewitched Sarah, was making her hate her, was leading Sarah into danger. She pictured them being arrested, their passports confiscated, locked up in some remote jail with no way of letting her know, even shot.... Somewhere she knew that she'd mixed up Patty and Sarah in her mind, but she couldn't stop. She felt Sarah spinning away, out of her orbit. She didn't want her to go to Cuba. The place was full of terrorists. Who knew if Mizmoon and Tania, as Patty now called herself, wouldn't make it a base for future operations.

Connie's first impulse was to tell Howard. Then she decided to wait awhile. She was afraid he'd turn it into the Jewish question.

Connie talked the whole thing out with Marc on the phone the next morning. A few days before he left for Switzerland, they had agreed he'd call her at his house. Luckily this was the day.

"I agree you're in a tough situation," Marc said. "But Sarah's not a baby anymore. Her friend is older. And if she's already been in Nicaragua, she's probably able to take care of Sarah in Cuba. Nothing terrible is happening there, anyway." Marc coughed at this point with what seemed to Connie to be impatience. She hated talking to him long distance, when she couldn't see his face and had to amplify his meaning by subtle changes in his voice. "But," he'd gone on evenly, "if you want Sarah to wait a year to make a trip like that, you don't have to justify it. Just tell her. Or wait a while. There is still time."

Sarah came into the kitchen before bed to fix herself a snack. Connie watched her rummaging around in the fridge, the bird on her shoulder trying to keep his balance.

"You know," she said, cautiously, "it doesn't seem fair to ask Joan to take responsibility for you. Wouldn't it make more sense to wait a year and do it before you go off to college?"

Sarah seemed to agree. She fed Rodriguez a grape and went back to her room without making a fuss. But the next afternoon, when Connie was out in the garden, she marched over to her with a determined look on her face. "I'm thinking of moving into Joan's apartment. I won't be in Latin America. I'll just be in Oakland. It will be good practice for later. A lot of kids from school are doing it. You can baby-sit Rodriguez for me. Pretend he's a grandchild."

Connie was squatting in front of her flower bed turning up the ground. Making holes like miniature graves. Next to her were the dwarf marigolds she was going to put in.

"How do you expect to pay for an apartment?" she asked, looking up at Sarah's blue-jeaned knees. She guessed Joan was angry about the trip, urging Sarah to pull away from her. "You can't possibly be earning enough money at La Peña. What do you earn two evenings a week? Fifty dollars?"

"Joan isn't asking me for money. We share stuff with our friends."

Connie was constantly amazed at how fast these friendships developed between teenagers. "You still have to pay for food and clothes. They don't just drop from the sky." Connie dug in her spade again. The soil smelled musty and tired. It needed fertilizer.

"I don't buy my own food and clothes now," Sarah said, kicking small bits of dirt onto Connie's marigolds. The girl seemed to be visibly changing, growing bigger and taller. Connie felt herself shrinking closer to the ground, like one of the seven dwarfs guarding a huge Snow White. Sarah was glaring down at her.

Connie got up and stretched to her full height. "That's because you're home with us. I'm not going to support this fantasy, Sarah." She brushed the dirt off her pants. "You'd better understand that."

"Why? You haven't given me any good reasons."

"Sarah, there are too many to count. It's bad enough that you're working in a bad neighborhood without living in one too. You'd be coming home at night alone. On your bike. On Alcatraz, one of the worst streets in the East Bay. It's a terrible idea."

"I'm going to learn to drive," Sarah said in a reasonable voice. "I've got my permit."

"You don't have a car, Sarah."

"I can get one second-hand for a couple of hundred."

"And where's the money for that coming from?"

"What's all this talk about money?" Sarah shouted, losing her cool. "What you're really afraid of is my getting mixed up with some black guy. Getting into wild sex in darkest Oakland."

"You know that's not true, Sarah." Why couldn't they ever

stop this? Why couldn't they ever stay on the same side for more than a week? It must be something lethal in mother-daughter chemistry.

"Or that I'll turn into a drug addict. It's parent-think. I hear you whispering to your friends on the phone." She imitated her mother's voice. "'Oh, that's perfectly awful! That nice Paley boy on drugs. Wasn't he an 'A' student too?'" Connie flushed. Her daughter could make a living as a comedian. Her inflection was perfect.

"Look," she said, drawing herself up to her full height. "I don't really care if you like my reasons. I'm still your mother and for now you'll have to do what I tell you. An apartment's out of the question until you finish high school. You're still a minor and your parents have to sign the lease. I won't, and neither will your father."

"God! Can't you see how hemmed in I feel?" Sarah withdrew to a defensive position. "It's claustrophobic living here." She flailed her arms like an epileptic having a seizure. "I hate it. I don't mean you. It's the whole thing. The way things are. I need to get away. Dad puts me down, won't let me explain how I feel, and you don't help me. Don't you see what I mean at all?"

"There is no reason I should understand. There is no reason why you have to run away from your problems. You can solve them here, sleeping in your own bed." Even as Connie said it, she was trembling, but she kept her eyes fixed firmly on Sarah until Sarah turned away and went upstairs.

Eleven

They went to the Sante Fe for dinner—Connie, Howard, Sarah and Mischa. In the two weeks since the Seder, Connie had been relieved that Howard had hardly spoken to her. She knew he was taking them to show he was sorry, but despite his intention he looked tense. Driving over, he listened grim faced to the latest news about the *Ma'alot* massacre. Twenty Israeli children killed. "They ought to blast Lebanon off the map," he said. She kept quiet but it didn't bode well for the evening.

Connie thought he'd probably chosen the Santa Fe because there was so much racket you couldn't really carry on a conversation. It had once been a railway station and was full of noise and fragments of speech. People trying to avoid connections. There was a huge grand piano at one end of the main room with a third-rate musician in tails hammering out John Denver's latest hit, *Sunshine On My Shoulder.*

Mischa moved his chair close to Connie, and began to tell her about the ladybug he'd found in the garden. He had to speak very loudly to make himself heard above the voices and the piano player.

"Can't you keep quiet for a minute," Howard asked. "Your incessant chatter is irritating." In the past, Connie would have shushed Mischa. But now, she simply took him with her to the salad bar and loaded his plate with shredded carrot, the only vegetable he liked. He was convinced it would help him see in the dark.

Weaving back, past a sour-looking couple with three overweight teenage boys, Connie felt oddly dissociated from herself, as though she were playing a role, pretending to be the lovely wife and mother out with her family. The children were watching Howard tensely the way savages eye the weather, waiting for the next storm.

"Mom, you forgot to put on salad dressing," Mischa complained, pushing his plate at her.

"You forgot to put gas in the car too," Howard said when she came back with vinaigrette drizzled over Mischa's carrots. "It's almost empty. Your mother is the only person I know who thinks a car can run without gas."

Connie carefully spread butter in the crevasses of her roll, trying to block out Howard's stupid joke. Like most of his jokes, it made her seem like an idiot in front of the children. She noticed his face looking unusually red and the grease on his chin from the steak and the way his lips drew back from his teeth when he laughed. The laugh meant he was in a good humor. A year ago that would have pleased her. But it didn't work anymore. Why am I still here, she thought, dismayed. Why am I taking this?

"While you were away in Israel, I never had any trouble keeping the car filled. You're the one who had it out all night. God knows where. Why didn't you fill it?" Connie asked.

He looked surprised.

"It's your job. I have more important things to think about." He jabbed at a piece of steak. Their life was like a surrealist movie, she thought. Bleeding meat and a man playing *Killing Me Softly With His Song.*

"Like what? What about the scrapes all over the car door? Did you get drunk and sideswipe someone? Is that what's so important? If it's my job to fix everything you screw up, I'm quitting." She heard the piano player smash into a final chord and the restaurant became oddly quiet.

Suddenly Sarah pushed back her chair and got up. "I can't stand this anymore. I just can't stand it. I have to go and talk to Joan."

"Why, why, Sarah?" Sarah's words came so close to Connie's own thought—I can't stand it—that it took her a minute to focus on what was going on.

"Don't you see? The way you two are with each other. It's unreal, crazy. I thought this was supposed to be a peaceful dinner. You can't even exchange a sentence without blowing up." She stood there her mouth working, almost crying. A man at a nearby table looked up, his fork halfway to his mouth.

"But why now, Sarah? Can't you sit down? Afterwards we'll talk about it." Sarah shook her head.

"She looks mad," Mischa said in a worried voice.

Connie looked at Howard.

"You heard your mother. Sit down and finish your food. Your friend can wait."

"Do you wait when you want to get out of the house? Do you listen to Mom when she asks you to stay home?"

"Ah, sharper than a serpent's tooth. You always were a difficult child. Even as a baby you had to get the last word in."

White, awkward, Sarah gathered her things, not taking time to put on her jacket, and ran out the door. Several people stopped talking and turned to look after her but then quickly went back to their food. Howard was smiling strangely. He avoided Connie's eyes and called for the waiter to order dessert.

Connie didn't know if Mischa was more upset by Sarah or by their silence. No one was talking or answering important questions. Mischa didn't eat the chocolate ice cream Howard got for him. Instead, he asked if gunmen could sneak into their house and shoot him the way they did the children at *Ma'alot*. When she said no, those things didn't happen in America, he whined for candy from her purse.

As they were getting ready for bed, Connie walked over to

the closet where Howard was bent over looking for his slippers. "What do you think about Sarah's running off like that?"

"I don't know," he said testily, straightening up. "Her behavior does seem very erratic. You think she's having a breakdown? Like your mother?"

"Oh for God's sake, Howard. You with your ideas about bad heredity. It's enough to drive anyone mad. I just wonder if she really went to Joan's."

"Oh that. Well, how should I know? As long as she's not going off her head." She found herself staring at his feet. They were so white, like a girl's. "Where are my slippers?" he asked her.

"How should I know? Find your own damn slippers."

He went back to rummaging in the closet, pushing the shoes from one side to another with his foot, then bending down and piling the shoes in a heap on the floor outside, trying to get Connie to intervene.

She ignored the mess he was making. "You know Sarah wants to move out. Live with that girl."

"Well, tell her I'm not paying the rent." He puffed out his chest.

"I'm not sure she cares. I'm worried about her, Howard. She seems so unhappy. About us too." She touched the sleeve of his bathrobe but he drew back and walked over to the bed leaving the closet in disorder. He still hadn't found his slippers.

"Women are always getting hysterical about one thing or another."

"Jesus, Howard. Can't you answer me straight out for once. Without trying to rack up points. I'm worried about Sarah. If you were any kind of a father you'd be worried too."

"I hoped she'd be different but she's just like the rest of them." He sighed and sat down on the bed.

"Dammit, Howard. Men always say women are hysterical.

Maybe there's a reason for it. Because men ignore their problems. You do it with Sarah. You leave all the worrying to me then you wonder why I'm frantic. Of course it's easy for you to be cool and rational."

"You're illustrating my point. Listen to your voice." He raised his to a high falsetto. "It's going up like a thermometer about to burst."

Connie wanted to throw things and scream but she didn't. It was what he was waiting for. And she couldn't reason any more. A little button in her head had switched off. There was just a black ragged pit of anger. She went into the bathroom and turned on the wall heater and sat next to the coils with her head on her arms.

How had she ever thought she enjoyed life with this man? She'd liked eating with him, watching him with the children. Even liked the synagogue where the women clustered together like sheep. Now she couldn't imagine herself there, huddled with praying women, their shaved heads covered with wigs. Separated from the men by a wall, unable even to see the service. It was hard to believe how much she'd changed in the months since Howard had been back. She used to think it was exotic that the rabbi wouldn't even touch a woman's hand. Now the women's submissiveness made her almost sick. What good did feeling unworthy do you? It certainly hadn't gotten her the love she wanted.

She remembered praying in the synagogue one Yom Kippur. The rabbi was conducting the service on the men's side. At a certain point, the wails grew more intense and she heard the thud of bodies as the men prostrated themselves on the floor. She peeked through a crack in the screen separating the men's and women's sections. There was an old man with a white beard who was clearly too weak to rise by himself. Howard had lifted him up with an expression of deep emotion on his face. How much she'd wanted to get some of that. She'd been a fool, Connie thought, wiping her eyes. She wasn't ninety years old, needing someone's hands under her arms. She should have gotten off her knees years ago.

She got up, splashed some cold water on her face and checked to see if Sarah had come in without her hearing. Then she took a blanket out of the closet and went down to sleep on the couch.

Sarah came home an hour later. Connie's instinct was to leave her alone. But when she saw her the next morning, she knew it was going to be hard so she put on her jacket and went over to Marc's house. He'd been back for two days now. Although she'd seen him briefly when he first returned, she hadn't really talked to him. When she got there, he was cleaning his skis.

"Switzerland was really magnificent," Marc said. "I forgot my work, forgot politics. Can you believe it? I didn't even care whether Nixon knew about the cover-up in April or March. The only thing I didn't forget is you." He stopped and wiped his hands. "I really missed you. Every night, I'd imagine you stretched out on top of me, your toes pressing mine." He put his arm around her and hugged her. "What's the matter? You seem tense."

"I'm feeling lousy about Sarah. She's been having teenage fits."

"It's the nature of the beast, *la bestia adolescente*." He rolled the words off his tongue. "Notice my terrific accent? An opera star I met told me I had an Italian voice. Hers was soft as butter. A real *diva*. I thought she was going to be a snob but she was a very nice person. And the amazing thing was that she had a magnificent chalet next to my hotel."

"Oh," Connie said coldly, "that is a coincidence."

"Not jealous, are you?" he laughed. "You don't need to be. She weighed about three hundred pounds."

Connie imagined him rolling around in a bed stained with sex like melted butter. The woman was big and gorgeous. "You know, Sarah wants to leave home," she said, sitting down at his desk and toying with an envelope of photos. "If she was ready for it, I'd let her."

He bent over her. She could feel the warmth of him. "Hey, let me show you the photos of my exploits. They're terrific." He took the envelope and spilled the prints across the desk. "Look!" He held up a photograph of himself with a dazzling blond in a fancy ski suit. "That's me with the off-slope guide." Marc was leaning forward towards her on his poles, talking animatedly.

"This is the ski trail looking up from the bottom." This time it was a brunette with one hand on her hip and a smile that could advertise toothpaste. "I just asked her to stand there for the scale," he said, "so you could judge the height of the mountain."

"Dammit, Marc, I have a problem. I don't want to hear any more about your vacation." She pronounced the word with a sneer. Or your flashy little chippies, she thought. "You might be able to go away for two weeks and totally forget your problems but I can't. I thought you were my friend."

She could see him trying to switch gears. "Sorry. I didn't realize you were that worried." He hastily collected the photographs into a stack, leaving the blond on top. "Look, a lot of Berkeley kids move out because they can't live with their parents. From what you've told me, Howard's a sick man. He's tough enough to hang on to his sanity by his toenails, but he's hurting all of you. If Sarah's able to leave.... Who knows," he said, "it might be wonderful for her to move out."

Connie blew up. "No, God damn it, it wouldn't be wonderful."

"Look, Connie," he said finally, "I'm terrified of alienating you but you must see how afraid you are of separating. You don't want to set limits because it makes you separate from Sarah—maybe from Howard too? Or did you marry someone you wouldn't feel close to?" He looked down at the desk.

Damn him. He was looking at that picture. She thought of him taking the snowsuit off the blond ski bunny and nuzzling her breasts. "I'm not sure you really know how to be close to anyone yourself," she said coolly. She felt like kicking him.

"You don't need to savage me just because you don't like what I'm saying. I'm trying to help you with your kid."

"There's no point in talking about Sarah, Marc. Your mind is on the Swiss slopes." And dark declivities, she thought.

"What's that supposed to mean?" he asked, his face turning red.

She picked up the photos and shook them in his face. "You know. Fun with Bunny and Sunny and all of the rest."

"Hey, what is this crap? Soon I won't be able to say hello to a friend on the street without you thinking I'm screwing her. Watch out, baby, you're going to wreck a good thing."

"It never was anything but fantasy to begin with."

"Maybe you should think about getting out then." His eyes seemed to grow a shell of ice. Black ice.

She was too angry to be able to stop. "Maybe I will."

Connie's stomach felt like prune whip when she got home. Part of her wished she'd made up with Marc, but the other was still furious. Her stomach was still churning when she sat by the window waiting for Sarah to come home. The longer she waited the more uneasy she felt. She'd probably messed things up by yelling at Marc that way. Maybe she was terrified of separating from Sarah. Certainly she was jealous of Joan. Almost as jealous as she was of those glossy women in Marc's photos. Maybe she just couldn't give anyone a bit of breathing space, Sarah or Marc. Sarah had a right to be close to this other woman. She even had a right to be bored with her mother.

A few minutes later, Sarah came home, walked straight into the kitchen and asked Connie to join her and Joan and Mr. Ramon for dinner at La Peña Friday.

Connie felt a wave of warmth flooding her chest. She couldn't be so bad if her daughter wanted her to participate in her life. “Aren’t you going to ask Howard?” she asked casually, sprinkling paprika on the chicken she was making for dinner.

Sarah shook her head. “Mr. Ramon would be certain to bring up the Jewish question. He’s really pissed now because the Israelis killed all those Lebanese after *Ma’alot* and he and Dad would get into an argument. Mr. Ramon says things won’t be better until the Palestinians have a state.” She went over to the sink and splashed some water on her face. “It was hot walking up the hill.” She mopped her face with a paper towel.

Connie badly wanted to go. She had such a burning curiosity about how Sarah looked and acted in that place, as though she might be someone altogether different there. Still, she hesitated. She was afraid they would use this as an opportunity to get her permission about Cuba or the apartment. Maybe gang up on her. But she couldn’t offend Sarah now, when she was making this offer. Connie spoke slowly, choosing her words carefully. “I’d love to see the place where you work, Sarah, get a sense of it so I can picture you....” She began cutting tomatoes in half. “But—I don’t know how to put this—let’s just make this a social evening. I don’t want to feel pressured.” She added the tomatoes to the salad on the counter.

“Don’t worry, Mom. We’re not going to put the screws on you. It’s only so you can see I’m not surrounded by monsters, so you won’t worry so much. You liked Joan. I’m sure you’ll like Mr. Ramon too.” It was on the tip of Connie’s tongue to tell her that she sounded very mature, but she didn’t. Sarah might have thought she was being patronizing.

Connie told Howard that she wanted to take Sarah to a potluck at school. He was relieved to hear that he didn’t have to go. She left some cold salmon and salad for him and Mischa.

They got to La Peña a few minutes early, so Sarah made her stand outside and look at the mural. Women and children, workers, musicians marched under the outstretched arm of a garishly colored apocalyptic figure with a guitar—an odd combination of resurrection and a salsa band. "Reminds me of Diego Rivera," Connie said, as enthusiastically as she could.

They went in past the bulletin board plastered with notices of events. A placard denounced anti-guerilla action in Argentina; the rounding up of left-wing Peronists. Next to it was a plea for starving children. Joan was there already when they arrived, sitting at a red formica table in the corner next to the bar. She seemed to be making some notes, though with the noisy talk and the strains of Latin jazz coming from the next room, Connie didn't see how she could concentrate. Sarah was immediately excited.

"Oh, you've got it. Let me see. Is it finished?" She grabbed the papers, brushed away the smoke coming from a man with tattered red pants and dreadlocks standing behind her, and started scanning the pages. Connie looked over at the bar. Two girls with beads braided in their corn-rows were talking intensely to a man in shabby tails he was obviously wearing as a costume. The casual mixture of black and white here made her nervous. Somehow she had expected a more Spanish looking group.

"I'm helping Mr. Ramon with an article," Joan explained, interrupting Connie's attempt to weigh the dangers of this place.

"What about?" She leaned back anticipating a discussion of Neruda.

"On the situation in Mantega. What that criminal Somoza did with U.S dollars after the earthquake. If they cut open that man's chest with a knife," she said passionately, "they wouldn't find a heart."

"I don't know much about it," Connie said, surprised, "only that the quake was a disaster. Destroyed a whole city."

Joan's face took on a fervid glow. "You should see those poor people, living in shacks sometimes without running water or any way to keep clean, while big luxury houses are going up downtown. It makes me furious. And they're so damn patient. Even the kids are out picking up rags all day for a few pesos."

Joan's outrage was touching but knowledge of Nicaragua wasn't one of Connie's strong points. "What kind of editing are you doing?" she asked before Joan could ask her opinion.

"Just helping Mr. Ramon with style. His English isn't quite perfect." Connie glanced down at the paper. The prose was bombastic, florid, pompous. Joan had apparently been trying to tone it down. She hadn't crossed anything out but she'd bracketed a lot and made little notes.

"That's not an easy job," Connie said, sympathetically. Joan's seriousness soothed her worries—the place didn't seem to be affecting her badly.

"It's a privilege for me to work with someone like Mr. Ramon. I've learned so much from him." Joan abruptly took back the paper, then turned and gave a radiant smile to the man who was approaching their table.

"Oh, Juan. Hello, hello," she said breathlessly. He reached down and gave her a perfunctory hug. Then he patted Sarah's shoulder—she was beaming too—and offered Connie his hand. He had a nervous handshake, but she could see why Joan was fascinated. He was proud of his looks. But flashy, too flashy. She noticed he wore elegant pointed shoes below the requisite bell bottoms and a medallion of some sort at the throat of his open-necked shirt. When he sat down she got a strong whiff of his cologne. He certainly wasn't Connie's idea of a revolutionary. After he settled himself in his chair, he gave her a gleaming smile. Like a Latin version of Marc. They had the same smile. Mr. Ramon had a beautifully molded mouth. A moment later its corners had drawn down into a sensual pout.

"Joan, you shouldn't have brought this with you to dinner. It is not something that interests anyone but us." He pointed at the papers. There was a nasty edge to his voice.

"I'm sorry...but I had a few changes to add. I kept thinking about it. I couldn't stop." She bowed her head. Connie studied her exposed neck; she looked a little like a peasant, about to be executed, in that coarse woven blouse.

"You've done more than enough already, I think." He turned to Connie. "Joan is a wonderful girl, but when she gets it in her mind to correct a revolutionary thinker...." He shrugged charmingly, but Connie saw Joan cringe.

"Only the expression. I wasn't...." Joan seemed suddenly as helpless as a young child.

"The same thing. You're not used to a virile prose style, that's all. There are some things—not many, of course—women can't grasp, and truly revolutionary prose is one of them." He was half joking. Still, it was a patronizing remark and Connie wished Joan would defend herself, at least joke back to show him she didn't mean to be put down, but she didn't.

As soon as he saw she was sufficiently chastened, he launched into a discussion of U.S. policy towards Central America.

"Kissinger made a trip down there recently, on a good will mission," Connie said. "It sounded like he was making a real effort to improve relations." Things about Kissinger always stuck in her mind because he had a face like her favorite uncle.

But Mr. Ramon didn't seem pleased. "Everyone says Kissinger's such a genius but the concept of economic aid is all wrong. It just creates greater disparities between rich and poor. Exploiting the people. That's one of the points I make in my paper." Connie noticed the way his chest puffed out when he talked. Proud of his mastery of newspaper jargon, she thought, meanly. God, he was pompous. But the girls didn't seem to notice. They were nodding their heads in agreement.

"Now I suppose they have to sort things out for themselves," Connie said. She hated political diatribes and Mr. Ramon was getting on her nerves.

"Do you realize, Mom, what people are willing to do for the Sandanistas?" Sarah asked excitedly. "There was a woman once who heard they were training near her village. She left her husband and baby, bound up her breasts to stop the milk, and went off to join the men. Now that's bravery."

Or insanity, Connie thought. Who was going to feed the baby? Sarah looked at Joan. "We're going to try to get some videos of women revolutionaries in Cuba."

"Runaway women are the least of the Sandanistas' concerns," Mr. Ramon muttered, smoothing back his hair.

"These groups scare me," Connie said, imagining Sarah off in Cuba with terrorists. Helping them find guns. Getting caught in a crossfire. "They sound so violent."

"It's not the Sandanistas you ought to be afraid of," Joan put in. "It's those generals with their mustaches." She swung her arms forward and back in march time. "Strutting around like uniformed roosters. You ought to support anyone who's against them."

"Good girl," Mr. Ramon said with a patronizing air. Connie wondered if he realized how much Joan's imitation of the generals resembled him. She was surprised at the way the girl deferred to him totally. Sarah was also rapt in open-mouthed adoration. But she was much younger and the man was her teacher, after all. Joan had seemed so strong and independent, so much a leader in her relations with Sarah. Now Connie saw Joan was hardly more than a kid herself.

"You'll see." Mr. Ramon threw back his shoulders, posturing. "By the time we throw Nixon out of the White House, the Sandanistas will be back. They're in the mountains now, more coming every day." He took a breath. "I can almost smell the smoke of their campfires. Proud men, squatting on their heels, spitting into the fire, making plans."

God, they were going on and on. Wouldn't Mr. Ramon ever tire of lecturing them about the Sandanistas? When

Sarah got up to go to the bathroom, Connie yawned ostentatiously, signalling that she was ready to leave. Mr. Ramon turned on her with his white smile.

"You have a wonderful daughter," he said. "Not just beautiful. Intelligent, very intelligent. You must be very proud of her."

"I am." Connie looked at Joan to see whether this praise of Sarah had disturbed her, but her face was calm. There was nothing strange about what he said, but for some reason it made Connie uneasy. The strangely proprietary smirk of self-satisfaction. He seemed so sure of his ability to confer favors, to charm. Still, there was something appealing about him. The way he stroked his slick hair like a big cat preening, the way he looked straight into your eyes when he talked, the caressing timbre of his voice, even when he was saying something unpleasant.

On the way home Connie thought of the way Joan had tilted her head and half closed her eyes with pleasure at Mr. Ramon's words. Somehow it reminded Connie of the way she'd been with Howard in the beginning. How grateful she'd been when he'd praised her grasp of Buber. It had been one of their first dates. They were walking around the reservoir in Central Park. Howard hadn't expected such deep knowledge, he said. Why not? She was suddenly sorry for Joan. She wondered how she could have felt so threatened by her.

Connie avoided saying anything negative to Sarah about Mr. Ramon. She seemed so pleased that Connie had come with her. And in spite of the neighborhood and the motley crowd at La Peña, it actually hadn't been as bad as Connie had feared. There was no back room like the one Sarah had told her about at the record store, where they took their shirts off and gave each other massages.

Marc had made up with Connie. He'd been tender and funny and she'd let herself be wooed back. "I wouldn't have shown you those photos if they were anything but innocent," he'd said, and though she didn't quite believe him, she had to agree that would have been pretty dumb. But their first fight had scared her. When she came over to his house Saturday, she resisted telling him he'd been wrong about her needing to let Sarah go. There was no need to score points or provoke him. "I had a great time with Sarah last night," was all she said.

"Good. It's hard to be passionate when you're worried about your kids. Now maybe you can relax a little and think about us." He pulled her down on his lap. "I was just planning my letter to Dear Abby. Want to hear it?" She nodded. "Dear Abby: What should I do? I want my girlfriend in bed with me when I wake up in the morning. She says she can't sleep over because she's married. Abby, does that seem reasonable?"

She kissed the tip of his chin. "I'll send you an astral vision tonight. You won't be able to tell it from the real thing."

"I don't want a spook. It's not fair to keep that mouth to yourself. Or those breasts. What if I told you to imagine me running my fingers *piano piano* over your nipples." He unbuttoned her blouse. "First the right...."

"You're getting to me." She relaxed against him. "Just put a little more *vibrato* in your voice."

"I have an idea," he said, circling her nipple with his tongue. "Come with me to New York."

"What's wrong with right here?" she opened his shirt and rubbed her face against his chest. "Why do you have to go to New York?"

"I've just been invited to a conference. Besides, it's stimulating to do it in different places. The top of the Empire State building or the subway in rush hour."

She laughed. "I'd love to but I don't see how I can." For a moment, she imagined lying in bed with him looking out at the East River, the gulls circling and calling, the rose and mauve of the sunset softly mirrored in the water.

"Sure you can. Use your imagination." He picked her up, lunged over to the bed, put her down and started to tickle her.

"Stop!" she giggled, trying to squirm away. "I'm horribly ticklish. I'm going to wet my pants."

He sat astride her, holding her still. "I won't stop until you tell me you'll come." He was tickling her under the arms and down the ribs.

Her chest ached and she couldn't catch her breath. She couldn't stop laughing. "Oh stop," she choked, turning red. He had slipped off her shoes and was sitting on her legs tickling the bottom of her feet.

"Say the word."

"Okay," she gasped. "Okay. I'll come." She didn't know how but it didn't seem to matter anymore. She felt a buzzing and tingling all over her body as though a thousand flies were having a party.

"Great!" He climbed off her, ran downstairs and was back in a minute with a bottle of champagne. He uncorked it, spurting a burst of froth onto her legs, then he took her shoe and knelt down beside the bed. "It's a charade. Who am I?"

"Prince Charming with a hangover? Crazy?" She hoped the shoe didn't smell too bad. He seemed to be kissing it.

"Right on both counts. You've won a trip to New York. All expenses paid. Before she could stop him, he poured champagne into her shoe, held it in both hands like a goblet and drank. Champagne was running in rivulets down his neck. He looked like that stone Triton she'd seen in Rome, head thrown back, drinking from his giant conch. "*Bouquet* Connie," he said, grinning up at her with his foam mustache. "Exquisite."

This romantic mood was abruptly shattered on Sunday when Connie caught Sarah in a passionate embrace with Mr. Ramon in front of the house. They were sitting in a parked car—his—and so involved with their kiss that they didn't even notice her drive up. At first she couldn't understand what she was seeing. She thought it must be Joan in the car. Wasn't she his girlfriend? But then she saw Sarah's red hair escaping from the scarf she had wound around her head. It was unmistakably Sarah's hair.

She parked and ran over to them and banged on the window. "Hey, what do you think you're doing with my daughter, you?"

"Please." Mr. Ramon motioned her back so he could open the door of his red Volkswagen. "You are making a mistake, *Señora*," he said, stepping out. "We were just looking at some maps. The print is very small. Sarah's eyesight is better than mine and we...."

"Looking?" Connie burst out, "Lip reading, I'd say. Or was it braille? Sarah, get out of the car this minute." Sarah climbed out sullenly with her backpack and stood buttoning her shirt.

"If I see you around here again," Connie hissed at Mr. Ramon, "I'll kill you. I'm going down to the school tomorrow and taking Sarah out of your class."

He stared at her, his eyes wide. "You're being hysterical, *Señora*. Certainly Sarah's old enough to choose her own companions."

"Who are you to tell me what to do? You're not her mother. You're a dirty old man picking on a child. You should be locked up."

"You call me a dirty old man," he said. "You with your privileged upper-class background. You have no idea what a real man is like."

"My background has nothing do with it. Politics isn't the same as lechery."

"You people are all the same. Suspecting dirt everywhere." He made large, excited gestures, flailing his arms as if he were stirring up a whirlwind. "You don't care if the third world starves as long as you can throw smut on some innocent man. Get him locked up so he won't threaten your power."

"Look at you. Who do you think you're kidding?" Hands on her hips, she looked him up and down. "Being Latin American hasn't stopped you from having fancy shoes and a Rolex. Even if it's knocked down it must have cost you plenty."

"You're small-minded," he said, stung. "It was a gift. Instead of insulting me you should be thanking me on your knees. I've done your daughter nothing but good."

"I'll be the judge of that," Connie shouted. Then she grabbed Sarah's arm. "Don't deny anything, Sarah," she said, pulling her into the house. "I saw you kissing."

"We were just being affectionate," Sarah said coolly, throwing her backpack and a new Stevie Wonder album onto the sofa. "You just care because you're afraid someone saw us and will think you're a bad mother. You're not thinking about what's right for me. He's done me a lot of good. Helped me to see things in perspective, get my priorities straight. And I don't care what people think." She glared at Connie defiantly.

"Sarah, wipe that look off your face and listen to me." Connie took her by the shoulders and sat her down on the sofa. "I don't care a damn about what good he's done you. He's taken advantage of being your teacher. Spent months making friends with you, getting your confidence. And now this. It's really unspeakable." Connie could feel her lip quivering. She pressed her hand to her mouth to stop it.

"But Mom...."

"And you're just as bad," Connie said, ignoring Sarah's attempt to interrupt. "How could you pretend to me that Joan was his girlfriend? You were lying to me all this time." Connie felt as though the veins at her temples were going to burst.

"What do you mean? I didn't. I never told you anything like that." Sarah sounded genuinely shocked.

"You did. I'm sure you did. You asked me to trust you with Joan and she was only your cover for...."

"Stop it." Sarah jumped to her feet. "I don't want to hear it. Joan has nothing to do with this. Don't go blaming her. My relationship with her is something separate. You don't give yourself a chance to really think, do you? It's just, wow, Mr. Ramon is bad, this is terrible." She pulled off her scarf and shook her red hair back like a flag. A call to arms.

"I've just seen him, remember? I don't like the way he weasels out of everything. Won't even own up to what he's doing. How can you trust him? Can't you really see what a sneaky little man he is? Self-satisfied. Totally macho." Connie's forehead broke out into a sweat. She wanted to take Sarah's arm and shake her into listening.

"He is not. But it wouldn't matter what he was," she said, punching a sofa cushion. "You would have felt the same way about anyone. You never like my boyfriends." She went down the row of cushions, punching them all. Bif. Baf. Right in the center. "Any of them."

Sarah may have been right. It probably wouldn't have mattered. Mr. Ramon could have been the God Shiva in his glory or a monkey.

"Sarah, I can't just sit here and let Mr. Ramon do this. I'm going to call the principal and tell him his teacher is molesting my daughter. There are laws against child abuse."

"God, Mom, you're really losing it." Sarah stamped her foot. "What do you mean, child abuse? That isn't even the right word. And how can you even think of calling the principal? I haven't done anything wrong."

"God damn it, I just saw this guy touching you...you're probably sleeping with him."

"No, I'm not," Sarah burst out, "but it's absolutely none of your business. And I warn you, if you tell the principal, I'll deny it. He's used to hysterical mothers. You'll just look ridiculous." She fluttered her hands, imitating the wings of some distraught bird.

"Sarah, I'm trying to protect you, for Christ's sake. I'm worried about you. And don't lie to me. I slept with boys when I was your age. Look, it would be a disaster for you to get involved with this man. He's twice your age! And a South American to boot. I mean, what do you know about Latin culture? You've never been out of the United States. How in the world are you going to cope with a man involved in revolutionary politics? Life isn't like a movie, Sarah, it needs experience to manage. You're still a child."

"I'm not." Her face was livid with rage.

"Sarah, you're driving me crazy. I can't seem to get through to you." Connie collapsed into an armchair.

"I hear you." Sarah stood looking down at her. "It's just that you're wrong. Mr. Ramon didn't abuse me or seduce me. I want to be with him. I love him as much as he loves me. We understand each other. We have a real relationship. It's not what you think at all."

"You love him! What do you know about love? You are sixteen years old, Sarah. Don't you think I was ever sixteen? You want to know what I knew about love then? Zip. Look, Mr. Ramon's a politician. He's got a compelling rhetoric. So of course you believe him. It's natural but it doesn't have anything to do with love."

"I believed him before he even said anything. I just had to look at him." Sarah put her hand on her chest.

Connie slammed her fist into the arm of the chair. "You must have heard stories about older men and adoring young girls. This is classic."

"Classic?" Sarah looked at her shrewdly. "Well, if it's classic then why isn't it natural?"

"It's only natural for you to be confused, yes." Connie tried to chose her words carefully. "It's confusing when a person who ought to be like a father to you, takes advantage."

"I can hardly think of Mr. Ramon as my father. I mean, my God, look at Dad."

"That's just the point. You're looking for someone to fill the gap. This bastard steps right in and exploits it." She remembered how it had been when her father died and she was looking. She knew what Sarah was going through. God, she wanted to spare her this.

"Mom, save your psychology. You know I hate it. Look, I've had about all I can take." Sarah's voice rose, "I'm not going to stand here and listen to you berate him and belittle my feelings. You might be satisfied with a messed up marriage but I certainly won't be. I'll never be in the situation you and Dad are in. I want passion and I'm going for it. Face it, Mom, there's no way you're going to get me to give Juan up. And if you try, you're going to mess things up between us so badly you'll wish you hadn't." She grabbed her book bag and slammed out of the room. Connie could hear her banging all the closet doors as she went down the hall.

Sunday night Sarah wasn't home by the time Connie was making her pre-bedtime camomile tea but since it was a long weekend, she felt only mildly uneasy. While the tea was steeping, she turned on the radio and ran through the stations looking for jazz. Caught by the mention of Patty's name, she stopped.

"The flames are unbelievable," a man's voice was saying. "They must have doused the place in gasoline." At first she couldn't understand what was happening. Then she realized what it was. The SLA was inside and the police, the SWAT teams, had set the house on fire. My God, the bastards! How could they do that? Not knowing if Patty was with them. "She's in there," an excited voice said. "We have reports that Patty Hearst is in the house." Would she even have time to get a wet cloth to put over her face?

Without thinking, Connie dipped her fingers into the tea and touched her mouth. Maybe all she could do was drop to the floor. The worst was probably not being able to breathe. Straining to bring in air, lungs clotted with smoke.

"That was an on-scene report," the newscaster said.

Connie imagined being set on fire. First the bright flare-up of her clothes, then the searing heat on her skin. Would there be pain right away or would it be more like a shock and then numbness? She imagined her blood heating up, her brains beginning to seethe inside her skull. No. She couldn't stand it. She'd take her gun and shoot herself first. The fragments of her skull expanded and opened like flower petals. Connie imagined her consciousness hatching out like a bird from a shell. Hovering over the scene, watching. Who? Her lover? Cinque? Did you still care when you were dead? Or was there a blessed indifference?

She woke up the next morning with a sour taste in her mouth and a sick feeling of foreboding. Wrapping her robe around her, she slipped down the hall to Sarah's room. She wanted to look at her, be sure she was home safely. She opened Sarah's door a crack and peeked in. Sarah usually slept with her bottom in the air like a baby and the covers pulled over her head. At first Connie thought she saw her, but her eyes were playing tricks. It was a pillow. She walked over quietly, still feeling that Sarah was about to emerge suddenly, and found a note written on Sarah's new stationery. "Am with a friend. Don't try to find me. Need to be alone for awhile."

Connie felt a sinking in her stomach. Her first thought was Mr. Ramon. Could he really have done that? Persuaded Sarah to spend the night with him? Connie looked for his number in the phone book but it wasn't there and the operator had no listing. Then she dialed Joan's number. She was sure Joan would know where they were. Anger tightened her chest as she listened to the rings. They made little flashes of sound. Then stillness. No answer. She had a vision of Sarah waking up in some seedy motel room, Mr. Ramon's arm thrown possessively over her back. The thought made her sick.

Connie went back to her bedroom. Howard was just getting into his pants. "Sarah didn't come home last night, Howard. I'm afraid she's up to something." She wished she'd told Howard earlier about Mr. Ramon. Now she was afraid he'd be furious at her too.

"Did you check the fridge for a message?" Howard tightened his belt.

"She left a note. But she didn't say where she was." The rumpled sheets made her think of the motel again. She drew up the covers with an expression of distaste.

"She's not an early riser." He looked at the bedroom clock. "It's only 9:30. Be patient. I'm sure she'll call."

"I don't think so," Connie said. If she were going to look for Sarah, she'd better get dressed. She slipped into a pair of all-purpose khaki pants and a cotton shirt with a wide collar.

Howard jammed his foot into his shoe. "This isn't the first night she's spent at a friend's. She just didn't leave the number, that's all. Most likely she's run off to see that Latin-loving girlfriend of hers. If you like, I'll go over to her apartment and take a look." He pulled his jacket off a hanger and started for the bedroom door.

"Wait." She followed after him and caught him by the sleeve. "She's not there. I called. I think she's with Mr. Ramon. I caught him kissing her."

Howard stopped dead. "Who's Mr. Ramon?"

Connie swallowed nervously. "Her Spanish teacher."

"Her teacher! And you call yourself a mother. You're supposed to be watching out for things like this. When did this business start?"

"She's been talking about him for awhile." Connie looked down at her bare feet. "I thought she just liked his ideas."

"What do you know about ideas? You dumb bitch! You're infuriating me. Wait a minute. Wasn't that Ramon the one who got her to work at the bar?" He put his hand to his head as if a new idea had struck him. "It's beginning to make sense. All that rot about Palestinian rights. Sarah giving up her Hebrew. It's all thanks to him—Ramon." He looked as though he'd touched an electric wire. "My God, how could you let her get involved with scum like that? Why the hell didn't you tell me?"

She winced. "I wasn't sure what you'd do." It was hard enough worrying about Sarah without having Howard yelling at her.

"Break his neck, that's all. And yours too. I can't believe you've been stupid enough to let things get to this point. I'm calling the police and reporting her missing." Howard ran over to the bed, sat down and started dialing the police station.

Connie put her finger down on the button, cutting the connection. "Let's try her friends first. I couldn't get Joan but maybe one of them."

"All right." Howard put the phone back on the cradle.

She went into the kitchen. It seemed less claustrophobic somehow than their bedroom with its odor of sleeping bodies. She fixed a pot of coffee, trying to think of who to call first, and settled on Chrissy. She was someone who might encourage Sarah's romantic fantasy. "She's picking up milk," Connie said to Howard.

"Damn the milk."

"Please Howard, don't make things harder. She'll be back in a few minutes."

While they were waiting for Chrissy to return the call, Connie poured them some cold cereal and made another pot of coffee. "Howard, what if she's been kidnapped?" She felt her hands go cold. "Mr. Ramon thinks we're rich."

"Don't be a fool. He didn't kidnap her. She followed him like a child chasing the Pied Piper. And you didn't stop her." He lit his pipe and blew a smoke ring in her direction.

She waved the smoke away with her hand. "Howard, you know that makes me nauseous so early in the morning. Quit it." She took the cereal bowls over to the sink and washed them, jumping every time she hit a dish and it clanged, sure it was the phone. When she finished, she put them away and glanced at the clock. It was a little after ten. Had they really been doing this only a half hour? She made herself wipe the counters carefully, getting all the spots. When Chrissy called back, Howard answered.

"She didn't know anything," Howard said. "This isn't working. You shouldn't have interfered with me when I wanted to call the police." He bit the end of his pipe.

"Just a couple more tries." She didn't want to call the police. She didn't think they'd want to help. Once when Howard had stayed out all night when she was visiting her mother in New York, Elsie had persuaded her to call the police and report him missing. Tell them he's a reputable person, a professor, she'd told Connie. The policeman had just laughed at her. "Jesus, lady. If every woman called the police when her husband didn't come home at night, we'd have the lines swamped." It had been humiliating.

Connie sat on the stool by the kitchen counter and twisted her hair around one finger while she questioned Sarah's friends. Howard paced up and down, puffing clouds of smoke. It was maddening. No one knew anything, or if they did, they weren't telling. By the end of an hour, Connie felt a burning, itching sensation behind her knees. When she bent to look, she saw she had broken out in a rash. Damn Sarah. Why was she doing this?

"This is ridiculous," Howard said, pushing her off the stool. "I'm not waiting any longer while you interrogate those teenage animals. I'm calling the police."

"Fighting with her?" Howard said to the police sergeant. "No more than usual." He picked at a hair on his chin, trying to get a grip on it. His pipe got in the way and he laid it down. "I can't see why that's any concern of yours." He gave a quick tug and the hair came out. He rubbed the spot. "What do you mean, this sort of thing happens all the time? Not with my daughter." He searched his jaw with his hand. "I don't care whether the time to report a missing person is forty-eight hours or three. She's missing, isn't she?" He found something behind his ear and squeezed viciously. "All right. I'm perfectly calm. Yes. I just want you to find her." Howard put the phone back and wiped behind his ear with his finger. "That man sounded particularly incompetent. I think we'll have to work on it ourselves."

"I'm going to call La Peña," Connie said, rubbing the inside of her elbow where a new patch of rash had broken out. "I don't know why I didn't think of it before." That worked. Joan had told a co-worker at La Peña that she was going up to her parents' cabin in Bolinas for the weekend. She'd left last night. Connie scribbled down the phone number of the cabin on the roll-down pad.

"Don't tell me you don't know where she is, Joan. She's probably right in the next room." Connie's voice was so flat and cold she hardly recognized it. She couldn't see why Joan would want to do this. Unless they had some sort of weird triangle going. She pictured Joan and Sarah sitting on Mr. Ramon's knees. One on each side. Dressed like little girls with identical bows in their hair. Mr. Ramon was fondling their legs. "I've already called the police. If you won't let me talk to her, I'm going to tell them I think Mr. Ramon has kidnapped her. The police are sensitive to kidnappings these days." For the first time, Joan seemed to believe Connie meant what she was saying. "All right." Joan expelled her breath, seemingly resigned. "She's here. I drove her up."

"Where's here?"

Joan gave her the address.

"You better let me speak to her. Sarah," Connie said when Sarah got on the line, "you come home or I'm coming after you. Is that clear?" Her voice was so hard, she could hear the echo of it in her ears. That wasn't at all the way she'd meant to sound. She'd wanted to be reasonable, soft spoken, but when she heard Sarah's voice—suspicious, distant, defiant—all the softness died in her throat. She wanted so much to reach out to Sarah along that black snake of a cord and pull her back.

"I guess you'll have to get me then," Sarah said.

Connie felt terrible, crazy. When Sarah hung up, Connie threw the phone against the wall so hard the plastic cracked.

"I'm going," Howard said, grinding his teeth. "Give me the address."

Connie handed it to him. "I'm coming too. Let me just call Mischa's friend and tell them we might be late picking him up."

They drove over the San Rafael Bridge to Route 1. "You're driving too fast, Howard. There's no point in getting stopped for speeding." The speedometer was pushing eighty.

"Don't be hysterical." He hunched over the steering wheel like a racing car driver.

"I don't want to get stopped, not to speak of getting killed. That's not hysterical. It's pure reason. But I suppose it's a reflex action with you by now to put that label on everything. Whenever I'm concerned about something—speeding or Sarah—wham, I'm a hysteric. My womb rising to my mouth." *Hystera-* was the womb, wasn't it? Womb vapors. But men were every bit as hysterical. What did Howard think he was doing now? Weaving between cars like a madman.

They were winding over the hills now. Objects zipped by them like the figures that pop out on video games—trees, poles, farm houses.

"If you'd taught Sarah how to behave, instead of always finding excuses for everything she did, you wouldn't have to put up with my driving. We'd both be home in bed. You should be grateful I'm driving you by the way, instead of bitching." The car bounced and came down hard on the springs as they went over a crack, and he slowed down a little.

"What about you? Where were you in all this?" She turned in her seat, pushing against the belt.

"You let her take the job. I told you it was a bad bunch."

The afternoon sun shone directly in Connie's eyes like an interrogator's lamp. She raised her hand to shield her eyes.

"So it's me again. I 'let her.' What a cop out. Why didn't you stop her if you felt that strongly about it?"

"I told you what I thought. You should have clamped down on her." He held the wheel grimly, staring out through the bug dotted windshield.

"I should have?" she repeated. "Who are you to tell me what I should do? You can't find your glasses or your slippers. You can't even find a glass of milk in the fridge. Where would you be if I didn't do those things for you?"

"I'd manage. I managed before." He ground his teeth.

She could hear the muffled ivory click through the layers of skin. She imagined him biting into her flesh. Chewing and swallowing.

"You never managed anything. You lived with your mother. She still washes out your underwear when you go home to visit. A fifty year old man who's still in diapers. I do those things too and then I pretend I'm not really doing them, to save your ego. I've even got myself believing that you're tough. But you're not. You're weak. You're a weak, needy man."

"Don't do them then," he said, hurt. "No one's making you."

"That's not true. When you don't have clean shirts, you shout like hell for them. You don't even pick up your clothes off the floor. You just step out of them. And then you complain about the mess as though you had nothing to do with it. You won't even change a light bulb. I could go on and on." She could, in fact. She felt as though a dam had broken and a torrent was about to rush out.

"You're no bargain, you know," he said. "Maybe instead of insulting me you should think about why your daughter runs off and leaves you. Maybe it's you. Did you ever think of that? Maybe your mother wasn't so crazy when she took that overdose."

"That's low, Howard, even for you." She felt her face get hot.

"If you don't like it you can get out of the car and walk."

"We have to get Sarah, remember?"

"Fuck Sarah," he said, "and you too."

Connie pulled herself together with an effort. "Look, whether we like it or not, we're here now. We're in this together. We've got to go ahead."

"Don't think I'll forget what you've said to me. All that nasty bile. And you call yourself a good woman."

"I should have called myself a doormat. Because that's what I was. Stretched out on the stoop for you to wipe your feet on. All your shit got scraped off on my hide. Talk about bile. You're the one who's seething with it. You want to run a lawnmower over your colleagues' faces, grind the Arabs into mincemeat."

"I should have knocked some sense into you, that's for certain." Howard screeched to a stop in front of an ice cream parlor on the main street and grabbed her by the arm.

She jerked her arm free, opened the door and jumped out. "Look, Howard, we're here. Just put it on hold, all right? I'm going in to ask directions." Her legs were shaking so badly she felt she was going to stumble and fall on her face. She felt in no condition to go in and drag Sarah out of someone's house. Beard the lion in his den. She wasn't even sure that Howard would stand behind her. She asked the boy behind the counter which way number 56 would be. The boy motioned vaguely to the left. When she came out, Howard was staring ahead, his face livid. Still, he followed her with the car, peering nearsightedly, while she looked for the number. We're in great shape, she thought. Like a pair of brawling Chaplin characters on some wild goose chase. It was almost funny.

The house, when she finally found it, was a small white shingle next to the water. The door was painted bright blue and had a knocker hung with a strip of brilliantly colored

Mexican fabric. Howard got out of the car, visibly adjusting his face into a look of composure. When he knocked, Joan opened the door.

"Where is she?" he asked hoarsely.

"In there." Connie looked where Joan was pointing and saw Sarah in a little room plastered with revolutionary posters, sitting on a rumpled bed. There was what looked like a man's shirt lying at the foot of the bed. No Mr. Ramon in sight, though Connie could almost scent him in the air. Howard walked over to her.

"Pack up your things. Move it. "

"No need to yell," Joan said, looping her thumb through the belt of her jeans. She looked like a young desperado.

"Move it," Howard repeated, clenching his fists. Sarah looked scared.

"I think she should make her own choices," Joan said stiffly. But she looked scared too.

"You shut up," Howard said, "unless you want trouble."

"Leave her alone, Dad. I'm coming." Sarah started to stuff her things into the backpack. Sarah's mouth was sullen, tight. Connie hated the expression on her face. Suddenly she was terrified by the violence of her own anger. If she touched Sarah, she was afraid she'd slap her the way her mother had slapped Connie repeatedly when she was a child, full in the face, losing control so completely she'd looked deranged. Coldly she motioned Sarah to come and stood aside while she went out the door and over to the car.

Howard opened the back door and pushed Sarah in. He seemed to think if he let go of her for a minute she'd scamper back inside. Like a jack rabbit. Sarah hunched up in the corner and put her coat over her legs. She looked away from them out the window at Joan, who was standing in the open door.

"Sarah, I want to talk to you," Howard said when they'd gotten back to the main road. "This is no way to behave. You've worried us terribly."

"I left a message. You knew I was okay." Sarah leaned forward, looking at his face in the car mirror.

He ignored her protest. "I'm surprised. I thought we understood each other. You've been doing something you shouldn't." He'd started relatively calmly but now his voice rose and Connie could see the muscle popping in his jaw. "I want to hear about this business with Mr. Ramon."

"Mom, tell him I wasn't doing anything wrong." In her confusion, she began talking and moving her body like a much younger child.

Connie turned and looked at her over her shoulder. "It's no use lying, Sarah. His shirt was on the bed, for heaven's sake. After what I saw in front of the house, you must take me for an idiot."

"You heard your mother, Sarah." Howard pursed his lips.

"Oh," she gasped. If she'd been less tired and frightened she would have thought of some excuse. But now she broke down.

"Yes, Mr. Ramon was there. Does that satisfy you? You've got a confession." She started crying angrily, putting her head against the back of the seat.

"You understand we can't allow you, one, to make out with your teacher, who is incidentally a bastard of the first water to take advantage of little fool like you, and two, to run off wherever you please without telling us. You're grounded for a month."

"What do you mean grounded?"

"I mean we will take you to school. We will pick you up from school. And you will spend the rest of your time at home."

"But I can't, I have a job."

"Don't you dare mention that job to me. That's where all our trouble started. But this is the end of it. You are not going to be out of our sight except when your teachers are watching you. And you are not going to be in Mr. Ramon's class anymore."

"Mom's taken me out already," Sarah said. "I'm in Mrs. Perez's class." Connie had gone down the day after she'd found her kissing Mr. Ramon and transferred her.

"I think she understands what she's done, Howard." For once Connie agreed with something Howard had done. But she didn't want him to push it too far. She nodded at Sarah, encouraging her to say something contrite.

"I had to do it," Sarah said. "I'd do it again too if I got the chance." She looked around desperately, as though wondering if there was a way of escape. If the doors hadn't been locked, Connie had a feeling she might have jumped.

"Then you're more of a fool than I thought." Howard accidently hit the horn and it gave a loud, startled honk.

"You've never been a father to me," she screamed. "I hate you. You're a machine. A robot. I don't think you even have a heart. Do you?"

They were trapped in the car. There was nothing to do but let that hang in the air.

Connie saw Howard take one hand off the wheel and massage his chest as though it hurt him. "I give you what I can," he said finally, when they had crossed the bridge and were almost home. "I can't do more than that. I'm sorry. Parents are often unsatisfactory. Mine were all wrong too. It's just the way things are."

"I don't care what your bloody parents did to you," Sarah said to Howard. "I don't care if they tied you in a chair and made you eat raw eggs and cream until you barfed. Just because they were monsters, it's no excuse."

"Sarah that's enough." Connie said angrily, "I'd hoped you'd learned something from this. That you were going to think a little. Not just blurt out every thought in your head." Sarah started to cry.

"I can't believe you did that," Sarah said to Connie when they finally got home. Sarah struggled to get some control of her voice but it came out like a hiccough. "Let him say all that shit to me. I'll never forgive you. Never." She shut her door and Connie could hear the click of the bolt.

That night Connie couldn't sleep. She lay in bed listening to Howard snoring until she couldn't stand it anymore and then she went into the washroom and plugged in the iron. At least piles of laundry made sense. You started at the beginning and slowly you got somewhere. Connie picked out a shirt of Sarah's and began ironing the collar. She'd been lucky, she thought. Luckier than Sarah. She'd begun with love. At least in the beginning her father had been there for her in a way that Howard had never been for Sarah. The farm had been the best. It gave her things she'd never forget. A blueprint for a good life. Even if somehow she'd missed finding it. Sarah's blouse was deep blue. Connie's father had a shirt that color that he wore in the summer. Connie remembered how he sat at the head of the table, sleeves rolled up, in front of a huge plate of corn from their garden. Awed, she'd watched his white teeth move along the rows, cropping off the sweet kernels close to the core. She could still hear the way he crunched. Stopping when he finished an ear to smile at her, his mouth buttery. She moved the iron slowly around the buttons, watching the steam. The corn had been steaming hot.

"You'll never make it," she'd say. "Not eight ears. You can't." But he always did. His appetite was mythic, gargantuan. She dreamed of entering him in a marathon. She was sure he'd make it into *The Guiness Book of World Records*. The most corn ever eaten by a single man at one sitting. With all that joy in life, how had he died? She folded the shirt and unplugged the iron. Even that little bit of ironing had made her sleepy. What would happen to Sarah later, she wondered, with a blueprint like this.

The next day, Connie got a letter from Saint Mary's. She sat down at the kitchen table and opened it with trembling fingers. She'd gotten the job for the fall. Her course was

Comp. Lit. 24 B. Sister McKinney was welcoming her aboard. She included the syllabus from last year, though she said Connie could change the texts. It was just to show her the format. Looking at it, Connie got cold feet. Could she really handle this? She felt herself trembling. She hadn't been in a classroom since graduate school. Kids were different now, less respectful. What if they made fun of her? She imagined them blowing up giant condoms and hanging them around the room for her first day. It's a Catholic school, she told herself, maybe they haven't discovered sex yet. Or rudeness. She looked at the letter again and saw she had two weeks to answer. She'd think about it quietly. Maybe if she went over some of the texts she'd thought about teaching, she'd feel calmer. Ideas would come to her.

Later that afternoon, Connie called Marc. "I've got some good news too," she said after she'd told him about her ordeal with Sarah. "I got a job at Saint Mary's starting in September. I'm excited and scared in equal parts."

"That's great," he said after a moment. "But have you thought what that will do to your leisure?"

"I guess I'll be spending more of it in the library."

"It's been so nice to be able to relax with you. To have you coming over on the spur of the minute. Are you sure you want to teach?"

"If I'm going to leave Howard, I have to. You still want that, don't you?"

"Of course I do." His voice sounded tired. "How can you ask?"

Connie was sitting in the sun in a little patch of foxgloves watching Marc change the oil in his car. "You know, maybe you're right," she told him, "I've been picking up too many pieces for Sarah."

"Now just have the guts to put her on her own," he said, crawling out from under the car. "It's her lookout if she fucks up."

Connie felt as though he'd dragged a piece of chalk across a blackboard. "When I'm agreeing with you, why do you have to be so harsh?"

"Look, I've got things on my mind too. I'm upset about Alix. She's got a new lover and she wants to know what I think about him. It's obvious the guy is after her money. She's lent him five hundred dollars already."

Connie stared. "What's her lover have to do with you? I thought you two had stopped talking."

He took off the oil cap, inserted a stained funnel and poured in a can of new oil. It was thick and viscous. She imagined it rising around Alix like a flood, closing her pores. Marc poured in another pint. "I can't ignore this, Connie. It might screw up Selina. What if she gives him the money she's supposed to be saving for Selina's college?"

"She makes a good salary, doesn't she? Let her borrow if she has to. She could do a lot of things but she doesn't have to run to you. She's a grown woman." Connie felt her heart sink. It occurred to her that she might lose him, not to the snow bunnies but to Alix.

"Connie this isn't a time to be jealous. Believe me, if Selina wasn't involved, Alix could fornicate with the whole Watergate crew. Fuck them backwards or forwards. I wouldn't give a damn. Look baby, don't give me a hard time." He washed his hands under the hose and dried them on a rag. "Let's stop thinking about our problems and think about the wild time we're going to have in New York."

"Jesus, Marc, I'm not sure I can leave Sarah now...."

"You can, you just have to want to. And if you haven't made arrangements, you better get popping. I've already reserved the tickets." He dropped down beside her.

She could smell the crushed grass, warm and fragrant. "Well...."

He pushed her back into the flowers and unsnapped her jeans.

Connie decided to try to talk with Sarah. See what state she was in. Try to assess whether it was safe to leave her. Sarah had a sore throat and was taking a day off from school. She was sitting in bed, surrounded by cutup magazines making a huge poster collage. She was fitting in the picture of a crying dark-skinned child with a distended belly.

"Sarah," Connie said after chatting with her for a few minutes, "I might be going to New York for a few days."

Sarah looked up like a dog sensing the wind. "Oh yeah? When?"

"Maybe next week." Connie could see she was pleased. She wanted her mother to get out. Oh Jesus, Connie thought, how can I go to New York now? There couldn't be a worse time. Howard won't pay any attention, and Sarah will cook up something with Mr. Ramon. She sat down gingerly on the edge of the bed, her thoughts ricocheting like ping-pong balls. But Marc would be so disappointed if she didn't go. He'd been planning this for weeks. Her head began to hurt.

"Sarah, I don't want to go if there's going to be trouble."

"Trouble, what more trouble could there be? I'm sick, I'm grounded, Dad looks at me like I'm a bum on a street corner. What do you think I'm going to do? Go on a rampage? Jump off the clock tower? Maybe I should."

"Sarah, you had a part in all this, remember."

"How *can* I forget it? I'm losing my job at La Peña, the only thing I really cared about. Those people counted on me. It just doesn't matter to you, does it?"

"Look, Sarah, I'm sorry about the job but actions have consequences. What bothers me more is that we don't seem to have any way to communicate." Connie rested her hand lightly on Sarah's leg through the covers. "Maybe you should talk to someone outside the family, someone impartial...."

Sarah started screaming at her before she even finished. It was as though she had triggered a volcanic eruption. "Nothing's wrong with me," Sarah yelled, scattering pieces of jungle scenery onto the rug. "What's wrong is you. You're afraid of me, afraid to really listen to me. You want to plaster things over, patch them up. You don't want to see how wrong everything really is. And now I've found someone who listens and really cares." She put her hand to her throat, swallowed and lowered her voice. "Besides, I told you, I love Mr. Ramon."

It was amazing, Connie thought, how puppy love had all the drama of the real thing. With her afghan pulled around her like a cape, Sarah was as flamboyant and grand as Bernhardt.

"You want to brainwash me, because I'm in love with someone you don't approve of. You think I can be deprogrammed like a Moonie. Well, I can't. Send me to a shrink, if you want. I've learned about passive resistance. I'll keep my mouth shut until he dies of boredom."

Connie bent and picked up Sarah's cut-outs from the rug. Brilliantly green trees clotted with thick vines. "Forget it. It was just a suggestion." How could she expect Sarah to be reasonable if she wasn't herself? Why didn't she give up Marc if it was so easy? Why didn't she stay home from New York and take care of her daughter?

That night she tossed and turned, rolling her sheets around her until she had to get up and untangle them. She thought of some of the crazy things she'd done with Freddy at college, climbing up on the roof of the president's house in a hurricane, running along the tops of boxcars. What was Sarah likely to do? Sneak out of the house to meet Mr. Ramon, the way Connie did to meet Marc? Sarah wasn't going to stay grounded unless Howard watched her like a hawk and Connie was sure he wouldn't. He'd probably be out himself on one of his night wanderings. Connie imagined Sarah waiting until Howard went out in the Pinto and then taking the keys to the other car. Thinking she knew how to drive because she'd gone to her first class of driver's ed. Doing eighty on the freeway to Oakland. Wobbling over the white line. Finally, Connie fell into a troubled sleep and dreamt of Alix as a mermaid with an iridescent tail and sharks teeth singing lullabies to Marc.

When she woke up, the first thing that came to her mind was that it was ridiculous to worry so much about Sarah. If one tenth of the things Connie imagined had happened, Sarah would have been dead long ago. Anything she can think of to do when I'm gone she would probably do when I'm here. I can't follow her to school, after all. She could be dropping acid in the bathroom. It's not as if I'm deserting her, she told herself, it's only a few days. She decided she would ask the housekeeper to babysit Mischa in the afternoons and keep an eye on Sarah until Howard got home.

When Connie said she was going to visit her mother for a few days, Howard looked at her angrily.

"Leaving me to keep Sarah grounded?"

"Well, why not? I've been doing it up till now. Why shouldn't you take over for awhile?" She didn't really expect an answer. After their last fight they weren't even trying to communicate. "Don't worry. You'll manage. I need a rest." It seemed to her that her need was like an iceberg whose tip was just beginning to surface.

Connie called her mother and told her she was coming to New York for a visit—next week.

"How lovely, darling. What's the occasion?"

"What better occasion than seeing you?" Connie could envision her mother sitting on her bed propped up by pillows, her small feet crossed at the ankles, a book on her lap.

"Oh, dear," Elsie exclaimed, as though she had a sudden toothache.

"What?" Was her mother worried about Louise again? She never wanted to overstrain her help. It was irritating not to be able to visit your mother because it might tire the cook. The funny thing about it was that Louise enjoyed Connie's visits. Probably more than Elsie did.

"The spare room is supposed to be painted next week. I'm not sure it will be ready." Elsie sighed.

"That's fine. I wasn't planning to stay with you anyway. It was so hard for you last time." Elsie had made the guest room into a storehouse for her paintings and she'd insisted on moving them all out and Louise had strained her back. "There are lots of nice hotels. In fact, a good friend of mine is going to be at the Stanhope. If I stay there, it'll give me a chance to see him too."

"A friend? What friend? Why didn't you tell me you were coming to see a friend in New York?"

"I'm not. He just happens to be there."

"Maybe you should stay with me after all." Elsie seemed to be thinking aloud. "I can put off painting the room."

"Don't be silly. It would upset your schedule," Connie said with a touch of irony. "You were very definite about the room being painted. I'll stay at the Stanhope. It's only a few blocks from you."

"Who is this friend?"

"You don't know him." For a second, she felt the way she had as a little girl hiding her favorite marble under her hand. If I show, you'll take it. The marble had been cloudy blue with intense midnight swirls.

"Connie, I don't think you're coming to New York to see me at all. You're coming to see this man." Her mother sounded indignant.

Connie laughed. "I'm coming to see you both." The desire to show her marble was overwhelming. "In fact, I was planning to bring him over to meet you. I think you'd enjoy him."

"Well, if you like, you could both stay here."

Connie almost laughed again. It was so much like a replay of her and Freddy. Elsie's taking them up to the Cape. Giving them a room next to hers. But this time Connie felt more in control. She could open the door a crack, let her mother glimpse her life, or shut it completely.

"That's very sweet, Mother. But no. Thank you."

"Well, then, let me treat you." Connie could hear the rustle of paper. Her Mother was probably looking up the hotel in the phone book. Preparing to call and make a reservation.

"There's no need for that." There was still something tempting in the idea of having her mother pay. Connie resisted, but when she hung up, she was sweating. She went into the bathroom and wiped her face and neck with a towel. The visit wasn't going to be as easy as she'd thought.

Summer
1974

Twelve

The Stanhope was much older than Connie remembered, though the big high-ceilinged room had a sort of decayed charm. Marc was at the opening session of his conference and she was sitting on the bed on top of the faded burgundy bedspread trying to decide whether to read Erica Jong or Sue Kaufman. Erica Jong was sexy and Jewish and from New York. Connie had bought *Fear of Flying* the day Marc tickled her until she said yes to the trip. It sounded like just the thing to take on a getaway weekend. Besides, Connie thought wryly, it might catch her up on the liberation she'd missed in the sixties. The legitimacy of casual sex. Adultery as a form of self-expression.

But now the garish cover, with its unzipped jumpsuit advertising the zipless fuck, made her feel sluttish and irresponsible. She turned it face down on the spread and skimmed the other book, *Falling Bodies*. The first thing she hit on was a scene with an unhappy little boy building machines out of junk he found on the street. The boy was about Mischa's age and his problems were probably the fault of his mother, a frantic, bored housewife. She started to feel chest pains over her heart. I've really messed up this time, she thought. My daughter has just run away to Bolinas. My son has nightmares every night. Howard is walking around the house like Moshe Dayan preparing a commando raid.

I've been thinking about getting out. And what do I do? I come to New York like a lovesick teenager, complete with dirty books in my handbag. What am I doing here? I must be out of my mind.

She got off the bed and looked out the window onto the avenue. Howard's not capable of taking care of those children, she thought, watching a couple unload their sleeping child from a taxi. Right now Sarah's probably doing something awful. What if she comes home from school stoned and tells Howard off and he gets furious? What if Sarah puts acid in their orange juice? She imagined them all crawling around on the floor mesmerized by the pattern on the carpet. When she came home she'd find three psychotics.

She was so deep in her imaginings that when Marc threw open the door she was shocked to see him looking unperturbed. It was as though someone had changed the television channel without her noticing.

"Sorry I'm so late," he said, skimming his hat onto a chair. "There was a dinner speech on Psychoanalysis. The questions went on forever." He kissed her, running his fingers lightly over the silk sleeve of her kimono.

She wanted him to hold her and blot out the thoughts ticking away in her mind like mini time bombs. After all she'd made the choice to come hadn't she? It would be stupid to ruin their few days by worrying. She rubbed her hand over his cheek. "Was it worth it at least?"

"Not very."

"Wasn't there anything exciting?" She undid the top button of his shirt.

"Well, there was a paper on the difference between insatiable desires and real needs."

"Oh?" She leaned against him, smelling his sweat. "How can you tell?"

He took her hand and put it between his legs, closing her fingers around him. "There. Good. That's how. If it's hard, it's real." She felt him throb against her palm through the light wool. A stabbing excitement flashed through her groin.

"You're outrageous." She pulled him against her, eyes closed, feeling the warmth grow.

"At least let me undress." He finished unbuttoning his shirt, suddenly shy.

"Forget about your shirt. I like you like this, in wild disorder." What had gotten into her? The more he resisted, the more she wanted him. She began to feel like a maenad drunk on sacred wine. He was trying to look dignified but even he had trouble doing it as he was stepping out of his pants. She touched the curve of his groin where it met his thigh. She wanted to rub her cheek along it.

Then he was caressing her again, running his hands down her side, moving her towards the tall four-poster bed. She leaned against it, bending back while he nuzzled her breasts, biting and licking. They were incredibly tender, almost painful.

Marc stopped. "Are you comfortable leaning back like that?" he whispered. "Do you want to get on the bed?"

"No, I'm all right." Actually she didn't want to get on the bed at all. She liked pressing her bare feet against the floor, the curve of her back against the bed. Her bed at home wasn't high enough for this. It felt deliciously abandoned. Like Isadora Zelda, she thought. She wished she had her dress on so she could just pull it up. Her kimono parted silkily along her sides.

He knelt, exploring between her legs. "My God, you're wet. Do you want me to kiss you?"

The warmth spread into her stomach. She tugged gently at his hair, pulling him up.

"No? You're ready? Just like that?"

"Yes. Yes. Put it in." She tangled one leg around his thigh, urging him forward. She wanted him where she could see him, his face next to hers. She wanted to see the rim of dark around his eyes.

His penis wasn't very hard. But it felt good anyway, like a

blind mole nosing, trying to get in. Move now, just keep moving. Only a little more and she would.

"That certainly didn't take much," Marc said. "Sometimes I think sex for you is all in the head."

Why did he have to spoil things? "It's you. You excite me terribly." She nibbled his ear.

"I hope so." He climbed on the bed and drew her up beside him.

She kissed his shoulder. "Believe. That's what you're always telling me."

"Touché."

Afterwards, though, she lay in his arms thinking of home. What if Mischa asked Howard to call her at her mother's? He'd been having dreadful nightmares since he saw pictures of the *Ma'alot* children on T.V. Howard had been making it worse by constantly talking about the massacre. Telling him how the children were playing, not suspecting anything, when the terrorists hit. Mischa became obsessed with them sneaking into his bedroom after he'd gone to sleep the way the tooth fairy did, except that instead of giving him a dollar, they'd kill him.

Marc was propped on one elbow studying her face. "Penny for your thoughts."

"I'm a little dazed," she said evasively, touching the warm underside of his arm. "It doesn't feel quite real."

"It's real, all right. The roller coaster's been climbing up slow but now's the downhill ride. So hold on to your hat. No one's going to keep me from having you. No one. Not your husband. Not even your daughter." His eyes shut on the last word. In a minute he was deeply asleep.

In the morning when she woke up, he had the television on low and was watching Barbara Walters chat about the impeachment hearings with someone. She had a sassy, scratchy voice. "You caught me being political before breakfast," he said.

"I don't mind," Connie murmured, rubbing her eyes. "But

if it were up to me I wouldn't even read the newspapers until it's all over. Anything new?"

"Not as far as I can tell. The lady's pretty high on herself though. I've never understood what they see in her. Too tough. She has no charm." He flicked it off and went into the bathroom.

"Maybe you don't need it when you're the highest paid woman in television," Connie called after him.

"You can't go to bed with your money," he called back.

He came out naked, with his toothbrush and toothpaste in one hand and a drinking cup in the other, and sat down on the edge of the bed. "I promised I'd take care of you, remember?"

"I didn't know that included brushing my teeth. She tried to take the brush from him, but he wouldn't let her.

"By sharing a toothbrush you're helping conserve our resources. One less boar will give up his bristles." He squeezed out a shining ribbon of paste.

"I thought it was plastics that were in short supply," she said, laughing.

"Quiet. You think too much." He moved the brush carefully up and down. Every time his hand rubbed against her lips, she felt a stab of excitement.

"I'm going to wash your hair too. Wash your everything. You'll be as clean as a newborn babe." He offered her the cup.

"I've got to spit," she mumbled, getting up.

"All right, I guess I can allow that." He followed her into the bathroom. "Go ahead. You can pee too." He put the plug in the tub and turned the faucets on full.

"I'd rather...." She spit the water into the sink. Her mouth felt minty-clean.

"Don't be shy. I'll do it first and you can hold my penis." He took her hand.

"Can I aim it?" It felt so warm, warm and silky like a small animal.

"Anywhere you want. It's yours." He concentrated and a thin stream arched into the bowl. It had the faint odor of asparagus.

She moved the stream around the bowl, feeling like a kid with a forbidden toy. "I'll do a figure eight. Oh oh, it's running out. Now what?"

"Shake it off. A little harder. Don't be afraid. It's not delicate. Good girl. If we get married I want to have two toilets side by side so we'll never be separated, even when we're...."

"You're crazy."

"About you." He pushed her hair back and whispered into her ear, "Do you want me to tell you a secret I've never told anyone before?" She saw their faces reflected in the bathroom mirror, flushed, touching.

"Let me guess. You broke into your chairman's office and stole the promotion files."

He looked annoyed for a minute. "It's not a public secret," he said. Then he took her hand and caressed it, building up the mood again. "Feel here," he said, putting her hand on his penis.

"It feels like a raised scar. What is...." She felt suddenly squeamish, the way she had when she first touched the ridged place marking the loss of her appendix.

"I don't know. Maybe it's a birth defect. Anyway, no one in the world knows about it but you." And a dozen other women, she guessed. She wondered whether he felt badly about it. It seemed like such a little thing. But then, maybe everyone feels doubts about their genitals, even men. There was something manic about his mood this morning. As though he were trying to absorb her. To charm her into himself.

"Your bath's ready," he said, turning the water off. "Get in. Don't slip." He climbed in back of her and held her inside his legs.

"I'm not sure it's big enough for both of us."

"Of course it is. Lean back and I'll soap your hair." He drew her back against his chest and poured warm water over her head. Then she felt a cool splash of shampoo and he was massaging her head with his fingers. She could feel her thoughts loosening. There was only the sensation of his fingertips kneading her scalp. "Am I doing it too hard?"

"No. It's nice." She relaxed, eyes closed, giving herself over to him.

She knew there was something excessive about all this but she didn't care anymore. She liked it. Marc would have made a terrific mother. He even made sure the water didn't get in her ears when he was rinsing. Maybe if she could have just gone back to being a baby for a while, sort of started over again, things would have turned out better. Her thoughts wouldn't heap up in such confusion. They'd come more slowly. She would have loved it if thoughts were like objects that you could set out in front of you on a table...oranges, bowl, knife, vase, flowers...all clear, all making sense together, even though they were so different.

"I feel like a mermaid. I wish I had hair down to my waist so you would comb it for a long, long time before you got all the snarls out."

"I'd like that." He helped her out of the tub and wrapped her in a big towel, rubbing her skin gently. From the next room, she heard the yearning harmonies of Ellington's *Satin Doll.* The Duke was dead and all the stations were playing it.

"What?" she asked, the saxophone tugging at her heart.

"I'm glad you want something for yourself. Once you start, who knows where you'll stop? Maybe you'll let me comb out your snarls forever." He hugged her. "Connie, I don't want to be just your lover. I want to be your husband. Will you marry me?" Still holding her around the waist, he leaned back so he could see her face. "No, don't look at me like that. I thought about it a lot when I was away. This is more than just another affair. This time it's right. I know it."

Connie was suddenly wide awake. "Marry you? Good

heavens, Marc, do you really think I'm going to buy that? Your wife still cooks dinners for you, for God's sake. How can you think of getting married? You're still as tied to her as Bebe Rebozo is to Nixon."

When his face got dark, Marc looked so handsome. He was angry now. He was pulling the hairs from the comb as if he'd like to pull them from her head. Squeezing out the wash rag, hard.

"I'm going to start divorce proceedings when I get back. I mean it. I want to marry you. It's what I'm working towards. I thought you were too. That while I was gone you'd think about leaving Howard." He took his shirt from the hook on the bathroom door and put it on. "Is this really such a surprise?" He smoothed his shirt, making sure it was flat all around before he fastened his trousers. His hands were precise.

"Leaving Howard isn't the same as getting married. We haven't even tried living together. I told you before, you're a romantic." She sat down on the bath stool and pulled on her stockings. She felt confused.

"Yes, I know, like Hemingway. But I'm not Hemingway. I'm not even in the habit of marrying my long-term mistresses." He tilted up her chin with his hand. "This is an entirely new script. There's a great part in it for the leading lady. Won't you take it? I want you down to the parings of your toenails." She ducked her head. "You know what your trouble is? You still don't trust me."

He was right, she didn't. But she was starting to want him again. The silk of the stockings set off little sparks in her groin every time her legs rubbed together. She took his finger between her teeth and pressed down.

He pulled his hand away. "Don't bite. That hurts."

She laughed and took it back, chafing the spot she'd nipped. "Come on, then. We'll be late to meet your future mother-in-law." She tried to imagine what it would be like being married to Marc but all she could picture was a succession of beds. A lifetime love affair, yes. That might be wonderful. Marriage suggested other things. Troubles with children, bills, grunted complaints over dinner. She thought of sitting opposite Selina while she blared Peter Frampton and blew huge pink bubbles with her gum.

Marc looked in the elevator mirror and straightened his tie. His face had the rosy glow of satisfied sex. "I think your mother will take to me," he said brightly. "Older women usually do."

"Just don't talk to her about Selina or Alix."

Marc frowned. "Why not?"

"Mother has a thing about broken marriages. I want you to come in and dazzle her. Understand?"

He nodded and patted her rump affectionately. "Don't worry, kid. You've got it made." Was she sure Marc would dazzle her mother? Elsie never liked Howard. But Connie simply couldn't resist showing Marc off.

They were remodeling the lobby. Connie missed the old heavy green drapes and the worn gold trim. She missed the old doormen too. Even Joe was gone, who had kissed her in the dingy service elevator. And the red-haired man at the front door. Now the elevators were automatic and no one seemed remotely Irish anymore. There was a sign on the elevator wall urging the tenants to conserve energy this summer by not turning their air conditioners below 78 degrees. It was depressing. But her mother's place hadn't changed. The Indian cowbells Connie had given her were hanging on the door that she still left unlocked. Elsie boasted that her friends thought she was insane. Maybe her innocence protected her; she'd walked through Harlem on summer nights hailing taxicabs and never had any trouble.

"Mother, Mother, I'm here," Connie sang out brightly in the direction of Elsie's bedroom. She heard the creaking of the wood floor in the hall. Elsie was hurrying. Connie suddenly imagined her tripping on the runner. She'd try and talk to her about getting wall-to-wall carpet, though she knew ahead of time she'd say it was hideous.

"Don't rush, Mother. We'll come to you." But it was too late. She was framed triumphantly in the hallway door, smiling.

"This is Marc, Mother," Connie said cheerfully, bringing him over to her.

"I've wanted to meet you ever since I saw your paintings," Marc gave her his most charming smile. "It's lovely finally to be here."

"Thank you," she said languidly, extending her hand as though she expected him to kiss it. Connie noticed her mother was wearing her Chanel No. 5. Its full, strong scent struck her like a gloved fist. Marc held Elsie's hand awkwardly, then shook it once and let it go. He should have bowed, Connie thought, and brought it close to his mouth, kissing the air. They stood for a moment looking at each other.

"Beautiful things you have here," he said finally. "That mobile reminds me of Calder." It hung from the ceiling over their heads. Slowly whirling blades of red and black, triangles of silver like birds' wings suspended in the air.

"It is Calder," Elsie said. "It was a present from him. I was working on my red and black series and I was so touched that he chose the same colors to give me. I think it does well in the entry way, don't you, where it catches the drafts?"

Marc looked nonplussed. "Yes, very well," he stammered.

"It must be worth a fortune now," he whispered to Connie as Elsie led them into the dining room.

Connie followed her mother with a sinking feeling that this might not work. Marc seemed suddenly as nervous as a child at a new school. "So what?" she whispered back, touching his arm encouragingly. "I thought you were above all that. Remember your contempt for the rich."

He gave a tight laugh. She saw his eyes flicking over the paintings. "I hope your mother has good insurance."

"Why, are you planning a heist?" she asked, a little too loud.

"Shhh." Marc squeezed her wrist, plainly afraid her mother would hear. Then he made an elaborate show of adjusting a cushion behind Elsie's back. It was amazing how uncomfortable most antiques were, Connie thought. Her grandmother's sofa, for instance, was a nightmare. You almost slid off the overstuffed silk seat and there was no way of leaning against the high carved back with its curlicues of grapes and flowers. No wonder Connie had filled her own house with comfortable sofas and deep chairs where you could curl up and read a book. Places where kids could play. It struck her how much of her life was a reaction.

As soon as they were settled on the sofa, her mother's Siamese cat brushed against Marc's legs, checking him out. Marc reached down to pet him and the cat suddenly arched his back and hissed.

"Please don't. You're upsetting him. He doesn't like strangers." Elsie snatched the cat onto her lap. "Oh, poor Ellsworth," she stroked the cat's head. "There's too much confusion, isn't there, pet?" Embarrassed, Marc started to leaf through the catalogue on the butler table, *Pop Art, 1950 to 1973*. Connie knew that Elsie hated Pop Art but she'd never let a show go by without checking out her rivals. She expected Marc to say how much he liked Andy Warhol but he didn't. Maybe he guessed that Elsie thought Marilyn Monroe was vulgar. Still, Connie was surprised to hear him launch into a description of his paper on new parameters in the treatment of adolescents who act out dangerously . It wasn't a subject that was likely to interest her mother. She swallowed, disappointed. She'd thought he'd be able to manage better.

"You really have to modify technique substantially," Marc was saying. "These patients just can't get by on silence punctuated by uh huhs. They need stronger interactions, less rigid rules." Elsie didn't look impressed and Marc's voice was unnaturally high.

Connie leaned against him, wanting to comfort him by her warmth. "Marc's done some brilliant work on this, Mother," she said firmly, trying to make her mother pay attention.

Elsie straightened her rings. "You don't go in for all that holding and touching stuff, I hope," she said in a bored voice.

"He doesn't run encounter groups, Mother. It's a piece of original theory."

"There hasn't been anything original in psychology since Freud," Elsie said. "And he was more an artist than a clinician. Connie, dear, you're looking really sallow," she exclaimed suddenly. "Are you all right?"

Connie felt a rush of blood to her cheeks and neck. Couldn't you just be civilized for once? she thought. You know damn well how uncomfortable I am. Instead of worrying about my health, I wish you'd find something nice to say to Marc. "I'm fine, Mom," she said, "just hungry."

"I usually have a light breakfast. I hope it'll be enough for you."

"I'm sure it'll be perfect," Connie said, the words sticking in her throat. This was getting worse and worse.

They got up in unison and walked the few steps to the mahogany table against the wall.

"You sit here then, Marc, if you will," Elsie said, lowering herself into the Queen Anne chair and pressing the buzzer hidden cleverly beneath the carpet.

Connie's heart sank when she saw Louise bringing in a silver tray with dishes of steamed prunes and a big bowl of what she recognized as "French," a concoction of sour cream, cream cheese and sugar that her mother had forced on her as a child.

"Hello, honey," Louise shifted her bulk onto one haunch. "Where are those children of yours? You sure should have brought them with you."

"Next time I will, for sure." Connie smiled at her. She saw Marc looking warily at the sour cream. He was a bacon and eggs man.

"Connie," her mother snapped, "you were the one who

was so hungry. You're interfering with Louise giving us our breakfast." She stamped her foot impatiently. "Well, Louise? Don't just stand there."

"It's a bit of a sacrifice not to have a hot breakfast," Elsie said as Louise served them, "but I'm trying to do my part and cut down on energy consumption. You know, not turn on the gas in the morning." That was a lie of course. Since Simon died, Elsie had always had strange things for breakfast. Lettuce smeared with honey. Caviar on toast. Connie thought her mother could have at least made a little effort to serve something normal.

"Looks delicious," Marc said, with false heartiness, "a real European breakfast." He dipped his spoon into the dish of prunes and put one in his mouth. Then he spit the pit back into his spoon and deposited it on the edge of his plate. He watched Elsie to see what she did with hers. When she spit out her pits, she held up her napkin in front of her mouth. The next time Marc did that too. He tasted a dollop of sour cream. "Mmmm, *crème fraîche*."

"My grandmother ate it every day of her life and she lived to be ninety-five and never had a wrinkle. I intend to do the same. Will you have some Coca Cola to go with it, Marc?" Elsie extended the bottle towards his empty glass.

"I'd like some coffee," Connie said, "and I have a feeling Marc would too." The sour cream glop was bad enough first thing in the morning without diet Coke.

"Not at all," Marc said, "Coke has plenty of caffeine." He took a large sip from his glass and smacked his lips appreciatively.

After Elsie had insisted on helping them to seconds, she started telling Marc how much she loved baroque architecture. "In Michelangelo's great dome, the function of space was emotional," she said, squinting her eyes at Marc. "But that must be hard for a rationalist like you to grasp."

"Oh no," he said, "a tour of the baroque churches in Rome was a high point of my trip. The Bernini chapel...."

"Ah yes," Elsie broke in, delicately licking a trace of sour cream from the corner of her mouth. "Too bad the facade has been ruined by pollution. I hear it's positively black. Connie said you'd just gotten back from Europe. I can't imagine what pleasure you'd get from seeing things in that state."

Marc's face was pale but he made another effort. "Well, actually, the Swiss Alps where I skied were absolutely pristine."

Elsie took a sip of Coke. "I wouldn't travel anywhere, not with all those terrorists. It's really a state of anarchy. A while back, I read that a leading publisher, Feltrinelli, tried to blow up an electric company and ended by blowing himself up. Almost every week someone is shot or kidnapped. You were there. You must have heard how they kidnapped the Getty boy and cut his ear off."

Connie shuddered, picturing his parents opening the box and unwrapping the bloody cotton. It had the primitive quality of the Greek stories where adulterous women are served their lovers' bodies for dinner.

"Violence is everywhere," Marc said. "Look at what happened yesterday on Morningside Heights. Two kids were shot in a gang war. That's only fifteen minutes from here."

Elsie sighed heavily. "Children are always the ones that suffer most. Look at the children of divorce. I know an eight year old, just the age of poor little Mischa," she looked at Connie, "who became autistic when his father left. That reminds me, how is Sarah, Connie, you said she was sick. I was surprised you'd leave her when she wasn't well."

Connie felt as if her mother had probed an open cut. "It's just a sore throat, Mother. Sarah'll be fine in a day or two." Would she? What if while Connie was in bed with Marc, Sarah was screwing Mr. Ramon? She imagined Sarah hiding in a storeroom at school with Mr. Ramon lifting her skirt. Leaning her back against a stack of textbooks.

"You know, Mrs. Silver," Marc said defensively, "some children do fairly well. It's worse to be in a terrible marriage. Even the Italians recognize that. They just voted to keep their divorce bill. My daughter, Selina, was miserable when I was with my wife. She's doing much better now that she has separate time with each of us. I think it's a relief to her. And I'm certainly much happier."

Connie couldn't believe her ears. She nudged Marc hard with her knee under the table. Jesus, this was all they needed. She'd told him Elsie was sensitive about broken families. Connie wanted to show Marc off, not get into some horrendous argument.

"That may be," Elsie said coldly, "but I read a study recently that said no matter how much life improved for the parents, the children were permanently traumatized."

"That study had no control group," Marc said, rolling a piece of bread between his fingers. "I've treated kids who've gone through hell with abusive parents and who've blossomed in a second family with a sympathetic step-parent."

Connie felt her neck getting hot. Oh God, when was he going to stop? If her mother started questioning him she'd find out that Selina wasn't doing well at all. And if Marc really thought Selina would be happy if he married again, he was deluding himself. And Sarah? She was exploding already. Connie put her hand on Marc's knee and squeezed, then she coughed so loudly that he had to stop talking and pat her on the back.

"That's enough," she said meaningfully. "Thanks." Then she picked up the paper and turned to her mother. "Mother, can you believe this? A Jasper Johns painting was auctioned for $240,000."

"It's outrageous." Marc was tightlipped, "Rampant commercialism and greed."

Connie had just mentioned it to distract her Mother. She was surprised at his vehemence.

Elsie looked at him coldly. "Would you rather artists starve? Most people feel that way. Millions to defense and not a penny for art. That's the crime, not selling a painting for $240,000. A truly new and unique creation is priceless."

"Oh." Marc glanced at his watch then pushed his chair abruptly back from the table. "I lost track of the time. If I'm going to pick up a present for Selina before I get back to my conference, I'd better get going."

"Do you have to?" Connie asked, trying to get him to look at her. What in God's name was going on? She had assumed they'd leave together but he clearly wasn't going to wait for her. He looked like a man about to catch the last train.

"Oh, you're leaving so soon. What a pity." Elsie had a look of barely concealed triumph. "*I* never forget to leave myself time when I buy presents. You never get things right when you rush."

Marc was already in the entry hall.

"We'll meet for dinner then?" Connie called after him. He barely managed to grunt a yes. The cowbells clattered as he went out, adding a sort of ironic commentary. Suitor leaves palace in disgrace, transformed to a cowherd. Queen Elsie reigns triumphant.

They had gone into the bedroom because Elsie had said she wanted to lie down. "Fix my pillows," Elsie ordered, climbing onto the maple fourposter.

"Fix them yourself." Connie would have liked to take the pillow and push it against her mother's face. She felt as if she were going to cry with rage. "Did you have to be so bitchy, Mother? Marc was a total stranger. Did you have to treat him like that? Couldn't you be civil for an hour?"

"The man's a total fool. I can't see why you'd be interested in him. He's weak. He's going to drag you down." Her eyes bored into Connie, shrewd hawk's eyes. "If you think of him at all outside the bedroom. I don't know what's happened to your mind."

"If he acted badly, it's because you made him. Every time he opened his mouth, you cut him down. Nobody could shine in that atmosphere." It was like asking a plant to grow in oil instead of water.

Elsie's delicate nostrils flared. "Nonsense, the man's a Don Juan, an adventurer and a fool."

Connie stood her ground, hands on her hips. "He's been perfectly faithful to me."

Her mother gave her a contemptuous look. "And you haven't been faithful to your husband."

"Why did you invite me to bring Marc if that bothered you so much? You sounded as though you thought it was perfectly natural."

Her mother crossed one ankle over the other as though she were punctuating an invisible text. "I wanted to see if your marriage could be salvaged."

Connie pictured a boat slowly sinking to the ocean floor with her inside. Furniture and bits of clothing floating around it. Children's toys. "Salvaged?" She shook her head to get rid of the image. "I don't know why you're defending my marriage when you know how awful Howard is to me."

"But he is your husband." She pointed a well manicured finger at Connie. "I was faithful to Simon. You have to be faithful to Howard. I didn't want you to marry him in the first place but you made that choice and that's what you have to stick with. It wasn't until Simon died that I had a lover. And even though he was a very special man, I never thought of remarrying." Elsie tilted her head and glanced at her profile in the dresser mirror. "You only have one husband."

Connie felt her brain spinning. "But you told me you were heartbroken. You made me feel so guilty that I couldn't stay at college. You kept saying I had such a wonderful life...You mean all that time you had a lover? Why didn't you tell me? Why did you make me think Steve and I were all you had?"

"I couldn't tell you, Connie. He was married. Don't gape. It makes you look retarded. Really, I don't know why you're so surprised. Did you think I could paint without joy in my life?"

Connie hadn't thought about it, about the energy of her

mother's huge canvasses of naked men. It hadn't occurred to her that the vitality of her mother's work had anything to do with sexual energy. "So you're talking to me about adultery when you did it yourself?"

Elsie jiggled her top foot in small angry flicks. "The point is, there's a difference between having an affair and marriage."

"I'm not planning to marry Marc, if that's what you're getting at."

Her mother sighed through tight lips, steam released from the valve of a pressure cooker.

"But regardless of Marc," Connie looked at her warily, "I don't think I can stay with Howard."

Elsie was instantly upright, gesticulating with a ringed hand. "Don't you realize this is going to end in disaster and then you'll only come crawling back?"

Her mother had hit Connie's nightmare on the head. "No," she said, almost shouting, "I've got a job."

"What on earth for? You have a husband who's supporting you. Stay with him." Elsie stared at her as though she'd lost her mind. "I don't think you realize how confining it would be. Working nine to five like a secretary."

"It isn't nine to five, Mother," she said firmly, wondering how many times she'd taken her mother's word for things that were clearly wrong. "Besides, it's work I like and I want to do it. I need to feel independent."

Her mother's face contorted in a way that made Connie's stomach churn. "Listen, just let me tell you. If you think that man's going to stick with you when you've broken with Howard and have taken your little job, you're wrong. He likes you because you seem like a rich woman. You have time to dally and play kissy kissy. He won't feel the same way when you're working your fingers to the bone, believe me. Or don't. Do as you chose. You act so meek but you're stubborn underneath." Elsie sank back against the pillows and closed her eyes. "I'm exhausted. I don't want to hear any more about this job. Get out."

Connie looked up at the photo on the bureau. Her father in a sweater and jodhpurs held her, a fat, laughing baby, in his arms. She conjured up the image of her father urging her to put her horse over higher jumps. She saw him bending over, lifting the bar up a notch. Her stomach quivered. "Don't think, princess," he'd called to her, "just do it." Straightening her shoulders, she walked past her mother's bed and out the door.

Steve's apartment was only a few blocks away. She'd said she'd go riding with him at the Central Park bridle path. On the way she thought about Saint Mary's. Until today Connie hadn't felt totally committed to the job. But after this morning, she realized that it was the only way she was going to break free. Not just from Howard but from Elsie. Just having the thought of it in her mind had made her able to talk back to her mother. Her knees were trembling now from the stress of it but she'd done it. Suddenly she felt a wave of panic. Talking back was one thing, but how did she know she was going to be able to teach those kids? She wasn't even sure she had her old notes from graduate school—she rummaged mentally through her closet. When she got home she'd have to look for them. But who knows how out of date they'd be? There was probably a whole new way of reading by now.

Steve met her at the door with a big hug. She hadn't remembered how small he was. Connie noticed that the bald spot in the center of Steve's head had been replaced by thick brown curls. "Steve, I thought you were never going to get a toupee." She couldn't believe he'd done it. He would have looked great bald. People with symmetrical heads always did.

"It's not a toupee," he said, pretending to be offended. "It's natural, it's an implant."

"Big difference."

"You wouldn't say that if you had experienced the

process." He looked at her and grinned. "Izzy left her riding clothes in the bedroom for you. She would have liked to come herself but she had to go to the dentist with Josh."

Changing in the light, airy room, Connie thought how lucky Steve was. His wife, Izzy, was one of the kindest, most supportive people she knew. Always there for the children with hugs and an ear for their problems. And as if that wasn't enough, she was sophisticated, learned and charming. As she pulled on the smart black jodhpurs Izzy had left for her, Connie wondered enviously how Steve had managed to find her.

They took a bus across the Park and walked the few blocks to the stables, where their horses were saddled up waiting for them. Connie's was a black gelding with a gentle face and a star on his forehead; Steve had a big bay. They maneuvered along Central Park West trying to keep the horses from spooking at the traffic sounds and then suddenly they were in nature. Huge leafy trees, their leaves still fresh, not marked by soot the way they would be later in the summer. If she hadn't been so angry at her mother and Marc, it would have melted her heart. But she was in no mood to be nostalgic about her tricycle rides in the playground. Even her memories of canters along the bridle paths with her father had a gray cast to them.

"You know what Mother just told me?" she asked him as she pressed her knees into the black's sides, urging him into a trot. "My father's been dead since I was fifteen and she just told me she had a lover after he died. Did you know?" Steve's horse was throwing his head and taking little mincing steps to the side. Steve stroked his neck with one hand, not looking at her. "You did know. Why didn't you tell me?"

"She asked me not to." He was making his horse walk in slow circles to quiet it.

Connie pulled up and waited for him. "Well, who was it, dammit?"

"Randolph Guest," he said, letting the horse move forward

again.

She saw Guest, short, balding, with wide sensual lips, intelligent eyes. "My God, Jeanne's husband? How could she do that to her best friend?" Connie's horse tried to snatch at a leafy branch growing beside the path and she yanked the reins viciously.

"You know how she is."

"But Jesus! That man!"

"Right. He's a pompous ass. A hopeless narcissist. Just like her. I went over for dinner once when he was there and he never let me get a word in edgewise."

Connie kicked her horse into a canter and Steve followed her. The thudding of the horses' feet felt like blows, striking and bruising the earth. Her horse was beginning to sweat but she didn't let him stop until his sides started to heave and she could hear him blowing. Steve reined in beside her and they walked their horses up to one of the stone tunnels that spanned the path. Boys were perched on the edge throwing spitballs.

"So why did it stop?" she asked when they came out on the other side. "This affair?"

"Very simple. He got sick. You know how she hates sick people. Remember when I had bronchitis? She wouldn't go anywhere near me. I thought I was going to die. Finally she hired a trained nurse to take care of me." Steve loosened his rein and the bay stretched his neck gratefully. He was calming down, sensing a good rider.

"She used to wear a face mask when I had a cold."

Steve gave her a crooked smile. "It's lucky we have each other. Most people wouldn't believe the stuff she did to us."

"Well, at least we had a sane father, who brought us handcrafted puppets when we were sick. He probably would have wiped our noses too, but he had to go to work." There was still a box of puppets and marionettes in her closet at home. A comic Punch with a long nose, richly dressed princesses and naive looking animals. "He was everyone's Rock of

Gibraltar."

A pregnant woman walked alongside the bridle path in a pink sweat suit pushing a baby stroller with a radio tucked in the back. "*Stop in the name of love*," called out Diana Ross and the Supremes as they rode by. Connie looked after the woman. Young and tired. She'd stopped all right.

"I don't see it that way," Steve said, taking his feet out of the stirrups for a minute and flexing his feet. "Elsie and he were made for each other. Do you know, when I was only a little kid, he took me into his office and told me how worried he was about his investments. I couldn't have been more than six. Can you believe it? Asking a six year old for advice." He caught the stirrups again.

Connie noticed how perfectly he sat, thighs tight against the horse, ankles and knees in line, heels down. "Strange. With me he acted as though life was a three-ring circus." She wondered whether Steve was remembering correctly. It didn't sound like the same father.

"That's because you were a girl. He believed girls shouldn't think about money. He even took me in and showed me the new toilets he'd had installed at the firm. He was so proud of his plumbing."

"He was fastidious. I remember that. Told me to keep my nails clean, change my underwear."

"He was tense as hell. You just couldn't see it."

They rounded the last turn before heading back to the stable. Two men naked except for tennis shoes and ties raced by them. Steve's horse shied and began to back up. His nostrils were flared and pink inside. A temperamental animal. He would probably have thrown someone else.

"Easy boy," Steve patted his neck. "That's New York for you. Streakers. Jesus, they were stark naked."

"More power to them," Connie said. "People are frustrated, tired of cover-ups. I'd do it if I dared." She urged her horse into a slow trot, wanting to use her leg muscles. "Steve, what would you think if I left Howard?"

Steve trotted after her. "I thought you were getting along better," he said when he caught up. "He seemed mellower last time we visited."

"How can you say that?" Connie pressed her heels against the horse's side. He speeded up. "Most of my friends would throw a party for me if I said I was leaving him."

"You're my sister. I'm worried about you. It's dog-eat-dog out there. Do you know how many beautiful, talented women there are climbing the walls in New York? I'm sure it's the same in San Francisco. Maybe worse, with all the gays and swinging sex."

"You mean I'll never get another man so I should keep the one I have?" The horse was trotting so fast she hardly had time to rise before the next beat came. She started to get a stitch in her side.

"I'm not saying you're not attractive. But men who couldn't even get a date in college are walking away with prizes. I see it every day. Women clients are always crying on my shoulder."

"You're lucky you have an understanding wife."

"Don't be mad at me. It's just the way I feel. I don't take risks in the market either."

"It's okay." Connie swatted at a huge fly that was buzzing around her horse's neck, attracted by the sweat. "Security's a priority for me too. I'm basically a coward. All my big adventures occurred before I was five."

"Is it really so bad with him?"

She shook her head. "I just wondered what you'd think. Now I know. It's the sort of decision you have to make for yourself anyway."

"Notice how discreet I'm being. I don't even ask if there's a third party." His brown eyes moved over her face.

"Oh Steve...." She wondered for a minute if her mother was right, if the only place for Marc was in bed. He certainly couldn't hold his own against Elsie. She tried to imagine him at the dinner table with Izzy. He'd probably shock her.

Start talking about something inappropriate like dangerous liaisons.

"My urge to control the situation with brotherly advice is almost overwhelming. But I won't say anything else. If you need an ear to bend later, you know where to find me."

"Thanks. I probably will. Only right now things are too confused to even start explaining. I feel as though I've been living in the Stone Age and I've just been transported to the twentieth century."

Marc and Connie were sitting at a table in the Stanhope dining room arguing.

"Jesus, your mother's a witch," Marc said. It was like some horrible replay of a scene with Howard. That was just what he called her. It made Connie's head hurt.

"You got her tee'd off by talking about Selina and your marriage. You promised not to do that, remember? We agreed before we went."

"I don't remember agreeing on anything," Marc said angrily. "I don't think I even answered."

"That's funny because I distinctly remember a long conversation. I told you exactly what kind of a woman Mother was. That's why I felt like clobbering you when you started in about the benefits of divorce."

"What difference did it make? She would have found out about it sooner or later."

"I don't care. It was rude. I asked you not to do it and you did it. You didn't care a damn about my feelings. How can I rely on you for anything serious if you can't even do a little thing like keep your mouth shut?"

"Your mother got me rattled. I couldn't let her go on with that nonsense about damaged children."

"Why not? What earthly difference does it make if she thinks they're damaged? You're not in court. You didn't have to prove yourself to her."

"Didn't you see how she was working on you? Trying to

make you feel guilty, make you stop loving me. Why'd you take me to see her in the first place if you didn't want to see if I could stand up to her? Or did you secretly want her to win? There's something really sick going on between you two. Why did you take me if you didn't want to show me she lives in a God-damned museum? Even the bathrooms are full of your family history. Soft-focus photographs of a country place that looks like Camp David. Wasn't there some message I was supposed to get?"

"I wanted to show you off to her," Connie said. "You think I wanted to embarrass you? You can't be serious." She took a drink from her water glass but her hand was shaking so that she spilled half of it on the table and the front of her dress.

"I don't think you understand what you want." Marc put his napkin over the wet spot on the table. "She clearly didn't think I was good enough for you. Though what Howard has beats me. Unless it's his fancy street address. Or the fact that he voted for Nixon. What are your mother's values anyway? Don't marry down." His tone had a bitterness she'd never heard.

The wet fabric felt clammy against her skin. "You're the one that brought up money. You had to aggravate her by saying art wasn't worth paying for. Why couldn't you have picked on stock brokers? You did it and then you blame her. Mother doesn't care about money."

"Not much she doesn't. My God, Connie. Can't you see how much she cares? It's the air she breathes. She's the...."

"You have no right to be so mad at her. She was being perfectly nice to you."

"Nice! She's right there between us like a glass wall. I can see you but I can't have you." He hit the table with his fist. "You'll never marry me. It's all pure fantasy on my part."

That night, when they went back to the hotel, they crawled into bed soundlessly. Marc slept with his pajamas on and they were careful not to touch.

Thirteen

Connie had brought Mischa a miniature Evel Knievel stunt car. The stunt man was dressed in stars and stripes. Antidote to America's depression. Mischa looked at it uneasily.

"I almost got killed one night while you were gone," Sarah said before Mischa could say anything. "A truck swerved out of control and almost hit me head on."

"What?" Connie felt as though her chest was being squeezed by a giant fist. "Are you all right?"

"They called from the hospital," Mischa muttered. "Daddy had to go and get her. He was really mad because she didn't have a helmet and...."

"Shut up, you little toad. Tattler."

"Well, you were telling...."

"But you're all right?" Connie repeated.

"I had five stitches." Sarah took off the cap she was wearing and showed a white bandage on the back of her head. "I was lying beside my bicycle crying and shaking and the guy turned his truck around...."

Connie's stomach started to churn. "You were riding your bike at night? Without a helmet?" She could almost feel the thud of metal.

"You didn't really think I'd let Dad keep me locked up in my room, did you? While you had your fun in New York?" Sarah scrutinized the mark, only partially concealed by make-up, on her mother's neck. "I needed to talk to Juan. He's canceled the filmmaking trip. He's going to stay here."

That meant Mr. Ramon would be lurking in the background all summer. Connie opened her mouth but nothing came out. Oh God, she thought, what can I say to her? She knows what I've been doing. Connie could see Sarah on the edge of the road, her hair matted with blood. Sarah could have been killed and where was she? Playing Juliet to a middle-aged Romeo. She felt sick. If she had to get on the scales now, her moral weight would be zero.

All through dinner, while Howard complained about Rabin's new cabinet, he was staring at Connie's neck. She had wound a light scarf around it, trying to cover the mark. Afterwards, when she was putting the dishes in the sink he came up behind her.

"You went to New York to meet someone," he said flatly.

Connie's hands started to shake. She set down the dinner plates she was holding and turned around, wiping her hands on her apron. "Whatever made you think of something so ridiculous?"

"I've been putting two and two together. Since I've been back you've been acting different. Fighting me, always flying off the handle. At first, I thought you were upset because of Sarah. But not now." He bent slightly forward as though he were davening in synagogue. "Going to see your mother usually puts you in bed for three days. This time, you went on a buying spree." He picked up the end of the purple chiffon scarf she'd gotten in New York and gave it a tug. She thought of Isadora Duncan who had been strangled when her scarf caught in her car wheels. "You look radiant. And I know why." He paused and Connie stared at him.

"You're wrong," she said, forcing herself to smile. "My

skin is just good because of all the walking I've been doing."

"Walking for hours on Saturday and Sunday? You never used to walk around the block unless I dragged you. You didn't like to walk. Remember?" He came towards her and she jumped up, afraid he was going to hit her. But he didn't even touch her. He stood quietly facing her.

"I'm getting older. I need exercise." Connie said.

"And what about all those phone calls? You used to blab your face off on the bedroom phone, never caring if you were making it impossible to hear myself think. Now you go into the study and close the door. Come on, I know you're talking to someone. And you never pick up my things anymore. The house looks like hell. You better tell me, Connie. Get it off your chest. It's a sin."

"Why, so you can stone me?"

He gave her a nasty smile. "It's that Price, isn't it? Isn't that what happens in those trashy novels you're always reading? A fast talking lady's man shows up at some stupid bitch's door and in five minutes they're screwing like rabbits?"

"Please stop, Howard. There's no one." She moved back a step and half turned away, her hand touching her scarf.

He reached out abruptly and pulled it off her neck. "You don't need to wear that scarf. I saw the mark when it slipped down."

The scarf must have rubbed off the make-up but she had the feeling that whatever she'd done to hide it, it would have come out. It was a sign of what was wrong with their marriage, like a fever blister or a plague sore.

"Well, I hope you know what you're doing," he said. "If you're planning to run off, you won't have a house or a car. You won't have a cent from me."

"That sort of tactic doesn't even work with Sarah, Howard. It's certainly not going to work with me."

"Don't you realize how lucky you are having me support

you? No. I can see by that look on your face you don't."

Connie hadn't told him that she'd gotten the job before she went to New York, because she didn't feel sure enough that she could do it. Or really wanted to. She didn't want him to shake her into giving up before she'd had a chance to think.

"Do you really feel like getting up every morning and being a waitress?"

"I don't have to be a waitress. I could teach. You get up in the morning, don't you?"

"Who's going to have you? Governor Reagan's trimmed our budget again. I can count the job openings on one hand." He splayed his fingers open, shaking them in her face. "And you know how many twenty-six year olds are out there applying for them?"

She wished she had a shot of brandy. She could imagine it going down her throat, giving her courage. "I've got a job already, Howard."

His jaw fell. "Oh, shit." In a minute he rallied but she saw his face was pale. "What is it, a community college? A holding pen for retards?"

"No. It's a regular four-year place, Saint Mary's." It was hard to keep the triumph out of her voice.

"A Catholic school? Oh, that's great. Good mornin' to you Connie, me dear. Did you hear the luvly sermon in chapel today? On the conversion of the Jews."

"Come on, Howard, it's a job. I'm not changing religions. And anyway it's none of your business."

"Since when isn't your life my business? You're still my wife, aren't you? Well?" He took her wrist. "Answer me."

"You should know. You don't need to ask me." She tried to pull away but he hung on.

"Look, I have nothing against your doing something useful with your time. Why not write another book at home? They'll just give you the remedial students and stick you with all the administrative details besides. Believe me, you'd hate it."

"I don't butt into your work. I didn't keep you from going to Israel after the Yom Kippur War even though I was afraid you'd get blown up by some terrorist." She wrenched her wrist free. "I have every right to try this if I want to." She moved away from him, rubbing the sore place. "And without your snide comments."

Connie was over at Marc's house pacing back and forth while he sat and watched her from his swivel chair. "That's it. I've made up my mind." She stopped in front of him. "Howard knows, and I'm leaving. I don't know quite when yet. I have to think out the details. But it's going to be soon."

"Good," he said, looking slightly bored. "At least you can make a decision."

Mischa had started an afternoon sports program and Connie had been coming early to pick him up so she could watch him at archery. She loved the sureness with which he pulled the arrow back to his ear. His physical vigor refreshed her. Today, though, he was in a special hurry to get home.

"Where's the fire?" she asked him.

"Dad's taking me somewhere." He rolled the car window down and then back up again. "Somewhere special."

She had barely parked when Mischa threw open the door and rushed into the house calling for Howard. When she came in, Howard was already putting on his hat.

"We're going to the pound," Mischa said, unable to contain himself any longer, "to get a dog."

Connie looked at Howard. "Am I hearing correctly?"

"I thought we needed some new life around here. It was either a dog or a baby. Would you like a baby brother, Mischa?"

Mischa pointed both thumbs at the ground. "A dog. I'm going to train it. Dad's already got me a book." He showed her a little paperback with a picture of a half-grown puppy. "I'm going to call it Pompey the Great."

"We could have another baby too," Howard said. "Your

mother loves children." Mischa made a face and ran out to the car with his book.

"Howard, I assume you're joking, but there's no way I'm going to get pregnant now. I've got things I want to do."

"Really, what? I thought nothing was as important to you as touching baby skin. I thought you'd be enchanted at the idea." His tone was ironic but she could see he was worried.

"I told you I was offered the job at Saint Mary's."

"Did I tell you the joke about the Mother Superior?"

"Yes, Howard, and it's not funny. Neither is the one about keeping women barefoot and pregnant, so you can skip that one. Having a baby is certainly not the solution to our problems, if that's what you're thinking. Though I can hardly believe even you would think that. You don't like children."

"I'd put up with another one if it would keep you happy." He reached for her hand.

She grimaced. "Happy! Since when have you thought about making me happy? For a brilliant man, you don't listen very well. I've been offered a job I want. I'm taking it."

His jaw set in the willful expression she knew so well. "We lost twenty Israeli children at *Ma'alot* just last month and you're thinking about a fucking job."

"Stop it with the sanctimonious crap, Howard. It doesn't work anymore. I'm not going to have another baby. Period."

"How long do you think you're going to last at Saint Mary's? You're fooling yourself if you think it's more than a year or two. While they look for someone better qualified. They're used to people with lots of teaching experience." Howard paced back and forth in front of her, stopping to shake his hand under her nose for emphasis.

"I T.A.'ed for a year when I was working for my doctorate," she said, holding her chin up, looking him straight in the eye.

"When was that, in the dark ages? How many years since you've gotten your degree? Mmm?" He put his face right up to hers, hands fisted on his hips. "Everything you've learned is out of date."

"I went through it once. It shouldn't be so hard to catch up." She tried to keep her voice steady. Tried not to think of the closet full of old notebooks, of her note pad with everything on it crossed out. She shouldn't be listening to him. She was having enough doubts about whether she could actually manage. She'd simply throw a coin. Heads she'd lecture, tails she'd have small discussion groups. Or maybe she'd alternate. The main thing was to decide.

"Do they know you can't spell?" He exclaimed excitedly, "That you're practically dyslexic?"

She felt tension creep up her back. "That's only when I'm flustered."

"Let's see. We'll pick something easy. *Appealing*." He paused with a malevolent grin. "Go ahead, spell it."

"Howard, this is silly. I won't." She felt a flash of paralyzing dread. She could see herself standing at the blackboard, a piece of chalk in her hand, trying to remember how to spell something. Even now, she couldn't remember if *appealing* had two *l*'s or two *p*'s.

"See," he said triumphantly. "You'll make a fool of yourself."

"Dad, hurry up," Mischa yelled from the car, "and bring me some cookies. Please."

"Where are his cookies?" Howard asked.

"In the cupboard. Where else?"

Howard opened the cupboard door and picked out some Fig Newtons. "Think about it, Connie. You're a good mother. You like babies. It's what you know how to do best."

The next day, Marc's father had a heart attack and Marc flew to Boston to see him. Connie went down to his house. She'd promised to water his philodendrons. It felt lonely in his room without him. She turned on the radio and listened to a commentator talk about Kissinger's resignation threat. Good for him, Connie thought. He has done too much good to get caught in the mud with Nixon. She pictured Nixon sinking in black slime with only his eyes showing while Kissinger waved goodby from a rising helicopter. Marc was right, Nixon deserved to be shot. Instead of cowering in the White House filled with shame for what he'd done, the man was actually touring the Middle East. How could he hold his head up, she wondered. Shake hands with President Sadat. But he was doing more than that. He was offering Egypt atomic power. Not content with being a thief and a liar, he wanted to increase the chances for nuclear war.

When she called Marc a few minutes later, she was shocked to hear that his father was dead. Marc said he'd tell her all about it when he got home. Now he was at his mother's helping her get ready for the funeral. He said his mother was taking it pretty well. It was a comfort to her for him to be there and he was glad he could do something. It seemed incredible that he could sound so calm.

After Marc came home, Connie took one look at his face—his eyes had a matte look—and simply took him in her arms and held him. When he didn't rally after a few days, she wondered if he were in danger of a serious depression.

When she came over to his house, he was lying on his bed, surrounded by newspaper accounts he had clipped of the latest discrepancies between the transcripts and Nixon's tapes. He hadn't shaved and he looked like a hobo. Besides catching up on the Nixon news, he said, he'd been making some notes about his father, but he didn't want to show them to her.

"It might help if you talked about him. It doesn't have to be awful. You could start with the good things you remember from childhood." This was a strategy she'd tried with her mother when she was depressed. To prompt him, Connie told him a few stories of things she'd done with her father. She described how they used to ride through the fields around their farm. "The horses always farted as they warmed up. Green hay music, my father called it."

"You're lucky," he said wearily, not at all amused. "He's as real to you as if you'd been riding with him yesterday. I can't remember anything like that."

Connie had an urge to pull him off the bed and into the shower but she thought he'd feel better if he did it himself. She limited herself to picking up the cigarette butts and orange peels from his bedside table. In the midst of the mess was a faded photo of himself in short pants standing next to his father.

"You said your father taught you how to play stickball." Connie thought the man had a mean face. Mean and dull at the same time.

"Please, Connie, I'd rather not talk about him. Not yet. I know that's how you deal with things. But I don't want to. Nothing connects for me right now."

One day about two weeks after his father died, Marc asked Connie to go out in the garden with him. There was a love seat covered with worn green cloth and they sat in it swinging gently and listening to the birds. Like brother and sister, she thought. "It was wonderful how Dad brightened when he saw me. Patted the bed next to him for me to sit down." Connie pressed his fingers gently, urging him to go on. "Poor guy. His hand was so paper thin you could almost see through the flesh. And what indignities they put them through. The nurse came in to fix the catheter while I was there. Fiddling around as if it was a drain pipe and not a man's penis. You almost couldn't recognize it anyway, all shrunken up. More like a child than a man." Marc cried telling her this. She put her arms around him, feeling a wave of fear, willing him to control himself. It's going to happen to all of us, genital rot, skin slough. Your father was an old man, Marc. Don't take it so hard. She thought about her father dying at fifty, his eyes still bright, full of his future. The good times they were going to have after the war. When it was finished, he was going to get her a colt to raise.

"He was waiting to die until I got there, Connie. Not my mother, not my brother. Me. He looked right in my face, told me he loved me, and died." Marc smiled and pushed his sneaker against the grass. The swing started up again.

"I'm glad you had that at least." Connie was relieved at how consoled he seemed. For a moment she envied him his chance to say goodbye to his father. She'd been at camp hundreds of miles away when her father died. But what would they have said to each other? They were too close to need words.

"I was always too hard on him," Marc said suddenly, pushing the swing faster. "It wasn't fair. I always blamed him for not controlling things at home." Connie listened intently. Was he finally going to tell her something? "Once my mother got so enraged she threw an inkwell at the wall. Yelled curses in Rumanian. He didn't do anything. Just stood there, embarrassed."

"I thought you told me your father was German," Connie said. She'd been picturing him in a dreary shop eating bread and bratwurst. Now she had a sudden image of castles set in wildly romantic landscapes.

"He was. But she was Rumanian. He met her on the only trip he ever took. He should have stayed at home." He jumped off the swing into the grass. "I shouldn't have told you that story."

"Why not? What's so terrible about it? It sounds exotic to grow up listening to curses in Rumanian."

"What did I know about exotic? I was just a kid. The point is, I thought he was weak. Well, in a way that was natural. If a man can't handle a woman, he's a passive wimp. But I was a shmuck. I couldn't see my hand in front of my face. My father knew what he was doing. Maybe you shouldn't sacrifice yourself like that, but my old man knew what he was doing."

Connie couldn't make sense of what Marc was saying. He

seemed to be tying himself up in knots. Why couldn't he accept it? He had a wimpy father. Did he have to turn him into Jesus Christ? She looked at Marc and felt her stomach turn over. This was worse than New York. He hadn't helped her then with her mother but at least he'd made an effort. Now he seemed to be moving rapidly backward and inward.

"I guess it was Dad who taught me to care for people. From the age of three I was taking care of everyone in the family. I remember when I was three, watching my brother's baby carriage. It was God-awful hot and I had to pee like crazy. Ma must have forgotten about me. She was out somewhere collecting new herbs for her elixirs. Finally I gave up and peed on the walk."

There was a whirring sound overhead and Connie looked up to see a hummingbird spiraling down in his crazy mating flight like a tiny dive-bomber.

"Elixirs?" Connie asked, brightening. "What was she, a medicine woman?"

Marc looked evasive. "Oh, she made all kinds of potions from flowers and roots. She sold them in the back of the store. Actually they did quite well, all natural ingredients. For cramps and headaches and love troubles."

"Sounds like she should have given some to your father," Connie said, curious. This was the first time Marc had said anything about his mother.

"Yeah, poor guy. He thought she'd settle down after he married her. But she never felt comfortable in the house. She was happiest when we lived in the country for awhile. I'd wake up in the morning and see her out in the yard collecting morning dew to put in one of her bottles. The kitchen was filled with piles of rose petals and herbs. But we always ran out of milk and bread," Marc sighed. "I helped Dad shop, carried groceries." Connie pictured him lugging a bag as big as he was up flights of dark stairs while his mother stirred a cauldron like a witch.

"I guess a lot of kids have to do that sort of thing." She

chewed on a grass stalk, squeezing out the drop of sweetness. Maybe that was why Marc had been attracted to her. Because she'd been such a proper wife and mother. "Your mother was probably overwhelmed having two babies so close together."

He snorted. "She wasn't overwhelmed, not Ma. Her astrology charts told her she ought to stay in bed and rub chicken fat on her stretch marks. I was up and down the stairs all day bringing her stuff. Cotton balls to wipe my brother's ass. Beer to give her more milk."

"Your mother sounds like quite a character," Connie said laughing, "and you were a *wunderkind.* Boy, I wish I'd had that kind of service." Marc had been a good kid, there was no doubt about it. But was he really such a hero? Marc was looking at her wide-eyed, as though he was waiting for her to give him a medal.

"Sit with me while I take a bath," he asked her. He climbed into the tub and lay back passive and relaxed in the warm water. "You know, when I first married Alix, she was having a terrible time at the office. I used to hold her in my arms night after night and let her tell me about her boss and ask me how to cope."

"Isn't that natural? To want to talk to your husband?" Connie listened to him with a sinking heart.

"Of course, I wanted her to feel better. I did everything I could think of to help her. When she was sick after Selina was born, I took care of both of them. Selina was a colicky baby. She cried half the night. I used to walk her back and forth, holding her on my shoulder. The minute I stopped, whammo. She had an amazingly piercing wail for such a fragile little thing. But what did it all come to? Sometimes I feel so bad." He sank down deeper in the water, closing his eyes. "I put so much into my marriage. But it was ruined. I'm afraid it could happen again."

"You were unfaithful, weren't you?"

"I told you, it was just sex. Alix couldn't give, she could

only take."

"You seem to have an excuse for everything. You took women to bed. Don't you have any guilt over it? Do you really think it doesn't matter? You seem to blame everything on Alix."

"Watch out," he told her. "If I really let go and told you what I think, you'd feel worse than you do now."

"Try me."

"Don't imagine I haven't thought about my part in it. I don't do it much, I admit. Usually it's too painful. I'm afraid if I looked deep enough what I'd see would drive me around the bend. Once I went away for a weekend determined to reach that place. I sweated and cried for a day but I couldn't reach it. I'm not looking at you now," his eyes were still closed tight, "because you are closer than anyone to knowing what it is."

"And you don't want me to?" He shook his head, evasive.

"You sound pretty attached to your mystery. Maybe if you got a closer look, it would be simply boring. And you'd be glad to get rid of it." She'd read somewhere that certain people treat their neuroses like sacred cattle. To calm her nerves, she started washing him like a child. She lifted his arms and soaped them carefully, cleaning between the webs of the fingers and under his arms. She had a vivid memory of his washing her hair at the Stanhope. She couldn't stand the yearning it set up in the pit of her stomach.

The dog Howard got was still only a puppy. She was a cute little thing, part terrier and part poodle with a tail that arched over her back. Mischa was teaching her to sit, patiently giving the command, pressing her rump down. They were out in the back yard on the grass.

"The thing has worms, Mom," Sarah said. Connie had expected she'd be happy because her grounding was over, but she'd been in an obnoxious mood for the last couple of days.

"She doesn't," Mischa yelled. "Make Sarah stop saying that." The puppy lunged away and came up hard at the end of the ugly red plastic leash Howard had bought Mischa.

"Just look at her shit. You can see them wiggling around. The worms crawl in," Sarah sang, "the worms crawl out, the worms play Pinochle on Pompey's snout."

"Sarah, that's not really necessary." Connie put a restraining arm on Mischa's shoulder. "It's nothing to be ashamed of if she does have worms, Mischa. Most puppies have to be wormed. It's okay."

"Sarah said the medicine tastes like poison and it'll make Pompey hate me."

"Then I'll give it to her. Or we'll take her to the vet."

"He calls her Pompey." Sarah looked scornful. "He doesn't even know it's not a girl's name. I'm going to call her Pom Pom. Here, Pom Pom," she called, and the puppy scooted over, pulling the leash from Mischa's hand, wriggling the rear part of her body, frantic with pleasure.

Mischa ran after her but Sarah wouldn't give her up. She rolled the dog over and scratched her fat stomach.

"Pom Pom likes this. Don't you, you silly dog? Maybe I'll put her in my video. Hola! Wouldn't you like Pom Pom to be a movie star, Mischa? I could dress her in a little red skirt." She lifted the dog up and twirled her around, singing mockingly, *My Ding-A-Ling*. "She could be our revolutionary mascot."

Mischa looked puzzled for a minute. Connie could see him trying to figure out what a mascot was. Then his face got very red. "She's going to hunt ducks. Not be in your stupid movie." He picked up the puppy and carried her into the house.

And this was supposed to be a pleasure?

"I don't see what's the matter with Borrega Springs. We could take the kids and our new puppy for a family vacation. See the flowers." Howard picked up his paper and followed

Connie into the kitchen. Connie could see the photographs of Israeli bombers on a retaliatory flight, this time into Lebanon. If they kill our children, we'll kill theirs.

She put the plates in the sink and turned on the water. "They're not blooming in the desert now, Howard. It'll be boiling hot." His idea of a vacation was always to go to the most uncomfortable place possible. London in winter. A tropical rain forest in mid-summer. If not that, it had to be a place where you could pick your own vegetables. He loved pulling radishes out of the dirt.

"You pick a place then. Come on. It'll be fun."

"I thought you said if God meant people to spend time outdoors he wouldn't have let them invent houses." Why the urgency all of a sudden?

"You have a perfect memory for the inessential."

"Four minutes." She looked at her watch. "I knew that even if you were trying, you couldn't be nice for more than five." It was like asking a leopard to change his spots. But she had to admit, Howard was making more of an effort lately. Even if it always broke down sooner or later.

"What would you do if I weren't mean? You'd be bored."

This time, it was sooner. "That would be my problem then. But so far I haven't had to cope with it, have I?" She tried to imagine a perpetually kind Howard without his negative wit. She only saw him stumbling around in a badly worn jacket looking for his glasses.

"So now you want to go out and be a liberated woman. With this bloody job. I still don't see why you can't work perfectly well at home."

"What kind of home life do I have? You're out all night. I get to cook and shlep." She stacked the dishes on the drain board.

"I bought Mischa a puppy, didn't I?" Howard said proudly. "He loves the dog." The night before, she'd found little notes scattered around the house imitating her handwriting. "I will try harder to be a good mother to my beautiful new puppy. I will remember to buy a new box of tiny doggy wieners."

"It's just another thing for me to take care of." Connie started to sponge off the counter, irritated at the way Howard stood there without doing anything. She threw him a dish-towel. "I haven't seen you cleaning up when she messes in the house. And now she has worms."

"That's Mischa's responsibility," he said, as though he were explaining an obvious point to a student. He dabbed at the plate with the towel.

"Well, how's he going to learn if you don't teach him?"

"What's there to teach?" He lifted his eyebrows, "You just throw some paper towels on it and scoop it up with the dust pan."

"And then I'm left to wash the floor. The maid's certainly not going to do it."

"We'll get another maid then."

"That's not the point. It's you and me and the way we do things together. Don't you see? It's just not working. Getting another maid won't help. I want to get out. I'm going stir crazy. I need to have people to talk to about my work, colleagues. Besides, if I make some money I could support myself." She couldn't bring herself to say, get divorced.

Howard clenched his jaw, the muscle ticking. "Support yourself? You're dreaming. Do you know how much those jobs pay? Eight thousand a year. Do you really think you can keep up a house and support two children on that? Give it up. It's crazy."

It didn't sound like much when he put it that way. "I could borrow."

"From whom? That lunatic mother of yours? I don't think even she is going to approve of this. Her daughter downwardly mobile. Joining the toilers and grubbers."

"I wasn't planning to ask her."

"Well, then." He blew out his breath and sat down on one of the kitchen chairs. "Who? You have no credit, remember.

It's all mine. And you can't think any bank is going to give you a loan just like that."

"I don't see why not, when I start working." She realized she didn't know what you needed to get credit. Maybe you had to have been working for years. She'd have to find out.

"Starting out in the hole, you'd end up in deep shit." He brought his hand up under his nose to illustrate just how deep she'd be. "You know that, don't you? You'll be lucky if you can grade your papers on time. If I were you, I'd concentrate on that and not mouth off about supporting yourself." The word seemed to grate on his nerves. He scratched his arm as if he was ridding himself of a biting insect.

"I'll do what I have to," she said with as much dignity as she could muster. Getting papers back on time began to seem easy in comparison to getting the bills paid.

Howard sensed her uncertainty. "Most people would give their eye teeth to be in the position you are right now," he said in his most convincing parental voice, authority tempered by mercy. "You don't have to do anything." He stressed the word "have," looking into her eyes. "Nothing at all. Just sit around on your tush and amuse yourself. Eat chocolates. Collect elephant tusks or old lace. Don't be so set on giving yourself heartache. Believe me, I've worked for over twenty years. Whatever you think you're getting, it won't be worth it."

That night Connie couldn't sleep. She went into her study and looked up their old income tax figures. Then she got a pad and pencil. Howard had been right, she wasn't going to make nearly enough to keep them going. The blackness outside her window was oppressive. She lowered her shade and turned on the overhead light. Her eyes burned. It wasn't going to be easy to make up the difference. She imagined whittling down their life. Expensive camps, extra lessons, private schools. A lot of that would have to go. Her gym, riding? She didn't buy expensive clothes. The housekeeper?

She wouldn't have any idea until she figured it out how much difference those things would make. I must be crazy, she thought. I can barely manage now with Mrs. Whitely coming in to clean. How am I possibly going to do it if I'm working? And the reason we put the children in private schools is that they're good and Mischa needs the extra attention. She'd have to think of something else. Do that only as a last resort. Maybe there was some way she could get a loan from St. Mary's. In the morning she'd call Sister McKinney. Maybe she'd call the bank too and ask about second mortgages. Could she even get a mortgage without Howard? There was so much she'd never had to think about. It definitely was not going to be a picnic, being on her own with the kids and a new job. She picked up her pen and tried calculating again to make the figures come out better but she was too tired. The numbers began to slide in and out of focus.

She went back to bed and slid in quietly so as not to wake Howard. The roses he had brought her were on the bedside table. They gave off a sweet, heavy smell. She'd thought he'd gone out for the night and then he'd come back with them. Long-stemmed too. And a card with a Victorian woman swooning in a man's arms. She reached out and fingered the card. She should have thrown it out. Suddenly she felt a strange sensation. As though she were a candle being snuffed out. Nothing left but a vague smoke. It was more frightening than the loneliness she'd felt when her father died. She wasn't missing anyone. But she couldn't find herself.

She tucked the blankets around her and tried to think. What if Howard had been frightened enough to really change? He was already doing things he'd never done before, like bringing her flowers. She pictured him bringing her chocolates, taking her on vacations. Even as she was running it through her head, Howard started to slip up, give an insult instead of a compliment. "Oh shit," she told the image in her head. "Come on, Howard."

"I can't stop," he told her once after a party when he was drunk and confidential, "any more than Swift could stop writing satire." Maybe for a month or two. Then the moment he was sure of her, he'd be at her again. Tearing her down. Probably worse than before because she'd made him uncomfortable.

She crossed her arms over her chest, hugging herself. Once when she visited him before they got married, she'd found his bathroom floor crawling with ants. She'd flooded them out with boiling water. But the next day they were back. Appearing from all the crevices. That had been a good thing to do then. It would be stupid now. She saw herself ineffectually armored in apron and headscarf. Tilting at ants instead of windmills. Fighting what was bound to come back.

Connie was sitting in the kitchen talking on the phone to Steve about her job. Just before she called him, she'd been looking at her calendar, counting the weeks until the term started.

"You have oodles of time," Steve said. "Come on, chin up. You're just having first job jitters. It happens to everyone. Think how Isabel Peron feels suddenly finding herself president of Argentina."

Connie thought Isabel Peron looked like a bitch. "What about you? Whenever I've seen you on the phone with clients, you look so calm." She couldn't picture him really frightened.

"Half the time my stomach's in knots. Bow knots, double hitches, the works. You know about men and their calm surfaces, don't you? Believe me, it's learned behavior." Connie couldn't imagine ever having a calm surface. She felt like one of those cows with glass windows in its side. Anyone who looked could see the cud churning, faintly green.

"Do you ever have those nightmares where you're falling slowly off a cliff without being able to stop yourself? I wake up at night drenched in sweat, my nightgown sticking to me." She thought at first what she was feeling was a practical fear that she'd be short of money, but that was just a cover for something deeper. It was really a fear of being responsible for herself, for the first time in her life.

"You should be congratulating yourself. You'll be the first woman in your family to have a job. The Queen Bee never worked, or Grandma or even Izzy. Mother couldn't even write a check after Dad died. She had to hire that mouse-faced Mormon secretary to do it for her. If you think where you're coming from, you're doing great."

She was horrified to feel a great clump of anger dissolve in her stomach, flooding it with bile. He'd had the guts to do something with his life. Found a way to feel good about himself. While she'd been busy being a God-damned service station. She fought it down. "Thanks, Steve," she said.

After she got off the phone Connie looked over her texts again. She almost knew them by heart but it didn't reassure her. The things she wanted to say seemed either too trivial to bother saying, or too complicated for the students to understand. She wished she could just read them aloud to her class. A famous teacher of hers had done that in college. Old Nick would read them a bit of Herbert or Marvell, lean back, smile, and say in that deep voice of hers, "Ladies and gentlemen, a gem." The *Aeneid* was actually beginning to get on Connie's nerves. Aeneas could be unbearably priggish. Well, let the students discuss it, she thought. Let them run the class for awhile. Debate, read their papers aloud. But no matter how many times she made reasonable suggestions to herself, she ended imagining standing in front of twenty pairs of staring eyes while her panties somehow slipped down and lay limply around her ankles.

That afternoon, she had an appointment with a divorce lawyer. She listened to the news on the way over. Nixon was meeting with Brezhnev. She was fascinated by the way Nixon continued to function as president while the impeachment process gained momentum. He was like a chicken that keeps running around even after its head has been cut off. But what was so strange? She was still functioning as a wife, wasn't she? More or less.

The lawyer had an office overlooking Lake Merritt in Oakland. His fees were less than the San Francisco lawyers she had called and he was what she had expected. Somber and a little down at the heels, in a brown suit that had seen better days and a tie with white dots the size of lima beans. He did counseling on the side.

"First, tell me what the status of your marriage is. Are you still living together?" She nodded. "Have you asked for a divorce?"

"No. Not yet. I thought I should check out what my rights are before I go blindly plunging into this thing," she said, taking the chair across from him. "Is there a chance my husband could get custody of the children?"

"He could fight you for them. But usually these things are by agreement. Would he have any grounds for finding you unfit? Excuse my bluntness." He smiled. A nice smile, not oily or slick and she felt briefly reassured. "Ever had a breakdown?"

That startled her. "No. But my mother has had a couple." She pictured Howard telling the jury about her bad genes. Latent schizophrenia.

He gave a little laugh. "Don't worry. That won't cut any ice. The best judge on the divorce circuit has a mother in Langley Porter." He scratched something on his pad with a stubby pencil. "If there was guilt by heredity, we'd all be in trouble. Nope. It has to be you. Do you drink heavily? Take drugs? Anything like that?"

Connie hesitated. He was tactfully studying his pad. "I've been having an affair. That wouldn't be something my husband could use, would it?" Her cheek began a slight annoying twitch.

"It depends. Have you involved the children? How old are they, by the way?" He gave her another smile. He had reassuring hands too, short and practical like a farmer's. But she was still afraid, as though he were merely soothing her, not telling her the worst.

She told him they were sixteen and eight. "And I don't know about involved, but they've certainly seen him."

"Water?" he asked her, pouring a glass from a pitcher on his desk. She nodded and he handed it to her. "Sometimes a father has been able to prove unfitness. If there have been several different men in a short span. Or if there's evidence that a woman's lifestyle makes her neglect the children. But if the child has seen something sexual. Or been touched." He ran the edge of his hand across his throat. "That's the kiss of death."

Connie thought of the time she'd come back from Marc's and Mischa had said she smelled funny. Could that be built into a case for corrupting her child? She felt as though moral spots were appearing on her face like the pox that was raging through India, killing thousands every day. It was suddenly impossible to swallow.

"What's really important in custody is whether you can take care of the kids financially."

"Well," she croaked. She was losing her voice. It sounded like a rusty gate. "I'll have a job starting in the fall."

"Full time?"

"Part-time teaching."

He pursed his lips. "I'm afraid that won't get you very far."

She felt as though she were about two feet high talking to a bemused giant. Like Gulliver with the Brobdingnagians. It was scary. "I figured I'd get child support," she said with as much conviction as she could muster. "And some alimony. Though I'm not sure how much to expect."

"A lot of women aren't taking alimony nowadays. But I think a woman deserves some recompense for years of service. That's probably old-fashioned of me. Anyway, the amount's very variable. Does your husband know about the job?"

She nodded. "Why, is that bad?" She caught herself watching his lips as though he were an oracle.

"He might want to claim you're self-sufficient. Probably he'd want a phase-out sort of thing, that goes down as your salary goes up. I'd fight it, of course. It's obvious you need the money."

"Thanks." She tried to smile. But she was feeling increasingly depressed. "Well, at least I'd have the house. I don't think he'd try to take that."

"Was it yours before you married?"

"No."

"Then by California law, it's at least half his." He cleared his throat, giving her a chance to take in the implications. "Have you considered he might want to sell it, take his half out?"

"No, no, I hadn't." The back of her head began to throb with the beginning of a headache. Was she really going to be able to go through with this? She'd counted on the low mortgage payments. Even imagined that she could borrow on the house. Jesus! What if Howard did decide to sell? With so much resting on it, the teaching job was beginning to feel as risky as a tightrope act. What if she couldn't do it? Maybe she'd freak out like Sylvia Plath the moment she got in front of the students. Then she'd be stuck with rent on an expensive apartment in addition to everything else. By the time she left the office and climbed into her car, her head felt like the sidewalk under a power drill. God, even the damn car was only half hers. She imagined Howard cutting through it, leaving an open section, like a sliced lemon. The half car would keep spinning for awhile on its two wheels before it flopped down on top of her.

When she brought Mischa home from rec camp, he wanted to play Sorry, so she sat on the terrace in the sun and threw the dice and they moved their men around the board. She should have put "expert kid collector" on her vitae, she thought, "great at children's games."

"I made an atom bomb killer in shop today." The puppy

was nibbling his shoe laces. He lifted his foot out of reach. "It looks like a rocket. Bombs fall apart when it hits them and nobody gets hurt. I called it Mischa the Great." There was a sort of desperate bravado in his voice.

They must have been talking to the kids about the summit in Moscow, Connie thought. "Good for you. You're helping make the world a safe place. You should send it to President Nixon." She patted his bare knee and he flinched away. She wanted to take him in her arms and rock him like a baby, kiss him and make it better. But sooner or later she was going to have to find a way to talk to him.

"I don't want to send it to him." Mischa's voice was querulous. "Tony's dad says he isn't going to be president anymore. Is that true? Can you really fire a president?"

All of a sudden she heard a noise from inside the house. Her first thought was that it was a burglar. "Stay here, Mischa, and move my piece for me." But as soon as she got to the stairs she heard Sarah's voice shouting at someone. "God damn it, I can't mellow out. It's not like sharing a book."

Without thinking she started up the stairs. When she got to the landing, she could see Sarah's door open. She burst into her bedroom. Mr. Ramon was standing right inside the door holding Sarah's arm. He was wearing a sweatshirt and tennis shoes as though he'd just come from working out. Working out? With Sarah?

"What in God's name do you think you're doing here?" Connie screamed. "Not just in my house but in my daughter's bedroom. Get out or I'll call the police."

He let go of Sarah's arm and made an appeasing gesture towards Connie. "You're the one who got her upset in the first place. I'm just trying to help her adjust." Connie opened her eyes wide. The insolence of this creep. "For such a bright kid, I can't see why she failed her math final. I told her she could take a make-up in the fall if she studied this summer."

"Don't talk about me as if I'm not here." Sarah punched him in the arm. "Don't use 'she.' I hate it."

"How can you act as if you're doing math homework?" Connie asked Mr. Ramon, "My God, you're in her bedroom."

"I have the book with me." He showed her. *Trigonometry 1*. It had a sickly green cover.

She pushed the book away furiously. "Do you seduce all your students, or only the prettiest?"

Just then the front door banged shut and they stood looking at each other. Someone had come in while they were arguing.

"It's Dad," Sarah shouted. "He's going to kill him."

Howard rushed up the stairs. "What's all this yelling?" he asked. Then he caught sight of Mr. Ramon. "Who the hell are you?"

Mr. Ramon drew himself up to his full height. "I am Juan Ramon, your daughter's teacher."

"My daughter's lecher, you mean." Howard balled his hands into fists. "Why you sly, sneaking little bastard!" Mr. Ramon tried to step around him but Howard grabbed him by the collar, his face red with rage. "What are you doing in her bedroom?" Mr. Ramon tried to answer but Howard took hold of his sweatshirt. "How do you dare show your face here, you brazen son of a bitch." Mr. Ramon had his hands on top of Howard's, trying to loosen them. "I was tutoring her," he gasped, "that's God's truth."

"Playing with her tits, you mean, don't you, you unprincipled scum. What do you think I am, an idiot? You could do math in a library." Connie was amazed at the strength Howard's anger gave him. He was shaking Mr. Ramon back and forth like a sack of flour. "You think I don't know what you do in a bedroom? Huh?"

Mr. Ramon was sweating. "Talk to her." He rolled his eyes at Sarah. "She asked me to come in. She told me you wouldn't mind."

"Not mind! That a man twice her age is in my girl's bedroom! You wanted me to throw you a party, maybe? Put out the welcome mat. Take tickets." A drop of spittle fell onto Mr. Ramon's face. "This is my daughter we're talking about, not some Latin whore. Sarah," he called, "come here." Sarah didn't move. She had one hand over her mouth as though she was going to be sick. Mr. Ramon suddenly broke free and lunged around him. Howard grabbed him, locking him in a bear hug.

"I'm leaving. I don't have to take abuse from you." Mr. Ramon said. "I'll have you charged with assault."

Howard shoved him towards the stairs. "You'll charge *me*? You bag of grease!"

Connie felt her stomach drop the way it did on a roller coaster. She imagined Howard pushing Mr. Ramon down the stairs, cracking his skull against the bottom. She stared fascinated at Howard's brown shoes, scuffling against the heels of Mr. Ramon's sneakers. He didn't go down the stairs fast enough! Howard kept with him, shoving at the small of his back.

"Take your hands off me," Mr. Ramon said furiously. "Can't you see I'm going?" When they got to the door Howard pushed him outside and slammed it. Connie suddenly noticed Mischa standing open-mouthed by the foot of the stairs. He'd been watching this whole thing.

Howard started back up the stairs with a face like an Old Testament prophet.

"Mischa, honey, go feed the dog," Connie said. She didn't want him hearing any more.

Sarah was standing outside her door hugging herself with both arms.

"Get back in your room, Sarah." Howard took Sarah's arm and yanked her down the hall. "You make me sick," he said.

"I should have gone with him," Sarah said in a dull voice. "Then you wouldn't have had to fight." She looked at his jacket where a seam had given way under the arm.

"You think I'd let him walk off with you just like that?

Like snatching a loaf of bread from a counter? This is my house. You're my daughter." Howard slammed his fist onto her desk. "What hurts is having a child who doesn't know how to behave. How much are we supposed to take of this crap? Running off to Bolinas. Putting us through hell. Didn't you learn anything from that? Are you defective? Do you have worms for brains?"

Sarah hung her head, her red hair falling across one eye.

"Oh baby." Connie was suddenly overcome with sorrow for her. "The guy is a bastard. You shouldn't be giving him the time of day. It doesn't make sense."

"It doesn't have to make sense to you. It's my life," Sarah looked her full in her face. "I'm tired of your interfering. It's only making things worse." She took a deep breath, gathering courage. "If I want to throw myself down a sewer or let Juan beat me black and blue, that's my right."

"Right!" Howard shouted, turning scarlet. "To let him rough you up? How can you even think of such a thing? It's disgusting. What's the matter with you?" He took her arm and started to shake her. "If you're that crazy, I'll lock you up in your room for a year. I'll get someone to watch you. Three years. As long as it takes to bring you to your senses."

"Howard, what good is this?" Connie asked him. "Why don't you let her see if she can manage her life on her own if she wants to? That's what I'd do. Let her handle her own troubles for awhile. Mr. Ramon, school, the whole damn thing. See what she comes up with herself. That's the only way she's going to learn to be responsible. It's her show, run it or not."

"That shows how much you know about psychology," he sneered. "She doesn't need less supervision. She needs more. Sarah," he barked, "you have no right to anything. Do you understand? That bastard is not going to touch you, not hurt a hair of your head. Not while I'm alive to stop him. You won't go to school next year, if necessary. You'll study at home under lock and key."

"You can't keep me home from school, it's illegal." Sarah

tightened her body like an alley cat on a fence.

"Look, Sarah," Connie said angrily, "you're so busy feeling like a victim, you're forgetting what you've done. Broken all the rules. Had a man in your bedroom. You've behaved outrageously and you have to take some consequences."

"Now you're talking," Howard said, moving closer to Connie. "Lock her up the way they do in reformatories."

"You don't own me. I'm not your slave. It's my body." Sarah's face was set as if her defiance had been baked on. "If you lock me up, I'll stick pins in myself or burn myself on radiators."

"Sarah, stop it! You know you wouldn't do that. Why are you saying such hurtful things? This isn't love, it's just stubborn willfulness."

"Isn't that what love's all about? Hurting? Don't you hurt Mom all the time?"

Howard put his hand over her mouth. "Do you want me to gag you?" he asked. "Put a strait jacket on you? Because I will, if that's what it takes to shut you up. You won't be able to move a finger." He took his hand off.

"You control freak," she spat at him. "You don't know how to love anyone. Juan does. He'll get me out."

"I'll shoot his balls off if I see him within a mile of here. Can you get that through your thick skull?" He took a handful of her hair and tugged it.

"Don't, Howard," Connie held his arm. "That's not convincing her of anything." Furious as she was at Sarah, she didn't want him to hurt her.

"Can't I discipline my own child? I thought you wanted me to take an interest. Isn't that what you're always harping on? She's been throwing our life into turmoil for months. I'm fed up with it to tell you the truth. I think it's making trouble between us. That's what I think. And I'm going to deal with it."

"By making her into a mental patient? My God, Howard,

there must be some better way. This isn't the Soviet Union."

"You shut your mouth. I've had enough of your interfering. If you don't like it, get out. Get out," he repeated, livid. "Right out on the street if that's what you want."

Connie turned on him with a ferocity she hadn't known she had in her. "It's you that will go first. You," she shouted, "not me."

Howard went pale. "If it comes to that, it's my house," he said.

"Half yours. There's community property in California."

"We'll see about that." He let go of Sarah and started pacing.

"Don't threaten me, Howard. It won't do you any good."

He grabbed her arm so hard it hurt and started to twist it. She hit him in the muscle with her closed fist. "Take your hands off me," she hissed at him, "or I'll kick you."

He dropped his hand. "You always were a crazy woman. Even before we married. I should have sent you back to your mother and saved myself a lot of trouble."

"What was crazy was staying with a bully for seventeen years."

"Why don't you get a machine gun," Sarah screamed, "and just shoot her. Like the Israelis in Lebanon."

"I'll slap your mouth," Howard shouted. "Maybe that's what you need." He lifted his hand. Sarah ran into her bathroom.

"Lock the door, Sarah," Connie said. "Hurry."

"Bitch!" Howard banged on the wood. "Open up!"

Sarah didn't answer.

He kicked it. "I'll get an axe."

"Howard, come on." Connie spoke to him firmly, the way she had to the drunk who accosted her once in the park, "Leave her. She can't get away." He stood glaring at her, panting like a bull who's been charging at shadows all afternoon.

Fifteen

After the fight with Sarah, Howard holed up in his study with a bottle of white wine and Connie went into the kitchen and sat down at the table, chin cupped in her hands. This is it, she told herself, I can't take any more. We're killing each other. She could see Sarah turning into a delinquent if Howard pushed her hard enough. She wasn't the sort of girl who would stay locked up in her room. She'd find a way to get out. Run off to some street commune. Get pregnant. She felt her own stomach swelling with bile. She imagined ulcers forming, eating her insides. She was tired of playing twenty questions, hinting at leaving and letting Howard bully her into silence. Scared as she was, she had to tell him they were done for. Done in. Undone.

No one was in the mood for dinner. Connie made a sandwich for Mischa. Sarah stayed in her room. By the time they were ready to go to bed, Connie could see that Howard's anger had gotten tangled with lust. Despite the wine, he was tense. He wanted sex. She was determined to talk to him about a separation. The idea of sleeping with him made her feel physically sick. She kept looking at his mouth and she imagined his tongue tasting rancid as bad butter. She wondered if he'd drunk too much to be reasonable. Maybe she should just tell him she had a headache, take a sleeping pill and conk out. No. Then she'd have to key herself up to talk to him again tomorrow.

She put her pills on the bedside table and slipped under the covers, watching him undress with a sort of horrified fascination. She felt like the girl in *Dracula*, who watches the vampire slowly move towards her bed but is too terrified to scream. He was so thin he made her think of a wax figure of a corpse. His elbows seemed like flinty points. His collarbones jutted out. Even his skin had a yellowy, wax-like tone. When he had undressed and he turned to her in bed, she knew she had to do it now.

"I have to talk to you," she said, raising herself against the pillows and yanking her bathrobe down from the bedpost. "This marriage has been rotten," the words stuck in her throat, "for a long time."

His hand had been groping for her breast. Now he sat bolt upright next to her. "It's this business with Sarah," he started.

"No, it's not." She drew the robe around her shoulders, sliding her arms in. "That was just the last straw. You're in a rage all the time. About everything. It's torture to be around you. You make everything worse. What if you had broken Mr. Ramon's head? Getting yourself put in jail for life wouldn't have helped Sarah. Locking her up won't help either. This isn't the Israeli army."

"Tell me what you want," he said, as though it were simply a question of a broken dish and not a marriage.

"What am I supposed to tell you?" she asked him, crossing her arms over her breasts, holding herself firm. "Be sane, reasonable, mature. What's the point? You can't do it. It would be different if there was anything positive left, Howard. But I can't think of anything you do that gives me pleasure. No support, no love. It's an impossible situation."

He looked stunned. "If it's doing things around the house...."

She interrupted him with an impatient gesture. "You're years too late with that one. You know, the funny thing is, I never really minded doing things for you. I kept thinking one day you'd wake up and say, 'You're wonderful. You slave your ass off for me and I'm grateful. I don't know what I'd do without you.' I was a fool. I couldn't accept the fact that I married a mean man. But that's what you are, Howard. You make me feel small in every way you can. You tell me my work is shit. I have to beg for shopping money. You dole it out ten dollars at a time." She spoke downward toward the blanket, her legs neatly rounded under it, like the legs of a corpse. "You're sarcastic, you put me down." Keep going, she told herself. Don't think, don't feel sorry for him, just get it all out fast. "You're so rude to my friends that they won't invite us anywhere." She put her hand in front of her mouth. "I want a separation."

"Please don't do that," he said, pulling her back down beside him on the bed. "Please don't." He clutched her against him as though expecting her to intervene against this danger. To her horror, she felt him trembling violently in all his limbs. He pushed aside her robe and tried to enter her. "Let me, let me please." As though he had to get inside to warm himself and take off this terrible chill that was rattling his bones.

She felt herself choking, but she was angry at him too. If he cared so much, why hadn't he shown it? Done something, anything? Now it was too late. She pushed him away with both hands.

"No," she said, "I can't now." She edged away from him. "We have to talk about what we're going to do." Keeping her eyes on him, she swung her feet over the edge of the bed and stood up. She'd expected him to try and stop her but he just lay there, rigid, pale.

Now that she'd told him, and he seemed so subdued, she couldn't keep up her anger. She talked to him as though she were explaining to a small boy why he had to be punished. Firmly but with tolerance. She couldn't even remember the really bad things he did, like slapping and terrifying the children. And while she was telling him those other things, she wasn't really breaking with him inside. It was as though they were playing a sort of game in which she had unwittingly stumbled on an advantage, but she wasn't really imagining that he would disappear from her life. She would have been willing to bring him medicine if he were sick or help him find a car. She didn't hate him. She just wanted something better than what they'd had.

"I won't accept a separation," Howard said when he'd recovered himself a little. "If you ask for that, it will have to be divorce." He had gotten up and was standing in front of the dresser at the far end of the room.

She stood behind him, in her robe. She knew he was trying to frighten her. "I'd rather take things slowly," she said, "but if it has to be that way...."

He saw that, mystifyingly, she wasn't intimidated any more and took a different tack. "Maybe it's time for some changes," he said, turning around, "a program of improvement." Connie could see the effort he was making to try to grasp her thought.

"Being together makes you miserable too. Can't you see that?"

"I'm happier with you than without you."

"What are you saying? That you'd rather be alive than dead. That's not enough, Howard. I want a man whose body gives off sparks when I walk into the room. A companion, someone to be my equal in things. Not someone I have to nurse." In all their years together he'd never changed a diaper, and the only time he ever fed a child was when she had pneumonia and couldn't drag herself out of bed. It was painful to remember. It reminded her how much she had wanted him to love her. "Dammit, Howard. You can't even take in what I had to give you. No matter what I do, you always find something wrong. Even if things were eighty-five percent perfect, you'd find a jar cap that wasn't tight or too much salt in the meat. That's no way to live, Howard."

She saw them framed in the dresser mirror, faces ugly with tension.

"I won't complain about the jar tops any more," he told her contritely. "I think I did it because I wanted power over you. That's over now." Connie had always assumed he wasn't aware of his motives. That was part of the reason she was so tolerant. How can you blame a man with no eyes for not seeing? So much for sainthood. Her tolerance had only made him worse, not better. If she'd said this ten years ago...but she couldn't think about that now.

"The first thing we'll do," he said, rubbing his hands together, "is have a big party and invite over your friends—John," a psychoanalytic critic he particularly despised, "the Waters...."

"I can't believe you're saying this. You hate them. You called them phonies. Just last month you said you'd like to run a lawn mower over their faces."

"We'll start again," he said. "I'll turn over a new leaf." My God, she thought, if I'd only stood up to him years before! He wouldn't have turned into a different man but at least I would have had some leverage. When he saw her staring without answering, he went on. "You like the movies. We'll go to the movies. Even ballet if you want. And I'll give you a thousand dollars the first of the month. You can shop as you like and you won't have to ask me for money."

"Stop," she said, putting her hands over her ears and walking away from him. "Please stop now. I can't hear any more." She felt a thin scream rising in her throat. It burst out abruptly, a banshee wail.

"What's wrong?" he asked, bewildered.

She stopped at the foot of the bed, her hand on one of the maple posts. She would have liked to uproot it and hurl it at him like a spear. Clobber him in the head. "Who do you think I am? A child you can win with treats? Zoo and popcorn? Is that as far as you can get in your idea of what people give each other?"

"I thought my offer was pretty damn generous," he said, following her. "What else do you want?"

"If you can't sense it yourself, there's no way I can tell you. I can't lay you out a list of one hundred things. Even if I could, your heart wouldn't be in it. Maybe you'd tell me you loved me a few times, or kiss me in the morning for a week. But in a month, you'd be right back where you started. And you wouldn't even have begun on the serious things. You can't teach a person to care."

He scanned her face nearsightedly, his heavy neck bent forward as though she were some unaccounted obstacle in his path, a thorny cactus or a bog. "Why did you tell me all those things then, if you didn't want to make things better?"

"Think about it," she said.

Howard's face darkened. "If you don't think I can change, what are we diddling around for? Just so you can have the pleasure of insulting me? Is that it?" He took a step nearer her. She moved around towards the head of the bed, eyeing the door. "Let me tell you something, Connie. I'm through listening to your complaints. If you won't accept my offer, I'll stay exactly the way I am. I'm calling my bank tomorrow and telling them not to give you any more money."

She felt her stomach turn. This was worse than a slap. "But my job doesn't start till fall."

"I'm not in the charity business. If you don't want to be my wife, why should I take care of you? You figure out how to live until you get your blasted job." Connie stared at him. All the weakness and pleading had gone out of his voice. He was his old self except angrier, like a boil she had drained on her thigh that grew back redder and hotter than before.

"I'll go on welfare."

"You'll have to. And don't think I'm going to let you have the house. I'll burn it before I do that."

"You're not serious," she said, but she felt frightened. She remembered him pushing Mr. Ramon down the stairs. She hadn't even begun to consider the harm he could do *her*.

What if he went round the bend completely and decided to shove her out a window? Or hack her up and throw her in the bay.

His eyes were blazing. "I've never been more serious."

"Don't be crazy, Howard. The kids need a place to live."

"That's your lookout. Don't think you're going to stick them with me." Connie wasn't ready to think about his selling the house. She felt like a juggler who's been handed ten balls instead of two.

"They're your children too, Howard. You can't just disown them like that. You denied you voted for Nixon when he got in trouble, but you can't deny your children. This is California. You're responsible for half their expenses. They're not just going to bring themselves up like lilies of the field." She saw him grinding his teeth, his jaw popping. "You brought this on yourself, Howard. If you hadn't been so mean, it would never have happened." It flashed through her mind that once when he was drunk he told her he couldn't help ruining everything he loved. But it was too late for pity. "I really wanted to make a family with you but it just won't work. Don't think I haven't tried. For seventeen years. I didn't just take care of you, shop, cook." She looked him in the eye. "I listened to you, read every word you ever wrote. It was like tossing hor d'oeuvres to a lion. It just whet your appetite for blood. Enough is enough."

"You liked me for my worst qualities," he said, hunching his shoulders. "You never liked me because I was a nice man. It's your fault too. Besides, my books bored you. Any fool could see the children were the only things that interested you in this marriage."

She had the urge to agree, to take her share of the blame, but she fought it down. "At least they react," she said, pulling down some extra blankets from the closet and taking a pillow from the bed. "They're open, they show affection. All the things you can't do. I'm going to sleep on the couch."

Howard ran over to the chair where he'd draped his suit and rummaged through the pockets. He took out his pipe and some matches.

"Please, don't smoke in bed," she said, keeping her voice calm.

Suddenly he snatched her dress and stockings off the other chair and threw them onto the bed into the furrowed place where she'd been lying. then he bent over and dropped her shoes and purse on top. At first she thought he was going to spit on them. His face was so full of contempt that it made her wince. But then she saw he had lit a match and was leaning over and holding it to her stockings. They flared. The filaments of brown nylon floated in the flames.

The hem of her light cotton dress caught and she saw black holes opening as the fire ate away the fabric. She stared, hypnotised for a minute by the way the colors boiled up like lava bubbles then went dark. He lit a second match, then a third and fourth, in rapid motion, throwing them onto the bed. New spots began to burn.

"My God, what are you doing?" she screamed, suddenly aware of what was happening. "Are you out of your mind? You'll set the mattress on fire." He was standing there, lighting all the matches in the matchbook, one after another. They arched like miniature sparklers before they hit the covers and caught. She ran to him, dropping her blankets on the floor, and hit him on the arm.

"I just wanted to show you how easy it would be," he said, grabbing her wrist. "How fast all your pretty things could go up in smoke." His face was so close to hers that she could smell the wine on his breath. A stale, stinking smell. "What's the matter? Not a big enough blaze for you?"

She noticed he was erect again. Her fear seemed to intoxicate him. She shrank back, tugging against his grip. "Howard, for God's sake! The sheets!" The rumpled bedding near her burning dress had caught. Tiny flames flickered along the ridges of the blanket towards the pillow.

They had bought the blanket right after they married, for their first double bed. Watching the fire climb down a hollow and up the other side, Connie felt as if red ants were crawling up her legs. Crawling and stinging. She jerked her arm away from Howard and ran into the bathroom for some water. The pillowcase had started to burn. Frantically, she dashed her glass of water on it. A small patch of flame hissed and guttered out, but a second spot kept burning. If the kapok inside the pillow caught, she was afraid the fire would spread to the wall in back of the bed, and the house would go up like tinder. It was a nightmare, the kind where you are screaming but no one can hear you. "Howard," she shouted, "get some more water."

He took off his wedding ring and dropped it on the bed, then he raised his middle finger at her.

She shuddered, feeling as though he'd hexed her. "Damn you," she said, snatching up a blanket from the floor and throwing it on top of the pillow. If she hadn't been afraid of getting burnt, she would have rolled the pillow up in it the way firemen do. She'd seen it in a movie. A woman burning. She remembered the woman slapping at her skirt with her hands trying to stop what was hurting her. She would have liked to press his head down against the burning pillow, smother him too.

Sarah looked in the door, her face white. "What's happening? Mom, why'd you scream? Are you okay? Is Dad hurting you?" Then she saw the bed. "Oh, God!"

"Call the police," Connie said.

"Don't you dare." Howard lifted a fist and shook it at her across the bed.

"Go ahead, Sarah. Do it!"

Sarah stared at Howard for a second then bolted out the door.

Howard started after her but Connie threw herself against him. He punched her in the back but she kept her grip. She could hear Sarah talking on the phone in her room.

"Help," she said. "My parents are fighting. There's a fire on the bed. Yes. It's 3250 Poppy Lane."

"Let go of me." Howard pushed her aside and ran out. "What are you doing, you little fool," she heard him yell. It's okay, Connie thought, struggling to catch her breath. Sarah gave them our address. "Listen," Howard was saying in his stiffest three-piece-suit voice. "I dropped a lighted cigarette. It's nothing. I've got it under control."

Connie thought of Mischa asleep down the hall. She suddenly remembered that his window only opened a couple of inches, not enough to get out if the fire got to his door. She went to Sarah's door. "Don't believe him," she shouted as loud as she could. "Send the police, hurry." Maybe Howard was going to beat her head in but she had to do it. What if he got up in the night and tried again? She had to get him out of here.

"She's drunk," Howard said. "Hysterical. No really we don't need any police. Shit. They're coming." There must have been a car in the neighborhood. Connie could hear a siren shrilling down the street. Howard slammed down the phone. "I'll deal with you later," he said as he ran back through the smoky bedroom to the bathroom and filled a decorative pot with water.

Connie told Sarah to get something bigger from the kitchen. Then she took the flowers out of the vase on the bureau and helped him, silently pouring water on the burning places. Her clothes had turned into a black paste and a nasty smoke was rising from underneath them.

She threw open the window to let in some air just as the police car pulled up in front, sirens wailing. The red lights on the top of the car twirled around, throwing off an eerie glow. Like strobe lights. She could hear the officers talking on the car radio and then they got out of the car and the doorbell rang. "Jesus, I can't believe you'd do this to me," Howard said, stumbling after her down the stairs. At the bottom, he pushed her aside, adjusted his expression and opened the door.

Past Howard's shoulder, Connie noticed the Johnson's lights turn on and their window curtain being drawn back. She felt a rush of shame. What would they think?

Howard ushered the police in with elaborate dignity. One was a woman with a short blond pony tail.

"I'm sorry to have brought you out here for nothing," Howard said, bowing from the waist like a samurai. "You know women's nerves." He grinned at the young woman, who looked hardly older than one of his students.

Connie's legs were shaking so hard she could hardly stand. "Please, you have to help me," she said, her breath catching in her throat. "You have to see what he did. He burnt up my dress, my underwear..." She felt for a minute as though she were a mental patient trying to explain a hallucination to her doctor. "Do you understand? I'm terrified of him. He burnt my clothes. Torched them. All gone up in smoke. Sizzled. Fried." She paused, wondering if they saw. "I told him I wanted a divorce."

"Oh," said the policewoman, glancing at Connie.

"For heaven's sake," Howard said primly. "Why do you have to make up crazy stories? We were just having a minor disagreement."

"That's not true," Sarah said, coming in from the kitchen with a pot. "They fight all the time. He's a bully. Get him out of here. He frightens my mother."

"We have discipline problems," Howard said, glaring at Sarah. "She's furious because I've grounded her."

"Bullshit," Sarah spit back. "He thinks he's Moses on a motorcycle."

"Please, you have to let me show you," Connie said, beckoning to the policewoman. What if they didn't believe her? If they left her and Sarah with Howard? His fists were balled tight against his legs. She saw him clenching and unclenching them, his knuckles white. She could imagine them smashing into her face. "Just let me show you," Connie repeated, not sure she'd said it strongly enough, "It's up there." She pointed over her head. The woman's partner nodded and she and Connie started up the stairs.

Howard started up after them. "Hey, this isn't Oakland. You can't just go barging into respectable people's bedrooms. You're invading my privacy. This is outrageous."

The policeman put a hand on his shoulder. "Why don't you stay here," he said with practiced restraint. "They'll be back in a minute and then you can say whatever you want to. Or talk to your daughter. She looks as though she's got plenty to say."

The room still smelled foul, even with the open window. The young policewoman rubbed her eyes and looked around. She drew in her breath sharply when she saw the gunk on the bed surrounded by puddles of water.

"We're going to have to get rid of this mattress. There's no mistaking that smell. Gag a maggot, we call it. It means the fire's worked its way inside. You're lucky the wall hanging didn't catch. Or the curtains. That loose weave is just what a fire loves. I saw this thing last year. A fellow who caught his wife with another man. Burnt the house right to the ground." She touched the charred handbag with the tip of her stick. "You wouldn't believe the things that happen."

"That's my purse," Connie said. "It could have been me." She started to cry. The young policewoman put an arm on her shoulder. "Easy. You're okay now." She offered Connie a crumpled Kleenex from her back pocket. The kindness hurt worse than anything. Connie felt as if she were dissolving. She just wanted to put her head on this woman's shoulder and cry.

When they went back downstairs, Sarah was sitting on the arm of a chair biting her nails and the policeman was leaning against the door watching Howard pace back and forth in the entry. "Well?" he asked his partner.

"He sure did a number up there. This lady's lucky she still has a roof over her head."

"Look at her," Howard said indignantly, waving a hand at Connie. "She's hysterical. She's got the shakes. How can you listen to her? I told you it was an accident. I wasn't watching my cigarette."

"He's a pyromaniac," Connie said, keeping close beside the policewoman. "He got thrown out of school for setting fires when he was ten years old."

Sarah went over to her mother. The three women stood in a little cluster. The policewoman, neat and efficient, Connie and Sarah in their robes.

"He doesn't even smoke cigarettes," Sarah said. "He smokes a pipe. It's over there on the table. When my little brother touches it, he slaps him in the face."

Howard looked at her grimly. "She's an incorrigible liar." He turned to the policeman. "Pipe, cigarette, what's the difference? I made a slip."

"Women don't usually pile up their stuff on the middle of the bed when they undress, buddy," the young policewoman said. "Her purse and shoes were there too. They couldn't have just walked. Someone put them there. You."

"I'm really scared," Connie said to the policeman. "My children sleep up there. I don't know what he'll do. He's capable of anything. Please. He shouldn't be here tonight. I won't feel safe. I couldn't even close my eyes. If anything happens to them...."

"You little bitch...," Howard said, advancing on Connie.

"Look, buddy." The policeman moved quickly forward and took Howard's arm. "Maybe it would be better to spend the night at the station. Let things cool off." The young policewoman took the other arm. Howard started to struggle but the policeman twisted his arm up behind his back. "Do you want to file a complaint?" he asked Connie.

"Tell him yes, Mom," Sarah said.

Connie looked at him, confused. "What would that mean? I don't want to prosecute him."

"It just means we can keep him at the station overnight.

That's what you want isn't it? Then the DA can figure out whether to charge him or not. Whether it's a misdemeanor or a felony."

The policewoman sat Connie down on the couch and helped her make out the complaint. "You're doing the right thing," she said, showing Connie where to sign. "What's awful is the ones that won't do anything to help themselves. I had a woman call with a broken jaw once. When I got there, she said she did it herself. And the guy was standing there grinning." She folded the paper up with a satisfied expression. "It's times like that I hate this job."

Howard was arguing with the policeman. "No, I'm not going upstairs to get my clothes. I'm not going anywhere. Take your hands off me."

"Don't give me a hard time, Mister, or I'll have to charge you with resisting arrest." The policeman was losing his patience. He twisted Howard's arm up further behind his back.

"You have no right to charge me with anything," Howard started, but the policeman took his other hand and pushed his head forward. "We're going to have to handcuff you, Buddy." The policewoman already had the cuffs off her belt and was snapping them over Howard's wrists.

All of a sudden Connie saw Mischa standing at the top of the stairs. She ran up and put her arms around him. He was holding his Evel Knievel, his eyes thick with sleep.

"How long have you been awake?" How much of this had he heard?

"I saw the black stuff all over the bed. Why did Dad burn...."

"Shhh," she held him close. "He had too much to drink. It's all right. The policeman are going to take him with them and give him some black coffee," she heard herself babbling. How many scenes like this were going to be engraved on Mischa's brain? What was this doing to him? He was clinging to her robe like a four-year-old.

"This trouble is all your mother's fault," Howard said when he saw Mischa. "You understand that, don't you, son? She wants to go off and leave us." Mischa looked at him wide-eyed.

"Mom?" his lip quivered.

"It's you I want to leave, not Mischa," Connie said, rubbing Mischa's head. "You're mean and you're violent. No one should have to live with you. Not even a dog."

Howard lunged towards her.

"Come on," the policewoman said, tugging his arm.

"I told you I'm not going anywhere, damn you," Howard snapped at her. "This is my house. I have my rights." The policeman quickly took Howard's other arm and while he alternately argued with them and swore at Connie they dragged him out the door and locked him in the police car.

When they had him secured, they came back into the house. "We've got to get the mattress outside," the policeman said. "Those things smoulder for weeks." Connie and Sarah went upstairs with them. First they wrapped the bedding and the pillow in a blanket, threw the whole mess in the bathtub and filled it with water. Then Connie and Sarah helped them drag the mattress off the bed and down the stairs. It left a trail of soot and charcoal on the new tan carpeting. "Sorry about that," the policeman apologized. They carried it into the backyard and the officers slashed it open with their knives and pulled out the filling. It was like disemboweling a sheep, Connie thought. Clumps of kapok intestine lay glimmering whitely on the grass. It stank. The only thing missing was the blood.

"Got a hose?" they asked Connie.

Mischa ran to uncoil it from the plastic stand at the edge of the garden. He turned it on and came back pulling it, spurting water over his bare feet.

The policeman watered each piece carefully, as though it were a plant. "I think it's out," he said finally. "But the fire department will come by in a little while to check.

Berkeley's crazy that way. Everyone's a specialist. They don't think a police officer is smart enough to see if something is still burning." He snorted. "You folks should probably keep the water going till they come."

"Thanks." Connie took the hose and began to walk around from clump to clump, watering each one the way she'd seen them do it. She felt as if she were being deserted by her best friends. A fog was blowing in from the bay and the air was getting chilly. The oak trees seemed as though they were hung with spider webs. Even the pine at the foot of the garden had a ghostly look. Mischa came and butted his head under Connie's free arm.

"I'll never leave you," she whispered, pressed him against her, trying to quiet his trembling. "Got that straight, big guy? We're all in this together. You, me and Sarah." Sarah kicked at a bit of kapok and pretended not to have heard. She rubbed her bare arms with her hands. Finally she shivered, gave a little sigh and walked over to her mother. The three of them stood there taking turns playing water over the soggy innards of the mattress, waiting for the fire truck.

Sixteen

In the morning, Connie woke up with a furry taste in her mouth as though she'd been drinking. She sat up trying to get a sense of where she was and saw that she was in Mischa's bed. He was asleep next to her, one arm dangling over the edge. It came back to her with a sickening immediacy. The fire, the police, Howard hustled out of the house yelling about his rights. He'd never forgive her for humiliating him like that. She saw his face twisted by rage into some kind of crazy mask. The jaws working, the eyes squinting up without any understanding in them. The image was so real she started to shiver. She pictured him brought into the station along with prostitutes and bums. Glaring at them, insisting on his privilege. How that must have infuriated him. He never forgave even the slightest injury to his pride. And this had been overwhelming. During the night in jail, he must have thought of revenge. She rubbed her arms, hugging herself close for comfort. What was he going to do now? Come back and break in? Beat her up? She jumped out of bed, threw on some jeans and a T shirt. Her first thought was to go over to Mrs. Johnson's house. Take the kids and go. But in a minute she realized she couldn't go. If she left even for a day, she was sure he'd find some way to get in. Once he was there, God knows what he'd do. Maybe she should ask Mrs. Johnson to come over and sit with her so at least she'd have someone with her when Howard came. She thought of Desdemona getting ready for bed on the last night of her life, sending away her companion, Emilia. That part had always sent little bursts of cold though her veins.

While she was thinking about it, she heard a car drawing up outside the front door and Howard's voice talking to someone. He must have taken a taxi. She imagined him standing outside in his pajamas shaking with humiliation and rage, asking the taxi driver to wait while he got his wallet. If he rang the bell she wouldn't answer. She thought of throwing his wallet to him out the window. Anything to make him go away again. Then there was the sound of a key in the lock. Oh my God, she'd forgotten the extra key under the mat. He was coming in. She held her breath, her heart pounding, and heard his footsteps in the front hall.

Her heart racing now, she ran into their bedroom. Whatever was going to happen, she didn't want Mischa watching. The smell hit her when she opened the door. Worse than rotten eggs. She tried not to breathe too deeply, keeping it out of her lungs. The room looked like a bomb site, she thought. Even the things that hadn't been damaged didn't make sense anymore. The four posts of the bed stuck up bleakly, like surveyors' stakes marking the place where a house had been. She circled the room wondering if she should have something in her hand to throw at him if he looked violent. For a minute she considered the paper weight but then decided against it. She'd miss and infuriate him more. And if she took the letter opener, he'd probably twist it around and stab her. She decided the best thing to do was to keep moving out of reach. When she heard the floor creak just outside her door, she tensed, ready for him. But he walked into the room without even looking at her. He hadn't shaved and his pajamas were crumpled and stained. Connie saw right away something had changed. He looked as purposeful as a demolition truck, one of those with a steel head that keeps moving forward and back taking huge bites of mortar and wood. He went over to the closet, pulled down a big suitcase and started throwing his clothes into it. He took the shirts, hangers and all, simply stuffing them in. Then he pulled his ties off the tie rack, dropped them on top, coiling like snakes, and wedged his sneakers and a pair of sandals in at the side. When he was finished he pushed the top shut and snapped the latches. Part of a tie was hanging out. He looked up at her as though she were a slug he'd discovered on his freshly mown lawn.

"You've done it now," he said in an icy voice. "This is it. I'm putting the house up for sale. I'm instructing the bank not to give you any more money." She could hear the suppressed rage in his voice. It cut through her skin like a blast of cold air. She paced nervously, as far from him as she could get, thinking it was better to be a moving target than a stationary one. Passing the mirrored dressing table, she saw his angry face reflected across the room, the naked bed between them, its springs exposed. Her own face in the foreground, pale, circles under the eyes.

"What about the kids?" she asked. "They have to eat. I'll pay you back later, if you want, when I get my paycheck."

"Don't talk to me about my children," he said. "You're a crazy woman, just like your mother. Don't think I don't know what you've been doing," his nostrils flared. "You're not fit to have the children." She felt her heart miss a beat. If Howard was angry enough, he might accuse her of involving the children in her affair. Setting a bad example. Making her daughter promiscuous. If it came down to her word against his, who would the judge believe? Howard would wear his vest and watch chain and quote the Bible. Could he talk away the fire? Say he was driven to it by an adulterous wife? For a minute she wished the police had taken photographs. Howard took khaki pants and a black T-shirt and went into the bathroom to change. Then he got another suitcase from the closet and started filling it with clothes from his side of the bureau. Grabbing handfuls of boxer shorts, undershirts and black socks, sweaters. Not folding anything. When the two suitcases were full he took them downstairs. Then he began to put his religious things in paper bags. His silver Kiddish cups, the menorah for Channukah, the twisted candlestick for the end of Shabbat. Prayer book, shawl and phylacteries. She imagined him wrapping them around his arm when he went into court. Armoring himself in righteousness.

When he finished, he went out and put his suitcases into the trunk of the Pinto. "Hey," Connie said, "you can't take my car."

"The Buick is at the shop. Use that."

"How am I going to pay for a thousand dollar engine job?"

"That's your problem. If I'm moving out of here, I need a car." He slammed the trunk shut. Could he do that? She pictured the Buick slipping away from her down Marin, crashing into a telephone pole with Mischa in the back seat. "Maybe you should have thought a little before you started all this," he said.

Connie didn't say anything. There was violence right under Howard's calm surface. She didn't want to risk a fight with him now. Not after last night. She had to talk to her lawyer.

He was still standing at the back of the car. "Don't think you'll get away with what you did to me," he said, biting off the words. "They put me in a holding pen with scum." He hit the car with his hand and Connie jumped back. "You can't imagine what it was like." His lips stretched away from his teeth in an expression of disgust. "Degenerates vomiting into paper bags. Wiping their mouths on their sleeves. Someone even threw up on my feet." He looked down at his Earth Shoes then up at her, outraged. "They wouldn't let me wash. I had to sit with that stink all night, surrounded by thieves and pimps. Everyone crapping in a common toilet. Making disgusting jokes. And you did this to me. I'll be back," he said as he got into the car, "and I'll take everything that's due me. Half of everything. The paintings.

The silver."

"Those things are mine," she said, shocked. "That's my grandmother's silver and my mother's paintings."

"You got the silver for a wedding present," he told her coldly, "and your mother gave you the paintings after we were married. They're community property. Ask your lawyer if you don't believe me." He gunned the engine and pulled out of the driveway fast, leaving her looking at the wheeltracks in the gravel.

When she went back to the bedroom, she found Mischa standing in the middle of the floor in his pajamas with the vacuum cleaner. His hands were smeared with soot and there was a long dirty streak of ash across his cheek.

"I can't get it all off," he said, frowning, "but it's a lot lighter than it was."

"You've done a heroic job, Mischa." She put her arms around him. "Thanks." After a minute, she drew back so she could see his face. "I'm sure you're wondering what's going on. Why all this." She gestured toward the bed, feeling a reluctance to name things. To say the words violence, burning, leaving. "I told Dad I wanted to live separately for awhile." Oh come on, she told herself. Be a person. Say I want a divorce because living this way is intolerable. Mischa's lived through it too. He knows. Why is it so hard to talk to him about it?

Mischa turned pale. The dark streak stood out on his face. "So it's true what Dad said about your leaving us?"

"Oh God, Mischa. No!" She sat down on the bed and pulled him down beside her. "I'm not leaving you and Sarah. I just can't live with Dad anymore. He's got to look for another place. He came back to get some of his stuff this morning. Look." She pulled a feather of ash out of his hair. "For a long time I thought things would get better if I was just patient. But they didn't. They got worse. I started standing up for myself and then all we did was fight. What ever happens now, it's bound to be better."

Mischa stared at Connie's sweatshirt. "When John Rae's parents got divorced they didn't stop fighting. His dad called up his mom in the middle of the night and said nasty things to her."

"There are ways to deal with things like that," Connie said, pressing her hands into her lap to keep them from shaking. "She should have had her number changed, or gotten an unlisted number."

Mischa studied an unravelling thread on Connie's midriff. "Once he even came over and let the air out of her tires." He hesitated. "Dad might come back and burn the house down."

"I don't think he's going to do that," she said, stroking his hair.

Mischa wouldn't meet her eyes. "Why not? Why won't he?"

"Because we talked things out," she lied. She could feel his body tense beside her. He was getting too old for her easy comfort. Up till now, she realized, she'd been feeding him fairy tales—more for herself than for him—because she hated to see him hurt. She wondered if she could cope with talking to Mischa honestly, about Marc, for instance. God, how was she going to manage that? She didn't even know if the man was going to stay around. She was relieved when the puppy ran in and started scratching Mischa's leg.

"What if Dad wants Pompey?" Mischa asked her, drawing the dog up on his lap. "Don't worry," he crooned, putting his lips against the puppy's caramel-colored fur, "I'll hide you in the cellar, the way people hid the Jews when the Germans were looking for them."

"I think he'll have enough to do setting up a new place without Pompey. Besides, he gave her to you."

Mischa kept stroking the dog. She rolled her eyes back in ecstasy. "She's part his then. You know that story about King Solomon and the two women fighting over the baby? Dad always told me they should have cut the baby in half."

"No one's going to cut Pompey in half." Connie looked at him thoughtfully. "Sounds like you're worrying about more than your puppy though. Want to tell me?"

He hung his head.

"Oh, come on. What could be so bad?"

"What If Dad wants me to live with him? Take me to Israel or something."

"Do you want to go?"

He shook his head vigorously. "I want to stay with you and Sarah."

"That's what I want too." She hugged him against her, the dog wiggling between them. "I love you and I'm going to keep you with me. No matter what." She meant it. Even if she had to spirit him away to Canada. Change her name and live in hiding. Mischa looked as if he was trying to solve an impossible math problem. She got up, took the puppy under one arm and pulled Mischa to his feet. "Come on, let's have some breakfast and get you off to rec camp. I'm going to call Robbie's mother and ask if they can take you."

Mischa looked at her doubtfully. "I don't want to go." He glanced down at the dog.

"Okay," she said. "After a night like that I guess you're entitled to a day off." She kneaded his shoulder through the light pajamas. Felt the thin blades. After her father died, Steve had obsessed endlessly about his toys, making lists, counting them, trying to keep his world stable by will power. She wondered if Mischa was going to be like that. Divorce did strange things to children. She imagined him tying up Pompey when he left. Calling up every day from camp to see if she'd been kidnapped. And this was just the beginning.

By the time she'd given Mischa breakfast, it was nine o'clock and she was able to call the lawyer.

"I've got to talk to you," she said, "Howard tried to burn the house down last night." She sat down on the stool in the kitchen.

The lawyer whistled through his teeth. "Are you okay? Was there serious damage?"

"No, but I'm pretty shaky. I had to call the police and Howard spent the night in jail." She leaned an elbow on the counter, "When he came back to get his things this morning, I was so scared, I couldn't think straight. I've got the feeling I'm making mistakes all over the place. And this isn't the time for them."

"Like?"

"Howard said he was going to close down the bank account. I thought of going down there and getting it first but he left with the car. I'm sure he'll be there by ten when the bank opens."

"We could try to call and freeze it. Even though they're not open, the officers are probably there. It's worth a try. Give me your account number." She gave him the number and he called. "We're lucky," he told her after a few minutes. "There's three thousand dollars."

"That's great," she said. "I was afraid I wouldn't be able to make it until my first paycheck arrived."

There was a silence on the other end. "You can't use it, you know. That's what frozen means. It's just there. Neither of you get it. But at least we know the money's there to draw from. I'm going to ask the judge to allocate some emergency money for the kids to tide you over."

"Will he give it?"

"I hope so. But it may take awhile. In the meantime, I suggest you put away some of your valuables in the bank. Use them for bargaining chips if he gives us a hard time. You know, jewelry, stuff like that...."

"He says my grandmother's silver is half his. She gave it to us as a wedding present. Is that true?"

"You might say she'd given it to you when you were ten. Your mother was holding it for you until you got married, something like that. Let him worry about proving it was a wedding present."

"And my mother's paintings?"

"Same thing. You had them in your room as a child. Are they worth much?"

She shook her head, trying to clear it. She wasn't used to thinking like this. "Yes. If I sold them. But I'd never...."

"You know Bekins warehouse. Get a box there and put your paintings in it. Put your jewelry in the vault. House papers, mortgage payment records, any other financial documents you can find. Now take a deep breath."

She started from her abdomen and worked slowly into her lungs and upper chest. "Good idea." She'd learned it in yoga. She thought she should go back to mediation, do it every morning to keep herself sane.

"My big fear is..." she took another deep breath "... that he's so angry now he'll try to fight me for the children."

"You're scared and upset now. You don't really know what he's going to do. But if he tries, there are some positive advantages to his having gone haywire. It may help you get custody if there's any kind of fight. Was he ever violent before this? Did he threaten you with a knife? Anything like that? So we could establish a pattern of abuse."

"He hit my son, Mischa."

"Oh," he said and she could sense his attention focus. "With his hand? With a belt? Really beating him?" She could visualize the lawyer's large, capable hands making notes in red ink on his pad.

"More like slapping." She found herself wishing Howard had used a belt. So the judge could see how bad he really was. My God. I'm really going crazy, she thought. "Look," she said, "even slaps can frighten a child, if they're given by someone who's out of control. Both my kids were terrified of him. Especially when he'd been drinking."

The lawyer sighed. "The court isn't much on emotional states. If there are no broken bones or bruises they're not likely to take it very seriously. A man's home is his castle."

Sarah had come into the kitchen while Connie was talking and stood at the counter fixing herself a bowl of cereal and listening.

"That doesn't make me feel very good," Connie said to the lawyer. Everything she knew about the law's attitudes towards women came from reading Victorian novels. It was hard to believe things hadn't changed since the nineteenth century.

"We still may be able to use it," he said kindly. "And if it doesn't fly I'll find another angle. Try not to worry too much. We'll work something out."

"I've got to call the locksmith, Sarah. Then I'll have a cup of coffee with you." Connie dialed Rex Key. While they had her on hold she thought about the possibility of Howard selling the house. Locks wouldn't help her then. She pictured a house she'd seen sheared in two by an earthquake. What could she afford with the proceeds of half a house? The locksmith came back on the phone and told her he'd try to get there before 1:00.

"Are you going to change the back door too?" Sarah asked her, "or just the front?"

"All the doors, front, back and side." Connie poured herself a cup of coffee and sat down at the kitchen table with Sarah. "I'm even thinking of boarding up the dog door."

"I doubt he can fit through that. His shoulders are too big." Sarah slurped some milk from her spoon. "I wanted to ask you about something."

Connie readied herself to reassure Sarah about some fear. "Shoot."

"Am I still grounded?"

Connie thought for a minute. Maybe this was the time to make a break with the past, to get out of the old patterns. "No, you're not. You have the makings of a responsible adult, Sarah. That's how I'm going to treat you from now on. You know what I think about things. You know my values. You've got a good head on your shoulders. Now's your chance to use it. If you want to flunk out, mess up in various ways..." she decided not to mention Mr. Ramon, "...that's going to be your business. I'm not going to interfere but I'm not going to bail you out."

Sarah gave her a guarded look. "Does that include Mr. Ramon?"

Connie took a yoga breath. "Yes."

"Can I ask you something else?" Connie nodded. "If you get a divorce, can I still go away to college?"

"I hope so, Sarah."

"If I get into N.Y.U., maybe I could stay with Grandma and cut expenses. That's really my first choice anyway."

"Sarah, I'm just not sure yet what we'll be able to do. But why don't you write to Grandma and ask her?"

After she finished talking to Sarah she called Marc and told him what had happened. "I don't want to leave the house with Howard wandering around on the loose," she said to him after she'd finished. "I won't feel safe until the locks are changed. Would you pick up a rug cleaner and some shampoo for me and bring it over? There's soot all down the stairs from where we dragged the mattress."

"Sure," he said.

"Oh, and bring your futon. I'll order a new mattress from Sears but they probably won't deliver for a few days. Do you mind?"

"Of course not. I'll be there by ten-thirty."

When the doorbell rang she looked out the peephole to make sure it was Marc. Then she opened. He was standing there with the rug cleaning machine in one hand, pole forward like a lance. Now that he was here like her white knight, she wanted to lie down with him on the couch and let him hold her, but she couldn't, not with the children here. She took the things from his hands and he went out to get the futon from the car.

"Are you sure you're up to this?" he asked her, leaning it

against the wall. "You don't look too good."

"I hate seeing this soot all over everything." She nodded at the dark smudges leading from the front door to the stairway. Each time she looked, it shocked her to see them muddying the clear, light beige of the carpet. It had been one of her few indulgences. Pure wool. She flicked some sooty dirt from under one of her nails. "I know what the theologians mean now when they say 'black as sin.'"

"Let's start at the front door." Marc opened the shampoo and crouched down, pouring the blue liquid into the dispenser tank. "I think it'll be easier to drag this thing up the stairs then to go down after it."

Connie took the cord and plugged it into the socket in the entryway in back of the umbrella stand. "I'm scared," she said over the whirring sound of the motor. "Howard's bound to do something. I know him. He can't stand feeling humiliated. If he was capable of burning the house down before, what's he going to do now? I feel like I'm surrounded by Indians. I don't know where he's going to attack first." She threw the empty shampoo bottle into the wastepaper basket. "Do you think he'll really put the house on the market? He's already closed the bank account."

Marc moved the hose back and forth over the stain near the door. The wool was turning a foamy gray-white now. Wet as a new-born kitten's fur. "I don't know," he said. "From the way you described it, he's furious. He wants his pound of flesh."

Mischa came down the stairs with the puppy, looking at Marc apprehensively. Pompey went up and sniffed the wet carpet then stepped on it gingerly. Marc held her back with one arm. "Uh, uh, pal. Your feet are dirty. I guess she doesn't wipe them on the mat when she comes in," he said to Mischa.

Mischa pulled the dog back and gave Marc a half smile. "Can I try it?"

"There's nothing to it." Marc turned off the shampooer and

let Mischa click it on again and stood beside him with a hand on his shoulder while he dragged it along towards the stairs. There was something so comforting about seeing them like that, as though there was nothing to be afraid of. Connie had a fantasy of Marc sleeping with her on the futon, guarding the house, like John Wayne, with a shotgun beside the pillow. She sniffed and a few hot tears trickled down the back of her throat.

"Hi," Sarah said, coming out of the kitchen to join them. "I remember you. You're Mom's friend." She emphasized the last word. "Are you going to be staying around?" she asked, looking him over.

Marc swallowed. "I'm just helping your mother clean up," he said.

Connie was surprised at how nonplussed he seemed. Almost prim. She would tease him about it later. "Mischa, you better take Pompey out back. She's getting restless. I think she has to go. Then if you want to help some more, you could put some of that mattress stuffing in those big garbage bags. Maybe Sarah would help you."

"In a minute," Sarah said, giving Connie a knowing look from under her long lashes. "I have to make a phone call up in my room. Come on, Mischa." She walked Mischa into the kitchen and came back with a glass of juice. Then she went upstairs.

Mischa was banging drawers. "Don't go out of the backyard though, okay?" Connie called to him.

"I can't find the bags," he yelled back. "Where are they?"

"In the drawer next to the oven," she shouted. "I better go help him," she said to Marc. "He's not at his best today."

When she got back, Marc had taken off his shoes and was starting to drag the machine up the stairs. His eyes had a faraway look, as though they were under water.

"What's the matter? You look strange." She stooped next to the shampooer, holding it so it wouldn't slip off the steps as Marc went up.

"This is hard for me," he said slowly. "Maybe when we finish the stairs, we should go out for awhile."

"I can't leave before the locksmith comes." She helped Marc move the machine to the next step. "I'd be too nervous."

"There are a lot of hard things to deal with here. Your house, the children." He turned his face away, working over a bad spot. "We started out having great times together. Going places, making love. Then you started telling me about your troubles with Sarah. Now it's Howard. I just wonder what this relationship's about anyway. Problems?"

She stood up and let the machine tug against the hose in Marc's hands. "You were the one who wanted me to leave him, Marc. You've been trying to persuade me for months to marry you. I'm sure you didn't think it was going to be easy. You know what happens when a family breaks up. Things are rough."

"The balance seems wrong." He hauled the cleaner up another couple of steps and wiped his forehead. "When is the last time we laughed about something?"

She stared at him. "How can you say that at a time like this? Jesus, what's going on with you?"

He moved onto the top step and stood looking down at her. "There's no telling what Howard may do. He's like a rabid dog. My life's in danger." Connie started to say something but he cut her off, his voice shrill. "You know, I saw him in the liquor store the other day. He came straight at me with a shopping cart. I thought he was going to crush me against a wall of bottles. And that was before you put him in jail for the night."

"I'm sorry," she said, "but I really don't think he'd hurt you."

"Look, just last month in San Francisco, a man shot his wife's lover in the head with a sawed-off shotgun. Point blank."

"That was some Mafioso, Marc, fresh from Sicily. People

don't do things like that in our circles."

"Didn't Howard just try to burn your house down? Next time he sets fire to your bed, you might be in it. Crimes of passion aren't confined to the lower classes, you know." He took a deep breath. "Let's not make love for a while. Let things settle down."

"What?" She couldn't believe she'd heard him right.

"Let's cool it for a while. Besides, it wouldn't help anything for me to be named as corespondent. You have enough legal problems already." He said it casually, as though it were too obvious to discuss, but his eyes were opaque, evasive.

She felt her little island of safety sinking. "There's no-fault divorce in California, Marc."

He started edging down the stairs, shoulders against the wall, carrying the shampooer. "I don't want my name brought into it. You know, the man who broke up Connie's marriage, that sort of thing. Particularly with all this violence. This could be a nasty business."

She followed him, trying not to step in the wet spots. "Life is a nasty business," she said. "That's no surprise, is it?" He was sitting on the bottom step putting on his shoes. "Marc, you told me to do this. I didn't expect you to marry me but...." The way he was concentrating on his shoelaces made her feel frantic. "At least I expected you to give me some support. Who can I turn to?"

"I better get the shampooer back to the store," he said, standing up and brushing off his pants. "The guy told me they're only open a half day today."

Connie knew he was lying. "Marc, I need you to help me through this."

"I am helping you, baby. What do you think I've been doing all morning? What do you think, that I'd run out on you?" Connie thought his eyes looked as if he'd raised metal shutters behind the lenses. She could see her reflection in the pupils but nothing else. "Listen." He pointed to the foam hardening on the rug. "After an hour you should be able to vacuum this stuff up." He guided her towards the door, handling her gingerly, as if she were a beaker full of some corrosive acid. "Don't worry," he said. "This is just a transitional period."

Mischa was out in front watering the fuchsia. Connie could see him from the kitchen window, his face puckered anxiously. Poor kid. He worried about everything now, from nuclear holocaust to the plants dying because Connie had forgotten to water. He was standing there with his thumb against his lips letting the water seep in slowly, the way she'd told him to. She hoped he wasn't going to start sucking his thumb again.

She picked up the newspaper with a sigh, put her bare feet up on the kitchen table, wriggled her blue-jeaned bottom into a more comfortable position and started to read about Nixon taking leave of his staff. Pure bathos. How sentimental and self-pitying the man was. He wasn't going to take responsibility for what he'd done anymore than Howard was. Once Howard was over his outrage, he'd probably feel like a victim too.

She could picture him telling some bartender somewhere, "I did everything for the bitch, but she didn't have a grateful bone in her body. She threw me over for a gigolo." It was amazing, she thought, how some people didn't feel guilt. She looked at the picture of Nixon hugging his daughter Julie, her arms tight around his neck. After using government agencies as his personal toys, all Nixon could tell the American people was that he was resigning because "he'd lost his political base." Jesus, politics.

She was so occupied with her thoughts that she didn't hear a car drive up and park in front of the garage.

"Mom!" Mischa came running in. "Dad's here with a lady." He squinted up his eyes at her anxiously. Howard followed him into the kitchen. Connie got up hastily, smoothing down her work shirt.

"Howard, call next time. Don't just surprise me. I don't like it." Through the open door she could see a blond woman in a conservatively cut linen suit pacing along the dining room wall.

Howard looked at a spot just beyond her left temple. "Have you gotten my response to that shit your lawyer sent me?" he asked.

"No, not yet." He must mean the articles of dissolution. She felt the fine hairs lift along the back of her neck. His tone was so ugly.

"You will," he said, pulling a salad bowl and some platters out of one of the cabinets. "In the meantime, I need a frying pan and something to boil water in. Where are you hiding the pots?"

"If you'd ever lifted a finger in this house, you'd know," she whispered so the woman wouldn't hear. Howard cursed and kept on pulling things out of the cabinets. An old toaster, an egg poacher. The woman came into the kitchen and gave Connie an apologetic smile. She was wearing stockings and neat flats.

"Oh goodness," she said, with a quick glance at Connie's flustered face and the messy kitchen. "Are we coming too soon? Before you've had a chance to get ready? Never mind, it's nice to see a place *au naturale*, so to speak." She looked at Connie's bare feet. "Don't worry," she added soothingly. "When I'm home, I never get myself together before noon."

Connie listened to the woman's barrage of words. "Who

are you?" she asked when she finished. Out of the corner of her eye she could see Howard rummaging in the knife drawer and she had a sudden image of him holding a butcher knife to her throat while the "nice" lady pushed Mischa into the car. He had burned the bed, hadn't he? People like that end up in jail or in the loony bin. Napa. She grabbed Mischa's hand and pulled him close to her.

"I've put the house on the market," Howard said.

"You've what?" She turned and stared at him.

"I've put the house up for sale. This is Miss Barth from Tepping Realty."

"How could you do that? We haven't even discussed it." She shook her head. "Have you really got it listed?" she asked the woman. She nodded. "You'll have to take it off then. It's not for sale. Howard. I can't believe you'd do this." She wished she'd listened to the lawyer when he'd tried to talk to her about selling the house. Now she wasn't sure exactly what her rights were.

"Maybe I should go," the woman said, without conviction, "and give you a chance to talk it over." She batted her eyes at Howard.

"No, don't go," Howard put his hand on Miss Barth's arm. "Look, Connie. I have a right to know what this property is worth. You're sitting on a gold mine here."

"Let Miss Barth come back another time, after we've talked."

"She's here now. Is it going to kill you?" Howard started getting red in the face. She could feel Mischa beginning to tremble.

"No. It's not going to kill me. I'm just not going to show it now."

"I understand how you feel, dear. Things are awfully complicated. But this is just a formality and it would just take a few minutes. Just to take a look and see. That way when you and your husband talk you'll have some facts to go on. It could be to your advantage, dear, believe me." She paused and looked at her watch. "I did give up a rather important meeting to come this morning. But naturally that's no concern of yours." She stopped and adjusted one of her gold twist earrings.

Connie sighed. She'd probably get rid of the woman faster by showing her the house than by discussing it for an hour. "All right," she said, ungraciously, "come on, have a look around."

Connie led the way, ignoring Howard. They walked slowly through the house, the woman taking notes on a little pad, murmuring things to herself.

"The studies should be turned into bedrooms. It would sell better that way," the woman said, "as a five bedroom. It's easy."

Connie wondered whether this could really be happening to her. What if Howard did insist on selling the house? Where was she going to live? All the apartments she knew about cost a fortune. She'd have to call the lawyer as soon as Howard left. "Yes, the fireplace works," she told the woman, "and the plumbing too, though it's pretty old. No. I don't think we have any termites." The last termite inspection had been seventeen years ago, when they bought the house. Who knows what larvae had hatched since then? Maybe if the place was full of termites that would make it hard to sell. "Isn't the market pretty bad now," Connie asked, "with the oil boycott and the recession?" She'd read yesterday that the Dow Jones had hit a four year low. 600 something.

"Oh, I think this would sell," the woman said brightly. "You have a lot of space here. Two lots. This is a premium property, even for Berkeley."

Connie remembered that her friend Jane rented out a studio apartment. Maybe she could afford that, though she wasn't even sure it was free. And how were three people going to squeeze into a space that small? As they approached Mischa's room, he started to pull on Connie's arm. She bent her head down to him. "I don't want her to go into my room," he whispered loudly into her ear. "Only friends come into my room, not strangers. Besides, Pompey's asleep in my bed. Tell her," he whispered urgently. "Tell her."

"This is my son's bedroom," Connie said. "He doesn't want any visitors right now. This whole divorce business is hard on kids," she explained to the woman.

"I understand," Miss Barth said, "poor little pet." She reached out a manicured hand to pat his shoulder. He shrank away from her as though her fingers were crab claws.

"Nonsense." Howard pushed open the door. "There's no reason why you can't see it." Mischa had a whole army of tin soldiers deployed on the floor. For the last week, Connie had heard him fighting imaginary battles. Imitating the roaring of canons and planes and shouting commands at his men.

Howard strode in, kicking the soldiers out of the way.

"Dad," he cried, "that's the Israeli fort. You knocked it down."

"Your room's a pigsty," Howard told him. "And what's that dog doing in your bed? I apologize," he said to Miss Barth. "He never used to keep his room like this." Mischa started to cry.

"Stop it, Howard," Connie said, taking his arm and pulling him towards the door.

"I've seen all I need to," the woman said, this time clearly distressed. "Please, really, there's no need to do this on my account." Howard came reluctantly. Mischa collapsed on his bed next to Pompey.

After Howard left, Connie called the lawyer. "Howard showed up this morning with a real estate agent," she told him. "He listed the house. Without even a word."

"That was a pretty stupid thing to do," the lawyer said calmly. "If he were rational, he'd probably have something worse up his sleeve. One of my client's husbands took another woman into the escrow office with him and pretended it was his wife. Actually forged my client's signature on the document. Got himself into big trouble." She could hear him flipping pages in his appointment book. "How's 11:00 tomorrow morning for you?"

"Fine. And thanks. I don't know why, but it helps to know other people go through these things too."

Afterwards, she gave Marc a call and asked if he'd like to take a walk with her later. She thought he might be able to give her some good ideas. "Sorry," he said, "I'd love to but I've got a meeting. I was just on my way out the door when the phone rang."

"You're a busy man these days," she said wryly, but he'd already hung up.

As she drove over to the lawyer's office the next morning Connie listened to excerpts from Ford's swearing in as 38th President of the United States. His voice was a change at least. She had gotten to loathe Nixon's sanctimonious righteousness. Ford vowed to follow his "instincts of openness and candor," ending a government "in which secrecy was the norm and lies the legitimate instruments of power." Connie felt a lightening of her heart. What a comfort to think it couldn't happen again. That Nixon was an aberration. Right now he was being whisked to California in his Air Force jet, to be jettisoned like a load of garbage. Out of sight, out of mind. A phrase from the articles of impeachment came to her mind. Nixon had "violated his constitutional duty to care...." She thought of Ford's first speech and her lips curled in an ironic smile. Instincts of candor indeed! If you were being truthful, how many ordinary people had them, not to speak of politicians? She wondered how long Ford's honeymoon with America would last.

The lawyer was wearing the brown suit and the white spotted tie that he'd worn the first time she came. "Look what I got in my morning mail." He pointed to a sheaf of papers in front of him. "It's the response from Howard's lawyer. It's no surprise to you by now that Howard wants to sell the house."

"What can I do?" She leaned forward peering at the tiny upside-down letters.

"First of all, stay where you are. Don't let him persuade you to move out for any reason. I mean, even if he threatens suicide. That's a mistake a lot of women make. One of my clients moved out for a few weeks, just to let things calm down, she thought." He shrugged. "She never got back. The court tends to keep the status quo. If you're there already, chances are you'll stay there."

She took notes on everything he said. Otherwise, she knew she'd forget it before she left the office. As it was, she was having a terrible time concentrating enough to understand what he was saying. Stress, she thought. Difficulty concentrating was the fourth symptom on the list she'd read in some magazine at the checkout stand. Or was it forgetfulness, or fear? She took a deep breath and read over what she'd written. "It can't be as simple as that. There must be a a..." she hesitated, "process?"

He smiled at her reassuringly. "Getting a divorce is like settling a boundary dispute. Even while the politicos are negotiating, the troops are digging in and the generals are planning strategy. If the negotiation works, the soldiers dust themselves off and go home. If it doesn't, the generals pull out their attack plans and they fight."

The war metaphor seemed apt. "And you're my general?"

"You know, I like you. You have a good spirit." He poured her a glass of iced tea from the thermos on his desk and again she noticed what a nice smile he had. "The best thing for us is to go on the offensive. Hit him with a list of the things we want. Not just the house but substantial alimony, child support. Do the kids go to private schools?"

She nodded. "But I'd been thinking of changing."

"Don't even think of giving up anything until you have to.

Think positive. The kids' education is important. He has a good job. He can afford to pay for it. Do you have a fund for college?"

"Yes, but there isn't enough."

"Then we should ask him to help. And there are medical costs."

She felt her throat getting dry. What if she didn't get any of this? How would she take care of all this stuff on what she earned teaching one bloody course, a measly four thousand dollars? She hadn't even remembered doctor's bills when she was calculating her expenses. Connie looked at the lawyer's hands. They seemed to have a life of their own. Opening and closing protectively around objects on his desk. Blunt and practical. More like a farmer's hands than a general's. She hoped he knew what he was doing.

"He should keep them on his health plan. He must have one from the university. Then there's his pension benefits and any savings accounts. That's joint property. Then I want you to make a list of all the things you have that he might want, jewelry, oriental rugs, fancy stereos. Those paintings you told me about."

She thought of a woman she'd known who'd been divorced. Her husband had taken so much that the house had looked like an empty barracks. And she hadn't been able to afford new furniture. Objects started to swirl in Connie's mind. She could see a big wind moving around her house, sweeping up everything in it, a whirlwind of books and furniture. Everything she loved vanishing out the door. "It would be worth a lot to stay where I am," she said, "but I wouldn't want to give up my mother's paintings."

"Of course not," he said soothingly, "no reason why you should. These are bargaining chips, that's all. I just want to know what they are. Look." He made a fist and softly pounded the desk between them. "If we play this right, we may not have to give up much of anything. It shouldn't be hard to prove Howard's violence. We could subpoena the policemen. This isn't your ordinary divorce. That bed burning was a pretty nasty business."

"And you think threatening him with revealing that in court will work?" She was afraid it might just make him furious and stubborn.

"I know Howard's lawyer. Ross is an experienced attorney. He can handle that. I'm going to take him out to lunch next week and talk things over. He's a pretty straightforward guy, not one of those super-adversarial types. I have the feeling that he doesn't know what kind of man he's dealing with. Howard has probably withheld a lot of material from him. I'll tell him how Howard pushed you around, slapped the children. I'll tell him about the bed burning." He paused. "But I have to warn you. If we push Howard's violence, he'll bring up your affair. How much did Howard actually know about it. Was there a diary? Witnesses?"

Connie felt herself break into a cold sweat. "He read some pages of my diary once but I tore them up." She tried to think if any of his friends could have seen her with Marc. They'd gone around everywhere together, holding hands, shopping. "A woman once said hello to Marc when we were buying coffee at Pete's. I thought I remembered seeing her at our synagogue." The sweaty patch spread between her legs. She surreptitiously dried it with her skirt.

"Did she know you were together?" Connie nodded. "Did she see anything physical? Anyone else who might have?"

"Howard doesn't have many friends," she said evasively, "and they aren't likely to volunteer things like that." The woman had made an arch remark that implied if you shopped together you must be sleeping together. Connie imagined facing her in court. Yes, I saw them, she'd say. They were feeling each other up in a store. "If it has to go to court, do you think I'd get to keep the house?"

"I think you'd have a pretty good chance. You have minor children living with you. You've never worked before. But look, there could be complications. We have to plan a strategy. If they insist the house is common property, I'll ask for a court order that will let you keep it until your youngest child graduates high school. After that you could sell the house and split the profits. At the worst I'd have to trade off alimony. The trouble is, by the time I got to that point you'd probably be up to your ears in debt. These trials can drag on for months. A year isn't unusual." Connie stared at him, horrified. A year? In debt? My God, she wouldn't have anything left. She'd be out on the street. Did Howard hate her enough to want to beggar them both? "I'll ask him to pay the lawyers' fees. But I can't be sure we'll get it." She put her head in her hands. Maybe this is what they mean when they talk about people falling through a crack. First you lose your husband, then your house. Little by little you slip down until you're sleeping in rest rooms like the loony lady at Live Oak Park. "Look," he went on softly, "I know you want to keep the house. I understand that's a natural first reaction. But you need cash right now. You're in a tight place. Two kids, a low paying job. It'll take you a few years at least to get something better. Your house must be worth at least two hundred thousand dollars. Think about it."

"The children have lived there all their lives. It's their neighborhood. All their friends are there. I hate to give it up." She made an effort to think reasonably. "But I do need the money. And if Sarah goes away to college next year, it'll be basically just me and Mischa. I suppose we don't really need a five bedroom house."

"Maybe you could find something nearby." His face was wide, friendly, a big moon lighting her through the forest.

"There is a small house for sale up the street. I could find out about it." She pictured them packing up, moving, Mischa carrying his hamster cage, Sarah the bird. Like gypsies.

"Good girl. Remember you don't have to do anything. Just keep an open mind and look at your options. It might make more sense to rent. Another possibility is getting a loan. You're starting a job soon. You might ask about getting a loan from your school. Buy him out."

"I thought of that already. Sister McKinney, the woman who hired me, told me Saint Mary's doesn't offer housing assistance. I might ask my brother for a loan, or my mother." Her heart sank at what that might mean. Elsie rushing out to take over her life again, "but I need to think about it."

On the way home she felt that her head was like a food processor filled with chunks of disparate foods—onions and butter and parsley, garlic—too much to grind up all at once. She stopped at a doughnut store and picked out two mocha twists, a plain glazed and a jelly doughnut. While the salesgirl was putting them into a bag, Connie decided that she'd have to call her mother and tell her what was happening. She couldn't leave her in the dark forever.

As soon as she got home, she slipped off her shoes and put her feet up on the phone desk in the kitchen. "I've got some bad news, Mother," she said when her mother answered. "Howard and I are getting a divorce." She heard a sharp intake of breath.

"Oh dear, that really is too bad. After all those years. You must be distraught."

"I'm doing pretty well, actually." Connie hesitated, thinking of how much she should tell her.

"Are you, dear? Well, that's good. I know how unsettling change can be. Since Louise left, I haven't had a peaceful moment. That new maid Steve found me just can't seem to learn the way we do things here. She starches the sheets until they're stiff as boards. You know how delicate my skin is. And she has no idea how to cook pasta al dente. She can't even pick out ripe fruit."

Her mother's selfishness enveloped her like a damp, low fog. Couldn't she even put her complaints aside for ten minutes? Her mother paused for breath.

"Howard is being very reasonable about things." Connie said into the empty space. She thought of him dropping lighted matches onto the sheets, the bed blazing. "We're talking. But it's rough on the children anyway." She pushed aside an image of Mischa shivering in his pajamas at the foot of the stairs, terrified. "Sarah's worried about being able to go to college. It doesn't look as if Howard's willing to pay tuition."

"It's outrageous what things cost these days. I remember when college cost twenty five dollars a semester with books." Her mother sighed. "Do you realize that the new maid charges almost double what Louise did and she doesn't work half as much. She won't even do the hardwood floors. She's afraid she'll ruin her hands. Her new boyfriend likes her nails long. She's always mooning about him, neglecting her job. It's disgusting." She paused. "By the way, are you still going out with that man you brought to see me? Marc? Is that what bolexed things up with you and Howard?"

Startled, Connie bit her tongue. "Well, actually that seems to be dying down. We haven't been seeing each other much." Much! Marc couldn't even find the time to walk around the block with her.

"What? He's not going to marry you? After breaking up your home?"

"I don't want to marry him, Mother. It wouldn't have been a happy marriage."

"Why, what are you going to do then?" Her mother's voice started rising shrilly.

Connie felt the little hairs on her arms stand up. "I'm going to sell the house." It struck her that this really was the best thing to do. She'd been clinging to the house like a spider crab, not willing to leave its outworn shell.

"Sell the house! You'll be homeless. My poor grandbabies will be rootless vagrants. So that's why Sarah wrote asking if she could stay with me next year. Of course I said she could. Even though a teenager is bound to be a strain on my nerves. Now you'll have to come and live with me too. You can sleep in your old room. But Mischa? I really don't know how are we going to manage. The maid already has trouble making my dinner. How's she going to cook for three more people? Let me call her. Marie, Marie!"

Connie could hear her mother frantically ringing the little bell she kept by the bed. She hoped she wasn't going to have a stroke. "Mother, don't get so excited. There's no need to call Marie. We won't be homeless. I'll buy a smaller house or rent an apartment. That's not so bad, is it? You live in an apartment, don't you?"

"But it's terrible to make changes like that. Especially for the children. Children hate changes. I've been so desperate with this new maid. It's really as if I didn't exist. When you come, it'll be better. We'll go shopping, have tea together the way we used to. Maybe I'll fire Marie and...."

"Mother, I'm not coming. I'm going to rent an apartment. Mother? Can you hear what I'm saying?" Connie heard her own voice rise harshly like a violin in an atonal symphony, each instrument on its own track. Squeak, squawk.

"I'll get on the phone right away," her mother said in her fake efficient voice, "and see if I can find a good boarding school for Mischa. It would be good for him to have an organized routine, somewhere out in the country where there's lots of fresh air. You'll see, it will all work out."

1974

Eighteen

It was the first day of classes at Saint Mary's. Connie put off preparing to face her students and listened to the news while she had her second cup of coffee. Ford was settling into the White House, the newscaster said. Connie wondered how Nixon felt when he found himself suddenly dropped out of the Oval Office into private life. No longer living out every action in front of the cameras. Did he miss all the drama? Her own kitchen seemed oddly quiet without being restful. Like a stage set after the director had gone home. Even though Howard hadn't taken his share of the things yet, there were potential empty spaces everywhere. The coffee maker for instance; she was sure he'd claim that. She took a sip of coffee and imagined Nixon wandering through his rooms muttering, "I'm citizen Nixon," to his mirrors. Redefining himself.

"I'm a single middle-aged woman," she said aloud. Trying it out. It immediately conjured up graying hair and lonely nights. "With two children," she added. That helped.

She spilled the coffee into the sink. She was already too jazzed up. Sparklers of random energy were zinging along her spine. She took the radio with her and went upstairs into her bathroom to take a shower and wash her hair. It's getting too long, she thought while she rubbed in the blue gel conditioner. I should have gotten it cut. The sides were unruly, fluffing out like tiny chicken wings as they dried. What to wear? A light suit? Something with authority but not matronly. I have no idea how to present myself out of this house, she thought, horrified. She wasn't even sure how to introduce herself to the class. Her name? Should she let the students call her Connie? Doctor? Professor? No, she wasn't a professor, she was just a lecturer, and Doctor sounded pompous. Remember, she told herself, you wanted to do this lightly, with style. She suddenly saw a whole class of Sarahs appraising her, full of hostility. Butterflies of nausea fluttered at the base of her throat. She rinsed, got out, towel dried her hair and flicked on the radio while she put on her stockings. It was a talk show and some man from Arizona was saying he thought he'd seen Patty Hearst looking at baby clothes in Phoenix. Connie tried imagining Patty in her classroom, her stomach swelling slightly against her jeans. Connie felt maternal, protective. She imagined the baby curled inside Patty's stomach. Learning, even before its head emerged from between Patty's legs, how to do better than Connie and Patty had. A phoenix born from the ashes. In the midst of her daydream, she heard Mischa calling her outside the door.

"Mom, I think I'm going to throw up."

"Just a minute." She wrapped her robe around her and opened the door. Mischa made a dash for the toilet and stood there heaving while she held his head and made comforting noises. Wiping off his face with a washcloth, she went through the list of sitters. They were all teenagers who would be in school. Sarah had already left.

"I hate to leave you when you don't feel well." She put her lips to his forehead. Thank God it didn't feel hot. She couldn't have left if he had a fever. How did people do this, she wondered, as she tucked him into bed with a stack of comics. What if he'd been five instead of eight? What if he had a fever of 104?

"Do you have to go?" he asked her. "Can't you read to me first?"

She shook her head. "I can't be late. It would be awful to be fired on my first day." She made a wry face trying to get him to laugh, but he just looked at her unhappily, rubbing his thumb against his lip. "I'll put on a record for you, though. How about *Peter and the Wolf*?" She eyed her watch. She wanted to give herself plenty of time to get there.

"That's babyish. I'd rather listen to some of Sarah's stuff. Elton John or something." She knew Sarah hated to let Mischa use her records. She said he scratched them and forgot to put them back in their sleeves, but she didn't have time to deal with it. She gave him an armful of records along with a pitcher of apple juice and a plastic bucket to throw up in if he couldn't make it to the bathroom. "Here's the number at Saint Mary's." She put it under his pillow.

"It's funny to think of you being a teacher," Mischa said, holding on to her hand and playing with her fingers, "teaching all those other kids. I'm not sure I like it."

"That's certainly honest." She gave him a quick kiss. Then she ran into her room and put on her suit and got her things together. She already felt guilty.

Connie had gotten the Buick out of the shop before they started on the engine. She turned the key and heard a grating sound as it tried to turn over. Each time she tried it got weaker. She stopped when she realized it was flooded and sat there for five minutes with the windows open, waiting for the smell of gasoline to lessen, knowing she shouldn't try again too soon. What if she was stuck in the garage right through ten o'clock? She imagined the kids all sitting there coughing and fidgeting, finally getting up and walking out. When she came, the room would be empty. A friend of hers had signed up to teach Dante at extension and then showed up on the day after she was supposed to teach the class. The students were busy taking out all her chairs for a lecture down the hall.

By the time Connie finally got the car started, her stomach was churning. She drove past the Claremont and up towards Moraga along Highway 24. She tried to let the hills quiet her mind. They were tawny as big cats, crouching with their manes of green pine. It didn't work. Halfway there, she was sure she'd forgotten her briefcase and had to pull over on the gravel shoulder to look for it. Then she stopped to check her notes. She felt sure she'd taken the mortgage instead. Her mind seemed to be turning to jelly. She was afraid when she tried to talk she'd stutter or squeak. She put the briefcase up on the front seat where she could reach over and touch it. It had been her father's and she had the idea it would give her good luck. A little bit of him to carry with her. Stiffen her up. She tried to remember how he looked when he kissed her mother goodbye at the door and went off every morning. But all she could see was an old photo of him on a bad day. Eyes serious, strain lines around the mouth. Not smiling.

While she was working on getting a clear image of her father, she got off at the wrong exit and lost her way trying to get back on the freeway. She stopped at a gas station and the attendant pointed a grease-stained hand and told her, "Right at the stop sign, then three blocks, hang a left, right at the next...." A few minutes later she found herself back at the gas station. She started again with her heart pounding, a sickening sense of panic radiating through her chest. She had the feeling that if she made another wrong turn she would drop into a dream landscape where the freeway went around in a circle. She'd be locked in forever, following a gray cement road with a line down the center, going nowhere. For months after her father died, her mother hadn't gone anywhere without her. Unwilling to take a cab or bus. Afraid the taxi would have a flat or be caught in a blizzard and she'd be marooned in Brooklyn. The game of what if. Expanding possibilities of disaster. Connie began to sense why she hadn't thought of leaving Howard sooner. Why she had to tell herself stories about her marriage. It was this stomach-wrenching terror of being out on the road alone. She was the little engine that couldn't. The confusion in her brain lifted a bit with this thought. After all this wasn't never—never land, it was Orinda, and the roads didn't generally go around in circles. When she found herself back at the gas station again, she swallowed her panic and made herself write down the directions on a piece of paper. She drew a map for herself, turning the corners right, left, right. As she drove she turned the map around so she was facing the same way as the line.

Still, by the time she got to the Spanish-style buildings of Saint Mary's, she had stopped so many people to ask for directions, she felt like the Ancient Mariner. When she got out of the car and picked up her briefcase, she noticed her hands were shaking. That would be all I need, she thought as she looked over the students lounging in the halls. To have the chalk make quivery, wavy lines when she was trying to write on the board. The students were talking in small groups or sitting on the floor reading while they waited to see someone. Oddly, she'd imagined only girls at Saint Mary's, but she saw that the students were at least half male. She asked a bearded boy with blue eyes the way to Room 104.

"Are you teaching that new Comp Lit course?" he asked. She nodded. "I think I'll give it a try. I need four more units to graduate." He hesitated and she could see him wondering if she would make graduation easier or more difficult.

"And you want to do it with the least effort possible?" she asked.

He smiled at her, not at all abashed. "Let's just say I'm hot to move along. I'm an Ed major," he explained. "I want to get out there and do to them what's been done to me." He pointed at a half open door. "There's the room. See you."

"Thanks." She stood outside for a minute watching the students coming out of the room jostle the ones coming in. While she was standing there, Sister McKinney, the nun that interviewed her, came along and stopped to chat. "Have you been down to the office yet?" she asked Connie.

"No. I'll go afterwards. I was a little late." She thought of Mischa holding on to her fingers. She wondered if he'd had to use the bucket.

"There's a flyer about our social hour and the schedule for visiting lecturers. We have a very nice poetry series this year. I expect you'll be coming." She didn't give her a chance to say no. Connie felt her heart sink. She'd imagined herself preparing classes, grading papers. She hadn't even thought of the extras she'd have to do. Her life was chaotic enough without obligatory social hours and evening lectures. Sister McKinney was looking at her soberly. She had a serene oval face like a nun in a medieval painting.

"I think you'll find our students a challenge," Sister McKinney said. "They're full of questions. They'll keep you on your toes."

"I'm sure they will." It struck her suddenly that Sister McKinney was waiting because she was going to observe Connie's class. The thought made her knees weak. She was sure if she was watched, her mouth would twitch. She'd be overcome by general paralysis. But of course, why hadn't she thought of that? They'd have to observe her sooner or later. She only had a temporary appointment. One semester. Her tongue was sticking to the roof of her mouth. She bit her lip to make the saliva run. What if she couldn't manage? If she wasn't good enough? Clear enough? Modern enough? She felt the little confidence she had leak away like water through a sieve. She'd been out of touch so long.

"Well, enjoy your first day," Sister McKinney said as she turned away.

At least her humiliation wasn't going to have an adult witness. Connie picked up her briefcase and went into the classroom. There were about twenty students. They were talking to each other, settling themselves in their chairs, opening notebooks. She got out her materials, feeling grateful to have something to do, delaying the moment she'd actually have to talk to them. When she finished, she glanced at the big clock on the wall at the end of the classroom. It was only five minutes past ten. She still had fifty minutes to get through with these people staring at her. She couldn't believe how slowly the second hand was moving. At that rate, she'd never have enough to fill the hour. Her hands started to shake so hard it sounded as if she were drumming on the top of her briefcase.

"Would you hand the syllabus out for me, please?" she asked a ginger-haired girl in the first row. The girl took the xeroxed sheets and started passing them back. Everyone looked at Connie.

She described the course in detail and told them about the term paper and the examinations.

"Will you give out the questions before the exams?" a student asked. He had greasy hair that tailed down his neck.

"No. I don't think so."

The student stared at her belligerently. "Most of the profs here do it," he said. "It saves a lot of time not studying what isn't important."

Connie tried to control the trembling of her hands by resting them lightly on the desk. "If you participate in the classroom discussions, you'll know what's important." The student rolled his eyes and there was a flurry of suppressed giggles. "You'll be glad to see you don't have many books to buy," she went on, ignoring a hand that was waving frantically in the back row. "But what we read, we're going to look at carefully." She looked out over the room. Except for the boy who still had his hand up, the students sat, pens poised above their papers and notebooks. "I don't like having to race through things pell mell. I want you to get a real familiarity with these works." She paused. "I want you to think about how they relate to your lives. In fact, I'd like you to keep a diary for this class." She glanced up at the clock and saw that miraculously a half hour had passed. She was going to have more than enough material after all.

"Do we have to keep a diary *and* write a paper?" a girl in pink and black stripes asked. "That seems like an awful lot."

"It's a short paper," Connie said, "only five pages. I'm sure you can handle it." God, if they thought that was too much how were they going to react to the study groups? "I'll be talking about the Dido episode in the *Aeneid* first. After we discuss the themes in class, I'd like you to try a variation of it yourself. Write your own abandonment scene. I want you to use it as a lever to get into Aeneas's mind. Why did he want to leave? What was pulling him?" She had a brief painful image of Marc dragging the rug cleaning machine up the stairs.

"A girl with better legs," someone said in a stage whisper. Connie looked at him over the top of her glasses.

"I don't think so," she said, "but if you do, that's your scene. Write it. What will probably happen is that you'll find you don't have enough information to understand why Aeneas left Dido. For instance, you might need to know more about what was expected of men in Roman culture. So I'd like you to make a list of questions. We'll divide into groups and report back at the next class."

"Wouldn't it be easier if you just told it to us in a lecture?" Connie stopped dead. She'd gotten so excited about her idea that she'd forgotten all about her nervousness. Now her hands started shaking again. She peered down at the boy who had asked the question. While she'd been talking, she'd seen him scribbling away and had been pleased that he was paying attention. But now she noticed he'd been drawing a huge phallic shape with a bow tie, glasses and a bowler hat. He grinned at her. All of a sudden, the bell rang and she jumped, surprised. She hadn't gotten through half of what she wanted to tell them and already her first class was over.

When she got home, she saw the Pinto with a small trailer

attached standing in the driveway. Inside the back she could see a heap of Howard's suits and a carton of shoes. Another carton had some pots and plastic dishes. Giving another quick glance around, she saw the wine rack, still filled with bottles. It was padded side and bottom by blankets. Her favorite lamp with a mica shade stuck up in a corner next to a pile of linens. The way he'd piled everything in helter skelter reminded her of the moving scene in *The Grapes of Wrath.* In the movie you could almost taste the desolation. But this wasn't a movie.

She shuddered. Moving his things out somehow made his threat of selling the house more real. Getting it ready. Her lawyer had said that the negotiations seemed to be working, Howard was softening, but she couldn't believe he'd give in that easily. On an impulse, she pulled the lamp off the truck. Damn him. At least he wouldn't get this. Brandishing it in one hand, she ran over to the front door and turned the knob. It was unlocked. How had he gotten in? Could one of the children have given him a key? Or had Mischa simply opened the door for him? At the thought of Mischa alone in the house with Howard, she felt a surge of terror, the short hairs on her arms stood out like tiny quills.

She set the lamp down by the door and ran into the kitchen. Mischa was sitting on the floor, holding Pompey on his lap. He'd turned up a paw and was examining a crack between the pads. She crouched down beside him and put her arm around his shoulder. As she settled her weight, she heard a crunching sound and looked down. A big splinter of glass was protruding from under her shoe.

"What happened?" she gasped. There were shards of glass all over the kitchen floor. She looked over at the back door. It had been completely shattered. Pieces of glass stuck out jaggedly from the sides like teeth.

"Mommy," Mischa said, talking very rapidly under his breath. "I heard this big crash and then someone came inside." He leaned against her. "I thought it was a burglar so

I crawled under my bed with Pompey and hid. I tried to keep her quiet but I couldn't. She ran downstairs...." He stopped with his mouth open. His face was so pale the freckles on his nose stood out like spots of blood.

"Are you okay? Are you having trouble breathing?" Connie wondered whether he was going to have an asthma attack but he shifted Pompey on his lap and after a minute he seemed to catch his breath.

"When I heard Dad screaming at Pompey to shut up, I knew it was him. I was afraid he was going to hurt her or take her to the pound so I came down."

"Did he hurt you? If he did...." Just then she saw a big yellow stain on his pajama leg. At first she thought Pompey must have had an accident, then she realized he'd been so scared he'd peed in his pants. She felt like killing Howard.

"He just went in the study and slammed the door." Mischa hung his head. She rubbed the back of his neck wondering how she could ever make up for any of this. Mischa was looking at Pompey's paw again.

"Glass?" she asked him.

"I think I got it all out. There were two pieces."

"You did good, Mischa." One looked like a bad cut. It was still bleeding. Connie had some clean rags in a drawer. She carried Pompey over, wrapped a piece of sheet around the paw and tied it. "That won't stay on very long but it'll keep it clean for now. You'd better take her upstairs so she doesn't step on any more. Mischa gathered the dog in his arms. Connie suddenly noticed his feet were bare. "My God, you have nothing on your feet. You could have cut yourself. Where are your slippers?"

"I forgot them." He started sniffling.

"That's okay, honey. I didn't mean to yell. I'm not mad at you. I was just scared you might have hurt yourself." She lifted each foot and brushed off the underside, checking for splinters. "Is Dad still in the study?" she asked him calmly. Showing her outrage at this point would only upset Mischa more. The door was still closed, but now that she wasn't concentrating on Mischa she could hear the sound of Howard moving things around in there.

Connie kissed Mischa and gave him a little shove in the direction of the stairs. Then she went over and pushed the door open. It slammed back against the wall.

"Howard, I can't believe what you did. How can you terrify Mischa like that? Do you want to traumatize him for life?"

Howard was standing on a stool taking books down from the top shelf. He looked at her coldly. "Me traumatize him? What do you think you're doing with this divorce? Mischa will need years of therapy for every time that bastard Marc comes over here. My breaking the door is nothing. I'm Mischa's father."

"He wet himself, he was so scared." She was almost crying with anger.

"The little sissy...."

She started shaking the stool, trying to push him over. "Don't you dare say that. You...."

"Stop that. I can say anything I please. And I will." He jumped down. "If you hadn't served me those papers, Mischa would be out playing instead of sniveling upstairs."

"He could have gotten glass in his feet. Did you have to break the God-damned door?"

"Can't he look where he's walking? Is he that dim-witted?"

"Attacking Mischa isn't going to get you out of this. It might have before, but not this time. The dog has a big gash in her foot. I don't expect sympathy from you."

"Fuck you."

"But you're going to pay the vet bills. And pay for the door too. Jesus, you could have called, Howard. You didn't have to break in like a thief." Adrenalin was pumping through her system. She could feel it. Howard's frightening Mischa like this made her forget her own fear of what he might do if she got him mad.

"You should talk about thieves. What have you done with the paintings?" He gestured angrily at the empty walls. "Sold them?"

"I put them away in storage until we get things settled."

"And the silver? I noticed that's gone too. Those things are half mine, remember. And don't think I didn't see you take that lamp out of the van. When I leave here, I'm taking it."

"Dividing our stuff isn't the issue, Howard. We're talking about you breaking in here and terrifying our son. Jesus, look at this glass!"

"How was I to know you'd changed the locks, huh? God damn it! This house is half mine and I don't have any keys. What did you think I was going to do, sit around all day waiting for you to let me into my own house? Crazy bitch." He shovelled everything off his desk into another bag. Ink bottle, pen set, clock, paper clips, ashtray.

"Howard, just get out of here. You'll only come when you've given me twenty-four hours notice and when I'm here to let you in. And you'll pay those bills." She felt her temples begin to throb. She wanted to lie down in a dark room with a wet cloth over her eyes. "If you won't, I'll get a restraining order put on you. You won't be able to set foot in this house again, or in the neighborhood either. I should have done that to begin with."

"Don't you threaten me." He came towards her.

Her heart raced. She backed off into the kitchen, moving toward the phone. "Howard, if you don't go, I'm going to have to call the police."

"Wasn't putting me in jail for the night enough for you?" he said, pulling the phone cord out of the wall. "You want to lock me up for ten years, twenty?" He paced back and forth in front of her, his Adam's apple working. "Did your lawyer tell you to do that or was it that smart-assed boyfriend of yours? I'd put a bomb under his pillow but I don't want to spend the rest of my days in jail."

"Look, Howard, we shouldn't be talking like this. We don't have a relationship anymore. It's finished. I don't even want to fight with you. I want you gone, period. Let our lawyers talk to each other."

His shoulders seemed to crumple inward as though his jacket had been taken off a hanger. "You know, you were right," he said finally. "We should have done this years ago. It would have saved me from years of boredom in bed. In, out, missionary position. Your ineffectual kisses." He made a disgusted sound.

She had thought he was going to yield, his attack caught her off guard. "You can't hurt me anymore by telling me how bored you were," she said. "It's past. I just want to forget it. Besides, you did it often enough." She bit her tongue. She shouldn't have reacted. He was looking at her maliciously.

"I did it the way a man eats stale bread. If I hadn't had something else, I would have died of starvation."

"I don't want to hear this, Howard. Enough." She heard a sound on the stairs. She hoped Mischa wasn't listening to this.

"I never got what I really liked from you. Did you know that? Or didn't you ever care? You were so namby-pamby when you touched me, I could hardly feel it." He took a wooden spoon from the counter and held it clenched in his fist. "You don't even know how to squeeze my prick." Connie stared at him. He was talking so strangely. In all the years they'd been married, he'd never mentioned what they did in bed. Never said a word like prick. She'd thought what he did had been automatic, a sort of nervous reflex like a sneeze. "You know what I really like to do, Connie? I like a woman to scratch me until it bleeds. Slap me as hard as she can until she's red in the face. I like seeing her wear herself out trying to make me hurt."

"Jesus, Howard. Stop." Connie felt her stomach lurch. Who was this man?

"What's the matter? I'm more than willing to tell you the details. There's this great room in the Tenderloin with whips and handcuffs."

"You let women beat you? Is that what you're saying? For pleasure?" She felt a fog in front of her eyes. "You did that and then you came home and slept with me? I don't believe you." Howard had been tyrannical and nasty but there were some things she couldn't imagine him doing. It was as if Christ had come down from the cross and started masturbating.

"You never knew me. I was just your husband."

It was true, she thought, squinting at him. His face kept changing from Howard to non-Howard like those trick illustrations of figure and ground in psychology textbooks. "All those years you bullied me about being a good woman. About being a pearl. You called Mischa a filthy little beast. When all the time you were getting beaten..." she hesitated, not sure what word to use. Prostitutes? Dominatrices? Maybe there were men too? "...by whores. How could you?" For a split second, she saw herself in high boots with spurs. Kicking him. Making him grovel.

"The Jews have never been Victorian about sex. That's one of the things that distinguishes them from the Christians. There's even a passage in the Talmud that suggests men take temporary wives when they're travelling."

"What are you trying to tell me? That the Bible encourages adultery? That sodomy, whoring and coveting your neighbor's wife are really okay? Oh, come on, Howard. You were always talking to us about being a good Jew, being truthful, having integrity. Did you take your prayer book with you to the Tenderloin?"

He turned red and for a moment she thought he was going to hit her. "You always were a puritanical little fool," he said. "If you hadn't been, I could have covered our bed in black velvet. Made your ass tingle too. But you would have gone screaming to your mother at the first slap."

She felt sick but she couldn't let him see. If he knew how horrified she was, he might keep going for hours. "I've read the Marquis de Sade," she said. "I always thought it was tedious. So just take your books and get out." She slammed his door shut. Her skin felt slimy, as though someone had thrown a bucket of raw eggs in her face. For a few minutes she couldn't move. She just stood at the sink splashing her cheeks with cold water. Then she called a carpenter and ordered a solid wood door. It would make the kitchen darker, but she didn't care. The house was too open. The glass made it vulnerable. While Howard was loading his cartons into the trailer, she walked around the house looking at its openings. No living creature would have so many orifices, she thought. It wasn't prudent. It would get eaten in a flash. When the carpenter came, she was going to ask him how to burglar-proof the windows and doors.

On the evening of Rosh Hashana, when she would ordinarily have been at synagogue celebrating New Year, Connie was at Safeway shopping. She bumped into Jane at the fruit bins. "I haven't seen you in ages," Jane said, eyeing her shrewdly. "How are you? You've lost weight."

"Howard and I are getting separated. Weight loss is one of the few beneficial side effects." Connie put some apples in a bag.

"Well, good for you. I've never been able to abide the way Howard treated you."

The words sounded right but there was an odd tone in Jane's voice. "But? You look as if you want to say something else."

Jane looked serious. "I tried to call you last night but your line was busy and then this morning I thought maybe it was better not to tell you. You know, kill the messenger and all." She paused, whipping up suspense.

"Look, don't tell me if you don't want to." Connie started to push her cart away. Whatever it was, she was sure Jane would exaggerate. "I've got to finish my shopping."

Jane came after her. "Of course I'll tell you. I'm your friend, aren't I? Well, I was at Saks the other day getting a new blouse for my midi-skirt. And guess who I saw?" Her face gleamed with the knowledge. "Marc and Andrea. Honestly, I wish I hadn't introduced you. It makes me feel so bad, as though it's partly my responsibility. But you can't say I didn't warn you that he was a philanderer."

Don't panic, Connie told herself. Remember who's talking to you. "Who's Andrea?" she asked quietly.

"His secretary."

A current of nausea flooded Connie's stomach as she pictured a young woman with hair like corn silk and Marilyn Monroe hips. "Well, what's wrong with that?"

"Most men don't take their secretaries clothes shopping at Saks."

"How do you know he was buying clothes, Jane? Did you see him paying for them? Or her trying them on?" Was this true? Had he really done it this time or was it just one of Jane's games of cat and mouse? Breaking up other people's relationships because her own was so lousy.

"He had his hand on her thigh. Right here." Jane slapped at herself as though a fly had bitten her. "I wish I hadn't seen it, but I did."

Connie had known this was coming but she felt a jolt as if she'd touched a live wire. "You're sure?" She stopped herself and straightened her shoulders. Jane might exaggerate but Connie didn't think she would lie.

"He was kissing her ear too," Jane whispered in an intense voice, "and laughing."

"That's okay, Jane," Connie mumbled, feeling her face flush. "I get the picture." She pushed her cart away fast, escaping down the second aisle. Then she headed straight towards the liquor shelves and got herself a bottle of Kahlua. Imported from sunny Mexico, the label said, over a picture of a sleepy Mexican town with palm trees. Connie thought the Kahlua would be good for making chocolate sundaes. She desperately needed something sweet. It didn't occur to her to buy any ice cream.

After she got home and put away the groceries, she checked on Mischa. He was already asleep. Sarah was on the sofa.

"Thanks for watching him, Sarah."

"Sure." Sarah swept the crumbs from the cookies she'd been eating off the sofa onto the floor. "Jeff's coming over in a few minutes. He's going to help me with my college applications." Sarah had started seeing Jeff again. Connie still didn't quite trust his judgment but he seemed to have quieted down and Sarah was being more cooperative. She even seemed to be developing a sense of humor, though it wasn't always in the best taste.

"Don't go out though, okay? It's late."

Sarah parodied Connie's tone. "And there's school tomorrow and a quiz." She wrung her hands mockingly. "Be a little cool Mom, will you. I'm fine. We're not going to drive anywhere and get killed, or stoned or anything. We're just going to talk and look at my essay. Remember, you're letting me take care of myself now."

"Sorry, Sarah, this doesn't seem to be my day. Thanks for not blowing up at me. You've really been doing things very sensibly lately."

"When they have sex, why is Pat Nixon always on top?" Sarah asked her suddenly. "Come on, give it a try. It will cheer you up. You can't guess?" Connie shook her head. The answer was probably something to do with prick and Dick. It was amazing how raunchy Nixon jokes were. That must be people's way of discrediting authority. "Because he can only fuck up!"

Connie felt as if she were going to cry. Sarah studied her for a minute. "You should get some sleep, Mom. You look bummed out."

It crossed Connie's mind that Jeff might stay the night but

that was part of the bargain she'd made with Sarah. She was going to have to figure out how to live her life. After Jeff came and they'd gone upstairs, Connie got out the bottle of Kahlua. I'll just take one drink, she told herself, and then I'll write Marc a letter. That would be better than calling. I can think it all out, keep cool. Then in the morning I can re-read it to be sure it makes sense. She poured herself a little of the chocolate colored liquid and added a topping of heavy cream. Then she got out her stationery and a pen and sat down at the kitchen table to write.

But instead, she started thinking about the last time she'd invited Marc to dinner. She unpinned her calendar from the wall and stared at it, jogging her memory. It had been Friday. She'd drawn a box around it with flowers in the corner, in anticipation. Marc had pleaded work on his conscience book. He'd finally started it. "I'm holed up in my house working my pants off," he'd said. And then he'd asked her about the kids, about her classes at St. Mary's, listened to her politely. She should have realized that was a bad sign. People who were really getting along didn't have such good manners. And when had he ever worked so hard he couldn't get out?

She poured herself another drink and drew a sip of the sweet liquid through the cream, feeling the warmth as it went down. Now she remembered. She had asked Marc for dinner the week before. She had bought squabs even though they cost a fortune, and wild rice, getting everything ready before she called him. It was the day after she'd talked to the lawyer. She was discouraged by the slow progress of the negotiations. "I just need you to hold my hand a little. I'll make you something good." She'd tried to keep her voice light, not pressure him. Squabs weren't food for kids, but that's what she'd served them only to be called a "bird murderer" by Mischa, who refused to eat and wanted to bury his squab in the garden.

Then there was the time Jane had given her tickets to the

theater and she couldn't bear going alone. *Who's Afraid of Virginia Woolf* didn't appeal to him. He'd seen it years before in New York. "Too much hostility," he'd said. "That woman's a killer." Marc acted as though Connie had written the play.

She got up and looked in the liquor cabinet for Howard's vodka. The cream was beginning to sicken her. She thought she'd try a white Russian. It was amazingly smooth and she could feel the tension beginning to leave her body. "What about going to the beach?" she'd asked Marc on one of those bright, hot September days Berkeley is famous for. "We could make sand castles, stretch out in the sun and relax." He'd really seemed tempted. But now, as she considered her diminishing drink, it seemed that it was the weather that had tempted him, not the idea of being with her. That time he'd said he simply had to spend some time with Selina. He'd been neglecting her. Connie wished she'd recorded their conversation so she could replay it and listen to the tone. The suspicious pauses, the guilty little intakes of breath. She added some more vodka to her drink. Suddenly she remembered how tense he'd sounded. "Work is bad for you," she had said. Work, nothing. It was guilt about all the bullshit excuses he'd been feeding her. Finally he'd offered to take her to Chez Panisse for her birthday. They sat in the sun on the terrace and drank champagne. They laughed a lot. Except for not sleeping together, it seemed just like before. He stroked her arm and she quivered, wanting him.

She was beginning to lose track of time. Her memories of each conversation spun out in her mind like the entrails of a sacrificial animal. As she pored over them, she gradually filled with new energy. She had no exact idea of what she wanted to do, but she had a new feeling of confidence. Whatever she did now would be right.

She straightened her clothes, looking at herself in the mirror. Of course, it was obvious. She should go to Marc's. She had a vague idea of finding him in bed with someone. She imagined herself pulling the other woman's hair out. Scratching her. Ripping her clothes, slashing her tires. Taking another shot for the road, Connie reflected that if she frightened the other woman enough, she could get rid of her. Then Marc would come back. It all seemed very clear. He was weak, yes, but it was the other woman's fault. That blonde secretary Jane had seen him with. Connie pictured her slanting, calculating eyes.

She took the key and drove to Marc's. Being active, doing something, exhilarated her. She felt strong, purposeful. Like Wonder Woman swooping down to avenge a crime. Bouncing bullets off her bracelets. Even the trees along the road seemed to be waving her on.

Marc's little house was dark and quiet. She tried peering through the glass door but she couldn't even make out the couch. She opened the door with her key and went upstairs.

"What the hell," Marc shouted, jumping out of bed. She heard something clatter and fall.

The anger in his voice confused her. He didn't sound at all repentant. "It's me," she said.

"Jesus, you scared the life out of me. I was just about to run you through with a ski pole." He threw something aside and came up to her. "What do you think you're doing? It's 2:30 in the morning, for Christ's sake!"

She kept staring at the bed but there was no one there.

"Where is she?" she asked, looking around. He switched on a small lamp and she could see that he was wearing shorts and a T-shirt. She stared at him intently. "She must be here somewhere."

"What are you talking about?"

"Your secretary, Andrea." She hiccupped uncertainly. "The one you took to Saks. Don't pretend you weren't there."

"This is ridiculous. You come here before dawn to talk to me about my secretary. What's the matter with you?"

"Well, were you at Saks or not?"

He stared at her. "I bumped into her at the desk when I was

buying a sweater for Selina. If you want to make a mountain out of a molehill, go ahead. God, I can't believe you're doing this," he stopped, staring at her, hit by her breath. "You're drunk."

"You're not sleeping with her?" She studied his neck as though the answer would be evident.

"No. Of course not. Look for yourself," he said, as though he were talking to an imbecile. "No marks on me, no evidence. You see I'm alone. You won't find anything."

She giggled into her hand the way she sometimes did at funerals when she couldn't stand the tension. It was wrong, horribly wrong. "I apologize," she said, her voice slurred. "I've made a mistake."

"You sure have," Marc chaffed his arms. "Hey, listen. I'm cold standing here. If you're through with your investigation, I'd like to go back to bed." He slipped back under his covers. Her angry energy subsided and she began to wilt.

"Let me stay with you tonight," she said. She was sorry for him because she'd misjudged him. He hadn't betrayed her. She wanted to hug him, snuggle under his arm. It seemed perfectly possible. She sat down on the edge of the bed and touched his arm.

"No, I can't," he said shortly. "That would be rewarding you for doing something you shouldn't."

This wasn't what she'd expected. "I don't understand," she stammered, confused. "This is my home. This is where I belong. Here with you. I need to be here. Why won't you let me?" Lying in his arms even for five minutes, having him stroke her hair, hearing his gravelly voice, was worth anything. She craved him like a drug.

He sat up and patted her shoulder warily. "Come on, Baby, pull yourself together."

She leaned against him. "I feel sick. I think I'm going to throw up."

Marc helped her to the bathroom and left her there retching.

She was fascinated by the color. It looked like a pink fountain. What had she eaten that was pink? She couldn't remember. Her head ached ferociously. As her stomach emptied, it began to dawn on her that she'd really messed things up this time.

She washed off her face and hands. "Sorry about this," she said as she went out.

"These things happen. Don't give yourself a hard time about it. Are you sure you can drive?"

She nodded, ashamed. How had she managed to do this? Going back in the car she cursed herself. My God, where was her self respect? She would have slept with him too, if he'd let her. Her mouth tasted sour. She felt so ashamed—as though her dog or her baby had crapped on someone's floor. But the horrible part was that it wasn't her dog or her baby, it was her. How could she have thought storming his house would help her? This was the last straw, that's what it was. She'd lost him for good.

Nineteen

The phone rang when Connie was still asleep and she reached groggily for the receiver. It was Steve. Connie tried to assimilate what he was telling her.

"I found mother on the floor in the hall," he said. "She must have been drinking. There was a half empty bottle of vermouth on the floor next to her. And who knows what mix of pills she'd taken. The Demerol was empty and her sleeping pills." Connie turned on the light next to the bed. It was 7:00 Sunday morning.

"I don't understand how it happened," she said, bewildered. "Where was the maid?"

"She'd gone to bed. And then she was afraid to touch her. Probably afraid she'd be blamed if Mother died. Still, leaving her there in her vomit like that. Maybe I should have listened more to Mother when she complained...."

Connie had a sudden vivid image of her mother lying there, in the narrow hall, her face smeared. "You can't blame yourself, Steve. You've done everything you could to help her. Is Mother..." she hesitated, her heart pounding, "...is she conscious now?"

Steve's voice was tight. "They pumped her stomach out

but she's still in a coma in intensive care."

"I want to come but I'm not sure when I can." Her mouth felt dry and furry, her tongue thick. "I'll have to call school and see what they say. It might not be until Tuesday after my class. Unless you think...."

"Right now, the doctors say her condition is stable. So I don't think two days are going to make a big difference. In fact if she's awake by Tuesday, it would make more sense for you to come then, to be with her. The doctors say the drugs ought to pass through her system in about seventy-two hours unless there's some kind of neurological damage. If she seems worse, I'll let you know right away."

Connie looked at the clock on her bedside table. The second hand moved forward in quick jumps like a heart beating. Seventy-two hours, Connie thought, that's three days. My mother could be dead in three days! As soon as she got off the phone, she got her little notebook and began to make a list of things she had to do.

1. Call Sister McKinney
2. Call the airlines
3. Pack. Her suit would be the most practical, with her rust and white turtlenecks. If her mother was going to die, what sort of a day would it be? Would the maples be their most brilliant red and gold or would it be grim and rainy? The subways smelling of wet raincoats and urine? She shivered and decided to take an umbrella. She didn't think she'd need a coat. Not yet. What about her class preparation? Though she didn't know whether she'd be able to get back by next week, she had to act as though she would. She'd have to take the books and papers she needed.
4. Talk to Sarah and Mischa. How much should she tell Sarah, she wondered. Should she tell her about the suicide attempt or would it upset her too much? And what about Mischa? How much was he able to understand? "Grandma's sick." She tried out a matter of fact voice. "And I have to go...." She pictured her mother in a hospital bed, eyes shut,

tubes running into her and began to feel dizzy so she sat for a minute holding her head, her eyes closed. Then she opened them and tried to focus on her list.

5. Call the housekeeper. Ask her to keep an extra sharp eye on things while she was gone. Sarah could probably manage with Mischa. She was old enough. If she didn't want to cook, there were some T.V. dinners in the freezer and she could help Mischa with his homework and remind him to feed his hamster. But Connie would have to ask someone to take her turn with Mischa's carpool. And his classes at Lawrence Hall? She'd have to get someone to drive him there too. And...the list seemed to magnify endlessly. But it wasn't the list that was making her feel so anxious, it was the thought of her mother. They said you could hear people talking when you were in a coma. Someone once told her that after an accident he'd watched from a spot near the ceiling while surgeons cut into his body. She imagined her mother's spirit, watching. How would she feel?

Enough, she told herself glancing at the clock. It's getting late. I'd better call Sister McKinney. "I'm really sorry to call you at home," she said to the surprised voice on the other end, "but I thought I should tell you right away. I wanted to get you before Mass."

The Sister was very kind. She told Connie she could miss her Thursday lecture. "But if you think you'll be gone for longer than a week, we'll need to get someone to take your class."

"I'll try to get back," Connie said. But what could she do if her mother died? Refuse to stay for the funeral, rush back to teach her class? Now I'm going to lose my job, she thought. With everything else that's going wrong in my life, Mother's making me lose my job.

Connie called TWA and made reservations to leave at noon on Tuesday with the return open-ended. There was a flight out of Oakland, so she could go straight from her class to the plane. It might be the last class she taught too. How many lectures had she given? Five? Her first job had lasted five classes. She felt like crying, but if she did, she knew it would be hard to stop. She went downstairs and made herself a cup of black coffee. Don't fall apart now, she told herself, picking up the paper. You're only losing a job. People all over the world are starving. Connie skimmed the paper trying to get some perspective. There was an article on Vietnam draft evaders in Canada. Since Ford had pardoned them last month, they had been talking about returning. There was a photo of a long-haired boy who refused to come back unless Ford offered unconditional amnesty. The boy didn't want to feel like a criminal. What if her mother never came out of her coma and Connie was never able to make peace? Would she feel like a criminal? The article was called "Healing the Wounds." But pardon couldn't heal the boys who had died, could it? Or their families. Where was all that outrage supposed to go? Connie wondered what would happen if her mother came back to life. She couldn't feel anything. She felt frozen as though she'd been exposed on an ice floe.

When Connie heard Sarah turning the water on in the bathroom, she went upstairs. Sarah, still in her long nightshirt, was filling her bird's water cup from the tap. Connie knocked on the open bathroom door.

"Grandma's sick," she told her cautiously. "I'm going to have to go to New York." There was an angry squawk from Sarah's bedroom.

"Shut up, Rodriguez," Sarah yelled, shutting off the water. Then she turned around and faced her mother. "Can I come with you?" she asked eagerly. "I could visit N.Y.U., maybe even sit in on some classes." Connie considered taking both children with her to New York. But then who would feed the bird and the hamster and take care of Pompey? Mrs. Johnson might water the plants but she wouldn't be able to deal with a half-trained puppy.

"I thought you'd stay with Mischa and help him feel comfortable. Besides, you can't miss school." If she took them both with her, what was Mischa going to do all day, with her at the hospital and Sarah at N.Y.U? And what if she had to stay longer? No, it wasn't going to work.

"Missing a few days wouldn't hurt. I can work on my paper. It would motivate me if I saw N.Y.U. and got to meet people. You know, visited some classes. Saw what the school was like. I know I'd work harder. Couldn't Mischa stay with Robbie? He'd take his best friend over his sister any day. Please, Mom, let me come. I could help you with Grandma." Sarah walked slowly towards her room, balancing the cup. Connie followed her. "I could play scrabble with her. Grandma loves scrabble." She dripped some yellowy vitamins into the cup and stuck it through an opening in the cage. Then she took out the food cup and emptied the husks in the wastepaper basket.

Connie felt as if she was in a dream where people talk past each other. Half of them have holes in them like Swiss cheese but the other half don't notice and keep smiling and waving paper flowers. "Sarah, sweetheart, you don't understand. Grandma's very sick. She may die."

Sarah stopped with one hand in the bag of parrot seed. "Die?"

Connie took a deep breath. "She took too many..." she hesitated, hating to have to tell Sarah, "...sleeping pills." Damn her mother, why'd she have to do this?

Sarah stood quietly for a minute, letting the seeds run through her fingers. "I guess there's no need to visit N.Y.U. then. If Grandma dies, I guess I won't be going anywhere."

How could she think about N.Y.U. when her grandmother was dying? "Sarah, you might think about someone else for once. But look." She frowned, wondering how to go on, and decided on directness. "Grandma's a rich woman. If she dies, you'll have plenty of money for college."

"But I don't want her to die," Sarah whispered, horrified.

"I know that." Connie put her arm around her.

"I don't think I even want to look at N.Y.U.," Sarah said, hugging her back. "But if you want me to, I'll come with you. I mean, wouldn't you like some company?"

How many problems was she going to have to deal with? Her divorce, her job, her house, her mother dying and now her sixteen-year-old wanting to come and look at colleges.

"Sarah, you have to take care of Mischa. I can't farm him out because I'm not even sure when I'll be back. And it's too expensive to have the housekeeper come in full time."

"Take him with us then."

"Sarah, I don't want to rip Mischa out of school. It's the only stable thing in his life right now."

"Do you understand how much I want to do this? I'd give up my allowance for a year. I'd babysit Mischa for free on Saturday nights. I'd...."

"Sarah, we'll have to find another time for you to go to N.Y.U. Right now, I need you here with Mischa. It's going to be easier and cheaper. So stop hassling and help me get ready, okay?"

On the plane, Connie thought about her class. Even though she'd felt lousy, the students had been remarkably lively. She hated the thought that she wouldn't see them again. She had planned to go on to *King Lear* next week. She looked at her notes on the scene where Lear banishes Cordelia because she tells him the simple truth. Her mother was like that, she thought. Never letting her say what she thought. Never even allowing a hint from her children that she wasn't perfect. Not only an Einstein but the most caring mother. The worst part was the way you couldn't confront her because she always felt she'd made heroic efforts even when she hadn't done anything. "I really wanted to come," she'd say when she didn't want to visit Connie at camp, "but the train made me so sick. Simon just had to take me off. I had spots in front of my eyes." Connie had sat alone in her bunk on visiting day and scratched the ringworm on her leg into a burning circle of hate.

She suddenly remembered seeing her mother standing in front of a huge canvas swaying back and forth as though she was dancing. Connie must have been about five. She called softly but her mother couldn't hear her. She just stood there, a look of ecstatic pleasure on her face. For years Connie believed that there were magic children inside the canvas. At night, she was sure, they came out and played in the studio in brilliantly colored clothes. Connie planned to spy on them and copy them and win her mother's smile but she could never stay awake.

When Connie and Steve got to the hospital, they weren't allowed to see their mother right away. The nurses gave them folding chairs and they sat in the dimly lit hall outside the room with the green door, like visiting a prison.

"I thought we were going to lose her for a while this morning," Steve said. "The vital signs went way down but they seem to have stabilized." Connie breathed in the harsh smell of disinfectant. Her mother might have been dead by the time she arrived, she thought. She had a vision of herself dressed in black listening to her mother's will. Jesus.

"How's it going with the divorce?" Steve was asking.

"Terrible. I'm losing my job and I might have to sell the house." It suddenly occurred to her that she probably wouldn't be able to get any references. It would look awful on her record to have left right after term started.

"The house? Why didn't you ask me for a loan? I could handle it. I probably could even give it to you interest free."

Connie felt the tears well up. "How could I ever pay you back, with no job, no prospects." There was a certain irony to it. Her mother was dying and Connie was the one who was dead. "No, much as I want to stay, I think I'm going to have to sell. The taxes alone are enough to sink me. Besides, if I keep the house, my lawyer says I might have to give up alimony. And child support for Sarah runs out in a year. I just can't afford to keep it." She imagined transferring her mother's money into her bank account and for a moment she felt joy, relief. Then she felt sick. She wondered whether the man in yesterday's paper who murdered his wife for her money had felt like that.

"That's ridiculous. Your lawyer is too soft. In this city we play a tougher game. Look, Howard has a police record. You shouldn't have to give up alimony. You shouldn't give up any of the basics: alimony, pension, medical costs. As for child support running out, I think you have a good case for psychological damages. Your kids will probably need therapy after all Howard's put you through. But if you do decide to sell the house, you should ask Howard to pay capital gains. They could be considerable in a house that's appreciated as much as yours has. And if you're going to sell, there are tax advantages from selling soon, before the divorce is final. I'll go over all this myself to make sure your lawyer hasn't missed anything."

"I haven't told my lawyer this but..." Connie took a deep breath "...you know what Howard told me? That he'd been unfaithful to me for years. Do you think I could use that? Would it help my case? It was all sorts of weird things. Beatings and stuff like that." Each time she thought of it, she got a shock, as if she'd seen Dr. Jekyll turn into Mr. Hyde. Praying to preying. It occurred to her that right now Howard was probably in the synagogue asking to be forgiven his sins. It was the Day of Atonement. The holiest day of the Jewish year.

Steve leaned forward. The green light gave his face an under-water look. "Of course you should use it. Push it for all it's worth. And you haven't told your lawyer?"

"No." She'd been too ashamed, she realized suddenly.

"If Howard won't be reasonable, threaten to tell the judge and keep him from seeing the children. Or tell him that if you go to court, all that stuff will have to come out. I doubt he'd want that. This could push him to settle in a way that's to your advantage."

Steve's words were like coins in some exotic currency. She wasn't sure how much they were worth. Words are cheap, her father had always said.

Just then, the nurse called them in and they went and sat by Elsie's bed. After a few minutes of sitting there in silence, Steve stood up and adjusted his belt. "Look, I hate to leave you but I've got an urgent meeting with a client to get ready for a court appearance tomorrow." He gave her an apologetic smile. "The woman's awfully nervous and I'm afraid if I don't reassure her, she'll...."

"It's all right. I don't mind. I'd like to be alone with her for a while."

After Steve left, Connie sat and held her mother's hand. Her eyelids looked like blue-veined violets. Her face was pale as death yet her features were undistorted, purely chiseled. She seemed so serene, so far away, it was hard to believe that she could live. Involuntarily, Connie began to think of the Yom Kippur service. The lists of the ways people would die, "Some by fire, some by water, some by pestilence, some cut off...." She imagined the God of the Hebrews sitting in the clouds, his great book in his lap, inscribing the names of those chosen to live. Below him in synagogues all over the world, people atoned and hoped while the sun went down and the doors of heaven slowly closed. Connie had always liked the poetic intensity of that moment when there was only a glimmer of light in the sky and a crack in the heavenly door open to the cries below. She didn't believe in the patriarchal God but the ideas of atonement and repentance seemed real and true.

She thought of Sarah back home with Mischa, worrying about being able to go away to college. How much of what went wrong in Sarah's life was Connie's fault? Maybe if she hadn't peered and pried, if she'd left Sarah's door open when her first boyfriend visited, if she hadn't chased him away from Sarah's window with a broom, maybe Sarah wouldn't have needed a man old enough to be her father. Connie put her clenched fist up to her chest and beat it softly in the ritual gesture of atonement. Sarah had a lot to forgive her for.

Two nurses were joking in the corner, hardened by the constant stink of death. They were dressed in green, ironically the color of hope.

And Mischa? How many times had she left him alone and frightened? Once on the sidewalk when she was making love to Marc. She had put it out of her mind right after it happened because it made her feel too bad. The time he was sick and Howard had broken in. Now, when she was here with her mother. And she'd yelled at him, besides. "Don't whine so much. Can't you play by yourself for ten minutes? You see I'm working."

There was a burst of laughter from the corner, quickly suppressed. "Gallows humor," one of the nurses said. "I love Rabinowitz jokes. Do you know the one about the two Jews who wanted to get rich scalping Indians?"

Connie wondered what Howard thought about when he beat his chest. What was he sorry for? She hadn't ever really understood him. She hadn't known what went on in his mind. What his needs were, emotional or sexual. She hadn't ever really tried to figure out what they were. Just shuffed them off as though he didn't have them. Instead of being a good woman, she'd been blind. She'd spent years trying to impose her way of living on him, thinking she was being accommodating. The complexities of it made her head ache. And Marc? She'd known what he was. She'd seen him batting his eyelashes and smiling his fallen angel smile. But she'd let her passion override her brain. And when she was able to think, she'd imagined her innocence would win him over in the end—like a Medieval saint out to make a convert in the most difficult circumstances. Sin of false pride.

Connie looked down at her mother. Thin, clear plastic tubes running from everywhere. Tubes sent blood and liquid food into her arm—the inside of it was bruised and blue, her blue-blooded aristocratic arm lying on the white bed as if on the finest tablecloth—and brought fluids out again from the distended bladder. Machines whirred and clicked like huge women knitting, watching her vital signs, humming their concern. She was like them, she thought, going through the motions like a mechanical doll. She'd hated her mother so much that she'd damaged her own ability to love. She had no mercy, no charity, no comfort. She made no allowances for age and weakness. She thought of her mother before this suicide attempt, lying in her bed and crying for comforting. Wanting someone, man or woman, to come to her and give her relief, to give her caresses. Feeling just the way Connie felt when she lay crying for Marc. She realized with a start that she hadn't cried once since she'd come to New York.

One of the nurses came over, motioned Connie away and brusquely pulled the sheet off her mother's body. Connie drew in her breath. Though her mother's face was ravaged, her body which the nurse uncovered, still had its milk-white flesh, its gently curving hips. Wasn't it worse for her mother because, old as she was, her appetite for life wasn't diminished one bit? She probably wanted to be made love to as much as Connie did.

"You'd better go now," the nurse said, stony faced. "I have some things to do for your mother."

When Connie got back to the apartment, she switched on the television set and made herself a cup of tea. They were showing clips of Betty Ford in the hospital after her mastectomy. A real trooper, her husband had called her. Connie switched it off and called home. Mischa answered.

"How're you doing, Mischa? I miss you."

"Miss Crampton sat on my paper maché elephant and broke off his trunk." Mischa's nose sounded stuffy. She wondered whether he was getting a cold.

"You probably could put it back with a little glue. There's some in my desk drawer upstairs. Maybe Sarah could help you."

"No. It's wrecked up," Mischa said dolefully. "And Sarah only read to me for two minutes last night. I timed it with my Mickey Mouse watch."

"Stop lying, Mischa," Sarah took the phone. "Mom, I read to him for a half hour and he still wouldn't go to sleep."

"That's okay, Sarah. I'm sure you read to him. He's probably worrying about Grandma." Worrying about broken toys was like worrying about Pompey. It probably meant there was something he was too scared to ask about.

"How is Grandma? Will she make it?" Her voice was quivering. Still a child, Connie thought, in spite of everything. They hate the thought of death.

"She's still unconscious. The doctors aren't optimistic. She could stay comatose and never wake up." Connie sat down on the sofa and slipped her shoes off. Her feet were swollen from the plane. The air in the apartment was humid and heavy. They were having a spell of Indian summer.

"It seems like our family's breaking up. First Dad goes, now Grandma's dying," Sarah said. "I feel like it's partly my fault. Making you and Dad fight more."

"You're wrong, Sarah," Connie wished she could reach over and touch her hand. "It would have happened anyway. The tension over you just brought it to a head." And Marc. Maybe someday she'd be grateful to him for giving her back her body. Senses primed. But right now, she wished he was buried up to his neck in the sand without anyone to bring him water.

"Maybe."

"I think you don't believe me."

"Dad said Grandma was a hysterical, crazy woman." Sarah stopped and Connie thought she recognized the slight cracking sounds Sarah's jaw made when she sawed it back and forth. "He said I had bad genes. Does that mean he thought I was going to get crazy later on? Does suicide run in families?"

"Oh shit. Why'd he have to tell you that? As though you didn't have enough to cope with. No, no one has to commit suicide because their mother did, or their grandmother. It's not genetic, like hemophilia."

"You have Grandma's expression sometimes when you're worrying," Sarah muttered faintly. "And people say I look like you when I smile. So what do you inherit, exactly?"

"Hair color, eye color, body type—physical things."

"There was a kid at school who overdosed because her boyfriend left her." Sarah had an abstracted tone as though she was following some inner movie in her head.

"And what do you think of that?"

"I see why she did it, sort of. But it seems like a real cop out."

"So you wouldn't do it?" Connie held her breath.

"I feel pretty good with Jeff. I don't think he'd hurt me. But what if he did? I'm scared. I mean, can you really tell what you'll do when it comes down to it?"

"I think you can." Connie felt a chill despite the warmth in the room. It was what she'd always wondered too.

"Maybe Grandma didn't know that the sleeping medicine would have such a bad reaction with alcohol. Do you think it could have been a mistake?"

"Maybe. Nobody knows. But it could be. She didn't leave a note or anything." Let Sarah think that if it made her feel better. Though the lack of a note didn't mean anything. Elsie hadn't left one the first time either.

It looked like it was going to storm. Connie watched the display of lightening through the open window.

"Is there a worry gene?" Sarah was still trying to figure it out.

"Look. If you're around a person who worries a lot, like Grandma—or even me—you tend to worry too. Okay? But there are tricks you can learn to get out of it."

"Like what?"

"Test each worry out. Is this real? Do I have to be frightened? Or am I just being a copycat?" She realized it was just pablum from a magazine but maybe it worked. "Am I just doing it because my mother did? Ask yourself, what's the worst thing that can happen to me in this case?" The worst is that she could lose her job, lose the house, lose her medical benefits. For an awful minute she saw herself rushing Mischa to the hospital with appendicitis and being turned away because she had no insurance. She gave a quick short laugh. "That last part's tricky. You can't let your imagination run away with you. It takes practice."

Connie was sleeping in her old room. The floor was bare now. Her mother had gotten rid of the pink flowered rug that Connie's father had bought for her. She had never liked it. It kept reminding her of how girls were supposed to be all sweet and rosy, disgusting pink. When she married Howard, her mother asked her if she wanted it. She didn't, not at all. Her favorite colors were blue and lavender. It never seemed fair that blue should be a boy's color. She told her mother to give away her desk too. It was too small and the light wood annoyed her. It didn't seem serious. Almost the first thing she bought for herself was a big redwood desk with a top wide enough to spread out all her papers and books.

Her mother was using Connie's room as a study now. She had bought a huge new desk that jutted out under the old bookcase. Her pencils were all sharpened and next to them was a letter opener that looked like a dagger. Dark volumes that Connie recognized as her mother's journals were stacked neatly on one side.

Connie couldn't sleep. The city noises had become unfamiliar—the horns of buses, the heavy squeals of brakes, the lights that never went off. She got up, took her papers out of her suitcase and started to prepare for her Tuesday class. It soothed her to pretend for a moment that she was going to get back to teach it. She thought she'd concentrate on the scene where Lear, driven out by his daughter, begins to lose his sanity. "Reason not the need," he says, meaning that need, like love, can't be measured. He is beginning to see that. She thought she'd start by asking the students about what she saw as the central paradox of the play: reason in madness. Writers are dangerous she thought. The more genius they have, the more harm they can do. Shakespeare almost made her believe that going mad was what made Lear understand love. Her mother would have approved. All her life she'd thought there was something romantic about being mad. Seeing things straight made you ordinary, boring, insipid. The sad truth was that her mother hadn't been able to do the ordinary things, couldn't even hold a baby without having it grow rigid and start to cry. There was no romance in that.

She thought suddenly of Marc's hands with their sprinkling of black hairs. He'd been able to hold her, melting into her, giving her back that easy sense of fusion that she hadn't known she was missing. He could touch and hold but when it came right down to it, he was as elusive and unavailable as her mother. It might have been worse, she thought. They could have stayed together. Married. She would only have gotten more desperate and more abject. God, that drunken visit. She shuddered to remember how out of control she'd been. But at least that had ended it fast. Like pulling a rotten tooth. One quick wrench. And she was free to go on.

She put down her pen and picked up her mother's journals. She'd read early parts of them before but they'd disturbed her too much. After five minutes she'd forgotten what was in them. Now she felt drawn by a new curiosity.

She read very carefully through the typed journal of the last month before this suicide attempt. Though she was trying to see her mother as a person, she kept slipping into seeing her as a subject for a psychological study. What she wanted to find out was why she'd done it this time. Why keep on pretending that she couldn't understand? She could understand all too well. That was part of the trouble. She was terrified because she understood too well.

Okay, her mother wrote that she wanted to die because she was alone. Louise, her companion for so many years, was sick. Her lover was gone and even her new maid was threatening to leave. This threat was simply the last straw. She couldn't muster the energy to face getting new help. The part of Connie that couldn't stand being like her mother started up a conversation with her in her mind. If she could at least state the case for reason convincingly, she might come to believe it herself. Mother, she argued, this is totally ridiculous, childish. Worse than childish, infantile. You don't have to raise a finger to get a new maid or cook or companion. It will all be done for you by your son and daughter-in-law. Another woman will come and take care of you more or less the way the last one did. Change is not comfortable, I know. It makes you a little anxious. Maybe the new one will be dishonest—one of them did steal groceries, another, small objects—but that's what happens when you're old. People take advantage. Still, it's not the end of the world.

Yes, her mother's voice insisted inside Connie. It is the end of the world.

Her mother's stubbornness shook her. Elsie seemed so certain. Connie couldn't help wondering if she was right, if it was unendurable—if she would have been crushed by it too. It struck her that she hadn't been able to sympathize with her mother because it was too frightening—too much the picture of what she was so close to being—helpless, infantile. If she was going to be so hard on her mother, oughtn't she be harder on herself?

Connie lay awake and looked at the rain streaming in sheets outside her window. Whatever her mother hadn't given her, she, Connie, was free to decide what to give her mother. Giving and giving up were different things.

"I'm afraid if she doesn't wake up by tomorrow, we're going to have to think about taking her off life support," Steve said while they were walking in the hospital corridor.

Connie felt her heart thud. "I think we should wait. That doctor...."

"He's the only one. Everyone else is sure there's brain damage. She wouldn't want to be a vegetable, Connie. You know that. That's why she wrote those elaborate instructions. Remember how she read them to us? She was terrified of being kept alive by machines."

"I know. But it hasn't been a week yet. Let's wait a few more days. The doctor still thinks the drugs will pass out of her system."

"They should have done that days ago, Connie. The coma's no lighter now than when you came Tuesday and every day like this makes it more likely there's been brain damage."

"I want to wait," she repeated. A dim greenish light came out of the intensive care door. The corridor was bleak. Connie sat down on one of the folding chairs the nurse had put in the hall.

"Look, what if she does get off the respirator in a few days but never opens her eyes? What if she opens them but can't see you or recognize you? Can't talk, can't move, can't eat. Are you ready to take the responsibility for doing that to her?"

Connie put her hands up in front of her eyes. "I'm not ready to give up on her yet, that's all." Through her fingers she saw Steve's defensive look. As though she were making him the bad guy. "But then I haven't been taking care of her the way you have. It can't have been easy for you. Maybe if she gets better, I should take her out West. Give you a break." When she sold her house, maybe she could buy something smaller, a house all on the same level so her mother could get in and out. She imagined herself pushing her mother's wheelchair through the front door.

Steve's face relaxed. "You've got enough on your plate right now," he said kindly. "Anyway, Mother would be lost without her analyst. Even before this, she was calling her up in the middle of the night whenever she was overwhelmed.

Now...."

Connie felt a pang of guilt, remembering how she'd told her mother not to phone her like that. "I wonder why she didn't call this time."

"Maybe she did. Did you know that she left Dr. Lowenstein a parcel of money for that research institute of hers? She had me add that to her will last year."

"Mother never showed her will to me." Connie suddenly wondered why she hadn't. Wasn't there some conflict of interest in having your son as your lawyer? "All she told me was that she didn't want us fighting over money."

"There's no reason for us to fight," Steve said. For a minute he looked like a little boy. Connie remembered herself at ten pinning him down in the dirt, her hand at his throat. "Aside from the money for Dr. Lowenstein and fifteen thousand for Louise, she split it pretty much down the middle. I guess we'd put the apartment up for sale." He noticed her expression and stopped. "Unless you want to let Sarah stay there?"

Connie shook her head. God, she'd been jealous. "It's too big for one person," she answered sensibly.

"While you're there, you might think a little about what things of hers you'd like...china, books, jewelry. Maybe even make a list. It would be easier for me to take most of the furniture. It would cost a fortune to ship."

She thought of telling him he was right, it would be extravagant. "I want the dining room table," she said instead. "I love the mahogany. If mother dies, I'll be able to pay for it."

One of Steve's eyebrows shot up in the lopsided movement of surprise he'd had since he was a child. "Sorry. I didn't realize it meant that much to you. Everything's open to discussion." He hesitated. "There's one more thing I wanted to ask you about. Along with the will there was a note..." he cleared his throat "...saying she wanted to be cremated and have us scatter her ashes over the sea."

Connie tried not to think about how much easier the money would make her life. "Well, why not?" It was romantic. It fit.

Steve rubbed his chin. He seemed to be struggling to say something. "Mother wouldn't have thought of sitting shiva, but somehow I'd like to do it, if you don't mind. It would give the men in the office a chance to pay their respects. Most of them are Jewish."

"Of course, do that. Do whatever makes you feel better. I just don't want to have one of those memorial services where a rabbi who never knew her talks about what a fine, upstanding woman she was. If she does die, let's rent a hall and fill the place with flowers and have someone play music. She loved Beethoven's string quartets, didn't she? Maybe we could get a group from Julliard to play. Let her friends come and talk about her. Make it a celebration." Connie imagined the flowers. Chrysanthemums in bright yellow and rust, white and red roses. A banner over the stage, "*Ars longa, vita brevis.*"

Her mother looked just the same when the nurse finally called them in from the hall.

Connie pulled up a chair next to her head and reached for her hand.

"I'm going to stay a little."

"It's no use talking to her," the nurse said. "She's in a deep coma, can't hear a thing." Connie ignored her the way she ignored the nurse who told her to stop panting when she was having Sarah.

"Hi, Mother," she said, "it's Connie." She held her hand gently, massaging her fingers one by one. "I was sitting here like this with you on the Day of Atonement," she said after a minute. "I know how you feel about religion. You didn't raise me as a Jew, but I still felt there were things I needed to atone for. For one thing, I'm sorry I couldn't really listen to you. I didn't want to know how hard it was for you being alone. I don't want it to be hard for you. I'm sorry I told you not to call me in the middle of the night. That was cruel. You can call me all you want. And sometimes I didn't ask how you were feeling because I couldn't stand seeing your pain." For an instant she wanted to tell her mother how angry she'd been with her all these years. Just to have it all out in the open for once and to hear her mother say, I'm sorry too. Real forgiveness, atonement. But she imagined how her words would sound to her mother, like the high, shrill notes of a singer, shattering glass.

"Mom," she lowered her voice, concentrating her energy on the pale shell of her mother's ear. "I don't know how you did it but you kept going. You've got to keep going now. I need you. I need you to keep going so I can too." Was it her imagination or did her mother's eyelid flutter? She bent over, watching the faint quiver like the wing of a butterfly.

"Nurse, come quickly. She's moving her eyelid." The nurse lifted the lid, looked at her pupil and told Connie that the coma seemed to be lightening. Then suddenly her mother started to moan and jerk her head from side to side. The nurse grasped her chin and held it firm. "Don't let her pull out her tubes. I'll have to tie her down."

"Is it really necessary?"

"I wouldn't be doing it if it wasn't." The restraints looked like swaddling bands or the wrappings you put on a corpse. While the nurse was tying her, Elsie opened her eyes for a second and stared at Connie with what seemed to be recognition. Then she shut her lids and started to mutter. Connie leaned forward with her ear next to her mother's lips. "What is it? What do you want? Tell me, Mummy."

"Strangle the bitch," her mother said distinctly. Connie sprang back.

"She doesn't know what she's saying," the nurse said, tucking in the last band. "Hallucination, most likely. Call me if you need me. I'll be just at the next bed."

"I haven't left you, Mother," Connie said softly as soon as

the nurse had gone.

"Mary, Mary, please don't go," her mother's voice suddenly took on the plaintive accents of a very young child. Connie shivered. Mary was her mother's baby nurse. Connie had seen pictures of her. A fair skinned, rosy Irish girl. She'd gotten pregnant and been dismissed when Elsie was two. Her mother had clearly gotten all the departures mixed up. Her nurse, the maid, Louise, maybe even Connie.

"There, Mother, no one's gone." She stroked her mother's arm, crooning to her the way you would a child.

"She is," she wailed, still in a child's high voice, her eyes tight shut. She started to struggle against the restraints. "Let me go too. Take me with you," she pleaded. "Please, I'll be good." The anguish in her voice was so strong that Connie looked over her shoulder half expecting to see someone but there was only the curtain dividing the beds. Connie realized with a shock that she'd always been confused about the reality of what her mother felt. Sometimes her mother's crazy fears—the danger of wet hair, of public transport, of being raped, of being alone—seemed more real than other people's common sense. They were so passionate, for one thing. And that seemed a sign of reality.

"Jesus, Mother, you're not a child." Connie leaned close to her again, holding her shoulders gently, "Listen to me. You're not two years old. I'm looking at you now. I see your gray hair. You're a grown woman." Her mother lay quiet and Connie began again, slowly stroking her arm. "You're not alone. I'm here and so is Steve, nearby. Try to open your eyes and see me." Her mother's eyelids fluttered. She was trying.

"You're going to be okay." Listening to herself say this, it seemed real. And she was going to be okay too. She didn't have to be so afraid of every ghost and demon her mother conjured up. They were her mother's. Not hers. And if she wasn't so scared, maybe she could see her mother more clearly. Not tie herself up into knots keeping distant or going the other way and making herself sick with yearning. Have compassion but live her own life. Learn to love without losing track of herself. She'd gotten a taste of something she wanted with Marc and she was determined to have more. Next time she'd do it better.

Connie ran to call Sarah from a phone booth in the hospital lobby.

"It looks like Grandma's coming out of it," Connie told her, after she'd asked how Sarah was. "She doesn't recognize me yet, but she was cursing like a sailor. I'm not so worried about her anymore. She has the vitality of ten horses."

"What was she saying? I didn't know she knew any curse words," Sarah asked, interested.

"It wasn't what she said, it was her energy. She looks so thin and frail, but believe me, Grandma can take care of herself. Nothing's going to keep her down long. The way she fought that nurse, I think she'll be out of here in a week. How's Mischa?"

"He's playing over at Robbie's. I fixed his damn elephant trunk."

"Thanks, Sarah. You've really helped me out. You know, I've been thinking about you a lot while I've been away. I know you're mad at me for the way I've interfered in your life and I just wanted to tell I understand and I'm sorry. I want us to learn to talk to each other. I want to do things differently when I get back." As soon as she hung up she thought of some things she'd forgotten to tell Sarah. That she wanted her to be her own person even if she was opposed to everything Connie valued. She'd forgotten to talk to her about boundaries. Where the other leaves off and you begin. Where the mother leaves off and you begin.

Steve came and joined her after work. Elsie was still slipping in and out of the coma.

"Give her time. She's going to wake up," Connie told him.

"To what?" he asked. "God, I feel ambivalent about this. What kind of a life is she going to have? Who knows how badly damaged she is? There's a man in my office who was unconscious for a week after a car accident and he's totally paralyzed. He has to turn the pages of his book with a gadget hooked up to his eyebrows."

"I don't think she's paralyzed. Look at the way her feet keep moving." They both watched the sheet lift as her toes wiggled it. "I really think she's going to be all right. Before you came, she opened her eyes for almost a minute, and she's talking. Yelling her head off, actually. You should have seen her."

"It'll take weeks before we see what she can really do. How are we going to take care of her? What if she's incontinent? Or bedridden? We'll have to send her to a home."

"Why? She has lots of money. We can get her round-the-clock nursing. She'd hate being in a home. Can you imagine her being wheeled around to arts and crafts and bingo? Forced to eat, tranquilized? She fought like crazy today when the nurse was trying to restrain her." Connie pictured her mother tied to her chair like some rare caged bird, immobile, her eyes frantic. "I'll call around to the agencies and just see what kind of care is available and what it costs. Okay?"

Steve nodded glumly. "Go ahead, but I think bringing her home would be a big mistake. What's to keep her from doing this again?"

"I think she's relieved to be alive."

Finally late the next afternoon Elsie opened her eyes and looked at Connie. She smiled, then she realized that she was in a strange place and panicked. Connie stroked her forehead and soothed her.

"You're all right," Connie told her. "You're in the hospital."

"I've been on a trip," her mother said. "A woman invited me to her house and I had to go. There were a lot of other guests and it was a very long way off."

"That must be why you stayed such a long time. It's good to have you back."

Connie called home and got Mischa. "I've got some really good news. Grandma's awake."

"Hey," Mischa shouted. "Grandma's awake. Mom's coming back. Are you coming home tonight? Can I stay up to see you?"

"I'm not coming home tonight, sweetie, but I will soon." She blew a kiss into the phone. "I can't wait to see you and Sarah. Is she there?"

"I'm right here," Sarah said. "I heard. That's great about Grandma. Will she get out of the hospital soon?"

"They'll probably have to watch her for a few more days. Her plumbing isn't quite right yet."

"She'll still be able to have me next year, won't she?"

"I doubt it, Sarah. If she is able to come home at all, she'll have to have a nurse living with her. Maybe two, one for night, one for the day. Whatever maid she has will have to cook for them and take care of the house. That's already quite a crowd. And Mother will need quiet. You play loud music." Sarah started to protest but Connie shushed her. "I'm not blaming you, but it would disturb her. I don't think you'd be happy either. Sick people have strange hours. She'd probably go to bed by six and get up at dawn. You'd have to tiptoe around holding your breath. You wouldn't be able to have friends over."

"Oh God, you mean I have to go to Cal? I've been in Berkeley since I was born. I know every inch of the Cal campus. Half my friends are going there. It would feel like going back to high school for a fifth year. Even if I could just get away for a year...."

"Look, I sympathize with your wanting to get away. Maybe we could work something out with Steve. Josh is going to college next year...."

"You think he'd let me stay in his room?"
"It's certainly worth a try."

In the morning, the nurse said Elsie could try some soft food. Connie sat on the edge of the bed and fed her jello. Elsie opened her mouth like a little bird.

"Remember how when I was sick you would always give me jello? I thought it must have magical properties."

By the afternoon she was much better.

"You're getting married again, aren't you?" she said suddenly while Connie was wiping her mouth.

"No," Connie said before she could think. "It's off. We quarreled." The look in Elsie's eyes was astonishing. It was a look of pure naked triumph.

"Maybe you'll do something else with your life now," she said, "be less of a sex object."

As if that were what it was about. Her mother had taken the pills to get her attention. Not consciously, she would be charitable about that. But just under the surface. All that talk about the nurse who'd gone away and deserted her—gotten engaged—had left Connie feeling that her mother was actually talking about her. Desertion. What subtle ways her mother had of making her feel guilty.

"When Howard abused you, sometimes I had to bite my lips to keep from screaming. It hurt me so much."

"Did it? But Howard never came between us," Connie said. She wondered whether if she'd really been on the verge of marrying Marc her mother's suicide attempt would have stopped her, made her feel hexed. It would be different from now on she thought looking into the hugely distended black pupils.

Her mother lay back against the pillows and stared at her in bewilderment. Connie was afraid she was going to start hallucinating again.

"My doctor told me I was jealous because you found a nice man and I wanted him for myself. Dirty liar."

"Never mind, Mother, I understand." Connie stroked her mother's cheek and she nestled her face into her hand. For a moment she took Connie's finger in her mouth as though she were going to suck it. Then she opened her eyes and smiled. Connie was sure she'd forgotten totally about what she'd just told her.

"Let me tell you more about the woman who invited me to visit," Elsie whispered, plucking her sleeve. Connie smiled down at her. Her rapt face made her seem even younger that Sarah. "She had round, full arms like a Greek goddess." Elsie raised her hands, struggling to show her how the drapes flowed.

Her mother's conversation had returned to its normal plane. Floating on some distant surface. Allegory, drama, all filed and shaped to some image of beauty just as her art was. Connie's struggles to wriggle beneath had been futile. There was no way in.

"I'm sure she was wonderful. But you've got to rest now. When you get well, you'll paint her and then I'll see. I'll see." She had stepped into her old role but it felt different. She felt detached, lighter, even playful. Let her mother paint all the goddesses from Greece to India. It didn't matter. What mattered was that Connie was going to stop trying to get what had never been there for her. Stop bargaining for mothering that wasn't coming. Any help she gave her mother now was gratis. No return expected. Given just because she was able to do it. She felt as if a weight had been lifted off her chest allowing her to breathe freely. She wasn't going to keep trying to fit a puzzle piece in where it didn't belong, an earthworm tail in the sky or a piece of bird under water. She'd meet her mother on her own ground.

"I've been reading your journals, Mother. I think they're wonderful. When you get better, we ought to do something about getting a publisher. I could edit them for you, write notes and an introduction. How would that be? Would that please you?"

"You've always understood me," her mother said, pressing her hand. "You have an artist's soul."